The Dreams
of Fair Women

—7

The Dreams of
Fair Women

The Dreams of Fair Women

Alexander Cordell

PIATKUS

Copyright © 1993 by Alexander Cordell

First published in Great Britain in 1993 by
Judy Piatkus (Publishers) Ltd of
5 Windmill Street, London W1

**The moral right of the author
has been asserted**

*A catalogue record for this book is available
from the British Library*

ISBN 0-7499-0201-9

Set in 11/12pt Compugraphic Times by
Action Typesetting Limited, Gloucester
Printed and bound in Great Britain by
Biddles Ltd, Guildford and King's Lynn

For Donnie, my wife

Acknowledgements

I am grateful, as usual, to many librarians for help, not least an ex-librarian, Mr T. W. Yang, my friend of many years, who accompanied me around Hong Kong during my research in the Colony; also to the following publications to which I have referred during the writing of this novel.

Chinese Coolie Emigration
Persia Crawford Campbell: Frank Cass and Co Ltd, 1923

Chinese Emigrations with Special Reference to Labour Conditions
Ta Chen A. M.: Washington Government Printing Office, 1923

Hong Kong 1841–1862:
Birth, Adolescence and Coming of Age
Geoffrey Robley Sayer, BA: Oxford University Press, 1937

Fragrant Harbour
John Warner: John Warner Publications, Hong Kong

The Hong Kong Guide, 1893
Oxford University Press

Hong Kong. The Formative Years 1842–1912

Chinese Creeds and Customs Vols 1, 2 and 3
V. R. Burkhardt: South China Morning Post Ltd, Hong Kong

FOXISM

The Fox Tower, Peking

With acknowledgement and thanks to V D Burkhardt, *Chinese Creeds and Customs*, Vol III (South China Morning Post Ltd)

From demoniac possession it is but a step to the intrusion of Fox Fairies, which figure so largely in Chinese lore.

Old China worshipped the fox, believing it to be endowed with supernatural powers of transformation, and contact with humans was considered dangerous since, having invaded a human body, the spirit of the animal could live (by changing host) for over a thousand years.

Vixens have a predilection for beautiful females, using their wombs to facilitate travel.

The belief that the fox invested humans with his cunning is thought to have sprung from the peasants' awe of the mandarins who, possessed by evil themselves, dominated others by their cruel deceptions.

Shrines to the fox still exist in China: one of the guard houses on the south wall of the Tartar city of Peking is known as the Fox Tower, built to house the King of the Tribe, thus isolating him from humans.

I am a ghost and you are a ghost —
    If you are there at all —
In a world where an eerie, bleary host
    Of blurred lights flicker and fall.

I am a ghost in a ghostly street
    That isn't a street at all,
But a chaos of wheels and shuffling feet
    That hesitate, grope and crawl.

I am a ghost and I've lost my way ...
    ... Can nobody hear me call?
Please, Sister Ghost, won't you help a ghost? —
    Or aren't you there at all?

From 'Some Perfect Morning',
The Poems of Myfanwy Haycock (1913 – 1963), by
permission of Gwladys Haycock and Wynn Williams

Situation of Hong Kong in Relationship To Canton, China

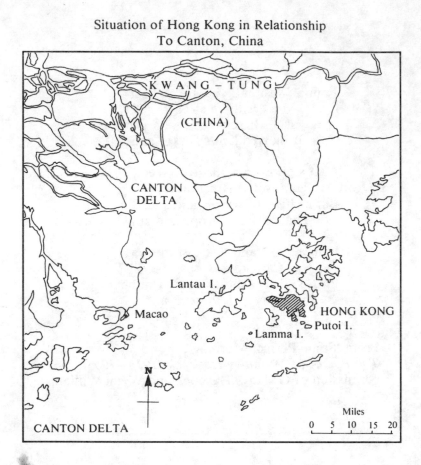

KWANG – TUNG

(CHINA)

CANTON
DELTA

Lantau I.

Macao

HONG KONG

Putoi I.

Lamma I.

N

CANTON DELTA

Miles
0   5   10   15   20

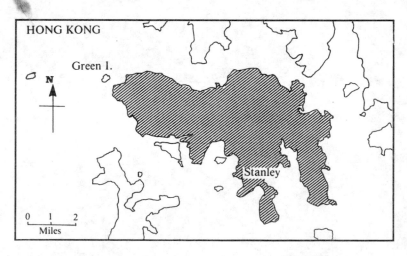

HONG KONG

Green I.

N

Stanley

0   1   2
Miles

Book One

Hong Kong
1850

1

Milly Smith, at the rail of the old *S.S. Mongolia*, watched the coaling coolies filling up the ship's bunkers. The sun slanted rays of incinerating light and oppressive heat from a sky of blue: summer, it appeared, had replaced spring in an otherwise typical Malayan morning. Earlier, Captain O'Toole, as Irish and diminutive as a Galway leprechaun, had come fussing down the deck to join her. 'Top o' the morning' to ye, girl! Is it me you're hanging about for, or the big handsome tea-planters comin' aboard from the jungle?'

'Forget about tea-planters,' said Milly, mimicking his Irish brogue. 'Shave off that beard, lose twenty years, and you're me boy.'

The captain leaned on the rail beside her, his eyes narrowed to the strickening light.

So far on this trip he carried only this passenger aboard, and he liked her: though young she was unpretentious, had a happy outlook on life, and since leaving Liverpool the pair of them had enjoyed interesting conversations; a rare commodity on a broken down old tub like this one, carrying a German mate and a mixed crew of Chinese and Lascars. In a minor way it was for O'Toole a finale to his forty years at sea; a tom-boy affinity which reminded him of someone out of his past. Vaguely the old captain hoped that their relationship would not be spoiled when the noisy, ill-mannered, up-jungle planters came aboard at midday.

'Dear God, it's hot.' Milly wiped her perspiring face. 'They tell me you can fry an egg on the pavement.'

3

'Aye, and worst of all is hanging around here before we slip moorings.' Cupping his hands to his mouth, he shouted, 'Hurry it along, Bo'sun, we're due out on the afternoon tide, remember!'

The pygmy coolies on the wharf below quickened under their loads; in varying hues of gold and quicksilver the harbour reflected rays of refracted light, slanting down upon the surrounding Malayan hills, dancing in the rippling wastes of translucent water.

'How long before we reach Hong Kong?' asked Milly, and O'Toole stared about him. White duck-suited Europeans and their servants scurried amid shrieked commands and flapping P and O bills of lading. Beyond the crane-spiked dockland the white façades of colonial government houses shimmered under the molten sun of a tropical midday. Somewhere out there, beyond the stink and swirling coal dust, thought O'Toole, clutches of civil servants eased their collars under the coolie-operated ceiling fans, chattering aimlessly about nothing in particular while their white-gowned wives and mistresses idly contemplated, within the soporific haze of lunch-time gin and bitters, the scandals of English social gatherings.

Out of the corner of his eye the captain saw Milly's youthful profile; beautiful with a very English quality, he thought, had it not been for the schoolgirl's freckled nose. Her hair was the colour of jet, a lustrous black which hung in plaits either side of her face. Privately the captain pitied her.

'I asked how long before we get to Hong Kong?' repeated Milly, her voice invading his thoughts.

'How long? About a week if the weather holds, though the glass is dropping.'

'What does that mean?'

'A rainstorm, if we're lucky. A typhoon if we're not. Then all hell breaks loose.'

'You're a happy soul!'

O'Toole patted her hand as it rested on the rail. 'Don't you worry. Come hell or high water, this old tub will make it. She's weathered South China Sea hurricanes, was nearly overturned by sand-piles in a dust storm off Port Said, and has been set

4

afire by pirates — she'll see us safe in Hong Kong harbour.'

'Pirates?'

He gave a grin. 'This is the Far East, and we're steering a course through the opium smuggling routes.'

'I thought pirates only appeared in story books.'

'Off the English coast they do, but this is the China Run, and we're a century behind the times.'

Milly looked at the sky.

'Are you all right?' he asked.

Milly did not reply.

She was thinking that her life to date, initially quiet and uneventful, was now racing towards its destiny, carrying her along with it at an alarming speed.

Within a few months of her seventeenth birthday her father's letter had arrived — a rare event that sent her into a flurry of excitement. But his message, as usual, was brief.

A marriage, apparently, had been arranged; James Wedderburn, a business associate, was to be the groom and Milly the bride. Which, she now thought bitterly, was apparently the way they did things in Hong Kong: without emotion, affection, and often without the agreement of one of the parties. In which respect she was lucky, some told her; other girls had been whisked away to the Far East as prospective concubines to fat gentlemen old enough to be their fathers.

Now, with the prospective bridegroom coming up on the port side, so to speak, the closer she got to the Hong Kong waterfront, the more appalling the prospect appeared. The one consolation, perhaps, was that Mamie, her beloved Mamie, would be there to greet her.

The black housekeeper, now over forty and employed since her childhood in the Smith household, had proved Milly's friend and companion in the days following the death of her mother. Indeed, had anyone asked Milly Smith who her mother was in those far off days, she would probably have said it was Mamie. But when, at the age of eleven, her father, returning to Hong Kong, had packed her off to the boarding school, he had taken Mamie with him: which

5

meant that there was not even an adopted mother to come home to. School holidays were therefore usually spent within the confines of a deserted school; wandering down empty, echoing corridors and taking tea with resident teachers who didn't really want to be bothered.

'Are you sure you're all right?' said Captain O'Toole.

'Perfectly,' she answered, coming out of her reverie.

In his time O'Toole had shipped many such young women East for marriage to prospective suitors. When it came to shot-gun weddings, he thought, the British colonials weren't far behind the Indians.

Beauty, of course, was the criterion when fulfilling a young woman's marital hopes; and often the hopes weren't hers, but those of a calculating relative. And while many a duke had been waylaid by the impoverished uncle of a beautiful serving-maid, mostly such marriages of convenience were nothing more than business negotiations.

Sweating badly, the captain moved uncomfortably in his white uniform. This poor child was just another such marriage contract, he thought, for he happened to know Sir Arthur Smith, her father: a man with his fingers in a dozen financial pies, including a directorship of the Peninsular and Oriental Shipping Company, which owned this old rust-bucket.

Milly's situation had become immediately clear to O'Toole; she was a commodity of doubtful value brought straight out of a dormitory school to be sold off as an old man's darling. Earlier, he had seen her portrait hanging in Sir Arthur's Marine Department in Pedder Street, Hong Kong: she was scarcely high value in the marriage stakes. However, what she lacked in womanly looks Milly made up for in personality, he thought: an unimportant attribute, perhaps, when it came to a society match. Reflectively, O'Toole cursed the system where unwanted daughters were brutally shipped back home to Britain or condemned to lives of unpaid and mistreated companions to some old hag twice their age. He hoped that Milly didn't prove to be one of these.

'Have you met your prospective husband?' he asked.

'No, but I know what he looks like.' Milly fingered a little silver locket hanging at her throat and snapped it open.

O'Toole saw the face of a middle-aged man, fleshy, florid, with greying side-whiskers; fifty if he was a day, he thought. He happened to know James Wedderburn Esquire, of Smith and Wedderburn, the shipping agents, and from what he'd heard Wedderburn's business activities were anything but savoury.

'What does your mother think about it – marrying by proxy as it were?'

'My mother died when I was born.'

'How do *you* feel about it?'

'It's what Father wants. He worries a lot, he says, about us being so far apart.'

'Sure to God,' said O'Toole, his anger emphasising his Irishness, 'it's what you are wanting, isn't it? What's it to do with yer feyther?'

A breeze blew between them, touching their faces with hot fingers; the deck beneath them trembled to the loading. O'Toole sensed a greater affinity growing between them.

'Are you making a mistake, young Milly?'

'Probably.' She lowered her face, then, glancing up, smiled brilliantly, instantly beautiful.

'Wedderburn's twice your age.'

The reply came quickly. 'The younger ones have all been snapped up by local beauties.'

This was true; the extraordinary good looks of the Chinese and Eurasians captivated the most diffident Hong Kong bachelors though not before they had served the usual male apprenticeship in the Mist and Flower bordellos then flourishing along the waterfront. Now the captain said, with a bold attempt at humour, 'Why not hold your fire until you take yer pick o' the savages due aboard?'

'Savages?'

'The equivalent – the jungle tea-planters from up-country.'

A smile touched her mouth. 'Now that sounds interesting!'

'If we survive them – because, from what I hear these days they're the spawn of the Devil.'

'Have you met any of them?'

'Only one, their present foreman. Time was he was

7

respectable; came down from Shanghai when he was still a boy and became a *compradore* – a supplier of goods to the shops and clubs. But that wasn't enough for Eli. He was a Baltimore lad and bound to get on. He wanted big profits and to get rich quick, so he went into tea-planting.'

'He's an American?'

'And as tough as they make 'em. Take my tip and stay locked in your cabin – he's a devil for the women.'

'Now it becomes even more interesting.'

'You behave yourself. It's my job to get ye into the arms of your feyther in one piece: a month from then ye'll be a respectable married woman, they tell me.'

'Don't remind me!'

The first mate, a big fair German, called him then, and O'Toole left to supervise the loading. But before he went Milly flashed him a smile, one he would always remember; most people he thought, smiled with their mouths, but this girl did it with her entire soul.

'You should smile more often, Milly Smith,' he said.

Sweetcorn, a pig-tailed Chinese waiter, so named because of his addiction to things American, brought Milly a cup of morning coffee as she sat in a deck-chair. His Mission English was good.

'You wait looksee for tea-planters come aboard, Missy?' And he pointed. 'Quick, *kwai-kwai*, they come now, eh?'

At the rail again Milly saw a gaggle of rickshaws come racing along the coaling-wharf: hooting like Sioux Indians their occupants arrived, all save one clearly drunk, urging their runners to greater speed.

'You know these people?' she asked.

Nodding, his round, yellow face regarded her. 'Sweetcorn knows everybody on the China Run, Missy.'

'You know their names, then?' She nodded down at the quay.

'Only one – Big Eli, the foreman. Others just drunks. All very bad men, Missy, and chase wicked, bad women.' He pointed to where the rickshaws had stopped, their six passengers getting out shakily; one, a big man in a white pith helmet to match his white suit, was paying off the coolies.

'See him – big fighter? That's Foreman Eli.'

'Big fighter?'

'Velly bad man. One time I work up-jungle way. Always fighting and chasing pretty ladies. For many months they all pick tea with natives, and Malayan girls run quick with Eli after them – I see it. *kwai-kwai* runnin', but that Eli quicker. You never heard such a hollerin' when he do catch 'em. Me Mission-trained, Missy, and read Bible, from Genesis to Revelation. You know Bible, Missy?'

She gave him a smile. 'Pretty well.'

'You know how many words in Old Testament?'

'I'm afraid not!'

'Then Sweetcorn say and one day you tell your children! Old Testament nearly 60,000 words, New Testament 182,000. I count them.'

'Good gracious!'

'No words in Bible more'n six syllables – you know this?'

'Really?'

'And littlest verse is 35 of 11th Chapter St John. You want more?'

'I can see you know your Bible, Sweetcorn!'

'Better'n Eli Boggs. Hell-smoke comes out o' his ears! Velly bad man.'

'What else do you know about him?'

'On Hong Kong side they do not like him in the English clubs. He got bloody rough talk, too, beggin' your pardon, but that's a fact. One time, too, I serve dinner at English table in Hong Kong Club, but I have not seen him since. You know this club?'

'Not yet,' replied Milly.

'Me waiter there when Eli was *compradore* man, selling groceries, see? And fat old English lady says to me: "Boy", she says, "you serve these shelled oysters frozen, do you? Not in Hong Kong you don't, so take them away and unfreeze them properly", she says. "Also, you call this meat lamb, do you?"

'"Very lambin', Missy," I told her. "Also, oysters out of ice-box from England, very cold, beg your pardon."

'"Don't argue with me, or you'll go out on the street,"

says she. And sitting beside her is that Eli getting stiff with whisky, but very kind to Chinese people, mind you. And he says, polite, "Ma'am, allow me to assure you on one point. You say this meat on your plate is not lamb?"

'"It is pork, young man. Allow me to know the difference."

'"Spring lamb, Ma'am,' says Eli, "for I am the *compradore* and I smuggled it in myself. As for the oysters, they always arrive frozen or don't keep." Lots o' gents up on their legs and with fists up at Eli, and the lady shouted, "Can anyone tell me how this drunken American got in here?"'

'Good God,' whispered Milly.

'Yes, yes,' added Sweetcorn. 'Good God I say, too, for this English lady said, "Get him out, you hear me? Throw him out!"'

'What happened?' whispered Milly.

'Then many people come, soldiers in blue and red uniforms, too, and get hold of Eli to throw him out, and the table goes over and the wine is spilled and men fallin' unconscious with Eli hittin' 'em out, and he shouted: "If she don't know the difference between pork and lamb, she's no housewife, damn her eyes! And if she wants her oysters warm, I suggest they go down here." And he shovels them shelled oysters right down the front of her — very large lady, you understand, very big topside.'

'No!' shrieked Milly.

'Yes!' cried Sweetcorn. 'And now there's trouble, with the fat lady fainting, people fanning her, and her husband fishing down the front for oysters. I tell you, Missy, this Eli causes offences tremendous, so the men got hold of him and threw him out and the Hong Kong Club don't get oysters off Eli Boggs no more. No sir.'

'Eli who?' gasped Milly, straightening.

'Eli Boggs,' said Sweetcorn, and Milly giggled helplessly.

'*Boggs*? I don't believe it!'

'Here he comes now,' added Sweetcorn, standing stiffly to attention.

Eli Boggs, striding down the deck, bowed low to Milly. His face was weatherbeaten; his hair a mass of black curls.

'Aha,' said he, 'this must be the passenger Cap'n O'Toole mentioned. Eli Boggs, Ma'am, at your service.'

Still stifling laughter, Milly curtsied demurely, her eyes cast down.

'I see you're enjoying the company of our good friend Sweetcorn.' And saying this he tapped his forehead and secretly pulled a face at Milly. 'You workin' aboard this old barnacle these days, my friend?' he asked the steward.

'Work for P and O now, Mr Eli. Don't work Hong Kong Club no more.'

'Thank God for that. Neither do I.' And Eli bowed again to Milly, adding, 'Later, with your permission, lady, we'll become better acquainted.'

'I look foward to it,' she replied, and the moment Sweetcorn had left them, asked, 'Isn't he quite the ticket, then?'

'Mad as a hatter,' said Eli. 'He's a good cabin steward — I've travelled with him before — but anything Sweetcorn tells you you take with a pinch of salt, so ye do.'

Good gracious, thought Milly, another Irishman, and mentioned it.

'As Irish as Killarney on me mother's side,' explained Eli.

Meanwhile Captain O'Toole was watching from his position on the bridge; knowing Eli's reputation, he decided to keep an eye on the pair of them.

11

2

The ancient *Mongolia* steamed along at a merry rate. With dolphins showing the way and flying fish skimming the wave-tops, she headed eastward for the wastes of the South China Sea. Eli was in a fine hearty mood as he joined Milly and the captain at breakfast.

'Top o' the mornin',' cried O'Toole, his usual greeting.

'And fair weather to you, me Irish friend,' replied Eli. 'Is the glass holding?'

'As well as can be expected, but if it starts to blow we'll be due for a tipsy. Do ye come this way often these days, Mr Boggs?'

Sweetcorn, his face expressionless, served egg and bacon to Milly and black coffee to Eli, who replied: 'When the season demands, for Malaya is the work-place and Hong Kong the playground.' He turned to Milly. 'They tell me you're packin' your bag for marriage up there. That true?'

''Tis a lucky fella awaiting her, for sure,' said the captain. 'I've proposed to her twice this trip so far, but she'll have nothin' to do wi' the Irish.'

Eli tipped back his chair, his hands round his mug of coffee. 'Do I know the lucky man? I'm in Hong Kong a lot, and swear I've seen you before.'

'This is my first trip East,' she said.

'Have ye been in the Marine Department lately, Mr Boggs?' asked the captain, and Eli snapped his fingers and sat upright.

'Got it! The portrait hanging in the Marine Superintendent's office! Spit and image of the girl!' He leaned foward,

12

interested. 'Then you're the daughter of Sir Arthur Smith — I heard you were coming out.'

'Heir to the family fortune,' interjected O'Toole, 'and she's already promised elsewhere.'

'I asked her if I knew the lucky man,' he said, watching Milly closely.

'Ah, it's a state secret till the date's announced,' replied O'Toole. 'But you'll know it soon enough, for there's not much misses the gossipmongers of the Fragrant Isle. Meanwhile, are your lads settled in?'

'Give tea-planters a bellyful of food and a hammock and they settle anywhere,' said Eli. 'I'm the one ye should be askin' about — last time I was aboard a P and O I got the stateroom cabin.'

He grinned at Milly, his white teeth flashing in his brown face, adding with a sigh, 'It's entirely unfair, so it is. There's the likes of me, out there in the jungle with never a lass to show a care, and these top Hong Kong fellas wi' the pick of the English fillies.'

'Me heart bleeds for you, Mr Boggs,' said O'Toole, rising from his chair. 'I've yet to see you up-jungle fellas go short on anything, includin' English fillies.' And he flickered a wink at Milly, and left them.

She stirred her coffee abstractedly, aware of the eyes of the man before her; they were dark brown beneath his jutting brows, eyes that constantly changed expression, she noticed; full of gentleness one moment, fiercely inquiring the next, silently voicing unspoken questions. Yet they were eyes that never betrayed the inner man.

Eli, for his part, was remembering a woman he had known long ago. The faint perfume of this girl's presence brought memories rushing back with unbelievable force, transporting Eli to the time when one like her had stood beside him on a wind-swept deck: a moment from another age. Ten years ago? he wondered. Was it really so long?

When he was twenty he had married the woman and taken her East to make his fortune. Annette was her name, a girl from Paris. In the second summer of their marriage in Hong Kong she conceived, and in childbirth caught the fever along with her infant and died. Now, in the tranquil, clear profile of the girl on the other side of the table, he saw Annette again, and it was if the long intervening years — a time when he had relentlessly pursued and possessed Chinese, Malayan and Eurasian — had never been. Momentarily, he was gazing once more into the cornflower eyes of that first love; reliving the days when she, with all her French charm, had come to him in the rollicking nights of the voyages between Hong Kong and Macao.

Milly raised her eyes.

'You are staring, Mr Boggs!'

'I'm sorry!' Eli moved awkwardly. 'I was thinkin' of your portrait in the Marine Office ...'

The old ship trembled to the rotation of her engines; below the fathomless sea swept in unseen eddies, and above, a June sun slanted down with searing rays into cool, translucent depths: home of countless strange and wonderful sea-creatures and the littered sandbed of a thousand wrecks.

'She was about your age, that's all,' he said.

'Who?'

'Oh, it don't matter. But I knew you long before I saw that painting in your father's office.'

'I don't understand.'

'Of course not. Shall we go up on deck?'

Eli Boggs, thought Milly, was an enigma; a man of half sentences who expected a listener's imagination to complete . his subtle pauses. Together they surveyed the placid ocean.

'Will you be staying in Hong Kong?' asked Milly.

'No chance. The lads and I work for eleven months of the year, then come east and let our hair down. There's five of us — myself, a Malay, a black, and two Hong Kong Chinese who have wives in Shaukiwan.'

'The pirate area?'

Eli glanced swiftly at her. 'You know of it?'

'My father wrote and told me. The scum of the China Sea, he called them.'

He shrugged. 'Depends upon your views. Perhaps the really dirty people are those running the opium trade; compared to them the Bias Bay pirates work for a pittance. The big opium *taipans* are the ones who make the loot.'

'He also said that the authorities are clamping down on smuggling and the British fleet is patrolling the Pearl River.'

He smiled. 'You're well informed.'

'As I say, I get it from my father's letters. And since we've become engaged, James writes almost every week. As head of the Marine Department under my father he knows most of what is going on.'

'James Wedderburn, the Superintendent?'

Milly nodded. 'The man I am going to marry.'

His face showed astonishment. 'But he's fifty!'

'What of it?'

The sea below them parted in swathes of white-laced foam as the old ship, creaking and groaning, blundered on like a plump woman in tight stays waddling off to market. Eli opened his mouth to speak, but she said, 'My business, I think?'

'I'm just a bit surprised, that's all.'

'So are most people.'

He began to walk and she joined him. 'I believe James Wedderburn is a good man and he's done a lot for the Marine Office. You know him well?'

'Fair to middlin'. I had a bit to do with him when he got the Piracy Ordinance through Government at the last Session — got a good legal mind.'

'That's what my father said.'

'Which is not to say that he'll make the best of husbands!'

'I'll be the judge of that.'

It was supposed to deter further questions, but did not.

'Certainly he's put the wind up the Big Eyed Chickens since he took over.'

'Big Eyed Chickens?'

'Pirates. When you see a Chinese junk with cannon aboard and two eyes painted on its prow, it's up to no good, folks say.'

'Until now I thought piracy went out with the last century.'

'Not in these parts. China's always behind the times. From

15

here up to Bias Bay and west to Macau, the place is swarming with 'em.'

He was handsome, thought Milly. And like most handsome men he knew it, and was possessed of that lazy grace that is the hallmark of strength. His jacket, open to the waist, exposed ridges of muscle; when he smiled, which was often, he was every inch the predatory male. She judged his age to be thirty, and wondered if he was married.

As if reading her thoughts, he said suddenly, as they strolled along, 'I saw my first Big Eyed Chickens ten years back, when I was just twenty. They came aboard off the Paracels — the day after tomorrow we'll be abreast of those — a cluster of islands off the Gulf of Tonkin. There's pirates and pirates, and these were the scum your father mentioned. The first thing they did was hang the captain, then threw half the crew overboard and tied up the rest.'

'How terrible!'

'I got away by lowering myself astern and hiding under the rudder. After they'd pillaged the ship they set it on fire and cast it adrift.'

'You escaped?'

'Or I wouldn't be here, me darlin'! I climbed back on deck and untied the crew.' He smiled up at the sun. 'Ten years . . . it seems a lifetime. I was on my way to Hong Kong to be married, just like you.'

'What was her name?'

'Annette — about your age, but you're dark, and she was fair. She had a waist like that,' and he made a circle with his fingers.

'And you're going to her now?'

'Good God, no. She died years ago.' He shrugged as a man does when empty of emotion. 'She had a French father, but her mother was Chinese. We were together for six months in Hong Kong, but being a Eurasian she was never accepted. Snobby damned lot!' He swore for the first time, turning violently away.

'To be of French extraction was frowned upon — Hong Kong never got over the Battle of Waterloo! But to be half Chinese . . . our marriage put the pair of us beyond the

16

pale. Social conventions rule that place. We suffered, the pair of us.'

'I'm sorry.'

'Don't be, Miss Smith. Just make sure, in your cosy little English corner, that you never get like that.'

She could not take offence, such was his sincerity.

'How did your wife die?'

'Childbed fever. The Chinese midwife had dirty fingers. I hunted the place for a European doctor, then couldn't raise the money; in the end I finished up in the slum quarter.'

'You didn't marry again?'

'At my age I'd be wantin' me head examined! I'm footloose, fancy free, just take life as it comes.'

'And the ladies too, I hear,' said Captain O'Toole, joining them. He patted Milly's hand. 'So you'd be best advised, sweet colleen, to give this rogue a wide berth, like I said.'

'Sure, I'm only after walkin' the deck, and my intentions are innocent entirely,' Eli protested.

Milly said happily, in her best Irish brogue, 'For certain sure, with an Irishman either side, I don't know who to believe!'

Later, with the midsummer moon hanging like a Dutch cheese on the rim of the world, Milly dressed for dinner, bringing out of her little cabin wardrobe the bright green gown that she had seen advertised in the *Journal of Modes*, a fashion magazine which had circulated the schoolroom. The gown reached to the floor, the skirt voluminous, the bodice cut low to a daring degree and off the shoulder. She remembered that somebody had said she possessed the best pair of shoulders in Broadhurst: 'Make the most of them,' a friend called Maisie had advised. 'Like me, you're better from the back than the front.' Milly was indeed sadly aware that in the area of womanly curves she was almost totally deficient.

Pulling on her long white lace-trimmed pantaloons, she tied them at the waist with a large red bow, an act considered by matrons to be the height of provocation. Then, sitting at her little mirrored table, with utmost care, Milly applied the first powder and rouge she had ever used: sufficient to enhance her peaches and cream complexion but insufficient to label her a fallen woman. Pleased with the result, she

17

stood up. By judicious bending before the mirror, she confirmed that although she was no beauty, she had seen worse. And while her waist could scarcely be spanned by a man's hands, the tight-laced stays had given it a certain delightful symmetry. She pondered the possibility of affixing a bustle, in the event deciding against it on the grounds that it diminished the already meagre curves of her bust.

Ashes of roses now, the chosen perfume of ladies bound upon conquest – in this instance, one who went by the name of Eli Boggs: tea-planter, sea-rover, womaniser and widower ...

And James Wedderburn? What of him?

A small, thin gonging echoed down the narrow corridors of the old ship, bringing Milly's romantic musings to an end. Sweetcorn knocked on the door. 'You come, please, Missy,' he called. 'Captain already sitting at table.'

'Coming,' said Milly, and stilled her racing heart.

Six men sat at the table: all save Captain O'Toole in various stages of tropical undress, and all spooning up soup with a chorus of ill-mannered noises. Eli raised his head briefly to acknowledge her presence, then lowered it again to concentrate on his meal.

'Make yourself at home, Miss Smith,' said Captain, blowing on his spoon.

'You sit here, please?' asked Sweetcorn, placing her chair. And whispered into her ear as she sat down, 'Oh, my word, Miss Smith, you look very pretty lady.'

The others completely ignored her.

3

Early on the third day at sea Sweetcorn knocked loudly on Milly's cabin door.

'Please, you come quick!'

Pulling on her clothes, she followed him up the companionway to the fore-deck. Here, clustered among the steam winches, stood the majority of the ship's crew, mainly Lascars; also Eli at the head of his tea-planters. One was an ageing Negro as black as watered coal; stripped to the waist and bulging with muscle.

'What's wrong?' Milly asked, surprised to be called when dawn was only just breaking.

'Nothin',' Eli answered. 'Just the cap'n having a roll call.'

'At this time of the morning?'

The men laughed among themselves. The big Negro said, 'Ah tells ye what, Missy — Ah'd have a roll call every dawn o' my life, just to set eyes on you.'

'Watch your mouth,' said Eli, and the big man took a step away from her. Strange, thought Milly, to encounter such discipline among tea-planters. Then the ranks parted and Captain O'Toole, his uniform immaculate even at this hour, appeared with his first mate beside him. Beyond them Milly saw the sea ruffling into white-topped breakers, an omen of a high wind to come. The world looked empty under the grey light crescent moon of dawn: the same moon, she thought, which was now peering through dormitory windows at sleeping faces on white pillows.

19

Standing on board a ship, surrounded by burly tea-planters, the memory of her schoolfriends seemed very distant.

The captain said in measured tones: 'Listen, everybody, this is important. At six bells a sea-going fishing junk passed us starboard, and he was flying a signal which Mr Bruner here picked up.' He indicated the first mate beside him. 'It seems that three Big Eyed Chickens have been sighted a hundred miles of Hainan, making east towards Bataan in the Philippines.'

A low murmur spread among the Lascar crewmen, usually the first victims of Chinese piracy. But the planters, Milly noticed, showed little interest. She glanced at Eli; his face was expressionless. O'Toole continued: 'If they keep to their course, well and good, but if they tack south they'll be astride our bearing, which is three points west of the Paracels.'

'Pirates − I told you, remember?' Eli whispered to her.

'And so,' said the captain, 'with the wind freshening as well, I'm changing to a course which will take us west of Lincoln Island and into slacker water.'

'Typhoon time,' said Eli. 'It never rains but it pours.'

'I tell you this,' continued O'Toole, 'because it'll add a day or so on to our arrival in Hong Kong.'

'Now that's real bad, Skipper,' said the Negro. 'Ah got a coupla flower girls awaitin' me on Kowloonside and if Ah come lately they'll go off the boil.'

'Nobody's worried about your women, Black Sam,' replied O'Toole. 'It's the demurrage that bothers me.'

'Demurrage?' asked Milly.

'Port duties,' answered Eli. 'He should worry! The P and O are rolling in it − ask yer feyther.'

'My father?'

'Smith and Wedderburn are major shareholders, aren't they?'

His knowledge surprised her, but she dismissed the thought as the crew returned to their stations, pushing past her. This brought Milly face to face with Mr Bruner, the first mate, whom so far she had seen only at a distance.

Clicking his heels, he saluted, saying in a guttural accent: 'This is a pleasure, Miss Smith. Hans Bruner at your service.

I hope you enjoy the voyage?' His cold blue eyes veered towards Eli. 'You enjoy the trip so far also, Mr Boggs?'

'Excellent, Bruner, and the company's even better.'

'Let us hope that a little piracy does not spoil things, eh?'

'Oh, a bit of drama livens up the place!'

Meeting Eli's hostile stare, Mr Bruner went on his way.

'You two don't like each other?' Milly said.

'No. It goes back a long way.'

She would have queried this but was distracted when some off-duty Chinese, part of the winch-crew, thronged beside them: weather-beaten men upon whom long years at sea had left their mark. Apparently unaware of their audience, they began to prostrate themselves before a little red altar set up on the fore-deck. Upon this they affixed a small scarlet-robed image: Tin Hau, the goddess of Chinese sea-farers. No more than six inches high, she sat in regal authority, her tiny Oriental features impassive before the mournful supplications of her worshippers, all now upon their knees before her with burning joss-sticks in their hands. Their sing-song incantations rose above the thumping of the *Mongolia's* engines.

'She is Tin Hau,' Eli explained. 'To the Chinese sailor she is what Horus the sun-god was to the Ancient Egyptians. Her flesh is said to gleam at midnight like the sun, a beacon to guide sea-farers into calm waters.' He indicated the kneeling Chinese. 'A typhoon is coming, also pirates, including Chu Apu, the most notorious pirate on the seas. They are terrified of Chu Apu, so they pray to her for safety. The legend says Tin Hau was born in Fukien, the daughter of a lowly fisherman. One Moon Festival, when her parents were preparing to go fishing with the village fleet, she was somehow left behind on the beach. As the junks sailed off her father noticed her waist deep in the surf, pointing at his sampan. Considering this an omen, he turned his fishing boat around and returned to shore. His was the only sampan to return home that day, all the others being lost in a squall. So the villagers credited Tin Hau with heavenly powers, and since her deification ...'

'Deification?'

'Since they made her a god — a little like an English

21

saint. She always has with her two attendants, Thousand Mile Eyes and Fair Wind Ears, to assist her in caring for fishermen and sailors. Between them they have cured countless ills, including healing an Emperor of a crippling disease.' Eli's face was aglow as he warmed to his theme. 'Gods are central to Chinese philosophy. Take the Kitchen God, for instance. Although he had every possible cooking utensil at hand – and every known food, from grouper fish to the great prawns, one of which would make a meal for a hungry man – he learned not only about cooking, but also about himself, with typical Chinese thoroughness.'

'Learned about himself?'

'To know oneself is important to China. Often the rich man will beg at a city gate, in order to know the poverty of the beggar; or pull a rickshaw so he learns of the puller's exhaustion.

'We burn special incense before the Kitchen God and offer him sweet foods, so that he will say sweet things about us on his journeys between Earth and Heaven. There is a special sweetmeat dedicated to him called T'ang Kua, which we must eat if our behaviour has been wicked. We also smear his mouth with opium or feed his effigy strong wine so that, if he intends a bad report of us, he will become befuddled and talk nonsense.'

'Good gracious!'

'The Kitchen God's name is Tsao Wang. He's one of the oldest deities and has been worshipped in China since the days of Wu Tu, a patron of Taoism in the year 133 BC. His food, when he is fasting for the sins of the household, consists of a few sips of morning dew and any spare moonbeams, which on dark and frosty nights means that he often goes to bed hungry.'

'You know more of such things?' Milly was enchanted.

'Ask me and all will be revealed.' He was suddenly no longer a reprobate with an Irish brogue, but had the intonation of an educated English gentleman.

'But how do you know all this?'

Eli patted the side of his nose with his forefinger.

'Ah now, me little English, wouldn't that be tellin'?'

Sweetcorn stood before Milly in her cabin; he seemed apprehensive, shivering beneath his white jacket.

'Missy in much trouble,' he began.

'So I'm beginning to think!'

'This Chu Apu is bad pirate man. He come so quiet in the night that he does not even wake up mice and is harder to catch than wind whistling in the sky.'

Milly gave him a reassuring smile. Sweetcorn continued gravely. 'You mind if I call you Milly? I am old Chinese gentleman; you young English girl.'

'Please do.'

'You leave quick before this Chu Apu arrive, please? Better for young girl to go into pig basket for drowning than live as Chu Apu's concubine.'

Despite the gravity of the situation, Milly stayed calm. 'You know about this man?'

Sweetcorn drew closer. 'Listen, like English soldiers say, him damned bad fella. In Shekki, where I was born, many pirates like Chu Apu lived on the banks of the Pearl River. My aunt and uncle, they rice farmers, and they take me and their harvest to Hong Kong market in sampan-boat. But always Chu Apu's pirates wait for us. "Good people," they would say, "what is the hurry? Please stay for a Celebration Tea." And this we had to do, or they would drown us. But always, when we go to sail off again, one bag of rice is stolen. Same thing happened many times before we reach the market, for other pirates were waiting to get their bag of "squeeze". In the end we have only one bag to sell for money, and we go hungry.'

'How terrible!'

The ship rolled and pitched beneath them, its rusted plates clanking at the onslaught of the swelling sea; a hollow booming sounded faintly from the depths of the cargo hold.

'Then Chu Apu become pirate chief and bring many men to burn Pearl River villages and carry away maidens,' Sweetcorn continued. 'And British gunboats no can find him. So I tell you now, leave quick when Chu Apu arrives, eh?'

'But where to?'

He pointed to the port-hole. 'Cap'n says big wind here

23

soon, so we sail east of Paracel islands to some quiet water. But Chu Apu, he will be waiting for us, you see!'

'How do you know all this, Sweetcorn?'

'Sweetcorn know plenty. I also see fishing junk go by last night. I read signal. Chu Apu is waiting two points off the Paracels, I tell you. Opium, see? And nobody except Bruner and Sweetcorn knows.'

'*Opium*?'

'Much opium for China on board this ship, and Chu Apu wants it.'

'And he is waiting to intercept us?'

'Come aboard at Paracel and steal opium, two tons.'

'I had no idea we were carrying opium. Is Mr Bruner a party to this?'

'What you say?'

'That the first mate is working with the pirates, is that what you are saying?'

'I *know*,' asserted Sweetcorn. 'I sail with Bruner twice before. Each time finish up with pirates.'

'Then why don't you warn Captain O'Toole?'

He shrugged. 'Me tell Captain? Who believe Sweetcorn? And if Chu Apu hears I tell, he will kill me. Also, if he do not come at the Paracels, Captain will give me to British to be whipped for lying. Perhaps even put in chains and sent on a slave ship from Hong Kong to Peru.'

'Slave ships in Hong Kong? I don't believe it!'

'Oh yes, Missy, plenty slaves. Coolie slaves, see? Hong Kong very bad place for poor Chinese people. Many black slaves in England, I read about that. Now coolie slaves in Hong Kong – merchants make plenty money. Big English companies like Smith and Wedderburn make rich on slaves and opium.'

'Now I know you're lying,' cried Milly. 'My father is a director of that firm – he would never do such a thing!'

The Chinese made a wry face. 'Me, Sweetcorn, I am full of years and have very big stomach. Man with *da douser*, big belly, very wise.' He smoothed his paunch with affectionate hands. 'I tell you true, Missy. I am sorry your papa make money out of Chinese slaves and opium. I go now.'

'You do that! Meanwhile I shall tell Captain O'Toole

24

everything you've said, and see what he makes of it!'

The steward passed a finger across his throat. 'You tell him, Missy, and Sweetcorn is dead.'

'Then why tell me this nonsense in the first place?'

'So you can hop *kwai-kwai* when we get to Paracel islands.'

'Hop where? I asked you that before.'

'Over the side of the ship and swim like a fish.'

'Oh, yes, and what about sharks? They say there are plenty here.'

'No worse sharks than Chu Apu, Missy. Back in Shekki I have pretty girl daughter like you. Since you come aboard you don't curse and treat me like dog, like other people: you my very good friend. So don't you talk to Captain about opium and slaves, or it will get me dead. You just go over the side and swim to the shore. Sweetcorn will see you later and feed you.'

'As I said, the sharks will get me.'

'Oh no, Missy, I pray to Tin Hau and she will see you alive and kicking.'

'I'm much obliged to you,' Milly answered faintly.

4

That evening, the fourth at sea, the sun sank low and blood red beneath the wave-capped ocean.

With dinner over, Eli suggested Milly might like to look at the phosphorescence in the ship's wake. It was a favourite excursion for ship-board lovers, but Eli was unusually quiet, a fact that Milly noted; his flirtatious Irish banter had diminished into a thoughtful silence. In this mood, thought Milly, he could almost be a man of breeding − an impression not usually supported by his raffish exterior. It was good, she thought now, to be attended by a mature gentleman after the boyish bumpkins of her Kent village, boys who trampled on her sensibilities with rough-hewn strength or trod on her toes in the village balls.

Eli, however, was thinking that he should have his head examined, allowing himself to be led such a dance by someone nearly young enough to be his daughter.

'Accordin' to the captain, you're still at school?' he said now.

'I'm not!' she snapped. 'I left months after my seventeenth birthday.'

He chanced a closer look at her. No, he concluded, she was not beautiful as Annette had been; the difference, he supposed, between a woman and a girl. Milly's was a child's face, immature, and nothing her long gown did for her lessened that air of adolescence. Had there been a mature woman aboard, he thought, he'd not have given her a second glance; but since she *was* the only available female, he supposed she would have to suffice.

26

Later, he thought, he might try to lure her down into her cabin; after all, he considered, everybody had to learn of life at some time or another, and better a man of maturity than some ham-handed bungling youngster. Back home in the up-country plantation he snapped his fingers and women came running. He cared for none of them, had not been capable of caring since he had lost Annette. But now the situation was urgent – he hadn't had a woman for a fortnight.

Conscience touched Eli then, and he stared down at the sea, immersing himself in the light of the churning phosphorescence. Milly watched him intently. How far could she go with this? The man who was now at her side was no callow boy whom she might push away with impunity, and the situation was becoming fraught with danger. Eli, meanwhile, deep within himself, was wishing her to the devil. Of all the females in the world he had to land up with a naive adolescent! And he smiled at the thought.

'Why the smile?' asked Milly.

He did not reply. Above the surge of the sea he imagined he could hear the empty-headed laughter of the plantation trollops. They came in all shapes and sizes, but had one quality in common – the ability to read the mood of a man, attend to his needs, and hold their tongues about it. It was strange, thought Eli, what variety in looks and character womankind possessed. God must possess a cupboard full of moulds . . . But while a mature woman could be trusted to be diplomatic, to put one's faith in the discretion of an impressionable child was asking for trouble. Out of the blue, came the memory of past carelessness for which he had suffered: an aberration that had nearly cost him his life.

At the time he was living with a Portuguese girl of charm and beauty, the daughter of a gunpowder factory manager based on Macao. She was also quick-tempered and handy with a knife. Having brought her to Hong Kong, the usual scene of his amours, he was lying beside her in that morning meditation which follows an exhausting night, when his manservant entered the room. And, before Eli could stop him, the man leaned over the bed, shook the girl by the shoulder, disturbing her slumbers and whispered: 'Wake up, Missy. Time you get out, go home.'

Such a scene followed that Eli swore to be more careful in future. Yet here he was again, embroiled with a young woman who had a powerful father awaiting her in Hong Kong. Might it not be best, therefore, to kiss her on the forehead and let her haul herself off to the safety of her bed? After all, there was always tomorrow with the chance of a better location and happier prospects.

Eli grinned ruefully, took Milly's arm in brotherly fashion and pointed down at the boiling wake.

'You know, it's said that the spirit of Tin Hau sleeps on the seabed, six fathoms down. It is she, they say, who is waving festival lanterns down there, making such beautiful sea-lights.'

'That's a new one,' said Milly.

'And when she sees a pair of lovers looking down over the ship's rail, she binds them together with ropes from the sea.'

'Really!' Her voice was heavy with irony.

'Tin Hau commands, lovers obey. And Milly Smith, if you were a woman instead of a girl, I would put my arms around you and kiss you – two becoming one, as Tin Hau commands.'

She stiffened. 'If I'm not a woman now I'll never be one, so don't patronise me!' She pushed him away. 'Meanwhile, I learned all about phosphorescence when I was at school. All you're seeing,' and she pointed down at the sea-lights, 'is the oxidation of natural elements, a phenomenon discovered in the year 1670. The same light is given off by glow-worms; it has nothing to do with magic lanterns, and even less with your silly old Tin Hau.'

'Good God,' said Eli. 'Is nothing sacred?' And he left her alone.

Yet moonlight was sacred to Milly. Since her schooldays it had played an important role in Milly's life – something which Eli had yet to discover.

Now, on board the *Mongolia*, a shaft of moonlight entering her cabin reminded Milly of the hypnotic beauty of the night ... and a command to be up and away to an unknown destination. In all of which, at one time, a village lad called Tom Ellery had played a vital part.

Lying in her bunk, watching the moon-shaft search her cabin, it appeared to her as a lantern: a solitary brilliance lighting the way. Her eyes drowsy with approaching sleep, Milly's mind returned to the school dormitory and the long lines of beds wherein lay sleepers in a chorus of sighs and snores. And, astonishingly, Tom Ellery, aged twelve (the same age as her), an early and unsentimental lover, also appeared, his snub profile silhouetted against the window beside her bed.

In the temple of her dreams Milly saw him again with astonishing clarity.

'Come on down, Milly Smith. Come on! *Come on!*'

And she, draping her nightdress modestly about her knees, obeyed.

Milly had first met Tom in a sunlit lane near Bredon village in springtime. The hedgerows were decorated with wild rose and he was running an errand: so it happened that the daughter of Hong Kong's wealthy tycoon met by chance the son of the local road-sweeper, and Tom of the freckled face and turned-up nose charmed her with his smile.

'I seen you a'fore somewhere, mind,' said he, 'and I thought you was a prim and proper old girl. But now I seen you here, and talked, I reckon I was wrong.'

'Really? Just because I'm at Gadfield High doesn't mean I'm prim and proper.'

'More'n likely, though. They got their noses so high up there they'd drown in a rainstorm.' And he looked her over: stared at the pink dress that reached to her calves, the high-buttoned boots laced to her knees, and the little gold crucifix at her throat. Never in his life had he seen such a hat, all floppy with sun and lying on her shoulders. White ribbons fluttered down her back in the wind and she smelled as sweet as a nut.

'The girls are all right — it's the mistresses,' said Milly, dreamily. 'Don't do this and don't do that.'

'Ay. Like me feyther says — fancy 'emselves proper, that lot, he do say. Where you off to now, then?'

29

'Evensong.'

'Where's that?'

'Church.'

'But it anna Sunday!'

'Harvest Festival.'

He gave her a grin from his smudged face. 'Oh, aye, us too. Me feyther takes us wi' the windfalls from Squire Oldroyd's orchard — but I never saw you in the pews, mind.'

'I'm new here,' said Milly. 'My father went to Hong Kong and I've only just come to this school.'

'Where's Hong Kong?'

'It doesn't matter.'

'I gotta go now,' said Tom.

'So have I.'

And he, who had never been so close to a 'gentry' before (as he told his father) watched her go with a sadness and relief.

'Where's Hong Kong?' he asked when he got home.

'Search me,' replied his father.

Later that year, in summer, they met again; and again after that, wandering around the first cutting of Oldroyd's big wheatfield. In dark they met also, and went on meeting year after year, undiscovered, in secret places, until one day Tom kissed her.

'Don't you ever do that again, Tom Ellery!' said Milly.

'Damn, that ain't much! My mate Alfie Owen do chase his Bronny Evans round the haystacks, and when he get her into one, kisses her like you never saw. She squeals when she's a runnin', mind, but when he do catch her she hollers blue murder. And she's got a shout on her like Satan's trumpet, our Bron.'

'Maybe, but I'm not Bronny Evans and you're not Alfie Owen, so remember that. And please don't touch me again.'

'No offence intended,' said Tom.

Unspeaking, they walked on with the grief of misconduct between them.

'A right ould codswallop you are, an' no mistake!' said Tom, 'Nobody's goin' to kill you, ye know.'

30

Her dress was brilliant white that day in the sunlight against the green of the fields; her hair was black and plaited either side of her face. From her wrist as she walked swung a little sun-bonnet, and larks rained down music upon them as they went. Here, in their season, grew wild ivy and blue-bells: blackberry brambles were now strewn across their path; Tom's hand was like a burn upon Milly's arm as he helped her over them.

'You're no gentleman, I can tell you that!' said Milly. 'You didn't even ask.'

'Aye. But I was never birthed a gentry, like you. But I love you truly, Milly Smith.'

'And I love you, Tom Ellery. Will you kiss me again, decently?'

'Hold your hat on.' And what began as a kiss of friendship ended in flushed faces and quick breathing, for they were now nearly sixteen.

'Time I was off,' said Milly.

'Ye can say that again,' said Tom, delaying, and his eyes were sober and serious in his face.

They went on meeting secretly, by moonlight in Squire Oldroyd's barn, talking away the night hours all winter; in summer they wandered at weekends within that easy quiet among the hills, in itself exultant. Humour was forged in them by Milly's gentility and the rough banter of the commoner to whom a mother, now but a memory in Tom's heart, was a distant but loving secret: to his mother they paid tribute, laying upon her grave summer and winter flowers. Jackdaws jinked by overhead, stone-chats scolded, larks nicked and dived in the endless blue which lovers call Paradise; down in the valley a short-eared owl flew above them in a rush of wings, and they dreaded the passing of the summer.

'Corbooger,' said Tom, 'I jist fancy a flavourin' conie picked off the hill and strewn wi' turnips, parsnips, tatties and onion. And one day you'll cook for me, Milly?'

'Only for you, Tom Ellery.'

'And I'll build ye a thatch, so I will, an' huddle ye clear o' the bad west wind, for they blow some'at fierce over Bredon. You hear me?'

31

'One day?'

'And share your body only with me, like you said?'

'Only for you, Tom Ellery.'

'Like as not you should be gettin' back now, lest those hoity-toity teachers snare you for good, and never again come to meet your Tom.'

'That will never happen,' said Milly, and heard beyond the sound of his breathing the starlings chattering in the elms and the distant shrieking of gulls. Above his black-curled head glistened, yellow-bright, eight-petal celandines, where hedge-spiders spun their webs of gossamer. Within the scent of wild thyme Tom held her, but even amid his kisses Milly knew the old, haunting sense of foreboding.

'Got to get goin',' said Tom. 'Crack o' dawn in the marnin', for harrowin' Squire's field with Maister, and he dunna reckon to start late.'

And Milly knew, through some terrifying intuition, that this was the last time she would see him. Laughing, he lifted her high in his arms, set her down upon her feet and kissed her again.

'Be seein' ye',' said Tom.

'Goodbye, Tom Ellery,' said Milly.

The week after, Milly went to the village to post a letter to her father in Hong Kong.

'Pity about young Tom Ellery, weren't it?' said a woman.

She was fat and choleric; the lines of her once joyous youth had died in smudges of sadness around her tight-pursed mouth.

'Tom Ellery?' asked Milly.

'Anna you heard? Talk had it that the pair of you was as thick as honeybuns. Killed on Monday — the horse shied while he were harrowin' Square Oldroyd's pasture, and the spikes went over him.'

Milly closed her eyes. 'Killed?'

'Buryin' him come Tuesday — he been gone nearly a week now. Don't time fly!'

'But it can't be ...!' Milly said. 'It can't be true ...' And she turned and fled, the woman gazing after her.

Unable to believe the evidence of her own ears, Milly Smith, on that same evening, kept to her promised Friday night meeting with Tom, their rendezvous being the entrance to Squire Oldroyd's big wheatfield. And, as usual she saw Tom approaching her, ambling in his loose-limbed way from the village. Yet Milly noticed that, perhaps through some strange trick of the moon, he possessed no shadow ...

Shivering with an unnamed fear (since others said he was dead), she waited; and Tom, with his happy smile, walked straight up to her and kissed her. But cold were his lips, and the arms embracing her were arms of ice. And Milly saw through a rift of his hair the scudding clouds that fleeced the sky; through his brow and cheeks she saw also the full harvest moon. All this she saw through the whiteness of his face before the bright clouds dimmed, bringing her world to darkness; and in that darkness, and only then, did Milly see the glaze of Tom Ellery's eyes, which were not the eyes of a living human, but the cold, fixed stare of one who was dead. And when in horror she stepped away, the vision before her, once the face of Tom Ellery, slowly melted and became dissolute, as flesh melts in fire; featureless, distorted, corrupt. Milly screamed, and stood with empty arms within the stench of his decay; watching with growing horror the decomposition of something once alive. And she fell, among the cornstalks, which were the cuttings of the first reaping; and lay there till morning, when, with the help of searchers, the teachers found her.

Her elders insisted that it was all a trick of the moon; an emotional aberration that would be cured with the passage of time. But Milly felt herself to be changed forever.

Worse still was the inevitable inquest by Headmistress Carver, a brittle-faced woman of bitter memories. She wasted little time in extracting from Milly the truth of her illicit courtship of Tom Ellery; innocent as it was, making certain, it appeared, that all the details of her foolish love for a road-sweeper's son were put about for the enjoyment of teachers and pupils. As the ultimate humiliation, a detailed report of her activities was sent to Sir Arthur threatening Milly's possible expulsion from Gadfield.

It was a shame from which she never fully recovered.

Now, back on the *Mongolia*, Sweetcorn, about to take a last breath of sea air before rolling into his hammock, saw Milly standing by the stern rail in her nightdress.

'Why, Missy,' cried he, 'you will catch death of cold up here undressed ...!'

But Milly did not reply; she was staring up at the moon.

'Why for you stand just lookin', eh?' The steward, seeing her expressionless eyes, passed a hand in front of Milly's face to no visible effect.

'Dear me, you very sick child, an' no mistake,' Sweetcorn said, worried. 'You come back to your bed with Sweetcorn.' And, taking her hand, he led her back to her cabin.

5

While Milly Smith was aboard the *Mongolia* sailing for Hong Kong, other things were happening to another girl who lived in China. Destiny had decided that the paths of their lives would cross. The second girl was called Anna No Name.

Around the fifth day of March in the Western Calendar, all insects in China awake from hibernation; this date is about a fortnight before butterflies may be seen on the wing in Britain. And Anna No Name, a foundling who possessed no living parents, remembered the date well for two reasons. The first because it was the season of the pussy-willow, upon whose yellow flowers the butterflies feed; the second because it was the time of Ching Che and the morning of her eighteenth birthday, which occurred when she was working for the Catholic nuns who ran the Mission school on the Pearl River delta.

Anna No Name was not Chinese but a Moslem, and her presence in Fu Tan village needs explanation. According to her parents, now dead, and in the absence of proof to the contrary, she was said to be descended in a direct line from Royal blood (though later it was discovered that Yung, her brother, would have none of this, and carried a secret to the grave). Their parents further claimed that Hsiang Fei, the widow of the Prince of Yarkand, was Anna's relation: the most beautiful woman in Asian history was known as the Perfumed Concubine, and in her time was the *grand passion* of the Emperor Ch'ien Lung, who once ruled China.

Captured by the Imperial Army, Hsiang Fei was brought

to the presence of the Emperor. Hypnotised by her beauty, he lavished upon her great treasure, even building for her a bazaar and a temple to remind her of her native land.

But Hsiang Fei would have none of him, even threatening to kill herself should he approach her, because she was in love with her foreign prince. Her name, Perfumed Concubine, was given to her by the courtiers, because from her skin arose a scent akin to musk. Legend maintained that on the skin of all her female descendants the same perfume could be detected − a birthright of those of her blood, even centuries after her death.

And so it was that the humble peasant girl born in Fu Tan, she who possessed no parents, exuded a perfume so pleasing that it was proof of royal ancestry: and because her parents were wandering nomads upon the plains of Kwangtung Province, the villagers who adopted and raised her called her "Anna, the Child Who Possesses No Name". In due course they handed her over as a servant to the nuns of the Catholic Mission School, one situated near Fu Tan in the Pearl River delta.

Anna No Name had the ability to play most beautifully on the *p'i pa*, an ancient Chinese instrument resembling a lute. It was her practice to travel the area as a musician, giving entertainment to surrounding villages; however, she was on her knees, scrubbing the floor of the Mission hall, when the Mother Superior found her that morning.

'Anna,' said the Mother, 'I have news for you. The people you call your parents, those who adopted you, have been murdered by Chu Apu, the pirate.'

Anna, being a peasant and used to death, closed her eyes, and asked: 'What of Yung, my brother?'

'Thank God your small brother is safe,' replied the nun. 'It was he who brought the message. He is waiting outside.'

'It is necessary for me to return with him to Fu Tan, my village?'

'Of course, child. But first you must go to the chapel and give thanks that your brother's life was spared. God has been generous to you, understand?' But Anna, who until now had shown devotion to the Holy Catholic Church, raised her face like a woman being baptised, and said: 'If this be proof that your God is generous, Mother, leave me to worship my Taoist gods in future.' And after saying this, she left the Mission.

Outside in the sun, ten-year-old Yung was waiting. He stood alone, unheeded by passing labourers; in rags, with rivulets of tears on his grimy face, and his legs and feet bare and skinny from the famine.

'They have told you?' he asked in Cantonese, his mother tongue.

'They have told me,' replied Anna, at which Yung began to cry, until she said: 'Stop wailing! Remember what Mama said? "Cry when people are born in this world, do not grieve when they are dead".'

She took his hand and together they went down the road that led to the river.

'Where are we going?' asked Yung.

'After we have greeted our friends the butterflies, I will tell you,' replied Anna.

As they walked together over the rice-fields the hedgerows became alight with pussy willow and sallow, also swarms of Atlas Moth and the beautiful Erasmia butterflies which rose about them in the sunlit day; for, as is known in China, butterflies love both the petals of the purple buddleia and the aroma of musk, and this was the Feast of Excited Insects.

'Our parents will never return to us now,' said Yung as they walked.

'Not as mortals,' replied Anna, 'but as Hungry Ghosts they will return, as certainly as the butterflies are born to us in the spring. *Look*!' and she held out her bare arms and the butterflies descended upon them; more and more came in clouds from the hedgerows until she was almost covered. The floating flowers of splendid wings vied with a dozen other varieties – they were in her hair, covering her face, folding and unfolding their wings in their loveliness.

'They will not even sit on me,' grumbled Yung moodily.

So Anna knelt and put her arms around him, and the scent of her skin was transferred to him. The closer she held him, the stronger the perfume of musk became, so that soon he too was nearly covered with a hundred hues, beautiful to see.

After a while Yung grew tired of this and asked, 'Tell me, Gold Sister, where are we going now?'

'We are going to our village, to kill Chu Apu the pirate.'

He did not question this, because he knew well that everything his sister had ever promised had unfailingly come to pass.

This, indeed, was part of the secret he carried in his heart.

The journey was long, and it was late dawn of the next day before Anna and her brother arrived at Fu Tan village close to the town of Shekki, which stands on the bank of the Pearl River; the village is famous in Chinese lore for being the home of Haiti, the giant turtle, an animal so gigantic that a family could build a house upon his back.

Soft rain was falling upon the red roofs of Fu Tan, and hearing strangers arrive, the Head Man came out of his door.

'Ah, at last! The orphan Yung has returned to us, and if I am not mistaken, he has brought his sister.'

Anna elbowed Yung to bring him upright, for he was sleeping on his feet.

'You will take food?' the Head Man asked. 'Upon my stove are noodles made by the widow of Shekki.'

Yung's eyes grew big in his boy's face, she was a famous cook, but Anna said: 'Later we will eat, Head Man. First, please tell me why our parents died.'

'Because they could not pay their rice dues to Chu Apu the pirate,' came the reply. 'He killed them with a rope around their throats and a little stick to tighten it.'

'You have reported their murders to the British?'

'I have, but the English Commissioner says he can do nothing about it. What is one peasant more or less? said he.'

'May we see their bodies?'

'Their poor faces are not for the eyes of a child,' said the Head Man, and indicated Yung.

'You are mistaken, sir,' said Anna. 'Let him see their sadness, so that when he is a man he will remember the debt.'

'What debt? This is not a money transaction.'

'The debt Chu Apu has incurred, which he will repay in blood.' Hearing this the Head Man smiled tolerantly, as old people tend to do, and replied: 'You, a slip of a girl, threaten this pirate? Listen! In this village he is known as Chu the Terrible. It is ridiculous to speak of revenge. Come.' And he led the way to a small bier where the bodies of their parents lay, covered with spring flowers and lucky red paper, for the next day they were to be buried. He asked gently, 'You would like to say your Christian prayers over your parents, Anna No Name? Although such prayers are not of my belief, as a Taoist, I respect the religions of others.'

'I have no prayers to say,' she replied. Yung, upon his knees by the bier, was shaking with sobs. 'But if I have prayers to spare later, I will say them over the grave of Chu Apu.'

This time the Head Man did not smile, such was the expression upon the face of the girl before him. Then a strange thing happened, something of which the people of Fu Tan speak of to this day. Suddenly, out of the dawn sun, there descended two great butterflies, both with snow white wings; one settled on the forehead of Anna and the other on the forehead of Yung. Seeing this, the Head Man was afraid, for snow white butterflies had never been seen before down the length of the Pearl River; and it must be remembered that white is the colour of funeral clothes in China.

Also, upon the wings of each white buttefly, plain for all to see, was painted the mask of a fox.

Taking the butterfly from her face, Anna held it before her. 'When next you stupid people pay your rice tribute to Chu Apu the pirate, tell him from me that before the next Feast of Excited Insects he will die, and in a worse manner than that in which he killed my parents.'

The Head Man covered his face at this, being afraid.

Anna and Yung lived for three days in the village of Fu Tan, so that Yung could regain his strength. On the morning of the fourth day, the Head Man said: 'Anna No Name, it is time that your parents were laid to rest, so they may go to their ancestors in a decent state. I have good things in mind for them.

'For many years my wife and I have been saving up for a happy burial, for what is death but a happy transition from this sad life to the fields of Paradise? With the money saved we have built a stone grave; within it is a little chamber with a red door to guard against the entry of devils. The grave is built to accommodate two, that they may lie hand in hand, husband and wife, and begin together the journey into the Afterlife. Do you hear me?'

'We hear you,' said Anna.

'You possess money?'

'I have ten Mexican dollars in my pocket,' she said, and showed them to him.

'Then it is agreed? For the sum of one dollar every year for six years you may hire this grave from me. And, at the end of that time, when the bodies of your parents have been purified, we will meet here and draw them out of the chamber. You have seen this done?'

'Yung has seen it, perhaps,' explained Anna, 'but I was adopted by the Mission nuns when a child: I know only the Christian rites of burial.'

'Then listen, for if it is done perfectly, you will guarantee your parents a happy eternity.

'As I say, we will meet here in six years and draw out the bodies. Then it will be the duty of Yung here, being a son, to hold in his hands the skull of each parent while the undertaker identifies every bone, first those of your father, then those of your mother. These bones he will clean with perfume and sand until each is sparkling white. No children will be allowed near during this process, for children often play with the skeletons of the departed, and this angers their spirits. Aged grandfathers, as you know, can often be short-tempered.

'Then,' the Head Man continued, 'the undertaker will place the bones of each parent in an urn, laying them in their natural order − the feet bones first, then the others, placing each skull on top. The mouth of each urn will be covered with oil cloth to keep out insects, evil spirits and hungry ghosts who are wandering in search of disregarding relatives, and the urns will then be transported reverently to their place of residence outside your door.

'Between now and then you must save ten more dollars, which is the fee of the undertaker; this will include the cost of the urn. One further dollar will be needed for tea money which must be dropped into the urn lest your parents suffer thirst in the heat of the Afterworld. You understand all this?'

'I know of it already, Head Man,' Yung confirmed.

'Thus your parents, whom you have loved all your lives, can be with you until you die, resting in their Golden Pagoda outside your door. More, if you buy a few thousand Bank of Hell notes and also lay these in the urns, they will never be short of money during their journey through Purgatory. Is that not wonderful?'

'It is marvellous,' replied Yung, but Anna did not answer.

'You will do all this for your people?' asked the Head Man.

'We will do it, because it is the custom,' she said, and for the first time since her parents died, she wept.

'Then our grave will be made ready for my wife and myself after the hiring, and the existence of your Pagodas properly registered with the Government.'

'We will attend to that also,' said Anna, and the three of them went to the house of the Head Man where they drank green tea and celebrated the journey of their parents to Paradise.

'You are at peace now?' he asked afterwards.

'I shall never be at peace until Chu Apu and his murderers are dead at my feet,' said Anna.

Later, at sun-go-down, Yung cut long branches of fern and with these thrashed about the grave to drive away evil spirits while the bodies of his parents were laid to rest in the tomb.

Anna watched all this happen, and did not speak: she heard the wailing of the villagers and smelled the incense being burned by the Taoist priest who was brought in from a neighbouring village. And seeing all this, hearing the incantations, Anna looked at the darkening sky where a single ray of golden light was burning and felt the outline of the little iron crucifix she held tightly in her hand. When the celebration of the dead was over and all the people had gone, she still stood there, watching until the light faded from the sky.

'You going to pray now, Gold Sister?' asked Yung, pulling at her, 'or are you staying here all night?'

Left alone, Anna said to the sky, 'I put my trust in you and you failed me. Now I will put my faith in the beliefs of my clan.'

And going into the Head Man's house, she joined him, his wife, Yung and the Taoist priest, and knelt with them before the little scarlet altar of Tin Hau, the Queen of Heaven.

Nearby, lying hidden in the grass, was the discarded emblem of a crucified man.

6

And so, while Milly Smith's ship, the *Mongolia*, was approaching the doubtful shelter of the Paracel Islands on its way to Hong Kong, Anna No Name and Yung were about to leave Fu Tan village for the bandit lair of one called Barby Lo, a comrade of Chu Apu.

The Head Man came down to the river as Anna and Yung were preparing to go.

'I warn you,' he began, 'no good can come of this. Within a week this sampan will drift back here on the tide with your two bodies aboard it. That is what the pirates did to your parents.'

'You see these four bags of rice from the last harvest sir?' Anna said. 'They have been given to us by the villagers because we have no rice of our own. How could we sit here in disgrace, and eat like lazy locusts through the winter, when we can use it to trap the delta pirates?'

'You are being ridiculous! To search out Chu Apu's bandits is to walk into the jaws of a tiger.' And, turning, he gesticulated angrily towards the villagers who had gathered around the sampan.

One, a giant with one eye and a wooden leg, shouted: 'Look, everybody, look! Once I was whole. I had two eyes and two legs, but when I refused to pay my rice tribute, Barby Lo the bandit took out one of my eyes with a spoon. "See how a man with but one eye can find his way home," he said, "he who refuses to pay tribute!" Then, a harvest later when I still refused to pay, he cut off my right leg. "Now let us see how he can hop," cried he, "and at the

43

next harvest, if he still refuses to pay, he will lose an arm,''
Good people,' said the cripple, 'these two young people are
asking for death, as did their heroic parents.'

'You hear this man who speaks for your good?' asked the
Head Man.

'We hear him,' replied Anna.

'And you refuse his advice?'

'Yung, prepare the boat for poling off,' she commanded.

While he was doing this, a ragged old crone who begged
at the North Gate shrieked in a voice filled with hatred: 'Oh,
dear me, what a clever little bitch we have here! And what a
stupid brother! Why do we worry about them? This girl, for
a start, is not even Chinese! She hasn't got a name, being
a Turk or some kind of foreigner. Being a fool as well she
is entitled to nothing. Did not her ancestor go wandering
outside the comfort of her husband's arms and end up in
an Emperor's bed?

'They say her skin gives off the smell of musk, that she
comes from an ancient court. I say she is descended from
the loins of some foreign beggar whom her mother bounced
one night outside the city gates!' This brought shouts of
laughter. 'And if she angers Chu Apu or his comrades, they
will descend upon us and demand more than rice — they will
take our heads!'

This frightened the people, even the Head Man; all stood
silently looking at their feet.

The old beggar shrieked: 'Look at that face! It has not
even been cooked properly in the oven of the sun, for it is
as pale as watered milk. We Chinese have black hair, but
the hair of this one is as brown as a fox, with tints of gold
and silver. As for perfume — I can smell her from here. It
is not the perfume of the lady concubine, but in my nose the
stink of a vixen. So if she insists upon it, let her go after
Chu Apu, and he will send her back home with a litter of
pups. Then we will tie her in a pig basket and drown her in
the river!'

All but the Head Man bawled their approval of this.

'Go,' he said to Anna. 'May the Taoist gods be with you.
but go quickly while the going is safe.'

Without a backward glance, Yung bent to the pole

44

and took the little craft out on to the breast of the river.

Once upon the current of the river, Yung asked: 'Gold Sister, are you certain that this is what our parents would have wanted — for us to kill the bandits?'

'Certainly, for the sake of the villagers of the delta.'

'It could be difficult,' he said. 'Chu Apu is so tall, they say, that he has to duck his head to get under the sky.'

'Then we will see to the smaller pirates first,' Anna replied abstractedly, busy decorating the interior of the sampan with lucky red and gilt festival paper, like the Macao girls decorated the Mist and Flower boats into which they attracted European sailors.

Yung said more for he was a great chatterbox; but later, when dusk fell, Anna silenced him and brought him to his knees before her in the boat, saying: 'You trust me, Small One?'

'I trust you, Gold Sister.'

'You love me also?'

'As the kittens love the cat, I love you.'

'And you will obey me in everything I ask when once we reach the quay of Barby Lo the bandit?'

'I will obey.'

The crescent moon, lying upon his back with his feet in the air, watched the sampan with Anna, Yung and four bags of rice make its way down the black velvet waters of the Pearl River; meanwhile polishing his reflection in the water, as all new moons do, being very young and vain.

Yung slept, but Anna did not; she lay wide-eyed upon the decorated cushions of the hooped sampan and listened to the reed warblers making love to the river. This she did until the sampan, out of the tide swim, ground its keel upon a sandy beach; and this, Anna knew, was close to the lair of Barby Lo, the first pirate she sought.

A bonfire was burning on the river bank, sending sparks and smoke into the night sky. And around this fire, which was close to a wayside quay, five pirates slept while the sixth kept watch for sampans coming to pay their protection money.

All were awakened by the sentry and trooped on to the quay in the moonlight. The biggest was Barby of the Hooked Hand, who had once possessed ears and a nose; these having been removed by Chu Apu, his commander, for a minor indiscretion.

'Aha!' he cried, rubbing his bearded chin with his hook. 'What have we here, eh?'

'A brother and sister come to pay our rice tribute,' cried Anna eagerly, jumping on to the quay.

'A woman with sense,' growled Barby, and brought out his notebook, very official. 'Names, please?'

Beginning to write, he then sniffed vulgarly at the night air with what was left of his nose. 'By the gods,' said he, 'do not tell me we have collected the Perfumed Woman of Fu Tan?'

'The same,' she replied.

'Then am I not in luck? Until you arrived, oh Scented One, my life was pestered by pig wallowers and scabby beggars! So let me assure you that you have come to the right place, for I am a romantic pirate if ever there was one.' He chuckled harshly, rolling an evil eye. 'Invite me aboard, I pray you.'

'All in good time. And if I pay my tribute in virtue, do you promise to let us keep our rice and pass unhindered down river to the quay of Cross-Eyed Wong, the next bandit?'

'To my bandit friend, Cross-Eyed, you shall go unmolested, my beauty, but only when I have had my pleasure of you. Make way, make way!' And he cuffed Yung's ear in passing, so keen was he to get aboard.

Taking him by the hook, Anna led Barby Lo into the prettily decorated canopy of the sampan, meanwhile holding him away while he tugged at her clothes.

'No, sir, wait!' cried she. 'In my country, according to the Book of Rites, I am bound by law to give you the welcome due to your rank as the great Barby Lo, one feared by all on the Pearl River delta. Therefore, we will first drink Celebration Tea, which my ancestors drank in greeting to the Mongol hordes during the reign of Genghis Kahn. This, believe me, sir, will so sharpen your desires that you'll be able to make love all night.' And Anna poured him

46

a cup from a pot that was freshly made, saying, 'Meanwhile, Master, be assured that you will miss no privileges. I am such an expert in the delights of lovemaking that you will never again know such pleasures, even were you to live for the next thousand years.'

'I shall die of impatience in the next five minutes unless you do something about it,' said Barby, gulping down the tea. 'By the balls of my dead grandfather, never have I known such urgency. Are there many more like you in Turkey?' His bulging eyes, which were like those of a frog, drifted over Anna as she knelt before him. He saw her simple robe of scarlet and silver; the wreath of her long brown hair; the slanted eyes and skin that was the colour of gold.

Meanwhile, as planned, Yung was on the quay serving Celebration Tea (to which had been added the petals of the oleander flower) to the other five pirates who were squatting on their haunches, awaiting the pleasure of their master. Settled comfortably back upon the silken cushions of the love nest, Barby already dozing off, Yung put his head around the door.

'Have they all had their tea?' Anna whispered.

'All five are snoring.'

'Right, listen carefully. Go into the woods and cut me twenty-four sticks of stout willow, each two feet long; bundle them and bring them to me.'

'What for?'

'Obey! Do not ask questions.'

'And when I have done that?'

'Make yourself scarce.'

Later, while the moon hid his face in terror, Yung helped his sister to drag the pirates, one by one and snoring, down on to the shore of the river. And one by one she pegged them with the willow sticks, their hands and legs outstretched, on their backs in the mud. By their wrists and ankles Anna pegged them out, there to await the incoming tide; each to greet the dawn in his own terrified fashion.

While Yung slept, Anna sat on the side of the sampan and, with her bare feet dangling in the river, played and sang beautifully on the *p'i pa*, watching with pleasure as the tide rose. First it reached the chests of the pirates, all of whom pleaded with her while frantically struggling at their bonds. She watched intently, enjoying the sight which ended in gasps and gurgles when the water covered their faces.

Then, still singing, she poled the sampan around them, looking down with satisfaction at the death masks shining beneath the surface of the water. Afterwards, as the sampan drifted down-river, she prostrated herself before the little red altar of Tin Hau, the Queen of Heaven, and prayed.

Her incantations over, Anna then put her arms around Yung and slept, a woman at peace, to awaken hours later when the sampan ground the mud of the delta.

'You are awake, Gold Sister?' asked Yung, also waking.

'I am awake,' she said.

'The pirates are dead?'

'Yes. Never again will they demand rice tribute.'

'So what happens now?'

Anna stretched, yawning at the sun. The day was beautiful in its early beginnings. 'Now we go down-river to the next batch of bandits,' she replied, 'the ones led by the second of Chu Apu's butchers, the one who is known as Cross-Eyed Wong.'

'And then?'

'We will kill them also,' Anna No Name replied.

7

A night later, upon the *Mongolia*'s deck, all was chaos. Men, tipping out of hammocks in various stages of undress, were rushing helter-skelter in anxiety, while Captain O'Toole and Bruner were bawling commands; others, as nimble as monkeys, were climbing rat-lines for a better view of the tumultuous sea. From the crow's nest came a faint wail.

'One cannon junk away to starboard, Master! Another coming fast on the port tack.'

Milly brushed away her flying hair; Eli, beside her, as cool as ice, even found time to flick her a wink.

'What will happen?' she asked fearfully.

'He's only after comin' alongside to board us.'

'In this sea?'

'That won't bother Chu Apu none. He's a sea-louse, and loves this weather.' He pointed at the nearest junk, a big three-master with a twenty-foot stern and bat-winged sails, bellying in the wind. 'See that one — and the one to port?' He swung around. 'They're trailing a steel hawser between them. Our old tub runs into it and this draws the attackers alongside — the oldest pirate trick in the world.'

'Then what?'

'Then, like I said, he'll board us. If the ould fella's in a good mood he'll likely shoot a couple of us to show who's boss; if he's in a bad one he'll tie the lot of us to the anchor-chain, heave it overboard and leave us to wriggle as bait for sharks.'

'He's done that before?'

'It's standard practice. Not that the fella's all that wicked
– just that he likes the occasional bit of fun.'

'How dreadful!'

'Meanwhile, you may get away with it if you do as I
say,' continued Eli, steering her back to the companionway
steps. 'Get below, lock yourself in, and don't come out for
anyone.'

Back in her cabin, Milly considered the tea planter. This
man, she decided, was an enigma. Even on the brink of disaster he was cool and contained. Nothing seemed to frighten
Eli Boggs.

He, in turn, was complimenting himself on the success of
his plans to date. Everything was happening with clockwork
precision.

His pirate gang, listed on the passenger list as tea-planters,
had aroused no suspicions, and Mr Bruner, his associate,
appeared to have the situation on the bridge well in hand.

The passing junk (owned by Eli, not Chu Apu) had arrived
at the correct time and flown the right signal, and happily
Captain O'Toole had seen it himself; more importantly, he
had taken Bruner's advice and altered course to one that
would take the *Mongolia* west of the Paracels.

And while this silly little English girl could prove an unnecessary complication, her presence, if properly exploited,
might be used to advantage. Indeed, the ransom her devoted
father might pay for her could be of even greater value than
the opium the *Mongolia* was carrying ...

Standing at the stern rail now, watching his 'tea-planters'
surreptitiously dropping scrambling nets down the ship's side,
Eli pondered this. What, he wondered, was Milly Smith
really worth? Ten thousand dollars? More like a hundred
thousand!

Indeed, the more he thought of it, the more interested he
became. Her father and intended suitor were reputed to be
the richest tycoons in Hong Kong, and Eli inwardly cursed
himself for not realising her potential earlier. To date, having
dealt almost exclusively in smuggling, with a little piracy
thrown in, the possibility of taking hostages and demanding
ransom money had never really occurred to him.

The important thing, of course, was to keep her out of

the hands of others. Chu Apu had barbaric habits where women were concerned: more than one shell-like ear having been lifted from the head of an unsuspecting peasant girl and sent in the usual bloodstained envelope to agonised relatives . . .

But, thought Eli now, while all was fair in love and war, certain things had to be considered when it came to kidnapping, which was a capital offence. Somehow or other he had to smuggle this girl away before Chu Apu got wind of her. Meanwhile, with the wicked old devil a couple of hundred miles distant, the coast was clear for Eli Boggs.

The sight of Captain O'Toole striding down the slanting deck towards him brought Eli to the matter in hand.

'Which junk is Chu Apu aboard, de ye think, Mr Boggs?' The old captain screwed up his face against the spray as a pea green sea came pouring over the rail. 'Can you make him out from here?'

'I can't make Chu Apu out at all,' replied Eli, and bringing out a long-muzzled pistol, presented it at the captain's head. 'If my calculation is correct, sir, Chu Apu and his mob are miles away. So get back to the bridge, me darlin' – you're about to do business with Foreman Eli Boggs.'

The dawn sky broke above the Paracel Islands in vivid splendour as sun-shafts of brilliant light searched the emptiness and white-winged gulls and little shags rose in flocks to greet the day. Calm after its white-walled tumult, the ocean lay placid and smooth, as if contrite for past wickedness; the wind was at whimpering peace, like a child who had cried all night. The ancient *Mongolia*, anchored in the lee of the islands, lay motionless.

Milly looked up as Eli turned the key and opened her cabin door.

'You – up on deck,' he commanded.

'What's happening?'

'Just do as you're told or it'll be the worse for you.'

'It'll be worse still when my father finds out about this! Tea-planters, indeed!'

'Just move, and bring your belongings. We're changing ships.'

51

'Where am I going?' She stood defiantly still; anger had now replaced disgust at his betrayal.

'Off this old crate for a start.' Opening the cabin door wider, he bawled, 'Sweetcorn!' and the Chinese steward came running. Reaching out, Eli hauled him into the cabin. 'Bring her things and take them over to my junk.'

'Right now, Master?'

'Of course right now! D'ye think I mean next week?'

'You take Missy? This bring very bad trouble!'

'And some for you if you don't move your backside!'

'I no come for kidnap, please?' protested the steward.

'Yes you do. You're in this up to your neck, like me. Get her things, I said!'

'What does he mean – kidnap?' asked Milly.

'Kidnap, me eye!' came the reply. 'It's just by way of a bit o' business. I'll hand ye back to your feyther if he pays a bonus for me trouble. Now, are you comin' – or do I carry you?'

Up on deck, in the blinding light of the cloudless morning, Captain O'Toole was standing under Black Sam's guard. More of his pirate comrades lounged nearby, eyeing Milly as she came up the companionway. The old captain's face, Milly noticed, was heavily bruised.

'I told you to lay off the rough stuff, Black Sam,' Eli commented. 'I won't tell you again.'

'Are you all right, Miss Smith?' asked the captain.

'As well as can be expected in such company.'

'It appears that these damned thieves planned this weeks ago.'

'Better us than Chu Apu, Cap'n,' said Eli. 'The ould fella would have ye tied to the anchor chain by now. Behave yourselves and ye'll all land back in Hong Kong in one piece.' And he shouted over his shoulder, 'Liven yourself, Mr Bruner! What ails ye?'

'I'd never have believed it of Bruner,' said O'Toole, bitterly.

'When you sup wi' the Devil, me boy, you need a long spoon.' Eli patted the captain's shoulder. 'Meanwhile, tell

52

me the difference between runnin' opium and a wee bit o' standard piracy?'

'There is no opium aboard this ship,' said O'Toole.

'Tell that to the Marine Department when you hit Hong Kong, Cap'n. You know, and so do I, that you've been on the Opium Run since the beginning of the war.'

'It is true,' said Bruner, appearing from below with a heavy box which he prised open at their feet. Milly saw neat rows of water-proof packages. The mate added, 'There's half a hundredweight of raw opium here and more stored amidships.'

Captain O'Toole replied calmly: 'All right then, let's get to business. Half and half. You take your share, leave me mine, and I'll report a boarding by Chu Apu when I get to Hong Kong.'

'Dear God,' said Eli, 'he's changin' his tune from minute to minute. But the ould fella gets the blame for most of what happens round here so why not this?'

Milly said, turning away, 'I think you are all disgusting!'

'What about her, then?' asked somebody, and the men closed in about her.

'She goes to Hong Kong with me,' answered O'Toole.

'To hell with that!' interjected Eli. 'Let her loose in the Marine Office and she'll blab us all to the Navy.'

'Put her over the side,' suggested someone.

'Now that would be a real waste, sure to God,' said Eli. 'I've got plans for the darlin'.'

'Kidnapping's a hanging offence, remember,' observed O'Toole.

'And I'll see that you do hang,' added Milly.

'Bless me soul to hell!' complained Eli. 'Did ye hear that, Bruner? And us just simple fellas tryin' to earn a bit on the side. How much is she worth, do ye think?'

'Twenty thousand?' The German moved away but Milly heard him add, 'Her father's big in Hong Kong, according to O'Toole.'

And Eli replied: 'She's no great beauty, but she's English. I say fifty.'

'Fifty thousand dollars? No concubine fetches that kind of money.'

'Right then,' said Eli. 'You get the opium, but she stays with me. Make up your mind.'

'You take the risks also, you understand?' the German insisted.

'I'll take a chance,' said Eli. 'I came aboard this old crate for the opium, but I know a bargain when I see one. She'd be worth a fortune to some respectable old Chinese gent!'

Captain O'Toole, going up to them, said audibly, 'I don't know what you're hatching, you two, but I'm telling you again – take her out of my hands and you're into a hanging offence. The Navy won't rest until they lay us all by the heels.'

'God save the Pope, just listen to it!' exclaimed Eli. 'Everbody's after stretchin' our necks. Me soul's mortified.'

'It will be when they bring you to trial,' said Milly, and the sound of her voice cut through the rough banter of the men. 'If Captain O'Toole's taking this ship to Hong Kong, I'm going with him. I'm warning you two, it'll be worse for you if I don't. My father is waiting for me and I intend to join him.'

'And supposin' ye don't,' said Eli suavely. 'Supposin', for once in your life, you do as you're told, me little firebrand.'

'Then my time will come, and I'll dance on your grave.'

There was silence; bound to their native lore, cowed by generations of witchcraft and voodoo, the Lascars and Chinese alike recoiled. Captain O'Toole stood motionless. Bruner bristled angrily. But Eli gave her a smile and a wink, saying: 'Aye, the filly's got spirit sure enough. Meanwhile, Black Sam, get her over to the *Ma Shan* – but keep your hands off her. Put her in a hammock and I'll be along to see to her later.'

To O'Toole he said: 'Get up steam and sail on the night tide. You can keep my share of the cargo but distribute it fairly – equal portions, man for man, from Captain to greaser. I'm making my profit another way, ain't I, my love?' And he patted Milly's cheek. 'But if anyone here breathes a word of what they've heard today they won't live an hour. If the Triads don't get you on Kowloonside,

54

Eli will. Better them than land in the hands of Black Sam. If you doubt me, go and ask Chu Apu on Lamma. Even he don't set foot on Lantau Island while Eli's activatin'. Good luck to you, and good sailing. Are the junks ready?'

'Ready and shipshape, sir,' said his bo'sun.

The night wind was stilled; the Paracels, great mounds of uninhabited land, lay black under the bright moon when Eli's two junks sailed out of the sheltering lagoon.

And history relates that the *Mongolia*, raising steam, followed them out on to the waters of the Gulf of Tonkin, on a course bound for Hong Kong.

Such was the evidence given at the trial of Eli Boggs, but never verified. Of only one fact were the harbour authorities of Hong Kong assured − that the *Mongolia* sailed: several sightings of her confirmed this, right up the China seaboard to within a hundred miles of Lyemun Gap, the entrance to Hong Kong harbour. But the old ship never arrived; her loss, together with that of Captain O'Toole and his crew, is a mystery spoken of in the Marine Office to this day.

The 1850s were bad years for Hong Kong.

Piracy was growing in Chinese waters. The steamer *Fei-ma*, attacked by Chu Apu, escaped, but the *Thistle* was boarded and burned by mandarin soldiers disguised as passengers, eleven of its crew being murdered. Following this, the steamer *Queen* was captured and sunk by piracy, as were the *Lola* and *Zulu* and rumours abounded in Hong Kong that an immense pirate fleet was about to attack the colony in force.

Dozens of ships were looted and sunk, but all were accounted for in the Marine Office on Peddar waterfront. Only the fate of the *Mongolia* remains unresolved.

Marine history lays the blame for this, rightly or wrongly, at the door of a European pirate; one who sailed under the name of Elias Boggs.

Therefore, when on the 29th day of February 1850 the steamship *Mongolia* did not arrive at the Hong Kong godown, ships were sent out to scour the northern approaches of the South China Sea, but returned to port with no news. It appeared that the ship, with Captain O'Toole in command (one of P and O's most experienced captains), had disappeared with the loss of all hands, including a woman named Mildred Smith, daughter of Sir Arthur Smith, one of Hong Kong's most illustrious sons.

Within a month of the tragedy the following announcement was made in *The Hong Kong and Shanghai Times*.

Tomorrow, March the 31st, a service will be held in St John's Church to pray for the soul of Mildred Elizabeth Smith, daughter of Sir Arthur Smith, a Director of the Peninsular and Oriental Shipping Line; pray also for the captain and crew of the steamship *Mongolia*, likewise lost.

A tablet will be erected to their memory and situated on Upper Peak Road at its junction with Glenealy and Caine.

In the midst of life we are in death.

At the presumed loss of his daughter Sir Arthur Smith wept bitterly, it was said, and would not be comforted.

8

In China the surname of a person is the name his friends and neighbours use; if further identification is needed, his second or third name is employed. The name of the second bandit leader Anna sought was Wong Tung Yuen, but his henchmen dispensed with formality and, because he was so cross-eyed, called him Cross-Eyed Wong.

Cross-Eyed Wong was not only famous as a bandit of the delta; his ability as a shark fisher had spread throughout the Celestial Empire, and he exported as far north as Peking and south to Canton the delicacy choicest to the Chinese stomach — shark's fins.

In youth Wong had been an ideal son and the pride of his parents but, by an unhappy accident in middle age, one day found himself on the port side of a fishing-boat when he should have been starboard: thereafter he not only walked with a limp to add to his optical disability — but was also possessed of the highest soprano voice in the Cantonese operatic repertoire ... the result of an unsuccessful argument with a shark.

Thereafter Cross-Eyed Wong not only took to banditry to revenge himself on a jeering society, but waged war on sharks: catching and keeping them alive in his shark pond two miles north of the delta. Here, in captivity, he relieved them of their fins, leaving them to wallow in an aimless search for food. Friend of Chu Apu, the pirate chief, hated by men and despised by women, Wong spent his days without the solace of female company. At a time when a man of riches might laze in the comfort of opium with women of large brown

57

eyes and breasts of gold, Cross-Eyed Wong smoked alone.

All this Anna No Name knew as she made her way to his quay to pay to him her rice tribute.

Let this be clear: no fiercer pirate (with the possible exception of Chu Apu) existed on the waters of the Pearl River. Only recently, to punish a villager for the non-payment of his dues, Wong had executed him by an ancient formula – The Death of a Thousand Cuts. Therefore it should have been with some trepidation that Anna and Yung approached Wong's encampment. Barby Lo, whom she had recently disposed of, was a monk compared with him.

Strangely, instead of the deathly quiet that preceded all such rice tribute visits, the river now echoed to music as sweet as anything it had heard in its history – and this was Anna No Name's singing. So beautiful was the music she made, accompanying herself on the *p'i pa*, that the birds of dawn joined in: the night-jar and the black-capped kingfisher sang, the wren and the wagtail, the green dove and his cousin the turtle dove, also the blue-tailed hummingbird (recently flown in from Africa). All sang to the evening stars in glorious unison.

'Stop that damned noise!' bawled Cross-Eyed Wong, dallying, as always to no avail, with his numerous concubines before settling down to a night of opium and depravity with five of his comrades in sin: brawny torturers of dissolute appearance, all former pupils of Chu Apu, from Big Son (which doesn't bear translation) to Piggy Ho-bun and Makee-learn, aged twelve; also Come-Dead-Quickly who was wanted in Peking for the garrotting of his mother at the age of ten. Hearing the noise continue, Cross-Eyed took up his personal blunderbuss (a large affair which fired stones and nails and was guaranteed to strip a man down to a skeleton), and, going to the door, fired both barrels, hoping to put an end to the dawn chorus for a fortnight.

Hearing the report, Anna knew that she was close to the lair of Cross-Eyed Wong, and made preparations accordingly.

Paddling the sampan closer to the river bank, she saw a villager planting in the fields. She jumped ashore, and hailed him.

58

'Is this the camp of Mr Wong, the great bandit, to whom I have to pay rice dues?'

'Poor soul,' cried the peasant, straightening. 'Who is asking?'

'Sniff the wind and you will know,' cried Yung.

The old man did so, saying as Anna approached him: 'Perhaps my eyes deceive me, but my nose does not. Surely I am speaking to the famous Perfumed Lady of Fu Tan, the up-river village?'

'The same. Does my perfume please you, old man?' She noticed that his white beard was stained with the juice of opium.

'Please me? Not even from autumn roses have I known such pleasure. What can a beauty like you want with such a man, who is more evil than life itself?'

'You slander your neighbour?'

'Slander him, you say? I am not a man given to obscenities, but may lice infest his crotch and donkeys piss in his nuptial bed. Meanwhile, fair one, beware. He has beauties like you for breakfast.'

'What harm has he caused that you hate him so?'

'He steals our rice harvest and starves us; he has brought the curse of opium upon us, and sends the profit to the Great White Queen across the sea, she who drinks our country's tears.'

Anna said angrily, 'You have the poetry of the peasant but the brain of an idiot. You complain but do nothing. Even while reviling British opium you are eating the stuff.'

And the old man wiped his stained beard and moaned: 'Do not judge us harshly! If we rejected his opium we would be executed. Even our nursing mothers are forced to eat it so their milk infects their babies. My own daughter-in-law lost her head last spring for refusing. This man is a devil. Even tonight he and his bandits go to their chamber to smoke the drug, and when the lust is upon them strangle a concubine for their evening's pleasure.'

Anna considered this. 'I am here to help you rise against this cruelty. Go now. Summon the young men of the village, and tell Cross-Eyed Wong that the Perfumed Lady wishes to smoke opium at the rise of the moon and that I await his summons here. During the smoking I will give a signal. At that signal bring the young men to bind the bandits with ropes, then leave the rest to me.'

The old man was appalled. Shivering, he cried, 'To attempt such a rising would bring death!'

'Are you not dying now?' asked Anna. 'Obey me. Go!' She pointed to the village.

'He won't be a lot of use to you,' said Yung when she returned to the sampan.

'Tin Hau sent him to me. She always has a reason.' And prostrating herself before the little scarlet altar of the Queen of Heaven she prayed that all she hoped would come to pass.

After this she stroked the feet of the little god, comforting their pain: for the feet of Tin Hau had been bound on the orders of the Emperor when she was eight years old. On this birthday her father had come to her and, taking each of her feet in his hands, had broken their insteps and the bones of her toes after which he compressed her feet in tightly laced leather shoes; each day thereafter tightening the laces until Tin Hau's feet, once beautiful, were only a little longer than her ankles, after which all but the big toes withered and dropped off.

'I dedicate my life to your pain, Mistress,' said Anna now, 'and will now share your pain, as the Catholics of the Mission share that of Jesus.' And such was the agony Anna evoked within herself that sweat beaded her forehead.

'What now?' asked Yung, when her supplication was ended.

'We rest until nightfall when Wong and his men retire to smoke opium. Then we wait for the miracle.'

'Miracle?'

'That the village will rise against the bandits.'

'The old man promised this? I did not hear him.'

'Tin Hau promised.'

Yung turned up his nose at this. 'Often I have begged favours of her and she did nothing. Last time, with Barby Lo, we were not dependent on others. You will die attempting this, Gold Sister.'

Before Moon-come-high, Cross-Eyed Wong, resplendent in

robes of yellow and purple, came down to the quay where the sampan was moored, and cried in his squeaky soprano, 'Is this the sampan of the Perfumed Lady of Fu Tan — she who was once in the service of the Catholic Mission?'

'It is,' Anna called back, and clothed in the scarlet of a sing-song girl emerged from the hooped canopy of the boat.

'What is happening?' cried Cross-Eyed, angered. 'I was promised carnal knowledge of a Christian child, and now I am offered a flower-boat harpy!'

'On the contrary,' replied Anna. 'Not only am I a virgin, but a disciple of your beautiful poppy. Drink and smoke with me and your impotence will be exchanged for a dozen sons. This I promise.'

'You know of my malady? How?'

'Because I am the witch of Fu Tan, and know all things. Allow me to lie with you, my lord, and I will educate you in the business of red and purple opium dreams.'

'You know the penalty if you fail?'

'Let us not talk of penalties, but of love,' replied Anna; and bowing to him, she took his arm, and walked with him up to the village.

Seeing her go, Yung made obeisance before the altar of Tin Hau, and prayed.

Within a little red room in Wong's mansion lounged many of his bandits, some with painted concubines, most already under the drug.

In the middle of the room was a table and upon this lay the pipes, which were long-stemmed, with bowls of silver: serving at this table was Makee-learn, being instructed in his apprenticeship to love and the poppy. Big Son was there with his new woman, also Come-Dead-Quickly and Piggy Ho-bun, the three being experts in both doubtful arts. Every face turned as Wong entered, pulling Anna by the hand into a room next-door.

The red painted walls of this room were adorned with a tiny gold-framed window, which was shut tight, excluding the air. The room was bedecked with scarlet cushions and tapestries looted from ships plying the delta. In the middle stood a single silver lamp.

'Remove your clothes,' commanded Wong, and Anna did so, save for a silken gown which he tossed her and which she fastened at the waist: a virgin's entitlement according to an ancient Book of Rites.

'You are the most beautiful female I have ever set eyes upon,' cried Wong, his eyes more crossed than ever. 'Indeed, already I am experiencing a rising of my hopes, so delay no longer. Come to my couch.' And, shivering, he lay there in ardent anticipation.

'But first we must smoke, my lord.'

'Later, Witch, later!' He held out fat arms to her.

'Be it upon your head,' said Anna. And crossing to his bed she knelt, caressing him and whispering as a lover. A moment later, fulfilling his destiny, Cross-Eyed Wong was dead.

Anna rose and stood staring down at him for a moment; then, going to the golden window, she opened it and looked out into the night. There was no sound but the chanting of the cicadas and the snores of the opium sleepers.

Lighting a taper from the lamp and putting it outside the window, Anna waved it so that it could be seen from the village. After doing this she went into the next chamber where the bandits and their concubines lay in an opium-induced stupor.

She knelt first at the body of Come-Dead-Quickly, and he instantly died. Then came Big Son, and after him Piggy Ho-bun. But at the sleeping Makee-learn, Anna paused, looking down at the face of the sleeping boy, who was not yet defiled. Returning to the window, she waited.

Led by the old peasant the villagers came, timid and fearful, armed with scythes and axes. Meeting them at the door, Anna said: 'Excellent. China could do with more of the likes of you. But the deaths of these are not upon my hands, or yours. When questioned you can say that your torturers went away, and since that will be the truth, it will be the end of it.

'Do not harm the boy or the concubines. Their souls can be saved through ways of peace. But carry the dead bandits and put them aboard my sampan where my brother waits. We have plans for them, you understand.'

The villagers went down upon their knees before her, kissing the hem of her robe.

'But how did they die, Lady? How?' asked a young man, kneeling beside the body of Wong. 'From head to foot I have examined them, and there is not a mark upon any of them!'

'By poison, all four of them,' she said. 'Ask Tin Hau, the Queen of Heaven, she who can stand on both ends of a rainbow. Be of good faith in her and none shall harm you again.' She led the way down to the sampan where Yung was waiting. Following her, carrying the bodies of the pirates, came the villagers.

The dawn was stretching pale fingers across the sky when Anna and Yung set off with the corpses of Wong and his three comrades. Within an hour Yung had poled the sampan to Shekki Po Tan, the old trading post that faces south to the Pearl delta. At this place is the shark pond of Cross-Eyed Wong, he who sent their delicacies to all the ports of the world.

'Take me closer,' said Anna.

Yung did so, carefully poling the boat.

'Closer still,' she commanded, and Yung protested:

'Any closer than this and we will foul the rope barrier, then we'll be shark meat.' Even then, as if scenting their approach, the starving sharks beset them, fins furiously cutting the surface.

'It is time for supper,' said Anna, and taking Come-Dead-Quickly by the heels she toppled him into the pond: a rush, a clash of teeth, and the water swirled with bandit's blood. Piggy Ho-bun went in next, followed by Cross-Eyed Wong and Big Son, and the pond, once golden in the light of the moon, became scarlet.

'It is finished,' said Anna, words someone had said before, and kneeling before the altar of Tin Hau, gave thanks.

This done, and while the sharks were feeding, she sang and played on her *p'i pa*, while Yung, at her command, poled the sampan around in circles.

The morning was sun-shot, the fields around the delta changing colour with each fresh rush of light: turquoise burned into gold on the breast of the river; the brown furrows of the fields shimmered into shades of emerald; pastures reflected brilliant light.

While the butchery of the bodies continued, Anna No Name, sitting in the prow of the sampan, smiled at the sun and played and sang most beautifully so that her music drifted down-river on the wind to the villagers of Shekki, who were planting in the fields; more than one raised a head to listen, so plaintive and peaceful did it sound.

'What happens next?' asked Yung, always bored when not engaged in killing.

Anna replied, 'We carry on down-river to the last of the delta bandits, and kill them also.'

'As you killed Wong and his men?'

'No, for these are the most guilty of all. Also Chu Apu, their chief; and another, a foreigner, who sails under the name of Eli Boggs.'

'How then will you kill these?'

'Witness it when we arrive. You will be appalled,' she said, and curled up before the altar of Tin Hau and slept.

Later that morning, while Anna still slept, Yung poled the sampan into a little inlet and rested there. He saw a little book of ancient quality lying near Anna's hand.

Reaching for it to pass the time, he read before sleep overtook him:

Outside the walls of the Forbidden City in Peking stands the mortuary of the dead Emperors.

The last Ming Emperor, Chung Chen, fearing death from rebels, retreated to this place and hanged himself from a tree. The Manchu dynasty that followed the Ming respected this and certified it by hanging the tree in chains, it being the guilty party to suicide.

Nevertheless, let Chung Chen be admonished by choosing a felon's death whilst wearing the Emperor's clothes: assuming that poison was not available he could have despatched his soul by a timeless and honourable method − inserting behind his ear a short length of bamboo, such wood being readily available in the vicinity. A little patience is all that is required − driving the splinter upwards until it pierces the brain, the effect being instantaneous.

If performed with dexterity the entry wound is small, and suicide unsuspected. Much used by the Mongols in unhappy circumstances, this releasing of the soul is known to the temples.

9

As early as 1838, years before Milly Smith set out for Hong Kong in the ill-fated ship *Mongolia*, China and Britain had been squabbling over the importing of opium into Chinese ports: this culminated in the first Opium War between the two countries, which began in 1839 and lasted for three years.

The Chinese Emperor in Peking, having made the importing of the drug illegal, sought to enforce it by arresting a Chinese accused of selling it and arraigning him in Canton before the warehouses of the foreign merchants. Then followed an announcement by his representative, Governor Tang of Canton, which read:

> It is stated on the order of the Great Emperor that his purpose is to cut off utterly the source of this noxious abuse; to strip bare and root out this enormous evil; and though his axe should break in his hand or his boat should sink beneath him, yet will he not stay his effort until the work of purification be utterly accomplished.

Despite Governor Tang's efforts, he was now being supported by the famous Commissioner Lin. This proclamation was ignored by the British, whereupon the arrested Chinese was brought before the asembled merchants, the British flag hauled down, and the man put to death by ritual strangulation.

The British representative, a Captain Elliot, was then required to hand over all chests of opium (which totalled over 20,000) under pain of death. This was done under protest and, by the middle of that year, 1,500 chests of the drug every day were destroyed by the Chinese authorities, the British force together with their leaders under armed guard being made to watch the destruction.

At this stage the Emperor also commanded the famous Commissioner Lin to go south to Canton to enforce his instructions, and he, one of the most authoritative officials in Chinese history, was present at the opium's destruction.

The destruction of the opium, under Lin's guidance, was carried out as follows:

Large trenches, each 150 feet long, 80 feet wide and 7 feet deep were dug: these were filled with two feet of water, into which the opium, having been previously broken out of the casks, were thrown; thereupon salt and lime was spread thickly until the drug decomposed, became liquid, and was drained off into a creek: thus was the opium sufficiently purified so that the fish of the delta, the livelihood of many, were not poisoned.

Chastened, the Europeans and their merchants retreated to Macao, away from the wrath of the Emperor, and the business of poisoning China was brought to an end.

The situation of the British in China was humiliating and Captain Elliot, in hopes of reviving the opium trade by rerouting it, requested permission of the Governor of Macao to store the drug in his waterfront warehouses. This was refused for fear of Chinese retaliation.

With this new failure Elliot then wrote to the British government begging it to send an expeditionary force to bring the Chinese authorities to heel; Whitehall acquiesced, instructing the East India Company to send military and naval units to enforce their demands. After much campaigning on the Chinese mainland and loss of life, a defeated China agreed not only to British peace terms, but to pay reparations exceeding fifteen million dollars to British shareholders for the loss of the opium.

Further, the Chinese agreed, under extreme duress, that Hong Kong should be ceded to the British as a colony dating from 31st December 1842.

This was the situation, one of open hostility and hatred of all things British, that prevailed in Hong Kong in 1850. Peace between the two nations existed only on paper, a state which continued until 1856 when the Second Opium War broke out, lasting four years.

Unaware of the politics of peace and war, Milly now stood on the deck of the *Ma Shan*, Eli's big junk, and watched dusk falling over the West Lamma Channel.

The Big Eyed Chicken sat motionless on the breast of Silvermine Bay in Lantau Island, and the stars looked so big you could have reached up and picked them out of the sky. Nothing moved in the endless panorama of sea and islands, save for the gentle lapping of waves and the creaking of the junk's giant hawsers.

For the past three days she had refused food, calculating that, upon reaching Hong Kong waters, she would be in a decline severe enough to panic Eli into action. All Sweetcorn's entreaties to her to eat were met with obstinate refusal, though there was one moment of desperate weakness when he had wafted the aroma of frying bacon towards her. She had heard him say to Eli in fretful tones: 'She anna eatin', Boss, an' you ain't goin' to make single dollar out o' a clay cold corpse.'

'Don't worry, she'll come to it,' came the reply.

'I don't know. 'Cause she's one obstinate woman. Three days now, and she ain't swallowed enough to keep mices alive.'

'Don't you worry about it, me darlin'. She'll be eatin' like a mule before she gets to her pa: only the soul can starve to death with food about.'

'I seen some velly skinny old souls in my time, Mr Eli.'

Then Milly sat upon her bunk, hugging her stomach, its voracious demands for food sweeping over her in waves of increasing intensity; griping, enveloping pains that turned to a heady swimming sensation with the slightest movement of the junk — a sickness that sent her reeling.

'How long before we get to Hong Kong?' she asked Black Sam, now up on deck.

'Tomorrow evening late, says Mr Eli. But if you don't

68

eat, Missy,' he added kindly, 'you ain't never goin' to see the skies over Hong Kong.' Towering above her, the black man steadied her at the rail. 'You eat, lady, jist for me?'

Another day of starvation: somehow, Milly told herself, she would have to hang on, even if they took her ashore at Hong Kong on a stretcher.

There was no lock upon the door of her cabin – a small untidy room situated aft within the poop of the junk: the high stern scientifically devised by centuries of sea-goers to handle the big rolling billows of the South China Sea. The cabin's elevated position allowed visual control of everything that moved on the deck below, and beyond lay the silver sands of Lantau – a tantalising route of escape, thought Milly, watching every movement on the junk. Anyone lowering themselves silently into the sea might cover the couple of hundred yards to the beach unobserved.

Earlier, in passing conversation, Sweetcorn had said archly: 'Nobody is on Lantau except us, I tell you. This island is much bigger than Hong Kong, but nobody lives here.'

'Yes, they do,' said Milly. 'Listen,' and she put up her finger.

Faintly, on the west wind, came an almost inaudible chanting.

'I do not hear,' Sweetcorn shrugged.

'Cantonese opera?' said Milly.

They stood listening, and the steward said, 'Ah, yes, I hear them. Not people, Missy, only the Buddhist monks. They bad Chinese, live in the temple on top of far mountain.'

'So there *are* people here!'

'Perhaps, but very bad fellas, I tell you.'

'If they're monks they must be good fellas.'

'Oh, my belly! I keep tellin' you — very wicked! Not Taoists, see?'

'I understand. Because they're not Taoists, like you, they're wicked old Buddhists!'

'You got it, Missy. Topside here velly dull.' And he tapped his forehead. 'Don't eat meat, no fried beetles, no chicken. Perhaps eat English girl though, if she go silly and climb up to the Buddhist temple.'

Milly did not reply. She was looking beyond his cherubic

face to the distant shore. Even a modest swimmer could reach it in ten minutes, she was thinking.

The dusk deepened and then came night. A moon as round and full as a Halloween pumpkin grinned down from the majesty of the Milky Way. The black shapes of Hong Kong's three hundred sister islands stood out in jet silhouette, like attendant witches beneath the lantern stars. Here, said legend, trolls danced and hungry ghosts wandered, looking for dependent relatives. And within the farthest westerly inlet of Lantau, unknown to any, the two pirate junks of Chu Apu lay at anchor, motionless, as if held by anchors to the bed of the sea. He who was the summit of Anna No Name's smouldering ambitions slept peacefully on the deck, snoring at the stars; while above him, perched in the shrouds, sat his white cockatoo, the emblem of a creature that ripped and tore ... Chu Apu, one of the cruellest men on the China seaboard.

With her stomach crying out for food − Milly hadn't eaten for nearly four days − she crept silently out of her cabin to the starboard side. Nothing moved on the silvered sea far below save the fry. Like handfuls of sand flung into the sea, they darted in shimmering cascades.

These, she learned later, were the teeming millions of tiny fish upon which lived the impoverished Hoklo fishermen of the little seaside villages. Cousin to the mightier Tangar tribe, nightly they paddled out of their ancient harbours to light their little bow-lamps and patiently beat their muffled drums to attract the swarming shoals. Darkness was the signal to countless sampans which peddled a living within sight of the Fragrant Isle, Hong Kong's early name: with their oil lamps gleaming like glow worms in the dark and their drums throbbing, they swept up the refuse of the sea, a life blood richer men despised.

With the faint drum-beat an accompaniment to the thudding of her heart, Milly found a coil of rope. Lifting it, she carefully uncoiled it over the junk's side and down into the sea. From somewhere aft she heard the unmistakable sound of Black Sam's voice; he was humming, on watch, some nostalgic tune she had heard him sing before, and the thought of discovery chastened her.

Lowering herself down the junk's barnacled timbers, and badly scratching her half naked body in the process, her feet touched water. The shock of it snatched at her breath. It was then that the dangers of her new situation seized her. Sharks! She had forgotten Sweetcorn's talk of sharks in inshore waters. But as she shook water from her face and the distant shoreline called her, stark as a white finger between sea and sky, Milly struck out for it, already committed.

It would have been sensible to have eaten something before beginning the escape, she realised; but neither sense nor forethought had influenced her. To escape had been her only thought. To swim ashore and climb the hill that led to the Buddhist temple. Milly swam with the grace of a natural swimmer, her long hair floating out behind her, every movement betrayed by the sea-lights of highly salted water.

Ten fathoms below, unknown to her, were the silver deposits from which the bay took its name. This was the home of the manta ray and octopus and the fiery encrustations of a world that was primeval before the ice caps melted. Strange and featureless creatures swam here in abundance: here lived the marine snake and the ancestors of the Chinese six-legged frog; giant turtles swam here, also the red snapper.

The homes of the little sea horses were here, their dancing bodies gripping the kelp so enemies mistake them for seaweed; also the star-shaped sea-anemones, their petal mouths gaping above the iridescent beauty of the mushroom coral, granite hard and most beautifully fashioned. Brilliant light moved here in a marvel of colours, flashing upwards under the lazy strokes of the swimmer whose white limbs were watched relentlessly by a thousand unseen eyes.

But Milly swam on, gaze fixed upon the approaching shore, unaware of the centuries old creatures lying beneath her, or the dangers that attended her every movement.

All was not friendly here. And suddenly the swimmer sensed approaching disaster. It was a new emotion, undefined, which began to contract her throat, impelling her tiring body into the

71

speed of panic. She was flailing at the water now, making slower progress. And was learning that which the victim knows within the final, gasping effort to escape ... And, as if on a signal, at the moment she felt herself lost, there loomed silently about her, up from the bottom of the sea-bed far below, an enormous body, sleek and beautiful; one with fins and snout and gliding tail.

Up from an unknown place came this threat, immense and frightening, and the sea about it boiled foam, bringing an icy coldness.

Milly, seeing a shadow under water, shrieked; but her cry was strangled by the suffocating sea, and she gulped down water, her senses clouding. Momentarily petrified, she was staring at a long snout surmounted by a single, fishy eye that rolled opaquely in the instant before the apparition vanished − only to reappear, leap high above her and land with a belly flop, spattering spray and foam.

Horrified by the encounter, she struck out with new strength, threshing about, her arms and legs colliding with the object moving silently beneath her. And in the moment when she again remembered sharks, she found herself lifted above the surface: now higher, higher, until nearly clear of the sea she went half in and half out of the water, propelled upon an acrobatic journey of flailing arms and legs as she balanced upon the body of the fish beneath her. At speed she went, with neither sense nor direction: now she was down, deeper, deeper, her lungs filling with water as she fought to escape. Her strength was leaving her. She rose to gulp at air before being balanced once more upon the driving snout and projected another twenty yards. Floundering along on the back of the creature she went ... before being dumped unceremoniously into the warm embrace of shallow sea and sand where she lay face down amid the sound of lapping wavelets.

With her white shift up around her neck and her pink, ankle-length drawers clinging about her thighs, she lay within a mist of fading consciousness, having cheated death.

'Hey!' whispered Sweetcorn, shaking Eli by the shoulder, 'Mr Eli, wake up. Missy gone!'

Eli sat up in his hammock. 'Where?'

'The English. She's away.'

Eli rolled out and stood there, bemused. 'Don't be ridiculous! Where could she have gone to?'

'Search me, Mr Eli! But her bunk is empty and she ain't on the junk. Me and Black Sam searched high and low.'

Rushing to Milly's cabin, Eli pulled back the tumbled bed-clothes of her bunk. He called Black Sam.

'You were supposed to be on watch, weren't you? You bloody idiot!'

'Yes, sir. Aye aye, sir,' said Black Sam. 'I go get her now, Boss. Quickly!'

There was tumult aboard the *Ma Shan*, with the crew rushing about poking in corners and pulling up floor boards. No one in all their life had heard such language. Up and down the deck went Eli, raging. He bundled a couple of the crew overboard to see if she was hanging on the rudder, and finally cornered Black Sam.

'If you've lost her, Sam, by jiminy, I'll have your balls!'

'Wait you!' wailed the bo'sun, for he had a telescope to his eye, and with one leg coiled around the ratlines, twenty feet up, he pointed. The moon, as if in contrition, suddenly flooded the world with light. Snatching the telescope Eli saw a small dot lying in the surf — Milly in her white shift and pink pantaloons.

'That's her!' snapped Eli. 'Get the sampan out, and quick! She's in the shallows and the tide's on the turn. Come on, you po-faced spawns of iniquity, there's ransom money goin' to pot out there. The moment I've sold her I'm away to Macao to live the life of Riley. Get movin'!'

And Joe Dolphin, a native of Lantau, seeing a life-saving sampan being lowered from the *Ma Shan*, turned upon his back and wallowed beneath the moon; then, playing in the little rollers of the South China Sea, he stood up on his tail. Looking shoreward, he smiled his fishy smile — as dolphins of any nationality are inclined to do when they have business with humans.

10

Milly opened her eyes to sunlight. In her ears, growing in volume, was the sound of Sweetcorn singing an aria from a Cantonese opera: a mixture of treble and nasal castrati noises which, said Eli, was enough to put the skids under the living, never mind the half-conscious. Milly, within this category, allowed her drooping eyes to drift around the little room.

'Ah, good!' cried Sweetcorn. 'Missy wake up, eh?' And he hurried, plump hands covered with flour, from an oil stove in the tiny kitchen and bent above her bed. Her lips formed words that would not come.

Slowly the room took shape, translating itself upon her consciousness. Through the window she saw in the distance the lush green of fields and the azure blue of a summer-lit sky: in the distance she could hear the faint roaring of breakers.

With Sweetcorn's grinning countenance still above her, her lips formed words that would not make themselves heard.

'Where are you, you ask?' he said. 'You come safe in this ole Lantau fort room, with me.' He shook his fist at the ceiling in delight. 'Now I got Missy back, and no more dead!'

She raised herself. 'How long have I been lying here?'

'How long? Perhaps two weeks – three? Ever since beginning of the Third Moon you lie dead, and Mr Eli unhappy, no money comin'. So now he go Hong Kong side for fifty thousand dollars ransom money, and no come back yet.'

'What happened to me?' Milly asked.

'You catchee bad head. You swim from junk, very silly. Also you no eat, and something come and bite you. You very sweaty, and shoutin' for your ma.'

'Fever?'

'I don't know. But Eli he go topside to the temple monks. One big fella monk give him medicine. I say no take it, girls not same as monks, but Eli makes you swallow. Bad medicine. Snake's bladder pee.'

'Good heavens,' said Milly faintly.

The sun blazed. In her sweating weakness she longed for the cold embrace of the sea and made no protest when the Chinese stripped and washed her, discreetly covering vital parts. Meanwhile he hummed the tune he had sung before, saying breathlessly: 'Don't you worry, small daughter. Home in Canton I had one like you, and you ain't got nothin' that she didn't have neither. So you just close your eyes and leave it to Sweetcorn.

'You know,' he continued confidentially, 'you very strange lady. All the time you ill I sit here and watch you like mama watching baby, and hear you say many funny things. Sometimes you shout and jump about but I hold you, and always you say same thing – crying about big foxes comin' to eat you. All same Red Riding Hood story like I tell in Chinese to my daughter when she was my baby. You know this story?'

Milly nodded, not answering. The old man continued: 'But your fox story different, see – all about men on horses trying to kill one. Sometimes you even bark and make dog noises.'

'You must have enjoyed that,' said Milly bitterly.

'No, no! Not enjoy, me velly sorry for you. Velly upset and crying. You keep saying you got animal's blood on your face, you savvy?'

Milly nodded.

'You tell Sweetcorn about this bad dream? Then it go away.'

'It's all very stupid.'

'We got same story in China, you know?'

'Red Riding Hood?'

'Other fox stories, too. You heard about fox fairies?'

'No.'

Sweetcorn warmed to the subject. 'Ah! Fox people very important in China, see? But our children also afraid of foxes. You know, Missy, Chinese children so scared of foxes that dead Emperors build one great house for foxes in Forbidden City in Peking. Ah, yes!' And he whistled softly, his voice quieter. 'Then all Peking foxes go and live in that Fox Tower and no steal little children out of their beds at night for eating. Many people come to the Fox Tower and leave food for King Fox to give to his fox fairies. Also, in Shansi, which is my home, there is an altar to all foxes roaming the earth, and people come to pray for them. You know why?'

Milly shook her head.

'Because, unless you pray for foxes' souls, they enter into the bodies of humans, kick out the human souls and do horrible things, and people like you and me get blame for it. You understand?'

'Of course, but I don't believe it!'

'Ah so, Missy. You gotta be clever Chinese to believe a thing like that. But I tell the truth, see? You want proof?'

'I'd rather not. I've had enough of foxes for the present.'

Beyond the open window of the fort room the sun blazed in the strickening heat of the afternoon. What with the thumping headache of malaria and talk of hated foxes, Milly longed for unconsciousness once more.

Here, Milly thought, in this lovely Lantau, men of strange lore and customs had flourished before the coming of the Golden Horde; strange rites had been performed. Within yards of where she was now standing an Englishman had arrived with a fleet of armed merchantmen, and landed for drinking water. In her mind's eye Milly could almost see the dory leave the assembled ships and row ashore; swarthy Jack Tars and cut-throat pirates from another age of England's history.

Eli had told her of the persistent and indomitable English buccaneer, Captain Weddell, who had arrived in 1637 and, representing the East India Company, fought his way up the Pearl River delta and past the Chinese guns of the great

Bogue forts, there to kill and capture until his task was accomplished in the face of an Emperor's defiance. Then came the planting of the Union Jack on Chinese soil and the establishing of commercial routes along the sea lanes between here and Southampton.

Within fifty miles of Canton, then captured by the English, one could smell the spices, said Eli: in this vast cantonment, a walled city some eight centuries earlier, once stood fabulous minarets and pagodas whose eight-tiered landings were embellished with turquoise metopis and cyma recta mouldings of solid gold. With buildings dominated by the White Cloud Mountain and its turreted embattlements rearing in ancient splendour, it was named as the country's most southerly city, one famed throughout the world for Chinese cultural splendour and commerce.

Then came the English, conquerors who brought for trade the curse of opium with all its attendant ills — smuggling, slavery in all its forms, and wholesale prostitution. Its crammed cantonments home to ten thousand brothels, Canton now flourished only as an opium centre, the anus of China — a nickname later claimed by Hong Kong once the Europeans obtained their grip upon its throat.

How infinitely small one appeared, thought Milly, standing here on the threshold of an ancient world; a minute and crawling microcosm set against a tapestry of savage beauty.

Would it really matter, she wondered, if Fate decreed that she might never return to her father? So many loves had failed the test of generations gone before; countless sons and a myriad of daughters whose ambitions had foundered upon the inevitability of Western greed.

Of the twenty-four Solar 'breaths and joints' of the year by the Chinese calendar, Clear and Bright, which is April the fifth, is the happiest of all, this being the time when the Chinese sweep the graves of their ancestors. This is followed by Grain Rain, and in early May the official Beginning of Summer sees the Chinese garrulous, excitable, and abroad in their brightest colours. Nothing is whispered, everything is shouted. No taciturn urbanity exists in the roaring markets where hawkers bawl their bargains amid tittle-tattling, raucous wives.

77

But that is in the crowded towns and cities. On Lantau Island, nothing transgresses the serenity of another placid day.

Milly wandered along the debris-strewn sands of Silvermine Bay, yesterday having brought a tempestuous night of storm. Now nothing but a warm wind stirred the exotic beauty of her surroundings.

With strength returning she wandered idly. Strangely she felt free from bitterness or recrimination, though the possibility of escaping to Hong Kong appeared remote. The illness had left her with a lethargic indolence she had never experienced before. Her earlier protests having come to nothing, she was now being forced into acceptance of her situation: that she would be returned to her father the moment he had paid the ransom money, and not before.

With only Sweetcorn left to her as a companion in the little ruined fort, the hours dragged by in wearisome pursuits: wandering among the rock-pools in search of crabs and minnows; lying in the sand and watching the antics of crow pheasants stalking the woods; listening to the moaning of the pearled partridges, plentiful here. And always the peak of Lantau's highest mountain tinkled its ghostly temple bells into her nightly dreams, and if the wind came from the west she heard the chanting of the Buddhist monks.

Standing within the brilliance of the early summer day she saw the dim outcrop of the old promontory fort. Upon a nearby crag stood the squat little figure of Sweetcorn who was furiously waving and pointing seaward. Then she saw it — a faint dot against the blue of the sky which slowly forged into the sunset-red sails of Eli's Big Eyed Chicken, the *Ma Shan*, returning from Hong Kong waters. Milly watched as the big sixty-footer came lumbering into the bay; saw it go about in a welter of foam, its batwing sail flapping before settling in isolated serenity, the great black hull rolling in the swell.

'Ahoy there, Milly Smith!' It was Eli up astern, waving joyfully.

'Leave me alone,' she snapped, and turned back for the fort.

Sweetcorn upbraided her the moment she arrived.

'It ain't no good treatin' Mr Eli that way, Missy. He

behave proper and decent. I reckon you need the likes of that old Chu Apu to show you. He'd cut your fingers off an' send 'em to your pa.'

'And you can leave me alone, too!' said Milly.

She was surprised that Eli didn't come ashore that night. His absence, just at a time when she longed for news of her father, made her fretful and indecisive. With illness still upon her she woke that night in a haze of sweating weakness and rose, looking out on to a night where a full moon raced across scudding clouds. A west wind blustered in the little coppice as she left the fort.

Faintly, she heard again the bells of the distant monastery. Soon, she promised herself, she would climb the far mountain and beg sanctuary from the temple monks. Alternatively, with hope of release no nearer, she might even swim out and send a message to Hong Kong by one of the many Hoklo fishermen moored just off the bay; the distance, she calculated, was well over a mile, so she would have to wait until she felt stronger.

Reaching a little cave which would shelter her from the wind, she went in, sitting cross-legged in the sand and staring out of the cave entrance to the sea beyond. Though sleep haunted her, she was alerted by a presentiment and found herself fully awake. Automatically she propelled herself backwards, deeper into the shadows.

What appeared to be an apparition had suddenly appeared outside the cave entrance: an animal of some kind which, intitially stalking as a cat does its prey, suddenly stopped and sat upon its haunches, its muzzle pointing towards the dark recesses of the cave.

Frozen by fear, Milly stared at it across the intervening yards. And then, as a flash of moonlight crossed the darkened shore, the eyes of the creature turned slowly into pin-points of red light, as the eyes of the trapped victim glow before the presence of a hunter.

Nothing moved. The wind was quiet beyond the cave entrance, as if witnessing a phenomenon. And suddenly, to Milly's amazement, the animal slowly advanced to within feet of where she sat. She backed away in apprehension.

Strangely, though, no abject terror seized her for existing within the encounter was an inexplicable acceptance that this was bound to be; a predestined arrangement by unknown and metaphysical design.

A moment of confrontation followed. A giant fox stared up, Milly stared down. And then, as suddenly as the creature had arrived, it began to waver into strange, contorted shapes before her eyes. To melt away, even as she watched: fur, flesh and sinew dissolving grotesquely. Within seconds, it was as if the dead remains of a living animal, long interred, had been lifted out of its grave by an unseen hand and deposited, in all its putrefaction, at her feet.

Milly began to shake, a little at first, then uncontrollably, opening her mouth for a scream that never came. She covered her face and shut her eyes. When she opened them, she saw to her astonishment that the thing before her, once sleek and full of life had diminished into a little heap of smoking bones and fur: even this evaporated, leaving nothing save the untouched sandy floor of the cave, as if the fox had never been.

In its place, slowly and clearly defined, there arose another vision, and this was Tom Ellery's face. In the fullness of his youth and strength Milly saw him clearly, his features unmaligned by death.

It was then that she screamed. With her hands to her face she screamed and screamed again like a madwoman.

The moon shone brightly: just as it had on the night when she had gone to meet the vision of a dead Tom Ellery.

That was the first shock of the night.

Milly ran. Gaining the cave entrance, she raced full pelt along the beach for the fort at the other end of the bay, fearing that with every step the mystical animal she had seen would pursue and overtake her: with the weakness of her illness encompassing her, her breath felt stifled by imaginary fingers around her throat.

The second shock came when, in near darkness, for the moon had now vanished behind glimmering clouds, she nearly collided with another apparition coming from the sea. It was Eli. Swimming ashore, having seen her from the

80

anchored junk, he caught her in his arms in the moment before she fell, and held her, gasping: 'In the name of God, what's the hurry?'

Milly fought for words that came with neither coherence nor sense.

'Settle herself! Now start again and tell me steady.'

Later, walking back to the fort, she managed to find the words.

'A fox, did ye say?' he asked. 'On Lantau? Oh, aye!'

'As true as God, I saw it − a giant fox!'

'In the cave, is it?'

'Not now. I told you, the thing disappeared before my eyes!'

'Had ye been on the hard stuff?'

'I might have expected that!'

Eli sighed as a man does when dealing with a child. 'Shall we go back and see if it's still there?' he asked.

Walking away, Milly said over her shoulder, 'It's not important anyway. I'll be out of here soon. It all depends, I suppose, if you've collected the ransom money?'

He said reflectively, 'You've been ill, ye know? It only needs a temple monk to get at ye now and he'd change ye into a ghost. Ye'd not be the first to start seein' things after a dose of malaria.'

'You still don't believe me!'

'Better if I'd seen the thing meself, but I'll take your word for it.'

Milly walked away, but again Eli caught her up and turned her into his arms, saying: 'Will you bide here for a bit, before we go in to Sweetcorn? I've something important to tell you.'

She pulled herself away. He continued: 'I'll be takin' you to your feyther tomorrow.'

'You mean that?'

'Wake up early and see.' Groping for her hand, he added, 'I've got bad news for ye, girl.'

'Bad news?'

'Say a prayer for your father. He won't be with us long.'

'He's ill?'

'According to rumour, he's dying. I don't believe in fussin'
about — best you have it straight.'

In silence they walked slowly back to the fort, but on
the steps leading up to its entrance, Eli said: 'About that
business with the fox ...'

Behind his head Milly saw the peak of the Lantau
mountain; heard again the faint chanting of the monks.
'What about it?'

He shrugged as a man does when judging a subject to be
one of minor importance. 'Only that perhaps it wouldn't be
wise to mention it to Sweetcorn.'

'Why not?'

'Well, you know what they are. Give a Chinese half a
superstition and he turns it into a national holiday. Also
he'd say you've been imagining things, as I do.'

'If it's imagination I can tell it to anybody.'

'And take a chance of looking a fool?'

'If you put it that way ...'

He said, ending the subject, 'Just as you like then, but
don't blame me if he puts it round the junks.'

'Why should I care? According to you I'll be in Hong
Kong by this time tomorrow.'

'Look, just don't talk of it to anyone! For once in your
life, will ye do as I say?'

The old steward, however, wasn't there to greet them.
And before they sat down to the meal he had prepared
(his pots were bubbling merrily on the stove) they went in
search of him. After a fruitless search Eli suggested that he
should swim out to the junk, in case Sweetcorn had rowed
over to it in the dory.

They found him eventually — dead behind one of the old
rusted gun-embrasures where he had clearly hidden in a vain
attempt at escape.

Most of his clothes had been ripped from his body, as if
by the claws of an animal.

Later, the crew of the *Ma Shan* came to the fort. They stood
around, looking at the body of Sweetcorn and shivering with
apprehension.

'A fox, did you say?' asked Eli, drawing Milly aside.

'A fox,' she repeated.

'A big one, you said?'

'As big as a good-sized dog.'

He spoke more of it, but she could not see him for tears, and did not reply.

'But look, Boss,' said Black Sam, still shivering, 'there ain't no animals at all on Lantau. I been comin' here these past ten years, and I ain't never seen so much as a rabbit.'

'Forget about it, I said.' And Eli adopted the attitude of a man who is ending a conversation.

11

With meticulous attention to planning (which was how he had managed to survive to date, he said) Eli returned Milly to her father's house during the birthday celebrations of Tam Kung, which was the eighth day of the Fourth Moon − the eighth of May by the Western Calendar.

A word about Tam Kung: another Patron Saint of the Chinese Boat People, he ranks second in their affection to Tin Hau, the Queen of Heaven. A god not to be trifled with.

'Today,' said Eli, 'I will take you to your father. But first you will have to wear the clothes of a Chinese. I'm not risking arrest by taking you to Hong Kong dressed like English gentry.'

Milly noticed the change of his accent; now, apparently, as English as hers.

'And what if I don't agree?'

'Then we hang around here until you do.'

With Black Sam waiting to ferry them out to the waiting junk, Eli led Milly to a little harbour of branches away from watching eyes. He put a bundle of clothes at her feet.

'Change into these.'

'If you turn your back.'

Removing her dress, she changed into that of a typical Asian sea-girl, putting on the cotton coat and trousers he gave her, also black stockings and low-heeled shoes which, a size too small, made her walk like a crippled donkey. Upon her head he put a wide-brimmed Hakka sun hat with a beaded rim which conveniently shaded her features.

'You'll do,' he said. 'Now for the face.'

From a little palette of village make-up he smeared yellow ochre faintly upon her cheeks and throat to give her the Chinese pallor; with infinite care he then painted her eyes with burnt cork, turning them up at the outer corners, the way the half-caste girls of Macao paint their eyes, trying to turn themselves into pure Chinese.

Pausing in these labours, Eli looked at her and she at him. Warmth and a fragile understanding that neither wished to dispel charged the moment, so that when the task was finished (Milly had meanwhile plaited her hair and hung it either side of her face, the ends tied with red ribbon) they did not move to break the spell that had resolved itself between them. Indeed, the longer they knelt there the more Milly wondered if he would try to kiss her, but the spell was broken when she heard herself say: 'Well, that's it. Are we going or not?'

She saw him then against a tapestry of sea and sky with the bat-winged sails of the *Ma Shan* billowing in the wind; the faint creaking of its great spars whispering over the sea towards them. Always she was to remember, now the time to part had come, the weather-stained brown of his face, which was the colour of the earth of Lantau and the gentleness of his calloused hands when he touched her.

'Now that it is time for you to go, I am sorry,' he said.

Milly did not reply. He added: 'Some women would never want to leave such a place.'

They rose, and she did not resist when he took her hand. Together they walked down to the sea where Black Sam was waiting with the save-life sampan. Eli said, helping her into it: 'But you'll come back one day, so get used to the idea. Rich or poor, nobody escapes from the Hong Kong islands.'

An early dusk was staining the early summer sky as the big junk, with Black Sam at the wheel, sailed into Shaukiwan typhoon shelter and moored near the shrine of Tam Kung.

Since early morning the Hoklo and Tangar sea people had been sailing in from the outlying islands and the southern coast of China, and the decks of the great Big Eyed Chickens were crowded with welcoming relatives. The craft were dressed overall, from bow-sprit to masthead, with flags, lanterns and streamers fluttering in the wind: eight lanterns covered with paper flowers announcing birthday greetings to Tam Kung were hanging over every poop and well-deck, with paper screens interwoven with fresh frangipani blooms decorating the bulwarks.

One junk – and Eli whispered to Milly that this was the lead-junk of the pirate Chu Apu – was carrying an enormous paper dragon with butterfly wings; its main deck filled with baskets of pink dumplings and hundred-year-old eggs. Here hordes of relatives were scrambling for bowls of steaming chow-fan. Sitting on every available space, they were sucking up with the aid of chop-sticks gallons of hot congee, the young with mouths of strong white teeth, the old with the champing jaws of age.

And above all a mad confusion of crashing cymbals, blowing bugles and clarinets, beating of kettle drums and banging of brass gongs: there being nothing the Chinese like better, explained Eli, than a cacophony of tuneless noise guaranteed to raise the dead. Hakka women (true-blooded aboriginals of an ancient tribe) sauntered up and down the crowded quays showing off their chunky gold jewellery amid the billowing smoke of Chinese crackers and rockets of red and green and gold.

'You promised to take me home to my father!' said Milly angrily.

'When it's dark, not before.'

They stood together in the confusion.

'You've collected the ransom money. You've no right to hold me any longer,' Milly protested.

'I've told you before – I haven't received a ransom. A few weeks ago I asked for one, but changed my mind.'

'Tell me why?' she asked sarcastically.

He turned away. 'That's something you wouldn't understand.'

'That's not what Sweetcorn told me! He said you got fifty thousand dollars out of my father.'

'Sweetcorn was wrong. And when I say something that important, I expect to be believed.'

'You're in no position to *expect* anything! Meanwhile, my poor father's dying, you say, so we'll never know the truth of it!'

To this he did not reply.

Finally he looked up into the dark sky and guided Milly through the crowds on the quay until they reached a side street. Here they were instantly surrounded by pleading beggars and coolies carrying sedan chairs. Selecting one, Eli helped Milly into it and put her baggage in after her.

'Goodbye,' he said.

She sat rigidly, staring straight ahead.

'Just as you wish.' Eli barked instructions in Chinese to the two coolies, who carried her away.

'Dang me, Boss!' said Black Sam, suddenly at his elbow. 'I ain't never seen one get away that easy.'

And Eli replied, hailing another palanquin: 'This is Hong Kong. I aim to get the chicken into the hen-house. She's no more'n a child now but give her a year or so and I'll pluck her off the perch.'

'Oh? You could have fooled me. You didn't even kiss her goodbye — I ain't seen that before, neither!'

The second palanquin arrived and Eli got in. 'Follow the chair ahead, quickly!' he commanded.

Black Sam stood watching, a grin on his bearded face.

Another was also watching from the poop of his big junk moored near the shrine of Tam Kung, and this was Chu Apu.

Milly's palanquin, with Eli's following, made its way up the Peak Road towards the English Mansion, her father's palatial home, which overlooked Hong Kong harbour.

Crunching their way up its gravelled drive, her two bearers stopped and lowered the chair. As if awaiting her through some sixth sense, Mamie the housekeeper was standing in the porch.

'Eh, dear, my darlin', come you here!' said she, and Milly was hugged to her ample bosom as if she were a small child once more.

In the absence of Milly's mother, Old Mamie had played the part. Now, over Milly's shoulder, the housekeeper saw the second palanquin arrive. Eli got out, standing in the shadows.

'And who might that be?' demanded Mamie, thrusting Milly aside.

'The man who abducted me,' said Milly.

With her hair in curl-papers, the housekeeper looked a fearsome sight.

'Then what you doin' here, you devil?' she shrieked.

'Just seein' she gets home in one piece,' said Eli, and left.

Mamie was halfway down the drive when Eli fled. With her fists raised and her vast bosom shaking, she bawled, 'You white villain, come back here! Hold on, you damn pig, while I fetches a gun!'

Afterwards Eli said that smoke was rising on the road behind him.

'Don't you bother none, ma honey,' said Mamie then, and putting a protective arm around Milly, led her into the house. 'Don't you worry, my precious,' said she. 'Mamie's got you now, and Ah'm right pleased to notice you got two ears.'

Chu Apu, the scourge of Chinese waters, was an aristocrat among pirates. Over the coasts from Shanghai to Canton he had cast his net; the very mention of his name induced panic.

Chu came from generations of pirates, being the offspring of the ferocious Cheng Yat of Bias Bay, he who was drowned in a typhoon; his mother, the infamous Shek Cheng, having succeeded to the dynasty, provided herself with many lovers (whose relatives infested the South China Sea), and using Hong Kong as her base, preyed upon shipping on the China Run.

Chu's mother became the first female pirate chief, ruling her horde with a rod of iron. Falling in love with her lieutenant (after putting her second husband to an ignominious death), she handed over the reins of her dynasty to him when in declining health, but when she died bequeathed her thieves' kitchen to Chu, her only offspring.

During the years in which Milly Smith lived in Hong Kong, Chu Apu held sway, at one time joining forces with another whose name was Eli Boggs. Both were wanted for piracy.

Meanwhile Anna No Name and Yung, after paddling into

Shaukiwan typhoon shelter, paused to follow the progress of Milly and Eli as they landed from a junk in the harbour. They watched as Eli hailed a palanquin; saw Milly get into it and her companion wave goodbye, then follow her departure in a second palanquin. Very strange behaviour, thought Yung.

'See,' he observed, 'the young woman goes, the man follows her. Why does he not travel in the same palanquin?'

And Anna replied, 'Such people are not important. In any case, there is no accounting for the behaviour of Europeans. The only important person in Shaukiwan today is he.' And she pointed to the figure of Chu Apu, the pirate.

On the basis that they who live by the sword die by it, Chu probably anticipated his end with Oriental fatality. He himself was pitiless when protecting his empire of opium, "squeeze", the gathering of rice tribute and protection money.

Nevertheless, while he still could he took retribution. When he heard of the deaths of his lieutenants of the Pearl River, Barby Lo and Cross-Eyed Wong, and of their henchmen — all executed, it was said, by the villagers of Fu Tan — he sailed there with his pirate fleet, burned down the villagers' homes and put to death everyone he could find. Only the Head Man and his family escaped.

In due course this knowledge came to Anna and Yung.

'He has sacked and burned Fu Tan,' said Anna. 'If fire is what he wants, believe me, Small One, he will have it in plenty.' And saying this, she commanded him to paddle their sampan close to the biggest of Chu's junks while she, sitting on the stern, played on her *p'i pa* and sang most beautifully. Many of the pirates, celebrating aboard their captain's junk, lined the rail carrying their chow bowls and waved greetings.

'Come aboard, Little Sister!' cried one, and lowered a rope ladder.

'What happens now?' asked Yung.

'We accept their invitation,' replied Anna, and climbed the ladder. Reaching the deck of Chu's junk, she played and sang until the moon came out and the stars shone over Shaukiwan.

Meanwhile the pirates feasted well, munching on delicious giant prawns, gobbling up chow-fan with clattering chopsticks and swilling it down with bowls of Tao-Tai wine. And even when the moon was dipping on the rim of the ocean and most of the Tam Kung worshippers had gone to bed Anna still sang, and the sweet notes of her *p'i pa* drifted over the sea.

'Come, my friends, make merry!' urged Yung, and brought more gourds of wine laced with arsenic and gunpowder. All drank deeply.

'How many are there?' asked Anna.

In the middle of the poop deck, where the drunken pirates had fallen, Yung counted twenty-two half naked bodies.

'Which is Chu Apu, their chief?'

Yung shook his head. 'I know not.'

'It is said that he is the largest of them all,' observed Anna, 'but they will be smaller when we have done with them, Little Brother. It is the way of people who die by fire. You have brought the rope?'

'I have it here.'

'Excellent. Now help me pull them into a circle and we will tie their feet together, so that they lie like the rays of the sun in a circle of drunken happiness.'

Twenty-two pirates soon radiated from the junk's binnacle, which shone in the moonlight like an orb of silver. Many snored; others were smiling in their drunken stupor.

EXTRACT FROM A LOCAL NEWSPAPER ON THIS THE EIGHTH DAY OF THE FOURTH MOON

Tragedy has marred the birthday celebrations at Shaukiwan of Tam Kung, a patron saint of the Boat People. Within the typhoon shelter, a great fire occurred aboard one of the junks; twenty-two of the Tangar fishermen being burned to death under foul circumstances, the victims being tied hand and foot. It is believed that it was the work of one of the Kowloon City Triads. Their captain, however, one Chu Apu, escaped; onlookers reported that he left the scene before the fire to visit relatives at Mongokok on the south side of the Island.

90

Yung said, when they had taken the sampan away to a safe distance: 'Well, that is the end of them. All the pirates and bandits have been cleared from the delta. Now we can return to our village — what is left of it.'

'Can you not read, you fool?' Anna showed him the newspapers. 'Chu Apu, he who burned our village, has escaped!'

'But he is only one, and we have our lives to live. Our luck may change when trying to catch him.'

'Our parents will not be avenged until he dies like the rest of them. Besides, we know now that he has comrades. The handsome American, Eli Boggs, for instance.'

'The American has never stolen from us or raided our village!'

'Perhaps not, but a pirate's friend today is our enemy tomorrow, Small One. Also, it appears that he has acquaintances among the hated Europeans, they who are flooding our country with opium against our Emperor's command.'

'This will never end if you take on the Europeans,' replied Yung hotly. 'I say leave it, Gold Sister. Let us return to Fun Tan.'

'When the task is finished, and not before,' replied Anna. 'Who, I wonder, is the girl with black hair? She who looked at the American with the eyes of a moonstruck calf?'

'She is no concern of ours!'

'If she is a friend of Eli Boggs she is very much our concern, as soon you will discover,' said Anna.

At which Yung wept, for he was sick of killing.

'Come,' said his sister.

'Where are we going?' asked Yung.

'To the village of Stanley,' came the reply, 'and the harbour where the pirate Chu Apu takes profits from his gunpowder factory.'

'You know of this?' Yung's eyes were big in his boy's face.

'I know everything,' she replied, and her eyes as she stared at the sky, were twin pin-points of light; as the eyes of an animal shine in the dark.

12

The English Mansion, situated some four hundred feet up Hong Kong's splendid Peak, was one of the principal homes of the capital.

Of Moorish design, its curved gables vied with the home of the manager of the Oriental Bank for splendour; its gardens, tended by specialists brought in from Seville, were considered the loveliest on the island. Access to this palace built with the profits of the Opium War was obtained by four-bearer coolie-chairs, of which half a dozen, plus lounging coolies, were continuously kept in the grounds for the use of visitors. All around lay the vast panorama of Fragrant Harbour and the purple mountains of China Beyond.

Such a view lay before Milly now as she wandered in the garden. From tiered paths of hanging frangipani baskets she was gathering flowers for her father's grave. Mamie Malumba, the beloved housekeeper who had helped to bring her into the world, came out on to the white-walled verandah of the mansion and watched her with a sigh.

'You comin' for coffee, Flower?'

'Yes,' Milly called back. With her arms full of flowers she wandered over the lawns to the verandah.

'Now don't you jist look as handsome as when you was three?' And Mamie took the flowers from Milly's arms. 'Dead or alive, your pa will be delighted with flowers from his own garden. You sad, child?'

'Of course.'

'You may not have your pa around these days, but always

remember, you got me. Ah loved you since the day you was born.'

'That's going back a bit,' said Milly.

The servant followed her into the vast drawing-room, a bandit's lair of rare ornaments and ornate decoration. The ceilings were hand-painted with murals depicting Chinese life through the centuries; the walls hung with priceless tapestries; the floors covered with Tientsin carpets. Gold and ivory abounded. It was the talk of the Hong Kong Club that Sir Arthur Smith's collection of Chinese artifacts challenged anything seen in the Celestial Empire since the days of the pillaging Mongols.

'You off to the cemetery right now, honey?' Mamie asked.

'When I've had coffee.'

Tang, the number one house servant, white-clad from head to toe, served her gracefully, his sleek black head, shining with pomade, bowed before her. For some unknown reason Milly didn't trust him.

'I come also, Missy?' he asked, almond-shaped eyes fixed on her face.

'No, I'd rather be alone.'

Mamie interjected: 'Best you take him, child. You ain't venturing abroad these days without an escort. Even I get shouted at, and Ah'm over fourty. You don't know the island yet. There's all kinds of bad things goin' on.'

'Oh, Mamie, I'm not a child!'

'Yes you is. To me you're jist a honey-pot baby, and I aim to keep it that way. That damned pirate snatched you once, and he's likely to do it ag'in. I don't trust that Eli Boggs no further than I could throw him.'

'It was he who brought me here, remember?'

'Yes, and it was him who collected the ransom.'

'Don't start all that again!'

'You can say what you like, but I got the proof of it. Fifty thousand dollars that no-good fella eased outta your pa, and him slidin' into his grave!'

'Did you see it paid?'

'See what?'

'The ransom you keep talking about.'

93

'Ah didn't need to see, for your pa told me everything. "Mamie," he says, and he was nearly expirin', remember, "that Eli Boggs has got my girl and is asking ransom money. Fifty thousand! Does he think it grows on trees? First he sinks the *Mongolia*, drowns Cap'n O'Toole and his crew, then gets my daughter on to his dirty old junk. To prove he's got her he sends me her earrings with a note saying that next to come will be her ears if I don't pay. What am I going to do?"'

'"Reckon you gotta pay, sir," says I, "or next it'll be her fingers."'

'So he paid up, as you said?'

'He told his partner, Mr Wedderburn, to pay it to a bank in Sumatra — lock, stock and barrel. Which just goes to show how much your pa loved you. Though he never was the same, mind, after partin' with all that money.'

'That I can believe.'

'But you was his darlin', remember. There was nothin' in this world that man wouldn't do for you.'

'No doubt.'

Milly rose, gathering up the flowers. It was bitter to think, she reflected, that Eli could behave in such a manner after giving his word ... She said, 'And now, Mamie, do you think we could have an end to talk of ransoms and pirates? I'm sick to death of both. And for heaven's sake stop calling me "honey".'

'Now, now. Don't you upset yourself, honey,' said Mamie.

In her room Milly changed into a black lace mourning dress, as was expected. Protecting her complexion with a little black sunshade, she took one of the house palanquins, managing to avoid Tang, Mamie's appointed protector. With no sound but that made by the four soft-footed coolies, she was carried to the Anglican cemetery in fierce morning sunlight.

Flowering azaleas and tropical convolvulus, bright bells of varying colours, bordered the path. The sea stretched beyond in placid beauty. Deep summer had come to Hong Kong.

Under cover of some wayside brushes, a fox watched the palanquin go by.

Hitherto unknown upon the island, this species had been imported by the sporting fraternity of English regiments, who then promptly hunted them almost to extinction. A few surviving animals snatched a precarious existence in isolated areas where few humans trod, their chosen refuges mainly cemeteries where the hand of enemy Man could not be turned against them.

This particular fox, a giant vixen, its rust-coloured fur shining in the sun, crouched lower on its belly as Milly went past then rose, with tongue lolling, and watched the palanquin wind its way down the valley to the Anglican cemetery. Raising its muzzle, it scented the wind then howled. Its cry, familiar to Milly from moon-filled English glades, echoed strangely among the foreign outcrops: she sensed the sound rather than heard it, momentarily inclining her head within the silk-padded palanquin.

The nearest bearer, turning under his load, asked: 'You hear devil-dog call, Missy?'

'The fox? Yes, I heard it.'

'Please for us to leave you here and not go inside cemetery?' His face was frightened.

'Very well. Put me down outside the lych-gate.'

This was the trouble with China, she thought abstractedly; the country's advance from the ancient into the modern was hampered by atavistic superstition. A fox barked once and the suppressed fears of grown men came flooding to the surface.

Yet, she wondered, was it not the same for herself?

Walking to her father's grave with the flowers, she remembered again her great ancestral home in Sussex: a vast pastoral acreage of uncluttered countryside, bequeathed by her paternal grandfather.

She recalled the string of racehorses; her first ride on her own little Shetland pony when she was three years old; the gathering of the local hunt, of which her father was Master; the stirrup-cup ceremonies, with flunkeys in breeches and red stockings carrying champagne from saddle to saddle amid the baying of hounds. All this Milly saw again in the eye of her mind, for the scream of the wayside vixen had revived childhood memories with astonishing clarity.

She saw again the steaming flanks of the hunting mares, the curling whips and yelping terriers, the choleric faces of men in the blood-scarlet they called hunting pink, and heard the excited shrieks of their women as labourers began furiously digging, the quarry having gone to earth.

'She's bound to 'ave gone down 'ere – near this old oak tree, Maister,' shouted a sweating hunt follower. 'I reckon she allus lands near these parts when she's a' carryin' cubs.'

'Stop talking and dig, man!' commanded Sir Arthur, sitting his big mare with fine military precision, whip upraised to threaten the challenging hounds.

His wife, Milly's American mother, standing nearby, shouted: 'For God's sake, Arthur, get the wretched thing out and kill it. I'm perished with cold.'

Milly, aged four, watching from a nearby carriage, trembled in terror.

'Got her!' The shout was triumphant, and out of the hole came the labourer's gloved hand, pulling the vixen by the tail.

'Get her into the bag. Quick, man!'

Sawing off the vixen's lower jaw so it could not bite the hounds, the man dropped it into the bag.

Hypnotised, Milly stared. To her horror there appeared at the entrance to the fox-hole three tiny cubs; unable properly to stand, they momentarily blinked in the sunlight until ejected by a terrier coming up behind them. Next the hounds pounced, seizing the cubs in a yelping tug-of-war. Blood scattered the upturned earth. The huntsmen backed away their horses. Milly, rigid, stared down at the carnage, and heard her father shout: 'Right, now the vixen if you please.' And a whipper-in stooped, picked up the wriggling bag, and threw it before the hounds. Tossing it high they then set upon it in snarling ferocity, tearing it to pieces. The mask of the vixen appeared momentarily before flesh and tendon, bone and sinew, were ripped apart in a barking, squealing free-for-all.

With the hounds whipped away, the labourer knelt and with one deft stroke of a knife severed the vixen's head from her body. Momentarily he held the mask high for the huntsmen to see. 'What's yer pleasure, Maister?'

'That my daughter be blooded,' replied Sir Arthur Smith. Dismounting, he took from the man's bloody hand the dripping mask. Milly sat wild-eyed in the open carriage as her father brought the face of the fox closer and closer to hers, then deliberately made a cross with a bloody finger upon her forehead. The mask swayed within her sight, the dead eyes of the animal appeared to stare accusingly into hers. In waves of mounting terror she saw it; the lolling tongue, the grinning teeth ... and before the sunlight faded she heard her mother say in her southern accent: 'Really, Arthur, I do declare that child is goin' to faint.'

They sent her to bed for a week for disgracing the family in the sight of their neighbours.

13

At first sight of James Wedderburn, Milly disliked him.

Long years of bachelorhood in tropical stations with the East India Company had taken their toll of the young and ambitious businessman who had earlier set out from England; his hawk-like profile reflected the acquisitiveness that characterised his financial dealings, and overindulgence in midday gin and bitters, coupled with lack of exercise, had brought upon Wedderburn a paunchy middle age and the loss of nearly all his hair.

His health he had exchanged for wealth: some, including Mamie (who, through his many visits to the house on the Peak, knew him well), said he was impossibly rich; the company he had formed with Milly's father being presently employed in property dealings that were beyond the dreams of avarice.

Having preceded Milly to the Anglican cemetery by a few minutes, Wedderburn turned as she approached him between the rows of monumental gravestones. Impeccably attired, he bowed to her brief curtsey.

'Good morning.' He replaced his top hat. 'You received my note?'

'Note?' Milly's face showed surprise.

'I sent you a note suggesting we should meet here.'

'I received no note, sir. I came, as usual, to bring fresh flowers to my father's grave.' Milly slanted her parasol against the sun.

'Ah, I understand! The inestimable Mamie no doubt received it as a matter of course, and did not deliver it.'

It was quite likely, thought Milly.

'It is almost routine in the East, you know?' Wedderburn said. 'When passing a friendly door one drops in a note to indicate that one is still alive.' He smiled a toothy smile, smoothing his stomach with slow, ponderous hands.

Paunches of this rotundity never failed to fascinate Milly, who had seen a few even during this brief spell in Hong Kong's society. She assumed it was due to good living, but Mamie had another theory.

'No,' said she, 'that ain't so, honey. The human race don't arise stomachs like hogs through over-feedin' − it's the force o' gravity. One moment the guts lie high, next it's on ma knees, an' Ah don't eat enough to keep a newt alive.'

Wedderburn continued, 'Everything's upside down. It's a difficult time for us all. Your father's death was untimely. Doctor Schofield thought he had years left in him.'

'Doctor Schofield?'

'The doctor who attended him − his personal physician. Your father brought him out from England.'

'Ah, yes, of course.'

'I assumed you knew the good doctor.'

'I did when I was younger.'

'Did he not attend your mother during her illness also?'

'I was only six when she died, I don't remember.'

'But you knew him on your own account, did you not? Was he not appointed to Gadfield School while you were there?'

'Yes, but I had little to do with him.'

'Then I am wrongly informed. Your father gave me to understand that you were very much in the care of Schofield; certainly he is looking forward to seeing you again.'

The mention of Doctor Schofield's name disturbed Milly; he was coincidental with her mental illness, a phase in her life brought on by the death of Tom Ellery, and its strange aftermath when Schofield, the physician employed by Gadfield School, had regaled her with a series of complex psychological tests. Further, she had discovered the phenomenon that the more one insisted that one was sane, the greater the need for such assurance. In the interim she had forgotten that

99

Schofield was now in Hong Kong as her father's personal physician.

Man and girl became silent and stood by the flower-covered grave, bound by the affinity of loss.

'He was my friend,' said Wedderburn.

'I scarcely knew him,' said Milly.

The sun burned down in smells of hot cloth and the pungent perfume of tropical flowers. Within the Gulf Stream, Hong Kong bequeathed a riotous tribute to life when it came to flowers: and a Colony grateful to an illustrious son had delivered floral tributes from as far away as Macao; overnight rain had strengthened their perfume.

Wedderburn rubbed at his eyes with a linen handkerchief. 'Would you like to walk?' he asked.

'If you please.' Instantly he took her arm. His touch was unpleasant to her; it was as if he was branding her as his own.

Amid the marble eccentricities they walked, between flying angels and little stone cherubs, the consequence of the Colony's mass slaughter of the young. Even these days, fever was rampant.

'Have you given a thought to the future, Milly?' Wedderburn used her name for the first time.

'It seems enough to have arrived.'

'And everything is strange? I quite understand.'

His voice, Milly thought, was surprisingly fine for one so changed by a lifetime of excess.

'Had your father lived to see us together like this, he doubtless would have broached the subject of your future himself. Now it is up to us to arrange it.'

'To us?'

She knew of the prospective wedding, of course, but did not intend to make it easy.

'Surely your father told you of his wish that we should marry?'

'Briefly. It was more an instruction!'

Wedderburn chuckled briefly. 'He could be brusque, but at least you knew of his wishes. I will make the necessary arrangements. Incidentally, I have been married before. Did you know?'

100

'I did not.'

He stopped her and smiled. His sparse hair was greying at the temples, she noticed; his eyes held the weariness of a man who endured constant paper-work. Also, and to Milly's astonishment, she realised for the first time that she was actually taller than he.

He said, 'The Colony doesn't suit women, you know. They do not possess the necessary constitution. Historically Hong Kong is supposed to have been conquered by female stalwarts in numerous petticoats sweeping down Spring Garden Lane and other such romantic places, ordering people around and imposing their will on the native population. But it wasn't really like that. Women get a rough time here.'

'From what I've seen of them some appear to survive,' she answered, reflecting at the number of fat ladies she had observed lolling in palanquins on their way to afternoon soirees.

'Perhaps,' came the reply, 'but they usually don't last long. Some succumb to fever; those who survive pine for home, longing to escape from the humidity. My wife was one who simply couldn't stand the boredom. The endless mah-jong parties, the social round ... Therefore, I think you should know that quite soon I intend to return to England.'

'I am sure that's a good idea, Mr Wedderburn.'

'Will you not call me James?'

'Not until we know each other better.'

'We should become better acquainted, you're right, be seen together at various functions. The Governor's annual ball for a start. It's next Tuesday.'

'I shall not be there,' said Milly.

He was clearly unused to being contradicted.

'And why not? Why is it not acceptable? After all, we are so soon to be married.'

'That is not acceptable either, Mr Wedderburn.'

His attitude was instantly contrite, 'Oh come, child, you are beside yourself. I fear I have rushed my fences – I was never one for the stealthy approach. And all this delay in your arrival, with that confounded talk of ransom money, has quite upset you. Believe me, I do understand.'

His voice rose. 'That damned Elias Boggs has much to

101

answer for! Not content with attacking the Company's ships and murdering their crews, he had the audacity to demand a ransom. It had a profound effect upon your dying father.

'I am the Marine Superintendent on this island, apart from other State duties, and will not rest until this scum is driven from our waters!'

His breathing was heavy now, cheeks bulging an apoplectic scarlet above his tight winged collar. 'Forgive my vehemence at such a time, Milly, also my premature talk of marriage. I shall come to the subject again when you have had more time to consider it.'

'I have already considered it, Mr Wedderburn. I shall not marry you or anybody else until I decide upon it.'

'But your father gave me to understand ...'

'He had no right! It is my life, not his.'

'But it is in his will. He expressly told me ...'

'The will is yet to be read, sir. And whatever it says will make no difference.'

He was agitated now. 'But you do not understand, child! Were our two fortunes to merge, we could become one great financial house. Millions of dollars are involved. The shareholders ...'

'Then the shareholders are going to be disappointed. I am sorry, but it was you who began this discussion.'

'Now, let us not be hasty!' Wedderburn patted her arm. 'The time is clearly not appropriate, and I apologise for my clumsiness. Nor does the weather help − it is confoundedly hot.' He eased his starched collar. 'May I call upon you next Tuesday before your father's will is read?'

'I shall always be pleased to see you, Mr Wedderburn, but not to discuss marriage.'

'I can see that you are quite overwrought.'

'On the contrary, I am perfectly calm. Come on Tuesday. Mamie and I will be delighted to see you.'

14

Hands on hips, businesslike, Mamie called from the garden up to Milly's window.

'Miss Milly!'

'Yes?'

'Where is you?'

'In the bath — I told you.'

'If you're still scrubbin' yourself clean for the month o' July, you'll have nothin' left. Is you in or is you out down here?'

'Why?'

''Cause you got visitors.'

'Who?'

'That porky Wedderburn. Is you in or ain't you? Ah'm jist sick and tired o' tellin' folks lies.'

'Say I'm in the bath.'

'I done told him that, but he don't move. Lest you come down he's a'comin' up, he says.'

'Mamie!'

'Don't you "Mamie" me. I ain't never seen a man so beside himself. What you been doin' to him?'

It was a morning of summer heat, with Hong Kong piling her coals on to the furnace of the sun.

'The sort of day when a glass of cold tea finishes more outside me than in,' said Mamie. 'Ah jist don't know what I've done to deserve this place. Dear God, Miss Milly, you does look beautiful cool!'

Milly, in her black lace mourning dress, had just come into

the drawing room. James Wedderburn heaved his bulk from a settee and greeted her, his own figure bulging in tight frock coat and fawn trews. Hands clasped benignly before him, he looked her over appraisingly.

Somehow, whenever she saw Wedderburn she could not help but compare him to the infinitely more prepossessing Eli Boggs. Hours earlier she had lain abed and watched the moon rise over the mountains of distant China; the same moon, she thought, that shone down upon Eli wherever he might be. Again and again visions of him returned, evoking a strange confusion of attraction and hatred. His betrayal still rankled.

'Milly Smith, you are more difficult to corner than a Chinese financier. Howqua, a prince of merchants – continually absent when needed – was ubiquitous compared with you,' Wedderburn joked.

'I'm always here,' she replied tonelessly.

'Not for me, apparently. Where the devil do you get to? Every time I present my card you're out.'

'I prefer my own company, Mr Wedderburn.'

'So it appears, but sooner or later we will have to talk.Today if it is possible.'

'Why today?'

'Because this morning your future will be determined. Your father's will is to be read. You have to face his last wishes some time or other.'

'So you keep telling me, Mr Wedderburn.'

He bowed before her. 'And will you not cease this ridiculous formality? My name is James.'

'If you insist.'

Footsteps and voices sounded on the verandah: people were arriving and Mamie reappeared suddenly. She was wearing a white dress sporting scarlet hoops that emphasised her bulk. Only Mamie, thought Milly, could insist on wearing that which suited her least.

'Mr Goodchild of Goodchild and Goodchild,' announced Mamie in a stentorian voice, and the solicitor, long a servant of the family, entered.

Twenty years of service in the East India Company seemed to have robbed him of height. Diminutive as a gnome, his face

104

was lined by years in the tropics. Giving Milly a sad smile, he took his seat at the head of a prepared table, arranging his papers before him.

'Dr Schofield,' announced Mamie next.

Schofield could have passed for an undertaker, burdened as he was with cadaverous features and a tomb-like voice.

'Miss Smith, how long is it since we have met?' He bowed over her hand, the servant of two tongues; a man who smiled, but not with his mouth.

After his initial greeting Dr Schofield took his seat beside Wedderburn, while Mamie, well to the rear, sat in stoical silence. The solicitor's voice muttered tonelessly in the stifling air of the room: 'I, Sir Arthur Smith, Baronet, of the English Mansion, Moors Gardens, Hong Kong, hereby revoke all former testamentary disposition made by me and declare this to be my last Will ...'

Milly was scarcely listening. Beyond the open window waves of reflected light from the silk-sheened harbour below hinted at the bounty of summer. The Hakka Guest People, she was thinking, would be working in the ricefields with their wallowing buffalo, their laughing brown faces fringed with the bead-veils of their tribe; Sai Kung mothers would be squatting along the old stone quays, smelling deep of their babies whose slobbering rosebud mouths were running with milk: Hong Kong amahs and "makee-learns" would be out and about in the red-roofed villages where the bald elders sat in morose silence, heavy with years, while little lads of the narrow streets raced about bare-footed, endlessly playing the 'finger-game'.

The Hong Kong of her peasant Chinese generations, thought she, had no place in this ornate and beautiful room where taipans of wealth sat dispensing ill-gotten gains to the already privileged. Like her.

Again Mr Goodchild's voice broke into the reverie of Milly's thoughts: '"I appoint my friend and business partner, Mr James Alexander Wedderburn, to be the sole executrix of this my Will, and bequeath the following pecuniary legacies:

To my daughter, Mildred Elizabeth Smith, at present of Gadfield School, Working Lane in the County of Sussex,

105

England, the sum of two million dollars, which consti-
tutes a percentage of my holding in the firm of Smith and
Wedderburn: consequent upon this bequest, I appoint the
aforesaid James Alexander Wedderburn to hold this sum,
and others which will later hereinafter be defined, in trust
for her until she attains the age of twenty-one years; until
when he shall hold such monies absolutely and unhindered
by any obligation ...'''

Where, Milly wondered, was Eli at this moment? Would
he be disporting himself, as old Sweetcorn had suggested,
among the Flower harpies who paraded the Macao waterfront? Or could it be that his junks were again anchored
off beautiful Lantau with its tree-fringed beaches, where the
wind held the music of chanting monks?

Her mind now escaped the imprisoning room and she
again wandered bare-footed among the rock-pools, where
little shrimps darted and blinding sunlight made sun-shafts.
She smelled again Sweetcorn's cooking-pots and the acrid
smoke of his fires; saw again the sun-stained ocean and the
bat-winged sails of Eli's Big Chickens bellying in the wind
off the Ninepins.

Mr Goodchild's voice droned on. Soon, thought Milly,
when all this is settled, I will go to Green Island where the sea
rushes through Lyemun Gap. There I will take over Father's
old Rest House, which, said Mamie, was the prettiest chalet
she had seen on earth.

'When God made Hong Kong he didn't forget a lot, but he
did the best of all for Green Island, which your papa bought
for a seaside home soon after he came to Hong Kong.

'I tells you, Miss Milly, you ain't seen nothing till you've
seen Green Island. So when you are sick to death of the
soirees, afternoon teas, and the ladies of Hong Kong Club,
you jist hop on a Hoklo sampan and paddle away to that
paradise; and all your troubles'll fade like they never even
existed. You heard about Green Island?'

One of the servants had mentioned it in passing, Milly
told her.

'Well, when I gets a day off, which ain't often in this house,
I gets meself a picnic hamper, call out some old junk and sail
off to heaven. You can walk naked as a baby there and folks

don't bother, for nobody even knows you're alive. Did I ever mention my fella Rastus Malumba? First time convenient I took him there ...'

'You haven't mentioned him till now,' said Milly, intrigued.

'Well, I ain't always been a spinster lady, ye know! Rastus Malumba was some man, I'm tellin' you! Six foot up was he, and shoulders on him like Bason's Bull, then some, and his head was snow white, but not with age, mind, for he was a bright young buck. Believe me, people looked up when my Rastus came by, especially the women, for they ain't never seen his like on the streets o' Hong Kong before he came.'

Milly asked her what happened to him.

'Well,' continued Mamie, 'he weren't born for the climes of this Far East. His mama made him good and straight under the sun of Africa, and that's where he should have stayed, I s'pose. "I'm takin' you out to Hong Kong, Mamie," said your father. "I ain't aimin' to go East again without your cookin', you got that?" "You think again, Master," I tells him, "for Ah'v just found a black fella who suits me, and I ain't shiftin' nowhere, for he and me are hot for marryin'."

'I was a jinky little madam in them days, you understand, and I knew a thing or two, but nobody had set me alight like that Rastus Malumba.

'"Is that the last word on the subject?" asked your pa. "It is," I said. "Oh no, it ain't," said he. "When I comes across a cook like you, I don't give up easy. You're comin' to Hong Kong with me, Mamie, and this fancy man you got ringed by the nose, he's a'comin' too, understand?"'

'So Rastus came to Hong Kong as well?'

'Sure enough, for I'd got him snared. I got that man so snared he couldn't do a walk on his own without takin' me by the hand. He were a bosom fella, see?' and she held herself. 'I only ever had one man and I got him right here. "Rastus Malumba," I says, "you want to go home to Africa? Well, you ain't goin': you're comin' to Hong Kong with Mamie. And after we done a spell in China we'll take a single ticket back to the tribes in Africa and live on goat's milk happy ever

107

after. That suit you?" "Wherever you's a'goin', Mamie, that suits me," said Rastus.'

'So where is he now?' Milly asked.

'He's six foot down where Hong Kong's poisons put him and I buried him on Green Island. And there was no place to go after my Rastus died ... so here I be.'

The reading of the Will was over. Mr Goodchild said: "That concludes the business for today, save for a letter written by Sir Arthur to all beneficiaries except Mrs Malumba, whom I now ask to leave."

Mamie did so, quietly closing the door behind her.

There entered from the verandah door two Chinese nurses dressed in white. Their faces impassive under their flowing nurses' hats they sat with open hostility at the back of the room. Mr Goodchild continued:

'Miss Smith, Mr Wedderburn, Dr Schofield ... under the terms of a codicil to the will, I have now a painful duty to perform; this particular codicil is of a most unhappy nature.

'I will explain its terms and instructions first, and afterwards read it to substantiate my statements.' He raised his face to Dr Schofield. 'It appears, sir, that at some time last year you found it necessary to give to Sir Arthur a medical report upon the behaviour of Miss Smith while she was in your care?'

'In my capacity as the school physician, I found this necessary,' Dr Schofield answered.

Goodchild rustled his papers. 'I have the original of the report in my chambers; this is a copy.' He handed it to the doctor.

'This is my report,' confirmed Schofield, glancing at the contents.

'It is countersigned by the Headmistress of Gadfield High School, I see,' said Goo the solicitor, adding:

'The Headmistress is also a signatory to the Report. As you see, she has supported everything I have written.'

There was a silence. Milly stiffened in her chair.

'Mr Wedderburn, the essence of this report and its effect is that from today Miss Smith has become a ward of court in chancery under English law; this same law obtains in Hong

Kong,' the solicitor said. 'Therefore, in your capacity as Miss Smith's appointed guardian I leave it to you to decide whether or not I should read this codicil in public – or merely outline the circumstances that have influenced Sir Arthur's request.'

James Wedderburn rose to his feet. 'It would be preferable to all present if you merely outlined the codicil, sir, restricting yourself to its salient facts. It is my wish to cause Miss Smith the least possible embarrassment.'

'I concur,' said Dr Schofield.

Goodchild went on, speaking to Milly as one does to a child: 'It appears that during your final years at Gadfield School you found yourself engaged in a – liaison – with a villager named Ellery, who later died. Is this correct?'

Mllly bowed her head. He continued: 'I ask you to be patient, Miss Smith. This is a subject your dead father has asked me to raise.

'As a result of this . . . this calamitious union you became seriously ill, and were for weeks under the protection of the school physician, Dr Schofield here, during which time you underwent treatment for mental disorder. Is that correct?'

Milly did not reply.

'Such was your condition that Dr Schofield and your headmistress felt bound to send a report of this illness to your father, and this codicil to the will is as a result of his receiving this knowledge.

'The effect on your father was traumatic. His health was already failing and you were far away. As a loving parent his only thought was for your future and to this end he went further, he instructed his business partner, Mr James Wedderburn, a single gentleman, to give you the maximum protection of the law as far as he is able, which included the offer of his hand in marriage. Your father wrote to you to this effect, I understand.'

'Yes, I received such a letter from him,' answered Milly.

'In which he made this suggestion upon Mr Wedderburn's behalf. Understand, Miss Smith, that as a family solicitor it is my duty to point out to you that, as a ward of court, you are not duty bound to accept Mr Wedderburn's offer of marriage.'

Milly raised her face proudly. 'I have already rejected it!'

There was another pause. 'Might you not give further consideration to the wisdom of that rejection? Mr Wedderburn is older than you, of course, but is much respected in this colony as a gentleman of untainted business acumen. It is also known that such a marriage would bring about the unity of two great commercial empires, an outcome that would doubtless prove economically beneficial. This, I repeat, was your father's dying wish.'

'And if I do not agree to the marriage?'

'Then, I fear, as a ward of court, jurisdiction concerning your future then lies in the hands of the family physician to whom your father − in his discretion, since you are under age − has given absolute licence.'

'Licence to do *what*?' Milly's voice rose.

'To return you from this colony back to England, where you would be put under the protection of the Board of Guardians of which Dr Schofield is an adviser.'

'And what advice do you intend to give me, Doctor?' Milly rose, facing him, but he did not reply.

Mr Goodchild said flatly: 'That you be put into Dr Schofield's care and returned to England, there to be held in the care of an institution for the care of those mentally disturbed in the city of York, until such time that your health improves to the satisfaction of your guardian, James Wedderburn. This we have the power to do under the Lunacy Act of 1845.'

Milly made no sound, nor indicated that she had heard the solicitor's words. Then she rose, staring down into their inquiring faces. The two white-clad Chinese nurses rose, too.

'The decision is yours, Miss Smith,' Goodchild added, 'but it is necessary that I should know it at the earliest moment. Dr Schofield's time is valuable; with your father's death he now has no employment in Hong Kong, and is desirous of returning to England at the first opportunity.'

'Then I shall marry Mr Wedderburn,' said Milly, and walked to the door, calling, 'Mamie, *Mamie*!' She had never needed her old nurse more.

110

Mamie came instantly. Gathering Milly to her, she glowered at the two nurses and raised a big hand, slamming the door in their faces.

The moment Milly and Mamie had gone Wedderburn was upon his feet. Sweating feverishly he mopped his face with a large silk handkerchief. 'Excellent, excellent!' he said. 'You can take it from me, Mr Goodchild, that this young woman will never regret the step she has taken here today. I will make her a good and dutiful husband.'

'I trust so, sir.' Mr Goodchild shuffled through his papers. 'The girl has certain rights and privileges that have yet to be fulfilled – you understand me?'

'Of course!'

'Then all appears to have passed off extremely well,' said the solicitor with a sigh. 'All that is not yet settled is my account. Do I take it that it is chargeable to the Smith estate?'

'Send it to me and it will be settled immediately,' said Wedderburn, and turned to Dr Schofield.

'I trust that you, too, will render to me your account for this service. I assure, good doctor, that I will not prove ungrateful.'

'First thing in the morning, sir,' Schofield replied.

15

It was clear, said the companions of Chu Apu the Pirate (although not in his hearing), that his virility was diminishing.

At the age of fifty Chu's physique was still a subject of admiration; his body, tanned by sun and wind, was that of a much more youthful man. If he did not possess all his former agility he could still get the better of most of his compatriots. But Chu, in his time, had enjoyed his fill of the fleshpots of Macao, where opium, drink (he took his gin and gunpowder neat) and hordes of concubines had begun to take their toll. However, forsaking the opulence of his ill-gotten riches, Chu had now divorced from his bed the harlots of his roguish youth and taken unto himself a girl-wife of charm and beauty.

Her name was Sulen, which means water-lily; Chu Apu, he of the wide chest, gold earrings and ferocious countenance, had fallen hopelessly in love at the first sight of her. With this emotion, new to him, had come the maudlin sentiment that old lovers bestow upon young mistresses.

Furthermore, it was said in Sai Kung that since acquiring Sulen the great Chu Apu, once feared by all, was not the man he was. A new banter was whispered around the loot market of Shaukiwan; Ladder Street echoed the slanders hissed around corners and bubbled through wine. The gossip came to a head when he was seen to sandpaper Sulen's firewood to prevent her from getting splinters in her fingers. While every other wife along the China seaboard was up and doing at the crack of dawn, this girl-bride

112

was lying abed in good weather or foul, eating sweet foods and lobster brought in especially from Macao.

Worldly proverbs that stand the test of time are much the same in any language, and the one applying to Chu Apu's stupidity was no exception: 'Yuht, lóuh yuht wùh-toùh.' Which, translated from the Cantonese, means: 'There's no fool like an old fool.'

People had been beheaded by Chu Apu for lesser insults.

Having heard of the burning of his junk and the death of its crew at Shaukiwan during the official celebration of Tam Kung's birthday, a chastened Chu Apu made his way to Stanley Harbour, a secondary watering-hole used by his pirate fleet in difficult times.

Within a mile or so of this harbour there is a little village called Wong-ma Kok. Recently Chu, unknown to the authorities, had founded a little gunpowder factory there, the village being so secluded that none suspected its existence. Even the local tax-gatherers, all of whom were in Chu's pay, never visited, so its villagers paid no taxes. Revenue from the sale of gunpowder paying better than outright piracy, it was Chu's ambition to retire to Wong-ma Kok, there to live in peace and amity with his new concubine for the rest of his life.

Such might have come to pass had it not been for a young officer of rank and distinction, Captain da Costa of the Ceylon Rifles, who had recently been stationed nearby to observe the comings and goings of pirates and contraband. Wandering in the tide-swim of Stanley beach Captain da Costa inadvertently encountered the beautiful Sulen, Chu's wife, dabbling her feet in a rock-pool and eating sugared locusts. She rose as he approached in awe at the sight of his fine gold-braided uniform.

'The evening, girl of marvellous beauty, was delightful until I set eyes upon you; now life itself is perfect,' da Costa said in Cantonese. And he clicked his heels and gallantly saluted while Sulen, used only to the grunts of an ageing and uneducated lover, returned the compliment with a gracious bow.

'How does it happen that one of such charm sits here alone?' asked the eloquent da Costa. The dusk formed a veil around the face of the girl before him. Surely, only in

Portugal, thought da Costa, do they grow such peaches.

'Have you no tongue?' he asked.

'I am awaiting my husband, sir,' replied Sulen, and pulled up the neck of her homespun coat, which, buttoned down the front, reached to her calves.

'You are a Hakka?' asked da Costa.

'I am not aboriginal.'

'Then Tanga?'

'A Tangar of the sea.'

'Of the fleet that sails in and out of Stanley Harbour?'

'That also.'

'Which brings your man to you, but also takes him away.'

'Takes him to the far fish shoals where the big grouper run,' said Sulen, for she was a fisher girl and knew what she was about. If you want to find a fool in the country, it is said, you bring him from the town. A uniform such as this, unusual in Wong-ma Kok, could fetch trouble – this she knew. But it could also bring, if one was sixteen, a quickening of the blood, the young man before her being handsome and well muscled. Not from him would come the ill-mannered jokes, Sulen thought: the filthy epithets of the galleys when the sea came roaring over the gunwhale in great green troughs, swilling thunderously down the thwarts. Not with this man's kindly eyes and sensitive mouth would a girl endure the sweating embraces of an ungainly lover. The face of this youth was serene, his manner confident, but not abrasive; the down of his years was still upon his cheeks, his eyes bright with an inner fire.

'Are there others like you at home?' asked da Costa.

'One other: Silver Sister is her name.'

'She is also beautiful?'

'Men turn their heads without her bidding.' Saying this, Sulen reached out her hand and a white cockatoo swooped out of the dusk and settled upon her forearm – a cockatoo who usually crowed harshly on the pennant of Chu Apu when he was in harbour. Holding the bird against her cheek now, Sulen knew that Chu Apu was approaching, and that it was time for the officer to go.

'My husband arrives soon,' she said simply.

'Would he be away if I returned tomorrow? Would a meeting between us be possible?' asked da Costa, thus giving his own death sentence.

'It would be possible,' replied Sulen.

'Can we meet at this place in the evening?'

'It will cost money, of course,' said Sulen, who as mistress of a pirate naturally had a head for business.

'Tell me what does not cost money these days! How much?'

'Fifty dollars. To buy sugared locusts.'

'Tell me of these,' said da Costa, and Sulen answered:

'We buy them off the village hawkers who catch them when the fireflies dance in summer. They come in great swarms from the mainland and the hawkers net them, kill them and fry them over fires; when sugared they are delightful.'

'I shall decline the sugared locusts,' replied da Costa, 'but were it possible to take sugared kisses from so beautiful a mouth, I would find this most desirable.' He stirred the sand with his boot, adding, 'In all such arrangements it is necessary to be discreet, of course. It would be a very large mistake to inform your husband of our intentions.'

'A larger mistake than you could possible imagine,' replied Sulen.

Chu Apu, having left the festivities of Shaukiwan to visit relatives in Stanley Harbour, poled his sampan into the shallows and leapt out on to hot, dry sand. Most of the night he had travelled and was now weary, but joy overcame surprise when he saw his beloved, Sulen, come splashing through the tide-swim towards him, her brown arms open in greeting.

'Husband!' she cried, 'I dreamed that you would come! All night long I have awaited you in the warm bed of the *kang*, in my father's house. My life is empty without you.'

And this but a few minutes after she had been in the arms of Captain da Costa, his kisses still warm upon her mouth.

'I come for comfort,' said Chu Apu, like a child. And Sulen, kissing away his tears, led him to her father's house the better to hear his whining complaints.

'All is lost,' sobbed he. 'My spies tell me that my biggest junk has been burned in Shaukiwan by my enemies, and my entire crew murdered. Indeed, my lotus flower, I was lucky to escape with my life.'

'My beloved,' whispered Sulen, 'you still have me.' And somewhere nearby a rooster crowed thrice.

Sulen reached up for Chu Apu and drew him down to her, covering his face with kisses; it being necessary to dispel any doubts he might have if tongues started wagging about her in Wong-ma Kok. Chu, mindful of his duty as well as his desire, tried to enjoy her, but could not. Because of the succession of lovers with whom his reckless youth had been fulfilled, Chu, alas, was now impotent.

'A son! Give me a son, Sulen, that I might live again within his loins!'

'One thing is certain, old man, you are never again going to live in mine.' Sulen muttered under her breath, rising from the bed and looking out at the sea where the moon was staining the glassy tide with beams of silver. And to her astonishment she saw, looking through the window, the unmistakable mask of a fox. She saw this only for a moment, a silent apparition which slowly withered and faded into nothingness.

'There was a fox looking at us through the window!' she whispered.

'A fox? It is the Japanese wine you drank last night,' mumbled Chu ungraciously.

'I tell you it was a fox!'

'Come back to bed and do not be ridiculous. You are in a worse state than me!'

'Is that possible?' She stood looking down upon him with growing disdain. 'What kind of a husband are you for one such as me? Release me, I beg you, from this apology of a marriage.'

'I tell you what,' said Chu, sitting up, 'I will wire you by your feet and tow you through the Ninepins off Shelter Isle, if you insult my manhood. I am good for a dozen like you, if you proved even half a wife.' Reaching out, he gripped Sulen by the wrist and pulled her back upon the *kang*; there he bent over her again, fighting the battle of his lost youth. Unseen by them both, the fox again peered through the window.

This was unusual, but not impossible: foxes had been seen before in Hong Kong, even farther west than Stanley. One, it

116

was recently reported, had been seen near the Anglican Cemetery, and one earlier still on the island of Lantau.

Rarely, however, did they peer through bedroom windows.

Chu Apu sat up in his bed, alone and miserable.

Drawing from its pouch his silver opium pipe, he rolled a little ball of raw opium and lit it beside the bed. Not once, but twice he drew great draughts of opium into his lungs, and lay there staring at the moon within the scarlet curtains of his oncoming opium dream. Red, blue and scarlet lights he saw in that dream; he floated delightfully upon a zephyr cloud of moonbeams: drifting, drifting within the brown arms of females who fed him grapes of luscious sweetness, and never once scolded him for his impotence. In noontide and moonlight ... floating, floating; in witching dusk and sunshine, shimmering in splendour, he floated. On an Ali Baba carpet of silver, he flew above a spinning earth. And at the height of this dream of excellence there arose within Chu Apu a determination that *opium* should be the doctor of his ills.

Gradually, the dream left him and he saw not a world of insubstantiality, but one of reality as the opium grew fainter in its grip upon his brain. And there arose before him then, so vivid he could reach out and trace its shape with his forefinger, the sight of a beloved face; and this was the face of his Sulen. But even as his arms embraced her, so her features began to wither.

Chu Apu, amazed, lifted the white hand that lay on the *kang* beside him, and saw to his astonishment that the hand he held was covered with a faint sheen of hair; this was not the hand of Sulen. And even as he stared in disbelief, the arm beyond the hand changed from his wife's soft skin to the fur of an animal. Knowing the tricks of opium, Chu, shuddering, raised the hand to his lips, hoping to banish the phenomenon, but the hand he kissed had become the paw of an animal. And the face above the hand was not that of Sulen, but the grinning mask of a fox, whose furry body was now clamped against his own. Widening his mouth to scream, he made no sound. He saw the bared teeth of

117

the fox, its lolling tongue, its slavering mouth; and as the paw he held bared its claws and reached for his face, Chu shrieked. Again and again he shrieked, and Sulen, beyond the bedroom door, heard his cry as it diminished into a strangled moan.

Thus died the soul of Chu Apu, the pirate of the South China Sea, he who had burned the village of Fu Tan, though his body remained alive.

And Sulen saw through the window, as she bent above the *kang* in terror, the brown body of a fox loping away into the cover of nearby trees. Reaching shelter it turned, and its eyes were twin points of light shining from the darkness.

Thus was Chu Apu sent into the depths of incurable madness.

There remained but one more pirate from whom revenge had yet to be exacted. And this was Elias Boggs.

'That then, is the end of our work,' said Yung to Anna. 'We have cleared the pirates from the Pearl River and we have heard of the insanity of Chu Apu, who burned our village. What more do you want? Cannot we now safely return home?'

'We cannot,' replied Anna, 'for our work is not yet ended. Can we return and say it is done while men like Eli Boggs still live? I told you before – he dies also.'

'For what crime?'

'For the crime of being a pirate!'

Yung, who was becoming more worldly in his opinions, answered, 'Start upon men like him and you will finish up in Bias Bay where there are pirates in swarms. No, Gold Sister, I am returning to Fu Tan. Stay and kill hundreds more if you wish, but I am going home.' Saying this, he hauled up the bundle he had carried from Stanley and put it upon his back.

'You would leave me to finish the task alone?'

'When it is done, and all are dead, then return to our village, and I will kill a chicken to greet your homecoming. Meanwhile, goodbye, for I am away.'

Anna stood watching as he trudged away to Pedder Street,

which was the site of the ferry that would carry him up-river to the village of Fu Tan.

'You will regret this,' Anna called, her voice louder.

'No doubt,' replied Yung. But he went on his way just the same.

Book Two

16

Great social and national upheaval greeted the day of Milly's marriage to James Wedderburn, which was celebrated during Sir George Bonham's term of administration as Governor of Hong Kong; the marriage being performed by the Reverend George Smith, recently consecrated as the first Bishop of Victoria.

> Today, the first of April 1851, a marriage was solemnised at the Cathedral Church of St John by the Bishop of Victoria between Mildred Elizabeth Smith, daughter of Sir John Smith (recently deceased), and Mr James Alexander Wedderburn, the noted businessman and financier. The wedding was attended by personal guests of the two families and prominent leaders of the Colony and a happy time ensued at the wedding reception which was held in the gardens of Government House and presided over by the Governor himself. This opportunity is taken to congratulate the respected bridegroom and his young bride.
>
> In view of the Taiping disturbances on the China mainland it is understood that Mr Wedderburn and his bride will not be taking their honeymoon in Macao as originally planned.

The newspaper understated the situation, for mainland China was erupting in the flames of the greatest of its rebellions.

Throughout China's centuries scarcely one had passed without some sort of armed protest or rebellion. The

123

Taiping Rebellion, which broke out years before Milly's arrival in Hong Kong, was a classic example of peasant resistance to unbearable Mandarin exploitation.

With the oppressive Manchu dynasty losing control in the Pearl River delta to secret Triads, Canton, only a stone's throw from Hong Kong, was soon in the hands of the new rebels. Led by the fanatical student Hong, the whole of China, from Canton to Shanghai, was ablaze with dissent and the Manchu government, decimated by years of inflation, nepotism and corruption (themselves little more than dignified barbarians) failed to control Hong's activities.

A word about Hong: suffering a mental breakdown which left him on the verge of religious hysteria, he claimed that he was the brother of Jesus Christ. This came about after reading a missionary Christian pamphlet: and in an ensuing dream he became transported into a sort of presidential galaxy of angels and holy choirs. During his period aloft, he said, his bowels had been removed and certain unspecified organs of a lofty nature substituted, thus elevating him to equality with the gods.

His first task upon his return to earth was to destroy decay and violence, and raise in their place a new era of love and gentleness, as practised by his God of Love. But his God also possessed another facet to his nature, and Hong acted upon this behalf as well: the Old Testament God of Wrath and Fire.

By the time Milly had entered the Colony, China's rebels had increased to some 30,000 and Hong called his own rebels his God-worshippers. Arms and equipment, bundled protectively in grease-cloth, were hidden in ponds and lakes for a coming insurrection against the Manchu dynasty and a headquarters was founded at a place called Taiping Tianguo, the literal translation of its name being The Heavenly Kingdom of Transcendent Peace.

Under the text 'The Kingdom of God is at Hand', Hong began attacking provincial towns and cities and putting to death the families of landlords and any professed gentility that stood in his path. Working upon the theory that all land should belong to the State and that the present rule of the Manchus was nothing more than private anarchy, Hong asserted that, since all property belonged by right to God, then all taxes should be paid, not to corrupt officials, but to God's Sacred Treasury.

The ensuing plunder of private property passed to the new society of farm-soldiers, as the God-Worshippers called themselves; this, in the end, merely relieved one section of the community of its wealth and privileges in order to enrich another.

Massacre, rape and terror gripped the heart of China. A new hierarchy arose possessing the power of life and death over all below it; new legislation was passed as a result of which the Taiping leaders were permitted to create private harems for the rich and bordellos for the poor. And while commonplace adultery was, according to the constitution, punishable by death, sexual excesses were in fact the prerogative of all.

Massacre, often in excess of 20,000 inhabitants, was the usual practice after the capture of a city; uncounted millions from Canton to Peking were put to the sword before the Taiping Rebellion disintegrated, during which the entire Manchu dynasty was also destroyed.

The effect of the rebellion on Hong Kong was immense.

Tens of thousands of refugees flooded over the Shamchun River seeking peace in the Colony, which itself had scarcely recovered from the effects of the First English War, the international squabbling over the British importation of opium into China.

What began as little streams of refugees became a rapidly swelling river as the bloodletting on China's mainland increased. And the river became a flood as new generations of immigrants poured in to escape the inevitable mainland famines; their hordes threatened to sink Hong Kong's hopes for a century.

Wily Hong Kong and Macao investors, their profits lost following the end of the First Opium War, seized the refugees as they came over the river, cornered them into sub-standard housing and tents, fed them on starvation rations and shipped them abroad to places as distant as California and Peru. Private firms had earlier made fortunes out of the rush of stateless humans into Hong Kong, in what was later called the Coolie Traffic, but which, because of its numbers, became in effect a Yellow Slave Trade. Along the Hong Kong seaboard ship-builders were now throwing together unseasoned timber to construct second-rate, leaking ships to transport the human cargo to lands which they called Paradise.

Resistance by the immigrant Chinese was thrust aside; Hong Kong special constables were employed to beat them into submission. The great firms that had sprung up during the Colony's years to make it a nation of wealthy merchants and traders, now confined their energies to a trade of degradation and misery that soon assumed immense proportions.

Argentina, lusting for the new human traffic, began to expand her old railways and build new ones. California flourished with the wealth of this new and dirt-cheap immigrant labour: slaves who would work until they dropped for a handful of rice a day. Acres of cheap tenements arose on the American skyline to house the miserable inmates who arrived half-starved and sickly after the buffetting of the Pacific storms. Scores of such ships actually foundered within sight of the Colony's harbours, with their hapless passengers battened down below; or chained beneath the hatches.

Inevitably, mutinies began to occur aboard the slave ships and squads of bully-men were sent aboard to put the coolies down. Hong Kong's waters were littered with the floating bodies of those who preferred drowning to transportation into slavery.

In Macao, too, the Coolie Traffic flourished. And all this during the period of Sir George Bonham's administration which stands amiably in the annals of Hong Kong's history.

Clearly the activities of the military, the Governor of the day, and private companies ranging across the whole spectrum of Hong Kong's business community were profitably engaged. And foremost in any such ventures, illegal or otherwise, were Messrs Smith and Wedderburn, of which James, Milly's husband, was now the senior representative.

'Don't tell me I've lent my name to this disgusting business!' said Milly, furiously.

'This disgusting business, as you are pleased to call it, was conceived and operated by your father long before I had a hand in it,' James replied. 'Meanwhile, please confine yourself to domestic activities, and leave me to handle business affairs.'

James and Milly were walking in the garden of the English Mansion in bright moonlight. A night of stars heralded the beginning of an argument which was to be a prolonged and heated one. After less than a month of marriage, the Yellow Slave Trade, conducted under Milly's nose, so to speak, was their chief topic of conversation.

17

Leading to Milly's bedroom was a garden verandah of quarry tile flooring. This had the advantage of signalling to a light sleeper the approach of unwanted visitors.

'But that ain't fair,' said Mamie. 'Mr Wedderburn's your husband — and whether you like him visiting at night time or not jist don't count with me.'

'He's got me, hasn't he?' retorted Milly. 'Which means he's got his hands on the dowry of over two million dollars. Surely that should suffice.'

'But you got the Bible, too, remember,' said Mamie, 'which says you gotta cleave to your husband till death do you part. You can't run in the face o' that.'

'He can't complain,' said Milly. 'I warned him!'

'You'm askin' for Hell and damnation, child! Night after. night I hear that poor fella slitherin' his bare spags along them tiles. It must come terrible hard on his feet.'

'It'll cool him down,' said Milly, picking up her sewing.

It was a morning of birdsong and sunshine, with just enough wind coming up from the harbour to stir the tails of the banyan tree thrushes. Below the garden of the English Mansion stretched out a vast panorama of foam-crested sea, and the mountains of China were doing their weekly wash under the burnishings of a September sun; it was a month made for lovers in Hong Kong, asserted Mamie.

'Mamie,' said Milly, 'you are an incurable romantic!' And she got up from her chaise-longue, clenched her eyes against the sun and stretched her long slim body. Mamie, with a sidelong glance, saw that the months were turning the girl into the woman.

'You like this dress, Mamie?' Milly slowly pirouetted.

'Ah do, but it'll sure put the shakes up Mr Wedderburn. You got no pity?'

Milly lowered her arms. 'Do you think we could forget about Wedderburn?'

But Mamie didn't react to this; hypnotised by the drowsy heat, she went on. 'I mind my big Rastus when I were about your age. I'm tellin' you − he reckoned this Mamie was the best thing to happen to him since he were a sucklin' child. "Mamie Malumba," he used to say, "don't you move from that position. You jist stand there smilin' down at me like that for the rest o' ma life and Ah'll smile back. And while you're smilin', what you doin' tonight, Missus?" "Mr Malumba," I told him, "I ain't doin' nothin' but sleepin', for I've had a hard day. You jist settle yourself down in your cabin bed on the other side of the lake, and I'll send you morning kisses."

'"But we been married three weeks now, girl. When does Ah come visitin'?" "When this Mamie says so, and not before," I told him, "and it ain't no good you gettin' sore about it, for that's what the preacher says. Fastin' and penitence is good for your soul." "But I ain't talkin' about my soul, Mame," says he. "Up and down that tiled verandah Ah goes like a fella on night patrol, and Ah ain't seen my missus uncovered yet ..." "That's your bad luck, but what the preacher done told us, Sam," I said, "this marriage business ain't all lovey-dovey; it's good for a man's constitution if the groom do wait." "Is that a fact?" said Sam, "I bet the fella who makes them rules don't go short on nothin'."'

Milly was giggling despite herself, rocking backwards and forwards with delight on her chair.

'Did you let him in eventually?' she asked.

'Ah did,' said Mamie. 'After he'd done his penance for all his bachelor wickedness, like the preacher said, but it was very heavy on his spags, jist like your poor fella, and never in ma life did I see size elevens flatter than Rastus Malumba's. Night after night he was up and down them tiles, till they dropped their arches.'

Ignoring Milly's laughter, Mamie put down her knitting and smiled at the sun. 'Mind, if he came back, even this minute, I'd take him by the hand and lead him into Paradise. That Ah would, honey-girl.'

'Oh, Mamie!' Milly put her arms about her, but Mamie shrugged her away.

'Don't you Mamie me! You jist give some thoughts to the rules and regulations concerning marriage; a husband's entitled, remember, and dropped arches ain't no joke.'

They exploded with laughter, holding their sides, but their merriment was stopped as if cut by a knife when Wedderburn appeared from behind a rhododendron bush.

'Is this private, or can anyone join in?'

He was dressed in a white duck suit that enhanced his rotundity; upon his head was an Eton straw hat that gave him the appearance of an over-grown schoolboy.

'A word alone, Milly?' he asked.

Mamie rose in wobbling immensity, and left them. Milly sat motionless, her face averted.

Wedderburn said tonelessly: 'It would appear that we have absolutely nothing in common. You agree?'

'Wasn't that apparent from the start?'

'I hoped that you might eventually come to believe —'

'That you married me not for myself, but for what I was worth?'

'You know that isn't true!'

'It is precisely true — a marriage of convenience, planned in the cruellest way.'

He waved his small, plump hands at her. 'We have been married for more than a month and I've seen nothing of you. We sit at opposite ends of the table; the servants bring us food, but we share not the smallest dialogue. I possess many friends, people of charm and intellect; all inquire after you. Hostesses all over the Colony are waiting to receive you, but you shut yourself away with that black servant like a meditating nun.'

'Leave Mamie out of this!'

'I fully intend to. I am not an old man, and it is necessary

130

for me to have the company of a lady of charm and good breeding.'

'How exciting! Have you anybody in mind?'

'Not at present, but if you continue to ignore my rights as your husband, I will soon acquire one!'

'So long as she doesn't live here.'

'Oh, but that's where you are mistaken! It is my intention that she will. Then she will be the mistress and you the paying guest, which is precisely your status at the moment. At the first opportunity I will seek a bachelor's housekeeper. There are many available, you know, they abound in Hong Kong.'

For the first time Milly faced him. 'You wouldn't dare! You couldn't face the scandal!'

'On the contrary — it's practically all arranged. If you think I am allowing myself to be ignored and ridiculed by a slip of a girl, you can think again.'

'The moment she comes, I shall leave!'

James shrugged. 'Please do. Little can be gained by your staying. Hong Kong may be used to matrimonial scandals, but two women in the nuptial bed would give the clubs an absolute field day.'

There was a pause. Milly, fuming, fought to control her shaking hands while Wedderburn strolled calmly around the room. Slopping whisky into a tumbler he sipped it, watching her with dispassionate eyes.

'The choice is yours,' he said, and drained the glass.

'There's an alternative,' said Milly. '*You* go, and I will stay. You've got the money, but the house is mine.'

He turned towards her, his mouth twisted ironically. 'You know, I've always had my doubts about your integrity. Dr Schofield disclosed your true sense of morality when he told of your schoolgirl liaison; and recently something else has come to light.' Smiling triumphantly, he stared out of the window to the lawns beyond. 'This Eli Boggs man, for instance.'

'What of him?'

'The pirate in whose arms you so conveniently landed ... You were a little closer to him than you gave me to understand.'

'I don't know what you're talking about,' Milly said.

'Do you not? Doesn't the name Sweetcorn mean anything to you?'

'Of course. I told you about him.'

'Ah yes, but you don't know what he told us about *you*. We're not fools in the Marine Office, you know. We have our informers everywhere. This man bandied it about that while you were aboard the *Mongolia* you and Boggs had much in common — before you knew he was a pirate, perhaps, but you made a happy transition from West to East, we are given to understand. Sweetcorn may be dead, but his living comrades still have tongues. And one we beheaded in Kowloon City last week didn't know the length of his under interrogation. Ship's crews do chatter.'

'Ships' crews also lie to suit their own purposes!'

Wedderburn smiled, mocking her. 'Some went so far as to claim you were moonstruck by Boggs. Which gives me reason to understand why you have so little time for me.'

'Don't be ridiculous! He ransomed me, did he not?'

'I'm about to remind you of that — a demand that hastened the death of your father. A ransom most brutally extorted!'

Furious, Milly made to leave, but he stilled her with a gesture, saying: 'Indeed, in case you still foster kindly thoughts of the redoubtable man, I'll show you something that may dispel a cherished memory. No, Milly, don't go. What I have to show you may end, once and for all, another schoolgirl dream you may have been treasuring.' Going to a sideboard he unlocked a little drawer and opening this he drew out a glass phial and held it up to the light. Milly gasped. Within the small bottle, clearly defined, was a preserved ear. Wedderburn held it higher. 'This accompanied the ransom note which your father received on his deathbed. At the time he believed the ear to be yours; later, after his death, we realised that this was probably the ear of an innocent peasant girl.'

Milly closed her eyes; when she opened them the grisly relic held her gaze with astonishing force.

'If this does not dispel any romantic notions in your silly little head, what will? The friend who saw you safely home was the same man who sent this ear. The next object to arrive at the house would doubtless have been your tongue, and if that didn't persuade payment, next would have come your head.'

Sickened, Milly now stood with the phial in her hand.

'Can you imagine the agony of the victim?' Wedderburn said. 'And the vicious cruelty of the man who hacked off her ear? They come in all shapes and sizes, these seaboard pirates; some mere boys, some as old as Methuselah, some ugly, some handsome — and of many differing nationalities. But all have a common curse upon their souls — the love of cruelty and lust for money. And your old friend Eli Boggs is no different from the rest.'

Mamie was alone in her bedroom when Milly knocked on the door.

'You knew all the time?' Milly asked her. 'Why didn't you tell me?'

'Now, I ask you,' cried Mamie, 'why tell you such a horrible thing? Ain't there enough misery in this old world? Anyways, these godforsaken fellas are all the same. There ain't one pin to choose between the lot of them.' She held Milly at arm's length. 'What you cryin' for, honey? This fella Eli Boggs don't mean nothin' to you! So dry up quick. If you'd been the one to lose that ear, you'd have some'ut to cry about.' And she held her close, whispering words of comfort.

18

Months later Eli, to the accompaniment of a bawdy sea-shanty, steered the *Ma Shan* from Lamma into Stanley Bay, on the south coast of Hong Kong island, and grounded her keel on an incoming tide. Black Sam, stripped to the waist despite the March cold, joined him at the wheel.

'Are we seeing old man Tai this morning?' he asked.

'To catch him cold,' said Eli, 'before his brain is aired.'

'Ye need to be up a'fore dawn to do that, Boss! He's a sly one. How much you aimin' to pay for his factory?'

'Five thousand; not a dollar more. Gunpowder's on the slide.'

Together they went down the gangplank and along the beach of Stanley harbour.

'You reckon he'll sell?' asked Sam.

'He's just fiddled Mad Chu out of it, and questions are being asked by a Portuguese officer who's snoopin' around, so the price should have dropped.'

'We'll have to give him one between the eyes if we buy it,' said Sam. 'Portuguese Customs officers I don't like at any time.'

'If needs be,' said Eli.

'They tell me Chu Apu's lost his brain,' added Sam. 'He's begging along Sai Kung quay on all fours, they say. The factory was his till he went mad.'

Eli nodded. 'Nobody can think what happened to him. But it's dog eat dog if you're a pirate. The world belongs to the carnivores, but no dog's eating me.'

Papa Tai was the comparadore of Stanley Village. Five feet high and bald as a gnome, he had made his fortune by selling his daughters.

Wife after wife he had used and abused; concubine after concubine he had violated in search of children: half-starved, broken creatures, bought cheap in times of famine, and whom, after they had performed their natural function, he had cast aside. In this manner he had sired scores of sons and daughters, and the youngest and most beautiful of these was Sulen, now sitting on her father's doorstep painting her toes and fingernails.

At the age of fourteen Papa Tai had sold her to Chu Apu. But now Chu had been officially certified insane, Sulen was at liberty to be sold yet again.

Sulen's expression as she sat there that morning was serene. She had combed out her long black hair in the sun and tied it at the nape of her neck in a bun and decorated it with wild flowers; she was wearing a yellow kimono of Chinese silk, in expectation of another suitor; even Eli admitted to himself as he approached that she looked ravishing.

'You come to see my Papa Tai?' Sulen rose. And Papa Tai, hearing voices, emerged from his mud-walled house on Stanley beach.

'You come to do business?' He exposed blackened teeth. 'If it is women you are after, I have but one left, my youngest daughter, and she is priced above rubies.'

'I come to bid for Mad Chu's gunpowder factory,' said Eli. 'You own it now, they say.'

'Every stone, every stick!' The old man regarded Eli through slitted eyes.

'Name your price.'

'Ten thousand Mexican dollars.'

'Five thousand, and do not be ridiculous!'

'Six.'

'Four.'

'Six thousand, and my daughter Sulen.'

'Four,' said Eli. 'I haven't had a woman for a fortnight, but I'm not buying children. Innocence is priceless.'

Papa Tai screwed up his ravaged face. 'A child? Innocent?'

He guffawed. 'She who has been wife to the ferocious Chu Apu?'

'For which reason I wouldn't have her if you offered her free,' said Eli, and Sulen, hearing this, screwed up her hands into fists.

Meanwhile, Eli was thrusting money into the old man's eager grasp. 'There is talk that a Portuguese Customs officer has been sniffing around here,' he said casually. 'How true is that?'

'Searching for the factory? Not true! Unless I showed you the way, even you could not find it. Meanwhile, my friend, I have good contacts with the brothels of the Beca de Roza; if you want a grown female I can obtain one for you within hours.'

'There are twenty-six brothels in Hong Kong's Victoria. There are more brothels than there are English family houses. So I've no need to go to Macao, old one. Where is the contract?'

Papa Tai wrote the contract of sale for the gunpowder factory and both signed it.

'But please, what about me?' asked Sulen.

'How old are you?' asked Black Sam.

'I shall be fifteen in the Month of White Dews.'

'Apply again when you have become a woman, and I will speak for you,' said Eli.

'May fleas infest the bellies of you both,' said Sulen with hatred in her voice.

'And welcome,' said Eli, who was now the owner of the Stanley Gunpowder Factory, and taking the contract he went back to his junk.

'You will show me where the factory is, Papa?' asked Sulen, watching them go.

'But why?'

'Because Captain da Costa, my friend, keeps asking if I know its whereabouts.'

'He will pay for such information?'

'All he is asking for so far is me.'

'You can do better, my child. You can be sold at the next Canton meat auction for a few dollars, but the whereabouts of the factory could be worth real money. Now that the place

136

is off my hands, ask him how much he will pay if you will lead him to it.' He touched her face with a gnarled finger. 'You hate Eli Boggs for rejecting you?'

'As the dog hates the cat!'

'Then sell him. It is appropriate. All is fair in love and war, as these foreign devils keep telling us.'

19

That evening, by a strange and unholy coincidence, Anna No Name was aboard her little mist and flower sampan, quietly fishing; the way in which the painted ladies of the harbour attracted customers.

History does not relate that she was there for the purpose of luring Eli Boggs into the privacy of the sampan's hooped canopy (wherein clients were introduced to the delights of love) – but it was a fact that Eli made much of during his later trial for piracy: an accusation that might lead him to the hangman's rope.

Anna sang sweeter and better than ever she had sung before murdering other pirates and Eli, examining the records of the gunpowder factory he had just purchased from Papa Tai, paused in his work.

The evening was hushed and the waters of the harbour as still as black velvet. Inclining his ear, Eli listened. Then Black Sam put his head around the door of the little cabin.

'We're in luck, Master. We've got a mist and flower sampan singer comin' up.'

'O aye?' replied Eli. 'I've seen 'em all before. I don't go a lot on 'em.'

'She do arrive with the prettiest perfume,' replied Black Sam. 'I can smell it from here. It pegs the nose to the stinks of Stanley Market, and that's goin' some.'

'If she smells as sweet as she sings, haul her aboard,' commanded Eli.

At which the singing abruptly ceased; both wondered why. Black Sam went up on deck and his eyes searched the dark

138

waters, now silvered in ripples under the light of the moon. Nothing stirred: it was as if the hand of God had reached down and lifted the singer skyward into oblivion.

'Can't make that out, Master,' Black Sam called down the companionway. 'She's plum disappeared!'

'Don't lose sleep on it, Sam,' replied Eli. 'We'll sail to Macao in the morning and pick ourselves two yellow Macao roses.'

'Not for me, Master,' said Sam. 'Ye see,' he continued, 'I ain't just anybody when it comes to women. Like you, Master, I'm particular over the woman I bill and coo. They sail in all shapes, sizes and nationality in these waters, from little Burmese lovelies of five feet up to lanky pieces from north o' Pekin; I've even known a woman in Shansi with bright red hair ...'

'Tell me somethin' I don't know,' said Eli, already bored.

'The one Ah'm shackin' up with final has got to be big, like me, with plenty to get hold of, and got to have a smile like a Puritan's bedsheet, yessir!'

'I ain't that particular, myself,' said Eli, 'so long as she's got two legs and various other equipment, I don't care.'

'Yes you do, for I know! These ladies come and go, but you only roust one up when your need is great.'

'Please, no more,' said Eli, lying back on his bunk.

'But it's true, ain't it? Have you taken a woman in pleasure since that half-pint English girl came aboard? You've not, and that's months back.'

'Had one a fortnight since! Talk sense.'

'But you do love old freckle-face proper. Admit it!'

'The devil take ye,' said Eli.

'We go roving seaward and we trap the merchantmen,' Black Sam said. 'We swing the hawsers, go aboard, and pile the loot into Ladder Street where the *compradores* come to buy; and on those ships sit the prettiest women I ever did set eyes on. But you don't give 'em a glance.'

'Enough!'

'Since you meet that young 'un, you've only got eyes for her. I can't make that out, for she's sure no great beauty.'

'Leave her out of it,' snapped Eli.

139

'But I'm correct — ain't I?'

'She's right for me, but I ain't right for her.'

'How do ye know that when ye don't even try?'

'She's on the other side o' the world, Black Sam.'

'Jeez! She's only on the other side o' the bloody harbour!'

'That's a thousand miles away from me.'

Now there came a silence. Anna's singing, like the single string of a violin on the clear moonlit air went on, but neither heard.

After a while, Black Sam went on. 'There we are then! When ye come to think of it, we're two of a kind, you and me, Eli Boggs. Soon I'll come across a Negro girl with a mouth like a black rose and eyes like slanted pearls, and if I make love to that woman she'll know I'm the man for her. And one day, like it or not, you're going' to see a freckled face a'smilin' ... That'll be the one you let slip through your fingers — but never again, Master. You understand? I seen that in the stars. She's for you!'

'Get your head down,' said Eli, 'and let's have more sleep and less philosophy. You got more mouth than the gulley of a sea-goin' junk so get going!' And Black Sam, grinning, went.

The sea was flat and calm. Earlier it had rained with a soft pattering on the cabin roof above Eli's sleeping face.

Far away to the east a typhoon was raging, lifting up the little Tangar sampans and smashing them down into the grey wastes of a tumultuous ocean. But in the fragrance of Stanley Harbour all was quiet; the air soft-breathing.

Suddenly a face appeared at the *Ma Shan*'s cabin port-hole: the face of Anna, like a creature spewed up from the sea. Crowned by a tumble of wet hair she watched, her eyes taking in the detail of the cabin and every feature of the sleeping man. Then her face vanished, as if sliding back into the sea.

There grew upon the world a strange quiet, and in this quiet Anna entered Eli's cabin. He, deep in sleep, heard nothing; her bare feet were soundless on the boards. But deep in the recesses of Eli's sleeping brain there crept a perfume he had smelled before, in the hedgerows of wayside villages, where the wild musk grew.

There came to Eli then a strange invading dream ... that the girl with the long dark hair, the English girl of the freckled face, was lying in his arms. And in this dream she reached out and touched his face, so that where before there had been the roughness of his stubbled cheeks, there was now the smoothness of a petal. Where earlier there had been dawn coldness, there now was the warmth of another human.

It was a strange and eerie escape into delight, one totally unexpected. Now the girl was whispering ... it was the voice of Milly Smith, running on the sands of Lantau with Eli. He saw again the yellow clumps of sand that rose from her naked feet as she ran and her dark hair flying out behind her in the wind.

But when Eli opened his eyes it was not the face of Milly before him, but that of another. One of Asiatic beauty, with almond eyes slanted high at the outer corners. And whereas the features of Milly Smith were white and smooth, this girl's were brown and blunter, as are the faces of the Hakka sampan dwellers, who labour under their wide-brimmed sun hats and jabber to each other in Cantonese.

Eli caught his breath, sat up in the bunk and stared down at the woman now lying beside him.

Anna No Name smiled up, her teeth white in her beautiful sun-black face.

'Jesus, Mary and Joseph!' he said. 'How long you been here?'

'For hours past,' replied Anna. 'I was swimming in the bay, became tired and swam to your junk. Looking through the port-hole, I saw you asleep. The sea was cold, so I climbed aboard and got in beside you, and now I am here.'

'You can say that again,' said Eli.

'You will allow me to stay?'

He regarded her quizzically.

She added: 'I was born on a lobster junk and the sea flows in my veins, I can cook astern or net-float and darn and mend, and once I served an Old Man on the piracy run up north to Bias Bay. But now I'm down on my luck and am in need of work. Captain, do you have a need of me?'

141

'No woman ever had to ask that twice of Eli Boggs. Shift over.'

20

On the morning Eli took Anna No Name to his bed in Stanley harbour, Mamie Malumba, high up the Peak in the English Mansion, was on good form.

'Honeybunch,' she said to Milly, 'you ain't doin' no good sitting around here with a face as long as tomorro'. I suggest we dump this ole place and leave James Wedderburn to his grubbin'.' She tipped Milly under the chin. 'How d'ye fancy a trip in the family boat to the Green Island Rest House?'

Milly looked forlorn. 'Rest House?'

Mamie gave her more than a glance. It was strange, thought she, how cygnets grow into swans and ugly ducklings become birds of paradise. For now, with the full bloom of womanhood filling out the skinny schoolgirl that once was Milly Smith, she could take her place with the best in Hong Kong. Dressed in white, with summer colouring her cheeks and her lace-frilled dress going in and out in all the right places, she was turning heads in the street; meanwhile putting years on her husband James, who still couldn't get within a mile of her.

'Don't you know?' said Mamie. 'It's a part of your papa's estate. When times were difficult he departed to this Rest House.'

'On his own?'

'Well, no! He always took a couple of girls with him — to cook and mend, you understand.'

'The men round here don't miss much!'

'The men round here don't miss anything at all,' said Mamie. 'Let's get goin' while the sun's got his hat on.'

Down at Pedder's wharf the two of them went aboard the *Singing Kettle*: a little steam-driven craft of brilliant white and polished brass. When it came to possessions, thought Milly, her father had spared no expense.

His greatest extravagance was about to be made known to her.

The biggest source of income for Hong Kong merchants in the nineteenth century was opium. However, after the Taiping Rebellion against the Manchu Dynasty, followed by the deaths of some sixteen million people, the opium runners, from minor merchants to great cartels, found the trade risky.

True, small incursions were still made with opium into minor ports on the Chinese mainland by small-time adventurers like Eli Boggs, but the source of enormous profit rapidly dried up. In an attempt to keep personal incomes high, the merchants sought other means of profiteering at China's expense. So the Taiping Rebellion became the lynchpin of another trade. This time in humans.

As a result of the flood of war refugees from China, the population of Hong Kong soared from 22,000 in 1848 to 40,000 in seven years when the rebels devastated the adjoining province of Kwangtung: this brought with it a host of Triad members (the basis of Hong Kong's secret societies) and the realisation that landless immigrants could, by judicious planning, take the place of opium in terms of profits.

'I tells you,' said Mamie, aboard the family boat, 'there ain't no bounds to the ingenuity of wickedness when financiers become involved. And your pa weren't behind the door when cunning was handed out.'

'And James?'

'Accordin' to my ole Rastus, your husband worked hand in hand with your father.'

The sea was sunlit in great swathes of gold and green; about the tumult of the prow great hordes of fry, the minute sacrificial food of the ocean, sprayed in billows of light, iridescent in variegated colours as the little craft ploughed the sea.

To the north Milly saw the flat calm waste of Kowloon

disappear in brilliant light-spray; to the south the mountainous outline of Hong Kong Peak gave way to the distant silhouette of Green Island looming up to port. Seeing this she remembered the green slopes of Lantau where she had run along the sands with Eli: he who had subsided into a faint, but affectionate memory, just as Tom Ellery, her first love, had faded, yet remained sufficiently to touch her emotions.

Tom was in his grave, she thought bitterly − but what had happened to Eli? It was now over a year since they had parted at the festival of Tam Kung. A lot had happened to her since then.

Mamie's voice interrupted her thoughts.

'Best you face it, honey − your pa weren't no better than he should be. And that' saying' somethin' with folks like Wedderburn around, for he is the spawn o' the Devil.'

The boat reached a landing stage at Green Island; ropes were thrown, commands rang out, a little gangplank went down and they went ashore. Almost immediately the Rest House came into view; a small but palatial building with a curved red pan-tile roof, its gables decorated with golden dragons. A flight of marble steps led up to its entrance.

Walking upon a Tientsin carpet of blue and gold, they entered a splendid room, its ceiling decorated with oil paintings of classical beauty. Fauns and naked nymphs disported themselves upon walls crowned by priceless Italian friezes; marble flooring set off the enamelled artistry of doorways leading to unknown rooms. All was extravagance and opulence.

'All this is just a second home?' asked Milly.

'Some folks call it a pavilion,' said Mamie. 'Perhaps you'll love it, but my fella Rastus, he hated it on sight. Three years he stood it here, the boss-man of the whole establishment, with a staff of six, from houseboys to makee-learns, and the finest chef money could buy. But your pa only visited here once in a year of Sundays.'

'With his fancy women?'

'You're learnin' quick! You gotta keep things quiet when you're in Hong Kong high society.'

'And you − did you come often?'

145

'Only on days off, to visit Rastus. This is only the second time I come since he died.'

A diminutive man appeared in a doorway; Mamie called to him in Cantonese and he scurried off, to return with a lighted lantern.

'Mr Soong, the housekeeper,' she explained. 'All his life he didn't do nothin' here but scare off stray dogs − like nosey Customs men.' She touched Milly's elbow. 'Follow me, and I'll show you somethin' to make your hair stand on end.' Shrieking something in Chinese, she handed Milly a key.

'Now we go down into the cellars,' said Mamie.

At the bottom of winding stone steps she opened a heavy, iron-studded door. In the light of the lantern Milly saw a room full of hogshead barrels, all neatly stacked: perhaps a hundred either side of a path that disappeared into dimness.

'Opium!' said Mamie, and held the lantern higher.

'Opium?'

'They say the war is over, and the trade stopped. But night after night the cargo comes in − by ship from India to Green Island. They anchor in the bay, then store it in here.'

Mamie pointed into the darkness beyond the stacked barrels. 'Down there, leading to the waterfront, is a door. They bring it in, stack, rebale it, and push it out the other end. The richest Hong Kong tycoons reckon they've got the best of the Opium Trade, but when it comes to your Smith and Wedderburn, they want to get up in the mornin'!'

'Good God,' whispered Milly.

'Best you know it all,' said Mamie. 'There ain't no end to your husband's wickedness.'

'And what am I supposed to do about it?'

Mamie shrugged. 'My Rastus tried to stop it and finished up in the ground.'

'What?' Milly stared at her.

'They done for him. I'm warning you, Missy. Somebody tipped off the Customs fella who was makin' his rounds, and two were found dead in the mornin' − one was the Customs Officer, the other was my Rastus. They said it was the fever but I knows otherwise. These fellas don't play around.'

146

'You expect me to stand for this? It's my money they're using now!'

'And what do you propose to do?'

'Report this to the Governor!'

Mamie gave her whitest grin.

'Why not?' demanded Milly. 'Isn't he the law around here?'

'Honey,' said Mamie, 'I don't know for certain sure, but it's my guess that he's up to his ears in it as well. This is Hong Kong; it ain't back home in the school dormitory. When they savvy what you're up to here they cut your throat from ear to ear.'

'So what do I do?'

'Nothin'. You sit at home and watch the Smith and Wedderburn money get bigger, bigger and bigger. This time in your name. My Rastus tried it, remember, and all he got was a bellyful of poison.'

'Poison?'

'The standard death, honey. A little squirt in the bread, or a few drops in the mouth while sleeping. Arsenic − it's been going on in China for a thousand generations.'

'Then isn't it dangerous to show me all this?'

Mamie nodded.

'Why did you do it?'

'Because o' my Rastus. You gotta make up your mind, girl, for you're the only thing decent that has come to this place for the past hundred years, I reckon. And you got enough spunk in your five foot high to clean the whole mess up.'

'Don't believe it,' said Milly. 'I'm not as brave as Rastus.'

'We'll see,' replied Mamie. 'Opium isn't the only crime here at the moment. You heard of Coolie Traffic?'

'Slavery yes, but not Coolie Traffic.'

'You're about to,' said Mamie. 'Now let's get upstairs before ole man Soong gets wind that we're up to somethin'.'

21

The silence of the night, and the full moon shining through the windows were having their usual hypnotic effect upon Milly.

Lying in an ocean of a bed within a room of hanging tapestries, she stared sleeplessly at the decorated ceiling. On all sides priceless vases shone their cloisonné brilliance; prancing figurines depicting ancient Asiatic rites stood in grotesque and erotic poses. Vaguely Milly reflected that it would have hastened her father's final heart attack if he could have seen her now, lying on the mattress of his thousand conquests. How could anyone hope to reconcile the English gentleman of aristocratic pedigree with this cess-pit of depravity and corruption?

No birds sang; which was strange, for her Hong Kong garden was usually filled with the chanting of night-jars and the whistling thrush. This stillness, broken only by the distant lapping of waves, stultified Milly's senses. Indeed, the light of the moon seemed to enfold her within a cold embrace, so that she became one within a vacuum of stillness.

Within the yawn of approaching sleep, she rose, pulled her gown about her naked body, and went through the french doors on to the verandah.

All was white; shadows having been washed out by the brilliance of the moon, Milly stood within banks of convolvulus. And there came to her a sweet memory from the past; like a chord of half-forgotten music, it stirred within her. And upon the foliage of the convolvulus flowers the features of a beloved face took form — that of Tom Ellery.

148

So clearly she saw him: his smile, his shadowed eyes; and heard his voice: ' . . . a right ould codswallop you are, an' no mistake, Milly Smith.'

Now Milly held him again, and the corn-husks from Squire Oldroyd's barn, where they had met in such innocence, showered down upon her once more. She saw, upon the sleeve of her silken gown, the corn-husks floating in another life; a pure life, far removed from this adulterous place. Picking them off her sleeve she held them in the palm of her hand.

Tom's words came to her now, like an echo on the foreign air: 'I will love ye to everlastin' . . . till Hell freezes over.'

And she walked on through the garden, followed by the memories of her first and only love.

There came to her also a sense of freedom that snatched at her, caught her up so that she was no longer confined within her body; and Milly ran, through the golden sand dunes encompassing the Rest House, and down to the beach. Splashing through the tide-swim, knee-deep, then waist-deep, she cast off her restricting nightgown and dived within the rollers of the incoming surf. Blackness enveloped her as momentarily she abandoned herself to the numbing rush of water; then she swam against the incoming currents and found herself alone in the calm of the timeless sea. Floating upon her back, enveloped in coldness, she screwed up her eyes to the emblazoned moon.

In that moment when instinct turned her homewards and she struck out for the beach, there came a sudden swirl of the sea and a sleek, grey body dived beneath her, to rise and upend her in a floundering of limbs. Instantly hoisting her upwards, the great fish then deposited her head down in a shower of foam and, popping his face out of the water, regarded Milly with a fishy smile. And this was the dolphin from Lantau Island, whom she had met before: the dolphin who now lived with his mate on Green Island. The two dolphins were apparently overjoyed at coming across an old friend, for they swam either side of Milly now, escorting her back to the beach with a dignity wonderful to behold. Within fifty feet of her feet touching sand, the friendship having been confirmed, both dolphins retreated seaward, and left her.

Gasping, Milly waded up the beach, aware of her nakedness; seeing the robe she had been wearing cast up on the sand by the tide, she pulled it over her wet body, looking like a water sprite. As she did so, she saw the unmistakable form of another human lying but a few paces away from her; a man sprawled in the sand.

Uncertainly, Milly approached the body. The man was clad only in ragged coolie trousers, the legs of which were tattered. Reaching him, she knelt, her hand touching the cold face whose eyes, transfixed, stared up at the stars. The moon momentarily darkened, then blazed, and she saw the face of the dead man with clarity: a boy, not a man, for his cheeks were round and smooth. An Asian, tragic in the mournful symmetry of youth defiled, for his hands were chained together.

Milly rose, still staring down. A chained boy, recently drowned; but from where? Chained by whom? And washed up on Green Island, of all places. Pity for his passing encompassed her now; somebody's son, somebody's brother ... She put her hand upon his heart, but his body was ice-cold. And suddenly to her horror, another body came tumbling through the surf further down the beach. Uncontrollably, it rolled and tumbled, through the foam-topped tide. As she watched the hairy arm of a man appeared above the surface, splashing down into the shallows as if calling for assistance. And the head that loomed out of the swim was wild-eyed and bearded: a man, not a boy, a new rush of the tide bringing him in upon a wave-crash.

This body, too, had manacled hands.

It was then that Milly saw, against the shore of the mainland, a line of big sea-going junks tacking in the wind as they furrowed the West Lamma Channel. In line astern they went, six of them crowded with sail, white froth frilling their sterns as they ploughed the sea.

Milly straightened, shielding her eyes from wind and sea-spray. Clearly, the junks were heading in from Macao. The sightless eyes of the bodies stared up at her.

Was this the Coolie Traffic, the Slave Trade of which people whispered in dark places? The trade from which she knew her husband − and her father before him − had profited?

Walking swiftly north along the beach, with the mainland lights of Mount Davis glimmering behind her, Milly broke into a slow run, to arrive at a little cliff-top giving a panoramic view of Lamma Channel. From here she could now see the incoming junks clearly. In a disciplined array of seapower they bore south, slower now. With men on the leading junk making semaphore signals by lantern, they crept inland, their bat-winged sails set for a landing.

A rocket rose lazily, spluttering in sparks, to fall dismally into darkness. Then came another as the last junk went into irons. The thumping and clattering of spars rose to Milly's ears as she watched.

It was then that she heard the shouting of men above the breakers. Slipping, sliding on grass, Milly sought lower ground; and saw, through a fissure in the rocks, a scene that she was never to forget.

From a makeshift harbour small outbuildings spread inland to a big hut. The first junk berthed, its gangplank was lowered, and down it thronged a column of milling, confused men, all chained and brutally driven onward by guards. One, too slow, was set upon and toppled from the gangplank into the sea.

Horrified, Milly realised that she was witnessing a trade in human misery tolerated by a disregarding Parliament, with Governor Bonham at its head. This, she later learned, was commercially called 'The Pig Trade'.

The old convict system which provided cheap labour to Australian farmers having ceased, new immigrants were sought to replace it. Thus the business of Chinese indentured labour was first begun, the starving refuse of mainland Chinese cities being bought for a song, fed, re-clad and transported to Australian and South African farms. Fleeing from the famine-struck areas like Kwangtung Province, whole families succumbed to the temptation and delivered up their freedom to become virtual slaves. What Milly was seeing now had been standard practice for the last eight years: vessels engaged in the Yellow Slave Trade had been leaving Chinese ports in hundreds.

Packed like sardines into anything which would float, battened down in stinking, airless holds, often chained, the

151

miserable cargoes set out from ports like Amoy, Hong Kong and Macao. The ships for such voyages were mainly constructed in Hong Kong, under orders from private merchants who oversaw the trade; licences being granted by the Colony's Marine Department, of which James Wedderburn was the executive head.

Moving through the shadows, Milly reached the confines of a barbed wire enclosure, wherein stood the embarkation matshed, and peered through the torn rush-mat walls to the scene within.

Hundreds of prisoners, mostly naked, lay on tiers of wooden shelving. Patrolling among them, carrying clubs, were the *Samsengs*, the thugs of Chinese Secret Societies; the Triads having already gained a foothold in the alleys of Kowloon City where they openly ran prostitution, gambling and opium dens under the protection of the Union Jack. Sickened, Milly ran back to the beach.

Later, she approached the columned entrance of the Rest House where stood the old caretaker, Soong, as if waiting for her. In regal authority he stood, arms folded upon his skinny chest, and bowing subserviently, asked: 'You go swim, Missy?'

'I go swim,' Milly replied, and made to pass him but his hand went out.

'At this time of night?'

'At any time I choose.' She stared at him defiantly.

'Go swim down on beach with dolphin: dolphin very good to play with in the sea. Always Master, your father, swim out and play with dolphins.'

'Despite the dead bodies on the beach?'

Incredulity struck Soong's lined face. 'Dead bodies? This is not possible!'

'The bodies of two men with their hands chained together.'

He smiled, showing yellow, broken teeth. 'Oh no, Missy Milly, your head go moonshine. It is not possible!'

'Then come and see for yourself.' Turning, she led the way and the old man followed.

'Sometime poor fishermen fall of junks, you understand?

152

And always your father say to bring down boxes and give them good Taoist funeral, for which he pay. But men in chains? Oh no!'

'We'll soon see,' said Milly. As they approached she pointed out the two dead men; the bodies were still lying in the shallows, lapped by the tide.

'Chains, you say? But where are the chains?' Soong stirred one body with his foot, then stooped, turning it over. It was the younger, the boy.

The chains had been removed.

'They were chained when I found them!'

'Ah now, Missy, you mistaken!'

'I am certainly *not* mistaken!' said Milly, and left him, saying over her shoulder, 'Have them buried decently – and send the bill to me, you understand?'

'I understand that also,' said Mr Soong.

Back in the Rest House, Mamie was waiting; she listened patiently to Milly's tale.

'The place is spooky, child. Didn't I tell ye?'

'It's more than spooky, it's a haunt of criminals!'

'Perhaps. Take my advice and forget it.'

'Forget it? A slave trade going on under my nose, making me money, and you tell me to forget it?'

'Maybe your husband jist don't know, honey, so don't jump too soon.'

'Doesn't know? According to what your Rastus told you, James and my father worked hand in hand!'

'On the opium trading, maybe. But he never did mention anythin' about a slave trade.'

'Well, we'll soon find out.'

'Don't you do nothin' till you're certain sure, mind,' answered Mamie. 'Folks can disappear round here for just makin' a mention – remember what happened to my Rastus.'

'I'll bear it in mind,' said Milly.

22

Back in the English Mansion at the weekend, Milly found herself the object of her husband's doubtful affections.

'Soon,' said James, as they walked together in the garden, 'the anniversary of the consecration of the cathedral is to take place. Many important people will be present. We were married there, remember? ... Sometimes I wonder if you forget ...'

He continued coldly, 'The celebration includes a reception afterwards at the Governor's Residence, a social honour which so far we have managed to avoid.'

'And will continue to do so,' said Milly.

'Come, be reasonable. I'm the executive head of the Marine Office; as such I am responsible to the Governor!'

'Perhaps. But I am not.'

'Your behaviour at times, you know, is completely irrational. Indeed I often wonder − and who could blame me − if you are yet recovered from your nervous disorder; mental instability is such a curious complaint ... I am asking so little of you. The Governor thinks highly of my department,' he continued, 'and while it is true that I didn't see eye to eye with the previous administration, this Governor takes an opposite view. There could even be a knighthood in it. Sir James Wedderburn − it has a noble ring.'

'Don't bank on it,' said Milly.

'You disapprove of official titles?'

'Absolutely, after what I've seen masquerading as ladies and gentlemen around here.'

James snapped. 'Your attitude does you no credit! While

it is true that many baronetcies at home are undeserved, the same could never be said of our colonials – all are distinguished members of society.'

'And wonderfully wealthy!'

'What has that to do with it?'

'Their wealth is earned by opium running and promoting unnecessary wars.'

'Milly, you are such a child in these things! All the trading is legitimate. If we hadn't shipped opium to the Chinese, the Portuguese would have done so on a bigger scale.'

Pausing at a rattan table on the terrace he swilled whisky into a glass and drank noisily. 'I hope this stuff hasn't been tampered with,' he said. 'There's some queer things happening in Hong Kong these days.'

'I wouldn't blame the Chinese if they poisoned the lot of us!'

There had been a recent outbreak of poisoning in the Colony. A baker, who rejoiced in the name of Ah Lum, had decided to rid Hong Kong of all White-Faced Devils (the local name for Europeans) by poisoning the bread he served to foreign customers. However, in his enthusiasm for the project, he overdid the amount of arsenic dispensed in each loaf, with the result that those who consumed them vomited violently, ridding their bodies of the poison before it could take effect.

Awaiting trial, Ah Lum vigorously defended his action as a genuine mistake; and was offering profuse apologies to all concerned – including Mamie, who was still suffering symptoms.

James grunted, swilling the whisky around distended cheeks.

'It tastes all right, I suppose,' he said.

Milly chanced a glance at her husband. Marriage had aged him; its failure was stamped upon his features. Unable to consummate their union, his befuddled attempts had bred in Milly a disdain that had gradually become disgust. Talk had it that her husband possessed mistresses; such men as he, Milly thought, clung to failing manhood by means of an animal sensuality which was devoid of love or tenderness.

What kind of lover would Eli make? Milly wondered. At

155

times her own thoughts shocked her; but she was enough of a woman to desire more than James Wedderburn could provide.

They wandered aimlessly side by side. The wind gusted from the harbour below, bringing brine to their lips: an autumn typhoon called Mary (they always gave them female names and vaguely Milly wondered why) was raging somewhere out in the South China Sea. The evening sky was the colour of bronze.

When the typhoon arrived the little fishing fleets would run for the typhoon shelters and the great sailing ships, their sails tightly furled, would throw out double anchors and ride out the storm. Down Rich Man's Peak would come the landslides; boulders reducing to rubble everything in their path. Villagers would be snatched out of their mud-walled hovels and whirled skywards, littering the Praya with their broken bodies. Then the rescue squads would come out; the children, always the first to die in China, being carried away to the little hillside cemeteries.

But humanity could survive the worst of storms. During the last typhoon a tiny Dutch child had wandered away from her parents in the 'eye' of the storm — that moment in a typhoon when all forces subside and a quiet calm exists before the tumult is renewed. Aged two, she was last seen in the Red Light quarter of Victoria, and three days later was given up for lost. But a day after that she appeared in the arms of a fragile old beggar, who, snatching her out of the wind, had carried her to his pitiful dwelling and there fed and changed her, even washing her mud-stained dress, before handing her over to her distracted parents.

The saving of the Dutch child had bred in Milly a new appreciation of human goodness. Even in Hong Kong, she thought, amid its depravity, opium trade and legalised prostitution carried out under the British flag, there could exist this unbounded kindness and courage. When a beggar, despised by all, could risk his life for a child, anything was possible.

Milly mentioned this to James now, as he walked beside her, glass in hand.

'Ah yes, I heard of that at the Club.'

156

'Do you not think it wonderful?'

'Wonderful?'

'Well, the Chinese hate us – it is well known. This rich baker, for instance, the one on trial for trying to poison Europeans ... Yet this old Chinese beggar protects one of our children.'

'Why shouldn't he.' He made an empty gesture. 'The child wasn't three years old! It was his duty to save her.'

The wind moved between them. She said peremptorily: 'You simply don't understand, do you?'

James shrugged his fat shoulders. 'I understand perfectly. He was a beggar who found a lost child. It was his responsibility to take her in, and he did. I understand they gave him a ten dollar reward. I'd not have given him anything. If he hadn't done it I'd have had him flogged.'

Milly walked away. He called tersely after her: 'Now what have I said, for God's sake? If I say a single word you don't agree with, you immediately flounce off. *Milly*!'

But she had passed from his sight. Alone, she stood by a brook, watching the dancing water. The wind momentarily touched her face like a spray of ice-cold champagne.

Breathless, James arrived at her side. 'What have I said to upset you now?'

'It doesn't matter.'

'Are you going to come to this reception at the cathedral? It's the least you can do. People are beginning to wonder if I really have a wife.'

'Mamie isn't well and I'd rather not leave her.'

'Try hard enough and you'll find another excuse.'

Milly decided to change the subject.

'What's going on at Green Island, James?'

He was instantly on his guard as Milly outlined her finding of the two dead bodies.

'Oh, that. It is not unfamiliar; we pick up dead fishermen almost every week. It is the typhoon – the currents bring them ashore through Sulphur Channel.'

'These were not dead fishermen. They were chained prisoners!'

Disbelief lay upon his face. 'But you must have been mistaken! Manacled, you say?'

157

'Both of them had their hands chained together.'

'And you reported this?'

'To Mr Soong, the keeper of the Rest House.'

James drained his glass. His face, thought Milly, proclaimed him a cherub of innocence. Either he wasn't in possession of the facts of Green Island or he was a most experienced liar.

'And what did Soong say?'

'Like you, he said I was mistaken. So I took him to see the two bodies. By that time − within the space of an hour at most − the chains had been removed. All that was left was just two dead fishermen.'

'I am so sorry that you had such a bad experience,' James said kindly. 'Green Island is a tragic place; convicts laboured there in the ancient past, you know. I cannot think why your father chose such a place as an escape while the less fortunate lived there in captivity.'

The temptation to confront him almost overcame Milly. Either he was an abject fool to allow such crimes to occur under his nose, or he was completely uninformed. With difficulty she decided to keep her own counsel concerning the Coolie Traffic. To move too quickly might anger him unnecessarily, and his icy calmness was a shock to her; under attack James usually subsided into small whining protestations, a state usually enhanced by whisky, of which he had this morning consumed a considerable quantity. A silence came between them, fraught with increased tension.

'Milly, I really do wish you would see Dr Schofield again,' James said. 'What you're suffering now may be akin to hallucinations.'

'My eyes don't deceive me,' retorted Milly. 'I saw what I saw, I tell you. Two dead men in chains − and I am saying so again.'

He made a face. 'I sincerely hope you won't repeat it outside the house. It could have the most appalling repercussions.'

'It's the truth, and I shall continue to say so.'

'Do that and you'll start a hare nobody will be able to catch. The political situation here is fragile; talk of chained prisoners on our own private island could be extremely damaging to

Smith and Wedderburn. You're in this, too, remember.'

'So we just bury them and forget them, do we?'

'We give them a decent interment. Drowned fishermen were always your father's personal responsibility; he sought out and often recompensed their families.' He sighed deeply, adding, 'Dead Tangar or Hoklo fishermen are one thing, my dear; but prisoners, chained and drowned ...? God help us! The *China Mail* would have a field day!'

'So you're going to do nothing about it?'

James shrugged expressively. 'Such things are best left to Mr Soong on the island. He knows how I want it handled.'

'No doubt.'

'Meanwhile ...' and he touched her cheek with a podgy finger, 'be a good girl and keep away from there until this business quietens down.'

He turned as Tang, the house boy, appeared on the lawn nearby. 'Yes?'

'Missy Mamie, the housekeeper, she call for Mistress, sir.'

'Tell her I am coming,' said Milly.

'Meanwhile,' said James, 'please do as I ask. Seeing Dr Schofield again is in your own interest. For weeks now you haven't been yourself. You have absolutely no outside interests. Unhappily, we appear to have little in common, but I am sure that it would only require a minimum of effort to make us a united husband and wife.'

In this ingratiating mood Milly found him even less attractive. She was now convinced that he knew precisely what was going on at Green Island: the dead men, the Coolie Traffic and its appalling cruelty.

Fingering his glasses, with a smile playing on his mouth, James watched her go.

23

St John's Cathedral was crowded to full capacity. In order of strict social progression the congregation sat in silence; the only sound Milly heard as she sat beside James was the creaking of stays and the buzzing of a captive blue-bottle.

All here was defined within Hong Kong's particular discipline. The Governor and his wife being absent on holiday, the next in importance – Mr Alfred Denning, the acting Governor, and his wife – were in the front pew, the former unaccustomed to such authority, having been passed over more than once by the Foreign Office for the post of Governor; his wife, of plump countenance with the usual matronly girth that graced most ageing females in the Colony, contemplated the proceedings with resignation. Her moment of glory was soon to vanish, for the Governor and his lady were due to return in the morning.

Behind them sat the Big Business bonzos of Hong Kong's escalating bonanza: *taipans* of wealth and privilege, escorts to females all safely married, their mistresses having been left at home in spacious apartments along the new Bonham Praya which Chinese labourers were reclaiming from the sea.

The first five rows being reserved for Europeans, the next ten were reserved for Chinese; these, mostly *compradores* with countless children, sat in wheezing obesity, easing tight collars.

In stoical silence sat the Chinese females. First wives were more acceptable to the *status quo*, while the keeping of secondary wives nevertheless was permissible under the terms of Customary Marriage. Wizened, fat, often undesirable,

160

First Wives were treated with solicitous kindness by their British counterparts, while Little Stars (the household name for concubines) were ostracised when it came to official functions. Under the marriage system concubines shared all privileges accorded to legal wives, but a second wife could be divorced for almost any indiscretion, including gossiping. These, therefore, sat a pew removed from their superiors.

After the Chinese, whose business activities took them into the holy confines of Government House as equals, came pew after pew of khaki and blue-clad soldiers and naval ratings, acompanied by their whispering wives and noisy children, being perpetually hushed by feet-bound, Cantonese amahs. And behind them sat the survivors of Hong Kong's civil population, the red-necked sweating clerks of lower administration. To the strains of a rousing march on the organ they sat in disquieting silence, watching shafts of sunlight move in pools of gold around the stifling pews.

Well up in seniority sat James and Milly, heading the massed ranks of Jardine Matheson, Butterfield and Swire, and a conglomeration of merchants, from Eurasian orientals to their dusky beauties of Portuguese Macao. Thus was the pattern of Hong Kong's early history exemplified: all present, one and all, in the name of the God of Profit.

'God Save the Queen' rang out on trumpets and drums: in a thunder of ammunition boots and silk-clad slippers, all stood reverently, then sat once more as James Wedderburn, Superintendent of the Marine Office, rose and walked with dignity to an appointed position facing the congregation.

Tense, her hands clutched together in her lap, Milly watched, and listened, as her husband's voice rang out.

'Here begins the Nineteenth verse of Chapter Six of the Gospel according to Mark.

"Lay not up for yourselves treasures upon earth, where moth and rust doth corrupt, and where thieves break through and steal: but lay up for yourselves treasures in heaven, where neither moth nor rust doth corrupt, and where thieves do not break through and steal: for where your treasure is, there will your heart be also ..."'

161

At which James raised his face and his eyes met those of Milly, who sat in a shaft of sunlight. Deep in her mind she saw again the upturned face of a dead boy, chained.

James read on.

"'The light of the body is in the eye; if therefore thine eye be single, thy whole body shall be full of light ... but if thine eye be evil, thy whole body shall be full of darkness ... take therefore no thought of the morrow ... sufficient for the day is the evil thereof ...'"

He closed the book.

The sunlit cathedral appeared to Milly to echo his last words; and she heard within herself the words of another, saying:

'Even so ye also outwardly appear righteous unto men, but within ye are full of hypocrisy and iniquity. Woe unto you, scribes and Pharisees, hypocrites! Hypocrites, hypocrites all!'

Rising in her seat when her husband returned, ignoring the stares of those about her, she went out into the aisle, and walked to the church door. Her feet clattered on the cold mosaic tiles, as she rushed away from the oppressive corruption within, through the church entrance and out into sunlight.

The Governor's Residence, set in a cultivated area of trees and shrubs near the Botanic Gardens, was known as Flagstaff House.

Here, before its columned entrance, visiting dignitaries were entertained in regal splendour. Its corridors had echoed to consulate and ambassadorial staff from scores of countries, all eager to pay tribute to the enigmatic opportunist that was Hong Kong.

Milly was handed down from a decorative travelling chair of green and gold bolstered by scarlet cushions − a privilege accorded to those on a first time visit − and sailors in full

162

regalia sprang to attention as James escorted Milly inside, to be received personally by the Assistant Governor.

Slim and beautiful American girls, sent out for the season, vying with each other for pride of place, chattered nasally to uniformed escorts; silk-clad Indians, the *pankee-wallahs*, pulled listlessly at canvas fans to disperse the heat of an already crowded Banqueting Hall.

'Mr and Mrs James Wedderburn!' bawled the toast-master.

'Ah, Mrs Wedderburn, how are you!' The Assistant Governor kissed Milly's white gloved hand. 'At last we have your company. Have you fully recovered?'

'Recovered?'

Mrs Denning, his wife, interjected, 'We are aware that you have been ill, my dear, and noticed that you left the cathedral early today.'

'It was the heat,' said James.

'You know people here?'

'Scarcely anybody,' replied Milly.

James added hastily: 'When it comes to social functions my wife finds excuses ...'

'As well I might do, given that opportunity,' Mrs Denning said vociferously. 'Colonial service does so little to enhance the prospects of lasting friendship: here today, gone tomorrow. We exist upon a plain of total superficiality. You are right to keep out of the swim, Mrs Wedderburn. Don't I wish I could do the same!'

Milly made a mental note to like Mrs Denning.

'Are you now free of these confounded doctors, child?'

'If only I could be free of the heat!'

'How right you are! But your nerves are better, your husband tells us.'

'Nerves?'

'That has been your trouble, has it not?'

'Good gracious no. And doctors? I haven't seen one for the past two years!'

'Then be assured that we hope to see you more often,' said Mr Denning. 'Meanwhile, will somebody tell me why these Americans insist upon talking through their noses?'

'My dear, such lack of diplomacy will shorten your career,'

Mrs Denning said. 'I think they are all perfectly charming. Come we must circulate,' and she led her husband away.

Milly scarcely noticed them go. Intent, she was gazing at a man who stood at the entrance to the room. She raised her face, eyes narrowed. 'Who is that man?' she asked.

'Which one?' James was again beside her.

'The big fair man standing alone by the door.'

The man did not move; a glass in his hand, he too was observing the guests.

'Who is he?'

'Bruner.'

'Who?'

'Hans Bruner.'

'What's he doing here?'

'You know him?' Unaccountably, James was now whispering above the rising conversation. Glasses chinked a musical accompaniment to an increasing hubbub as drinks were refilled amid noisy banter and shouted laughter.

'I know him well,' said Milly.

James peered through the crush of bodies towards the door.

'I'd recognise that man anywhere,' she added.

Hand on her elbow, James briskly steered Milly away. 'It isn't possible. Really, you do make the most astonishing statements!'

Delaying a passing servant, Milly asked, 'That man standing over there by the door. Do you know his name?'

The man peered through the crowd.

'The big fair-haired man standing by the door – look!' and she pointed.

'You wait, please,' said the waiter. 'I find out, Missy,' and he disappeared among the people.

'Look, how can you possibly know *anyone* here?' James said impatiently. 'You don't see anyone from one year's end to another.'

'He is Hans Bruner,' said Milly. 'He was First Mate to Captain O'Toole on the *Mongolia*.'

'Oh, Lord,' said James. 'Not that business again.'

Milly raised her voice. 'I tell you it's him! I'm not an idiot,

164

James. I was on the *Mongolia*. I've talked with him, dined with him!'

James impatiently ran his fingers through his thinning hair. 'The damned thing went down, didn't it!'

His voice had risen and people were aware of it, turning round to stare quizzically. Softly now, James added: 'The damned thing sank, remember? And there were no survivors.'

'But he wasn't on it!' Pushing through the clustering people, spilling drinks in the process, Milly made towards the room entrance, calling, 'Bruner! Hans Bruner!' only to find herself face to face with Mr Denning again.

'Ah, Mrs Wedderburn! You have found a friend?'

'The ... the man at the door. I know him.'

'Which one?'

'The big fair man standing alone.'

'Akil? You know Akil? Knowing his reputation with the ladies it is perfectly possible.' Taking Milly's hand, Denning led her towards him, crying happily: 'Akil, I commend you! You have made yet another conquest.' And he bowed briefly to the big man, saying, 'May I present Mrs Wedderburn, the wife of James, my efficient Marine Superintendent?'

To Milly he said, 'Akil Tamarins, the Dutch Ambassador to Peking.'

The man bowed with grace, and taking Milly's hand, raised it to his lips. His steel blue eyes burning into hers, he said in a thick foreign accent: 'It is my pleasure, Madam, although I believe you are mistaken. Believe me, had we met before, I would have remembered.' Turning to James he added calmly, 'In Holland did you pluck her? Not only in England do they grow such roses.'

'What a surprise, Mr Bruner,' said Milly.

'Madam, it is said that two of a kind are to be found any-where in the world. I do assure you, we have never met.'

'Damn you, Bruner!' said Milly. 'Damn you!'

'Oh come, Mrs Wedderburn!' It was Denning's voice. 'This is quite outrageous. The Ambassador has said he simply doesn't know you.'

'He knows me right enough!' came Milly's reply. 'What is going on here?' And she stared around their expressionless faces.

165

'You making fools of the pair of us, that's what's going on!' James hissed between his teeth. 'And we are leaving at once!'

'The poor girl,' said Mrs Denning, after they had gone. 'They tell me she can be very difficult.'

'It is the weather, my dear,' her husband replied. 'It really is appallingly hot.'

'The child has been ill.'

'Talk has it that she first came out here soon after a nervous illness,' a man remarked idly.

'Nervous illness,' said another, 'is always tragic, especially in one so young.'

'It's James I'm most sorry for,' said Denning. 'They say he does his best, but she simply doesn't respond. Personally, I think she should be taken back to England.'

Another said, in a hushed voice: 'According to Dr Schofield she was involved in some sort of scandal at her school. Just before her father passed away. In his will he insisted upon her coming out to live under the guidance of Wedderburn.'

'A sort of guide, philosopher and friend?'

'Something like that. But then he married her, and it simply hasn't worked.'

Then Denning crossed to Bruner. 'Could I have a word with you, old chap? Somewhere in private?'

24

Milly knew that Mamie's condition was worsening before Dr Schofield's visit. The evidence of it lay in the housekeeper's face, an ashen pallor that told of her growing weakness in the grip of poison.

'Her age doesn't help, of course,' the doctor said. 'Arsenic poisoning is a most debilitating condition. Usually the over-poisoned suffer acute vomitting and purge themselves of the poison; your servant wasn't so lucky.'

'She is not a servant! She's the only friend I have,' Milly replied.

It had been three weeks since Ah Lum, the baker, had been apprehended. While most of his European victims had recovered, Mamie appeared to be sinking.

'I want her nursed here,' said Milly.

'This isn't the best place for her. At the new Fever Hospital she could have round-the-clock attention.'

'How long will she be away?'

'A week and she'll be a different woman.'

'What do you think?' Milly leaned over the sick bed.

'Is it true they're going to hang that Ah Lum?' Mamie whispered.

'Just as soon as I can get my hands on him,' said Milly.

'What's all this about a fever hospital? I heard you talkin' to the doctor.'

'It's for your own good,' said Milly helplessly.

'You put me in the Fever Hospital, and I's a'goin' out feet first,' Mamie said weakly from the pillows.

167

'Now come on, Mamie!' Milly bent over her, gripping her hands, but she continued tearfully:

'If ma Rastus was here he wouldn't have me heaved out and taken to no hospital. No sir!'

'Mamie, be reasonable!'

'It's that doctor that ain't reasonable. Ah've been in this old bed for years: time was I shared it with my poor Rastus. You fetch me out an I'll go down six foot.'

Her hands, care-worn, were trembling against the white of the sheets. 'You trust me, Mamie?' Milly said quietly.

'Ah trusts you, honey, but not this fella Schofield. I don't trust English doctors no more'n I could throw 'em. If he gets his hands on this ole girl, I reckon he'll eat me alive.'

'Mamie, don't be silly!'

'Ah trusts you no end − so will you promise me some'at?'

'Anything.'

'If Ah'm swimmin' the River Jordan in the next week or so, will you promise to put me in with my Rastus on Green Island? They poisoned him an' all, remember?'

Milly stroked her hair, her cheeks wet with tears. 'You're not going anywhere, least of all in with your Rastus,' she whispered. 'Listen! Go down to the Fever Hospital with Dr Schofield, and we'll have you back here fit and well in under a week, I promise.'

Mamie did not reply.

After leaving the sick room Milly and Schofield walked together on the garden terrace. 'And you − what about you?' the doctor asked.

'I didn't eat any of the poisoned bread, if that's what you mean.'

'That's not what I mean, young lady, and you know it. I saw James at the Club this morning and he tells me you've been having more hallucinations.'

'More?' asked Milly. 'I wasn't aware that I'd ever had any.'

'Mr Wedderburn tells me otherwise.'

'Nothing my husband says surprises me any more,' Milly dropped her gaze.

'What do you mean by that?'

168

'It doesn't really matter.'

'What about these visions of chained men on Green Island beach?'

'What about them?'

'Is it true that you're supposed to have seen them?'

'Certainly.'

'Chained? Dead fishermen, maybe – but not chained, surely!'

They walked on. The air was cool after a fall of rain and autumn scents assailed them.

'Chained by the wrists,' Milly said. 'I only reported what I actually saw.'

Returning to the house they entered it and a silence came between them, broken eventually by the doctor. 'Mrs Wedderburn, you must try not to be angered by people who don't believe you when you make extravagant statements. Dead fishermen, yes – we get them washed up every other week on Green Island, but not chained!'

'*Chained*,' said Milly imperatively.

He answered gently: '*Delirium tremens* is nothing to be ashamed of. It is an entirely accountable condition in one who has suffered a mental breakdown.'

'I have never had a mental breakdown!'

Schofield laughed softly. 'There you go again! One only has to hint at a mental disorder, and you become over-wrought. You know perfectly well that your illness just before you left England was as a result of an acute mental lapse.'

'That's not true!'

'Mrs Wedderburn, one clear sign of mental strain is the constant declaration by a patient that there is nothing wrong with them. The mad are always shouting that they're sane! Nobody's saying that you are mad, but unhappy situations like the death of Tom Ellery, for instance, can bring about acute instability.'

'If you're talking about instability, James is an obvious candidate. His hallucinations come out of a bottle!'

'The Devil's Solution! Yes, I've noticed it.' He rubbed his chin, a man perplexed.

'It's James you should be examining, not me, said Milly.

'Oh come, be fair! James wasn't accosted by a living fox,

only to see it disappear in a cloud of smoke before his eyes; it wasn't he who discovered chained convicts on a holiday beach; nor is it James who asserts, in the presence of the Assistant Governor, that he intimately knows a man, only to find that he has never seen him in his life.'

'Nothing will make me believe ...' began Milly.

'Mrs Wedderburn, you are illustrating my point yet again! This is a perpetual difficulty with hallucinators – nothing will make them believe that they need medical help!'

'I know Hans Bruner when I see him! I have good reason to!'

Schofield threw up his hands in exasperation.

'I *saw* him!' Milly shouted. 'I recognised him, and nobody will make me believe otherwise.'

'Calm yourself, for heaven's sake!' Schofield pleaded. 'The fact is that you made a fool of everybody at the reception, including the Dutch Ambassador himself. Do you realise what would have been the furore had a *China Mail* journalist been within earshot? The incident would have been blown up out of all proportion. Even now His Excellency has had to answer the most outrageous suggestions.'

'Suggestions?'

'That you and the ambassador have met before – and privately.'

'We have. But he wasn't an ambassador then, he was a pirate.'

Schofield closed his eyes. 'A pirate? Good God! Now we've heard it all! Last time he was First Mate aboard the *Mongolia* on the China run.' Taking Milly's hands in his, he said softly, 'Look, calm yourself, I beg you.' He waved away Milly's growing agitation. 'Can't you see the dangers of continuing such ridiculous allegations? People are already suggesting that you're in need of urgent medical help. And you know what that means.'

'I know that I'm applying to have him investigated!'

'Do that, Mrs Wedderburn, and it will be the end of you. For less than that I could have you restrained!'

'*Damn* you, Schofield,' Milly whispered. 'I said it to Bruner and I now say it to you – damn the whole lot of you! Meanwhile, get out of here!' And she picked up a vase.

The doctor took his medical bag off a chair; going to the door of the room, he said: 'I can only help you so far, Mrs Wedderburn. If you insist on these fantasies — it can only end one way.'

'Repatriation?'

'Detention. You will be sent home under escort. This nearly happened once before, remember?'

'That's what you want, isn't it — to get me away from here!'

'It would be for your own good.'

'Another thing. My housekeeper isn't going to the Fever Hospital, understand? I'll nurse her myself, and do it here where she's safe.'

'My dear girl, if I order it —'

'Order it then!' Milly's voice rose in fury. 'She isn't leaving this house and you can do what you like about it!'

Schofield slammed the door.

25

The *Ma Shan*, Eli's junk, lay at anchor in Stanley Bay. Anna No Name was curling her hair in front of the mirror of his cabin when Eli, accompanied by Black Sam, entered.

'Today,' Anna said with authority, 'my small brother, Yung, is visiting me from Fu Tan, my village. Therefore I will not be able to sail with you.'

'That is convenient, lady,' replied Eli. 'For the next two weeks we are sailing south.'

'Two weeks? I shall not be ashore that long!'

'This time you will be,' came the answer. 'We don't carry women when we're after a prize.'

'A prize? What ship is it this time?'

Eli and Black Sam laughed together, Anna, discomfited, asked, 'What is so funny? Isn't it known from here to Canton that your trade is piracy?'

'Aye, but we are not fools enough to put it around officially. Would you?'

'I do not betray my friends!'

'You're right, missus, for you know what would happen if you did. Meanwhile, return with your brother to Fu Tan. You've been aboard for weeks — long enough!'

Anna turned from the mirror and her eyes slanted up. 'Time was you would not let me out of your sight!'

'That was before you wore out your welcome, girl!' said Black Sam, slapping his thigh and roaring his delight.

Anna shouted, getting up: 'Get this pig away from me! He dances to your tune like a marionette!'

'Easy on Sam, please,' said Eli.

172

'I have not started! From the moment I came aboard, this fool has insulted me. Do you think you can treat me like a dog? I am Anna No Name and my ancestry goes back to the first Moslem empire. When I first came to your bed everything was beauty and kindness – now you treat me like a whore from the Beca de Roza, to pick me up and put me down as you please.'

'It is the way I have with strumpets,' said Eli.

'I'm gettin' out of here, Boss,' cried Black Sam. 'I say tip her overboard – she can paddle back to where she come from.'

'Pig!' cried Anna. 'Both of you are pigs!'

Eli said levelly, 'You came uninvited, lady. You stayed of your own free will, and no woman anchors me for more than a month. We sail on the midday tide. It's up to you to be here or not when we sail back.'

'You haven't heard the end of this!'

'That's what I reckoned,' said Eli.

'It is because of the stupid English girl, is it not?'

'I'll say one thing, Boss, she cottons on quick,' Black Sam said.

'The one you talk about in your sleep,' said Anna. 'She of the rich father and beautiful mansion!'

'The chance would be a foine thing,' said Eli, going Irish. 'Meanwhile, get goin' – we're about to slip cables.'

'I'll go below and get my things,' said Anna, suddenly contrite.

'You do that. And only take what belongs to you, remember.'

Going below to the little aft cabin where she and Eli had made love so many times, Anna collected her belongings. Seeing the key to the Stanley Gunpowder Factory which Eli had recently bought, she slipped it into her pocket; such an article, she thought, might be of incalculable use at a later date. Then she went back up on deck and confronted Eli.

'I am going, but you will never be rid of me! Understand?'

'Gee, that's rough,' said Black Sam, his head around the galley door. 'They usually go for good.'

'Nobody gets rid of me so easily!'

173

'I can get a dozen like you from the Beca de Roza. Just go, woman!' said Eli. And he watched as Anna went hand-over-hand down the rope ladder and into her sampan.

Later, as Anna watched the *Ma Shan* sail out of Stanley Bay, she said into the wind, 'First I come to kill you, then I fall in love with you – such a damn-fool me. But now, like an old shoe, you cast me off. Now I tell you: the others died cleanly, but you will hang by the neck.'

Saying this, Anna then went to an appointed place, alongside the quay of Stanley, and awaited the coming of Yung, her brother.

Yung, arriving, bowed before her, his Gold Sister being the elder. He had grown. Work in the fields of Fu Tan had made him muscular, so that he was no longer a puny boy but one who showed promise of manhood. Even at the age of fourteen, hair was upon his chest.

'Are you well?' asked Anna.

'But for worries about you,' said Yung. Stripped to the waist, his body gleamed brown in the sunlight; his head was bald, shaved in the manner of the mystic.

'How is the Head Man?' Anna asked.

'Well. He sends kind thoughts to you.'

'Did he order you to shave your head against the lice?'

'He did not!' Yung replied. 'He sent me to the monks of Lantau Island, to seek forgiveness for my sins, and there I became a novice in service to Buddha.'

'Sins? What sins?' demanded Anna.

'The sin for which we are responsible. Murder.'

'Murder of *pirates*?' She was astonished. 'Who are they to accuse us of murder? Does not the murder lie in allowing such people to kill us by starvation?' She swore silently. 'More fool you for becoming a part of such religious stupidity.'

'It was the Head Man who taught me of the gentle Lao-tse, who lived six hundred years before the Christ you used to worship,' Yung said, sorrowfully. 'It was the Head Man who cast me out of Taoism, telling me to report for mercy to the Buddhists of Lantau Island.'

'So it was the monks who shaved your head!' Her face was furious.

174

'In the manner of a penitent,' said Yung. 'For a year I have lived in their monastery, and they have taught me to be tolerant of all living things — even bandits and pirates.'

'You sicken me!' hissed Anna. 'Now you are worshipping a foreign god, one who is not even Chinese!'

'I pray to no God,' said Yung. 'In Buddhism there is only a Creator.'

'Believe that and you will go to Hell, with me!'

'Neither is there a Hell in my new religion.' Yung's voice rose. 'No hope, either, for an eternal life; there is only Nirvana, which is a state of eternal peace.'

'Fool for believing such nonsense!'

'There is more . . .' Yung's expression changed. 'Only through death can such peace be achieved. You and I have drowned and killed men by fire; one has been driven into madness; and now you seek the death of others!'

'To drive the bandits from our land! And you have sinned as much as me!'

'For which I must be prepared to die, say the Buddhists, or never will I inhabit Nirvana. For a year now, while in their monastery, I have been clearing ants from the vegetation around the pagodas, lest I might unknowingly tread upon one, perhaps the habitation of a wandering soul.'

Anna stared at him with comprehension: she had never heard him speak like this before. 'You are madder than that maniac Chu Apu,' said she. 'And he was madder than most after I had done with him!'

'You talk of madness? Perhaps we were mad when we left the womb of our mother. Certainly I must have been insane to agree to such killing. So I beg you to return to Lantau with me and seek help. True, there are no other women there, but my Master will help you find the same enlightenment as Siddartha discovered — the wonderful peace that he has granted to me.'

'May you rot in hell!' said Anna.

'I am already there,' replied Yung quietly.

'Look, I will make a bargain with you, Small Brother,' Anna said thoughtfully. 'In order to rid the Pearl River of its thieves I have but one more man to punish, and this is Eli Boggs. Help me to put him into the hands of the

Marine Police and I will come back with you to Fu Tan. How about that?'

Yung hesitated: then, 'Did you not say earlier that you were in love with this man?'

'Sick with love for him – heart-sick until he cast me off!'

'And because of this you would now betray him?'

'Certainly.'

'But this is also against the laws of Buddha. Betrayal is death of the soul.'

'If one is fortunate enough to possess a soul!' Anna laughed shrilly, a laugh Yung had heard before when vixens called from the forests of Fu Tan. 'Besides,' added Anna, 'being hanged for a sheep is the same as being hanged for a lamb, is it not? Am I not already condemned?'

Yung ignored this remark saying, 'Tomorrow I am to report back to the Holy Father on Lantau Island. When do you want me to help you put this man behind bars?'

'Tonight,' said Anna.

'No more killing – remember?'

'No more killing.'

So it was that, under Anna's instructions, Yung sought out the headquarters of the Portuguese Customs House, where he asked to see Captain da Costa, the man whose courtship of Sulen, the daughter of Papa Tai, had come to nothing.

Regal in full inform, da Costa descended steps to the road. 'You are asking for Captain da Costa? What do you want with me?'

Yung, pulling his saffron robe about him, said, 'Sir, you know the family of Papa Tai who lives in Stanley Village?'

'I know them well.'

'Also the girl Sulen, his daughter?'

'Passably,' answered the officer, now on his guard.

'My sister, who is a friend of hers, asks you to come with me and she will show you the whereabouts of a gunpowder factory.'

'How is it,' asked da Costa, 'that its whereabouts appears

to be common knowledge, yet I cannot find it despite many attempts?'

'I know nothing of that. Will you come, or not?'

Da Costa looked at the sky. 'Already it is dusk. I will come tomorrow.'

'Come tonight, says my sister, or do not trouble to come at all.'

Da Costa looked Yung over. To visit Stanley in darkness could be dangerous, but here the invitation came from a monk. 'By your habit you are a Buddhist monk of Lantau. A novice who is abroad at night? That is unusual.'

'To find a gunpowder factory is an unusual request,' said Yung stoutly.

'Shall I bring soldiers as an escort?'

'It is only my sister you are meeting. There is no need for an army.'

'Lead the way,' said da Costa. And by these words he signed his death warrant.

Anna was awaiting them in her sampan. Bowing to Captain da Costa, she said, 'I sent a holy man to bring you, since it is important that you should come alone. You are an old friend of the Tais, I understand – they who once owned the Stanley Gunpowder Factory.'

'I have knowledge of them,' answered da Costa warily.

'The daughter, Sulen, will not tell you its whereabouts, but I will. You know, of course, that Papa Tai has now sold it to one called Eli Boggs, a pirate whose name you have doubtless heard before?'

'One our Marine Office wants behind bars,' replied da Costa. 'Tell me its whereabouts and we will kill two birds with one stone. For it is now no more than a storehouse selling cannon, shot and powder up and down the Pearl River; close it, and we cut off the source of piracy. What is your price?'

'To see Eli Boggs in gaol.'

'You ask no other reward?'

'None,' said Anna. 'Is that not so, Small Brother?' Yung, unknowing, smiled his agreement.

Turning down the sampan bow lamp, Anna opened the rush door that led to the quay. 'Follow me, Captain da

177

Costa,' she said. 'Yung, you can now return to your monastery, for your task here is finished. Soon I will come to you.'

And Yung, unsuspecting, agreed.

26

There had been in Hong Kong, since the sixteenth century, a series of underground caves which were subject to flooding at full tide when the sea swirled in from the bay. Not only were the caves uninhabited, but the access to them was so tortuous that few living persons were aware of their existence. Two who were were Papa Tai and his daughter; a third was Eli Boggs, who had recently acquired the premises.

Within the deepest cave, like a small cathedral carved from a fissure in the living rock, was the Gunpowder Factory, misnamed since, all gunpowder manufacture having long since ceased, it was now merely an arsenal for the storage of ships' small cannon and deck boarding-weapons – from cutlasses to broadswords, from daggers to muskets. It was a pirate's paradise.

In other small chambers, separated by safe distances (the Chinese, having invented gunpowder, knew more than most of its devastating power), were separately stored the three elements necessary to successful manufacture of what was known initially as the 'Fire Powder': saltpetre, charcoal and sulphur. Such ingredients were best kept apart.

In the manufacturing chambers these substances were first ground by Papa Tai into a fine dust, mixed together into a paste, then pressed into small cakes and dried; in this condition they were then ready for use, either as explosive charges ignited by a fuse (also manufactured by Papa Tai and burning at the rate of two feet a minute) or for breaking down into sizes calculated to give greater or lesser range for the little square cannons carried aboard by unsavoury characters like Chu Apu, Bruner and Eli Boggs.

'At this stage,' said Anna from the darkness to Captain da Costa, 'you are likely to get your feet wet. May I suggest that you take off your fine boots and roll up your socks?' A strange request to one whom she was about to murder.

'Although you are asking for no reward for taking me to the factory, I shall insist that you accept one,' da Costa replied.

'My reward lies in the apprehension of these pirates,' replied Anna. 'And this Eli Boggs is not only an American fool, he is one of the worst villains in Hong Kong.'

They walked on side by side, now paddling in deeper water, for the Stanley tide was coming in; the officer now had his fine boots tied together and hanging on his shoulders. This, thought Anna, with a secret smile, would scarcely be a death with dignity.

'You have heard, of course,' said da Costa, 'that many of these thieving wretches have recently been put to death. Up and down the Pearl River delta they have been dying − executed, it is said, by a brother and sister whose parents were killed by them in a village called Fu Tan. Where do you hail from?'

'Not from Fu Tan,' replied Anna. 'Nor do I possess a brother.'

'The lad who bid me make this rendezvous with you . . . ?' Clearly he was now suspicious.

'He is a friend, not a brother.'

'It matters little who executed such scum − what matters is that they are dead. That is my feeling.'

'And mine,' replied Anna. 'In the business of crime and punishment, is it wise to ask too many questions?'

'I consider myself admonished,' said da Costa. 'How much farther?'

'We are now at the very edge of the channel; here we have to wade knee-high, then after a few steps the sand slopes upward. Keep close and follow me.'

'Who informed you of such an entrance? It is ingenious.'

'Sulen, the daughter of Papa Tai; he who sold the factory to Eli Boggs.'

'That is strange,' replied da Costa. 'Despite my efforts to persuade Sulen, she would not tell me anything.' Anna laughed softly at this as she walked, saying, 'Be content that *I* know of it. The mistake you made was to show her neither love nor money, both of which she finds irresistible.'

'I tried to bribe her, but she said it was insufficient. Love I cannot give her, because I have a wife in Portugal; besides, a decent man could not seduce a child.'

'Your second mistake, sir. She is a woman.'

'And you? Why are you showing me the factory's whereabouts?'

'I have my reasons.'

'One of which is hating the American, Eli Boggs?'

Anna smiled at him. 'Now, at last, you are learning about women!'

They went on and came to a niche in the rock face in which stood an oil lamp; Anna lit this and held it high as da Costa happily followed in a circle of wavering, yellow light.

Coming to a massively studded door, Anna unlocked it; the officer followed her, to find himself within a small room of racks upon which cans of gunpowder were stored. Ejaculating softly, he stared about him. This was the end of his search, he had found the gunpowder factory for which his superiors had long been searching.

Realising that the lamp-light was fading, da Costa turned, and was astonished to find that Anna was no longer there. All he saw was the slow closing of the massive entrance door in the moment before it slammed shut, leaving him in total darkness.

Groping, he found the door and cried out, but his voice merely echoed within the empty chamber. Hammering and kicking at the wooden panels in his panic, he realised that he was entombed. Lying upon the floor, his cries unheard, he listened to Anna's retreating footsteps.

Weeks later they found his body.

27

The First Conference of Sea-Farers — the official title of operators in the South China Sea, was held on Green Island in the spring of the year 1853. Eli Boggs was one of those who attended, albeit on an unofficial basis.

Hans Bruner, James Wedderburn and Dr Schofield (business man and physician to the firm of Smith and Wedderburn), were also present, together with Mr Soong, the Rest House caretaker, and Mr Goodchild, the solicitor. These and others, taipans of the East India Company, assembled in a hut standing east of the big matshed on the Green Island peninsula.

With the Colony's Governor again away in Peking on a diplomatic mission, another also attended; and that was Denning, the Deputy-Governor Milly had met at the Reception.

'Sam,' said Eli, 'we ain't been invited to the annual conference, but I reckon we owe that bunch of rogues a visit.'

'And likely get our throats cut?' replied Black Sam.

'It's the chance we take. Something's going on, and I reckon to be there at the death.'

'You say the conference is on Green Island.'

'That's right. They'll be discussing something new, I'm told.'

'Coolie Traffic!' Black Sam sniffed disdainfully. 'That's been around in Hong Kong since Jesus was a baby.'

'Something worse'n that, though. Coolies are being washed ashore, I hear, chained hand and foot.'

182

'That ain't likely, Boss. The brokers always sell 'em on the hoof. How can they walk if they're chained up?'

'Manacled,' said Eli.

'It's their business. Taipans like Wedderburn don't interfere wi' us,' said Sam brusquely.

'Listen! Gunpowder's on the slide since the war stopped. Opium's down the shoot an' there's no shekels in piracy!'

'If you think they'll share their loot, Boss, you're mad. Chu Apu didn't succeed and bigger men than him have failed too. Europeans are running the Coolie Traffic now and they're big trouble.'

'I'm still entitled to a share.'

'In slave selling?'

'Why not?'

'They're Chinese villagers, man!'

Eli tipped him under the chin. 'Don't tell me Sam's gone soft.'

The other shrugged. 'We ain't that short o' dollars, are we? Don't we have enough?'

'In this trade you can never have enough, for you're alive one minute an' dead the next. So rouse 'em up! Call back all crews on shore leave. Check shot and powder, in case things blow up rough; sharpen cutlasses, clear the decks. How many fighting junks can we call on a lamp signal?'

'Three,' said Sam. 'One's lying off Lamma, one's at Whampoa under repairs, and there's another off Chung Chau.'

'Then flag them to a rendezvous north of Sunshine Island — midnight tomorrow. Captains to prepare for armed landings.'

'Are ye tellin' Chu Apu's son that you'll be there?'

'I ain't notifying anybody. They're on my territory, so I'm just walking in.'

'The Governor's in it, too, mind,' said Sam.

'Wrong. The Governor's up in Peking — but his Deputy is. If ever Hong Kong's been run by a bunch o' crooks, it's now.'

'Well, we ain't all ashes o' roses,' said Black Sam.

'And we ain't bloody hypocrites, neither,' said Eli.

183

Now, it happened that on the morning Eli assembled his pirate fleet and prepared to sail on Green Island, Milly had decided that Mamie, now slowly recovering from her illness, needed a change of air.

For this reason she sent for the family steam pinnace and the two of them sailed to the Rest House on the same island.

Unknown to them both, Milly and James, for differing reasons, were on Green Island within two miles of one another.

'Swim ashore and get the lie of the land,' Eli commanded Black Sam as, in a choppy sea, their fleet passed west of Green Island.

'Damn me, Boss, there's sharks about!' protested Sam.

'Do as you're told!' And Eli looked at the sky, which was suddenly cast over with a threat of rain, and added, 'While you're ashore have a peek at that Rest House, in case the conference is being held there.'

'The conference is in the north of the island. You'd never get those Europeans that far south,' Sam objected.

But Eli was deaf to his pleas. 'Report back to me with any new information,' he said.

When Mamie picked wild spring flowers and took them to the grave of Rastus Malumba, in a quiet bower of dog roses near a brook, she did not at first see the face of Black Sam rising soundlessly in the rushes. Nor did she hear his whispered ejaculation as he saw before him a Negro woman with a black face.

Mamie, now nearing forty, was considered old; and Sam, seeing the bowed shoulders of her illness and the lines of her face, thought her even older; he himself being only thirty-five. Yet the sight of her thrilled him; possessing still the inimitable grace of the African races, her ebony blackness brought back memories of the hot savage earth of his childhood. So hypnotised was Sam by the nearness of this woman that when she turned, shielding her eyes from the sun, he did not lower his face within the rushes, but knelt still.

'*Jiminy!*' exclaimed Mamie. 'What the hell you up to, Rastus?' And she clapped her hands to her face.

184

Sheepishly, Sam waded out of the rushes and stood before her.

'God's Kingdom!' exclaimed Mamie, patting her chest. 'Is you come alive?'

'Alive and kickin', ma'am,' said Sam, grinning; his teeth were a white streak in the sunlight of his face. 'Don't you fear no harm, woman – not from this Sam.'

'May Jesus reign for ever,' said Mamie. 'I thought for a minute you was my livin' Rastus!'

'No such luck! I'm only Black Sam. Anyway, who's Rastus?'

'You ain't knowing nothin' till I knows you better. Meanwhile, what you doin' here? This ole island belongs to Smith and Wedderburn.'

'Lookin' for you,' said Black Sam, still grinning.

'And a damn cheek you've got for talkin' that way! We ain't met official! Who are you when you're home, and what you doin' where you ain't wanted?'

'Me name's Black Sam, and I'm over here fishin' – mainly for handsome women.'

'Is that a fact? This fishin' belongs to milady Wedderburn, and she has the skin off anyone fetchin' 'em out without her permission. So be off before I sets the dogs on you.'

'Aw shucks, missus, don't be like that!' Sam melted her with a winning smile.

'Well ...' began Mamie.

'Well, nothin'. That ain't good enough, for I come with good and honourable intentions.'

Mamie wriggled like a schoolgirl, looking at her shoes.

'I reckons I'm stayin'. Yes, sir,' said Black Sam.

An hour or so later, while Sam made his way overland to the north of the island, Eli's three armed junks dropped anchor in North Sound and came ashore at the matshed quay used for assembling coolie slaves. Usually this was a scene of high activity, with blacksmiths striking on manacles and overseers herding the coolies into ships' holds. But now, in expectation of an incoming delegation, all was quiet. No birds sang in a place generally invaded by screeching gulls; it was as if North Sound had been sealed off by the slam of a coffin lid.

185

A big armed guard was standing by a hut door near the coolie's matshed and drew himself up as Eli approached. 'They know you're coming, Mr Boggs?'

'They soon will,' said Eli, pushing him aside.

Within the hut sat five men: Hans Bruner; James Wedderburn; Dr Schofield, Mr Goodchild; and Mr Denning, the Deputy-Governor of the Colony. All raised blank faces when Eli entered. Bruner, once the First Mate on the ill-fated *SS Mongolia*, was the first to recover himself.

'What are you doing here, Boggs? I don't recall you being invited.'

'Just heard about it,' said Eli. 'What the hell's happening?' Dr Schofield raised his thin, aesthetic face. 'This is a private meeting of the Sea-Farers' Organisation. And we don't like strangers.'

'Whether you do or not, you've got me,' came the reply. 'These are my waters and you're all trespassing.'

Eli turned as another entered, and cried to him in furious Cantonese: 'You of all people should know better! This is *my* territory!'

This was the son of Chu Apu. He came from the same mould as his mad father: bearded, of swarthy countenance, his voice was strangely high for so big a man, coming as a pip-squeak cry from his bloodless mouth. Talk had it that he was more cruel than his father; women feared him and children fled.

'My friend Eli, yes?' This he shouted in soprano joviality, his hand out in a greeting. Eli ignored this attempt at friendliness. 'Aye! One who asks what you're doing on his patch!'

'Speak sense, for God's sake, man,' interjected Schofield.

'I will, and I still say you're out of order,' Eli answered. 'Five years ago when Chu Apu and I fixed the limits, the waters of Green Island were mine. I could come in on a westerly down the Sulphur Channel and lay off North Sound till the wind suited me, while everything west of the East Lamma was Chu's; all signed and sealed, a gentleman's agreement. So I'm askin' again, what you all doin' here?'

'And I'm asking you,' said James levelly, 'what is your

186

legal basis for making such a claim? Gentlemen's agreements don't wash. Do you know anything about such an agreement?' he asked Chu's son.

The man shook his head.

James continued, 'My firm, Smith and Wedderburn, have had a ten year lease on Green Island since the old man bought the Rest House off the Crown, and that was before you even sailed these waters.'

'Maybe,' came Eli's reply, 'but you still have no legal right to use them without consent. Ships come and go to Macao nationwide, but the place still belongs to Portugal. Opium running to the Chinese mainland is still unprofitable, remember?'

Schofield raised his head. 'Who mentioned opium?'

'I did, so we know what we're talking about,' said Eli. 'That's illegal, too, the same as the Coolie Traffic.'

'Not under Hong Kong law!'

'I bet the Governor's ignorant of it.'

'He is not. And nor am I. I know exactly what's happening, and I approve of it,' replied Deputy-Governor Denning.

'You may do, but you're only the organ-grinder, and what the Governor says in this place goes.' There was a silence. 'If he approves and it's all above-board, perhaps you won't mind if I have a look around?' Eli continued. 'I'd like to take a peep into that matshed, for a start.'

They glanced at one another, alarmed.

'I say cut him in,' Bruner said. 'Otherwise he'll root around till he finds something he does not like.'

'Very well. Five per cent,' said Wedderburn with finality.

'Oh no,' said Eli. 'You're in my waters without permission, so I want twenty per cent of the takings.'

'Twenty?' cried Bruner. 'We only pay the brokers five!'

'What happens if we refuse?' asked James.

'Then I'll lay two cannon junks in North Sound and blow you out of the sea.'

'Gentlemen, gentlemen, this is no way to bargain,' Denning, ever the diplomat, interjected. 'Let us open the discussion a little. Clearly, Mr Boggs has discovered that profits exist in coolie trafficking and wants a share of the

187

proceeds. This is fair, if we accept that the approach waters are his. Alternatively we could switch our enterprise to somewhere cheaper. We are no longer officially selling opium to China, so our profits are down. The Coolie Traffic is ideal when it comes to restoring profit margins. The Mandarins are demanding coolies, and who are we to argue? I say let the debate end here, and we will cut in a sixth party: Mr Eli Boggs. After all, now he possesses rights to the Stanley Factory we must try to accommodate him, for we are in need of his services, are we not? Gunpowder was necessary to reduce the Bogue Forts, and doubtless it will be needed again.'

'I also want access to your books,' said Eli.

'Do you not trust our word?' asked James.

'I do not. I know you long-nosed thieves.'

'He's a little on the rough side, I suppose,' said Dr Schofield, 'but he appears to know what he wants.'

'That he does,' added Bruner. 'We have done business before, eh, Eli?'

'Aye — business that ain't yet finished,' came the threatening reply.

'But best not discussed here!'

'What is this — more complications?' asked Denning.

'No complications,' said Eli. 'Just that I'll let daylight through a certain bastard if I don't get the answer I want.'

Bruner shrugged. 'It is nothing, gentlemen. Simply a small misunderstanding that requires discussion.'

'Not so small,' said Eli. 'Something that can get a man hanged, even in this country. The sum outstanding was fifty thousand dollars — ransom money, Mr Bruner.'

'Settle it amicably,' said James. 'Meanwhile, can we continue with the business in hand? The next shipment of coolies?'

'Tomorrow,' said Mr Soong.

'Where are they bound for this time?' asked Goodchild. 'I shall need embarkation documents, remember.'

'Peru, is it not?'

'It depends on the broker,' said Schofield. 'This convoy is going through Macao.'

'How many?'

'Four thousand coolies over the next ten weeks.'

188

'That'll take them into typhoon weather!' said Eli.

'One cannot be particular. We're bound to take losses.'

'After all, they're only coolies,' said Black Sam, pointedly, coming in, he sat by Eli.

'Exactly, and therefore expendable,' snapped James.

Eli raised his eyes to the face of the man before him. This, then was the husband of Milly Smith; to this apology for manhood, she had given herself in marriage.

Presenting himself as a righteous Christian gentleman in a pagan land, Wedderburn, thought Eli, had perjured his soul to the god Mammon: taking all, giving nothing. Men like Wedderburn knew neither pity nor compassion. Yet Milly's father, old man Smith, would take some beating when it came to corruption, for this was how he had made his money. Eli began to wonder if Milly, now living in the splendour of the English Mansion, had come to realise this and accept it; for Wedderburn, he'd heard tell, was the biggest crook in Christendom, including Hong Kong, which was going some.

Eli examined the puffy face, the spotty complexion, the adder-like eyes that darted around with apparent incomprehension, masking the man's greed and deviousness. God help Milly, he thought, straight out of school and into the arms of this monstrosity. No wonder tongues were gabbling about her mental incapacity, whatever that was supposed to mean. And Eli was gripped by such hatred that his hands, unmoving, could have reached out to take James Wedderburn by the throat.

'What's this about chained men being washed ashore at North Point?' he asked suddenly.

'Don't believe everything you hear, man,' said James.

'I have the information on good authority.'

'If chained men are being washed ashore on this island I would know about it,' said Mr Soong.

'Then you don't mind if I take a look around?'

'Where?'

'In the matshed where the coolies are housed.'

'Why the matshed?' asked Goodchild, suddenly suspicious.

'Because that's where I expect to find the dirt,' said Eli.

189

They made their way to the matshed in which the prisoners were housed like a delegation of inspectors, Eli and
Black Sam leading the way.

It was a single storey building of bamboo and rush
cladding, with a floor of broken stone. On either side of a
narrow corridor, down which Eli strode like a general, stood
narrow timber bunks two feet wide, each a bed for a coolie;
the bunks, with access gained by standing ladders, were
constructed from floor to ceiling. Four thousand humans
breathed the fetid air, for there was no ventilation save for
a few roof holes.

In the middle of the shed stood a galley, its open-ended
flu pipe belching smoke under a great boiling pot in
which bubbled an odorous mess of rice and vegetables.
A ragged coolie was ladling this out into bowls, it being
feeding time.

'Two good meals a day,' announced James. 'Rice
congee.'

'The idea being,' added Eli, 'to start them off on the
six week voyage in better shape than when they were
collected?'

'It is better fare than they would get in the villages,' said
Bruner. 'It is good, is it not? A free ride to a promised land,
food thrown in and a minimum wage arranged by brokerage
on arrival.'

'In Peru?' asked Black Sam.

'That is the destination of this particular convoy,' said
James.

'How many coolies did you say?' asked Eli, innocently.

'About four thousand per convoy; a total of eight thousand
over the next ten weeks.'

'They sail via Macao?' asked Black Sam.

'Yes. Portuguese middlemen take over from there; our
interest in them ceases after that.'

'How much a head?'

'You said you wanted to see the books.'

'As soon as we've finished here. How much?'

Schofield frowned, calculating, 'About two hundred
dollars a head — that's our cut. What the brokers and
Macao merchants get for them in Peru isn't our business.'

'Pretty good,' said Eli, smiling. 'I've just worked out my share — eight thousand plus on the first four thousand.'

'We still have to argue that,' said Mr Soong, warily. 'Do not forget, Mr Boggs, we also pay duty to other Government officials.'

'At this rate of profit we ain't goin' to quarrel.' Eli put his thumbs in the lapels of his jacket and grinned expansively. 'Yes, gents, it all suits me.' He paused at the bunk of a squatting coolie, a man emaciated by hunger and with the face of a starved ghost. Unheeding to all, he was gobbling with his chopsticks, sucking up the steaming congee in grunts and belches, lowering them only when aware of Eli's sudden interest. Then fear struck his peasant's face.

'Where are you from?' asked Eli in Cantonese.

The man stared, wiping the saliva off his bearded chin. 'Shantung, sir.'

'What did you do in Shantung?'

'I was a miner, sir — working for the Kailing.'

'So what brings you here?'

The man stared about him, his eyes narrowed; the blackness of coaldust had tattooed his wrinkled skin.

'Fifty dollars to the broker, sir, to employ me and my family, for my wife bore me ten children, six are dead in the famines, four still living, and when I get to Peru they will be brought out, too, says the Master.' At this he rose and bowed to Wedderburn. 'Free tickets, free food, to begin another life away from China. It is excellent.'

'You are a fortunate man,' said Eli, 'born in the birth-place of Confucius, and now the chance of a new beginning.' The man before him grinned, delighted.

'What more could you ask?' interjected Black Sam. 'Take it from me, Brother, you are a very lucky fella.'

Eli nodded, patting the man's shoulder; the peasant sat down and again began voraciously to eat.

'Gentlemen,' said Eli at the door of the matshed, 'you are doing a marvellous job here. All my life I have seen the Chinese provinces starve; Kwangtung in particular, for there is either famine or plenty. In the name of common humanity I am prepared to drop my share to ten per cent, as a contribution to this amazing scheme of rehabilitation.'

'Take a note of that,' said Schofield to Mr Soong, who, bringing out a notebook, did so.

'And now,' said Eli, 'I leave you to your good works. But one last question. What happens to this fellow when once he reaches Peru?'

'I have explained,' said James pompously, 'that their future after we hand them over to the Macao brokers is not our business.'

'But Peru is running a labour indenture scheme that is tantamount to slavery! Can you guarantee to this man what he has been promised − that his wife and children will join him there, so that he can continue a decent family life?'

'My good man,' said Schofield, 'we cannot be their nursemaids!'

'So the chances are that he will end his life alone, in slavery in Peru?'

'The vagaries of existence, Mr Boggs,' said Goodchild. 'How can any man control his life from minute to minute?'

'If his prospects particularly disturb you, Mr Boggs, you can always opt out,' said James.

'Count me in,' said Eli, and held out his hand to seal the bargain. One by one they shook it. 'Scruples come second when it's ten per cent of a fortune!'

Outside, in the sun, Black Sam asked softly, 'You talk in riddles, Boss. Is you in or is you out on this palaver?'

'I'm definitely in,' said Eli. 'I'll be straight into these bastards the moment I haul anchors. Their own mothers won't know them when I'm bloody done with 'em.'

'And the coolies?'

'I'll get them back to where they belong, man. Home to the Chinese mainland.'

28

When beset with the business of Coolie Traffic, James usually stayed overnight on Green Island in quarters near the matshed. Milly was not surprised, therefore, to see him next morning coming across the gardens of the Rest House with Mr Soong, the caretaker. Pruning roses, she straightened to greet him. His eyes swept over her. Gone, thought James, was the callow girl whom he had first met; the pink dress she was wearing now fitted her to perfection, emphasising her curves.

'How's Mamie?' he asked, unusually interested.

'Not as well as she should be,' replied Milly.

'Her service isn't what it used to be, either!'

'What do you mean by that?'

'Exactly what I say. The fact is that she simply can't manage her duties.'

Gripping a rose so hard that its thorns punctured her skin, Milly turned to him. 'Naturally people work more slowly when they're unwell. But I've been helping her, and I thought we'd been managing passably well.'

'Assisting the housekeeper isn't your job. Anyway, I've advertised for a replacement.'

'You've *what*?'

'In the *China Mail* a few days ago.'

'And to date there have been no replies?'

'Indeed there have. A number of applicants have contacted me at the Club.'

It silenced her. James added, 'And I've had a most impressive application!'

'From whom?'

'A Chinese convent trainee.'

'Don't tell me you've engaged a new housekeeper without me seeing her!'

A pulse in his temple was pulsating violently. 'She's a little young, true, but she is extremely capable. I've arranged for her to call on you next week.'

'Do you know anything about her?'

'She comes with excellent references — some time ago she worked for the nuns of a Catholic Mission School on the Pearl River. Certainly she's respectable; she has a brother who is a Buddhist monk on Lantau Island.'

'She'll be wanting to convert us,' said Milly resentfully. 'You might have mentioned this before. After all, I'm supposed to be running the house.'

'Your interest in household affairs used to be minimal.'

'Perhaps so, but I've grown up since those days.'

'So I've noticed.' James lifted his eyes to the french windows of a bedroom that faced the lawns. 'Indeed, I was wondering ...'

'No!' said Milly.

To date, Milly had approached the fulfilment of her woman's fantasies but once; and that in the company of a boy-man, Tom Ellery. All else, despite her own misgivings, had been the vision of another: Eli Boggs. And she never really explained to herself satisfactorily why, that night, she left the door leading from her bedroom to the garden unlocked.

Later, Milly met Mamie in the garden, humming so happily to herself that Milly looked again.

'You're supposed to be ill,' she said.

'Honey,' answered Mamie, 'I'm so light in the feet I'm steppin' on a cloud!'

'What's happened? You were half-dead yesterday.'

'But now I's come better, for it's jist like ma Rastus has come alive all over again. You ever had such a roustabout feelin'?' Mamie's eyes were big in her face. 'I've met a man!' she added.

'You've *what*?'

'A man come swimmin' in from the sea, and says to

me, "Missus, never in ma life have I seen a woman so splendid".'

Milly gasped. 'A man, here on Green Island? Pull the other one!'

'It's true. Six foot up if he's an inch, black as Rastus Malumba, and a smile on him to send a woman demented!'

'You've been seeing things, Mamie!'

Mamie clasped her big hands together and turned in a circle of plump joy, laughing at the sky. 'You're right, honey. One moment I was putting flowers on a grave; next a big black stranger was standin' before me. And d'you know somethin'?'

'Tell me!'

'Well, first Ah thought it was ma Rastus, like Ah said, but it were a big fella fallen off a ship and swum ashore. You remember those junks sailin' north yesterday?'

Milly nodded at her, and Mamie continued quickly. '"Woman," this black fella says to me, "Ah ain't seen one like you in a month o' Sundays. How you fixed for a walk down Wanchai? For you're the one the biblicals are spouting about in *The Song of Solomon* spit and image. You know your Bible?'

'"Try me!"' says I.

'"Why you standin' by a grave?" he asks next, so I told him about my Rastus, an' how he'd been gone six years, and he says — the cheek of it — "If he's been gone six years it's time he was dead and buried, woman, for I'm alive and kickin".' Mamie giggled, whispering, 'You think me terrible?'

'It depends on what happened next,' said Milly.

'I took him in and gave him tea, for he was shiverin' cold, havin' been swimmin' for his life. You know what happened then?'

'I hope you aren't going to shock me!'

'That no-good rascal, he kissed me! If I never move from here, he kissed me!'

'Good!' said Milly.

Mamie faltered. 'Then he did it again ... and I doesn't think ma Rastus would approve.'

195

'But he's here,' said Milly, smiling, 'and Rastus isn't, and what the eye doesn't see the heart doesn't grieve for ... He fell off one of the junks, did you say?'

'Aye, the ones goin' up North Sound yesterday.'

'Did he mention his name?'

'Black Sam, he calls himself.'

Milly smiled secretly. 'And you've taken a shine for him, eh?'

'He can unpack ma bottom drawer any time he likes!' said Mamie. She went on, but Milly didn't hear her. Undoubtedly the fleet she had seen sailing yesterday belonged to Eli.

'I bet he had a big white smile and big gold earrings!' she said now.

'Dang me! How did you know that?'

'They usually have,' said Milly, reflecting to herself that if there was one pirate active in the area, there might possibly be two. But it was unlikely. This was the Black Sam she knew.

'What you thinkin' about, Miss Milly?' asked Mamie, watching her. 'You're lookin' mighty wicked to me.'

The night was quiet, as if life itself were holding its breath, and a movement in the air brought the perfumes of garden spices.

Yet the summer moon somehow gave the scene an air of anticipation and excitement, for far below the streets that later became notorious Wanchai, glittered and gleamed with the licentious fervour of the harlot Hong Kong was becoming; vying as it did with the Red Light quarter of Macao, where another nation, if not under the British flag, flounced her national hypocrisy.

And as Milly stood beside the big french doors leading to the garden and waited, she knew instinctively that Eli would come to her, as Black Sam had come to Mamie.

She told herself it was inexplicable that she should feel such a longing. Had he not sold her as a common chattel?

Somewhere in the Rest House she could hear Mamie stirring; a clock struck midnight and through the open french doors she saw the moon, heavy with summer's heat, ride on silvered clouds above the distant hills of China.

Outside in the garden a night-jar warned its mate in squawks and screeches; as Milly raised her head to listen, a twig snapped and a shadow fell upon the ground in front of her.

In lonelier moments than this she had dreamed of Eli's coming. And as the moon flashed its quicksilver brilliance around the bedroom, the shadow unmistakably formed the shape of a man. Unmoving, he stood with the moon behind him and when the night-jar, in panic, fluttered in shrieks to branches above him, he remained still. Milly, her heart thudding against her nightdress, slipped from her position beside the french doors and dived into bed; as if her movement were a signal of acceptance the man opened the door and entered the room.

Romance was afoot on two fronts in the Rest House on Green Island that night.

Mamie Malumba too, usually asleep at this hour, opened her eyes wide as she listened to the screechings of the night-jar.

A low tapping came upon her door.

'Who's there?' She sat up in bed.

'It's Black Sam, Mamie Malumba,' came the whispered reply. 'I'm here, all ready and waitin'.'

'You shameless scoundrel!' exclaimed Mamie, her eye now at the key-hole. 'You'm sittin' outside a lady's bedroom, you realise?'

'Forgive me; I thought you was a woman.'

'Don't you cheek me, you no-good pirate. What you arrived about?'

'Give ye three guesses,' said Sam, as usual.

'You take yourself off! Come back next year and you'll still be too soon!'

'That's not what you promised last night.'

'Since last night I changed ma mind. So you get off before I gives you a piece of it.'

'I's always gettin' pieces of mind from people unable to afford it,' Sam said forlornly. 'What you got agin me, Mamie Malumba?'

'Nothin', save you ain't the right man for virtuous women.'

'Do they know what they're missin'?'

'Don't you dirty-mouth me, Black Sam! You sling your hook a'fore I calls a policeman.'

'I don't hear so good,' said Sam.

'I said get out of here!'

'Have a heart!'

'I ain't got a heart for you — it's a swingin' brick. Besides, you ain't up to no good tonight. I can feel it in ma bones.'

'You can say that again, honey. There's room for two in that bed if you slides over.'

'Shame on you, Black Sam! That an immoral suggestion! If I lets you in would you ravish a lady against her will?'

'More'n likely,' said Sam. And Mamie, unlocking the bedroom door, threw it wide and opened her arms to him.

'That's all I wanted to hear,' said she. 'In with you quick before you change your mind.'

In the moonlight Milly saw Eli's face, bearded and heavily shadowed. Momentarily he held her in his arms, then bending, kissed her cheek, as one friend greeting another.

'The door was unlocked,' he said.

'Yes, I thought you might come.'

'Why?'

'Because I heard Sam come, too. He's at the back of the house.'

'He never is!'

'Don't you know what your crew get up to?' She was flippant now.

'No I didn't know,' he replied reflectively. 'Sam, like me, keeps his own counsel. Where's your husband?'

'Back in Hong Kong, I hope. But Soong's around.'

'Don't worry — I'll take care of him.'

Now Eli was carrying her through the french doors over the lawn, in a natural progression of events which brought neither fear nor apprehension. To Milly it seemed the continuation of what had gone before on Lantau Island: land, sea, moonlight, and Eli.

Soon, she knew, Eli would make love to her. Was it not

198

for this that he had come? That it was illicit and adulterous did not occur to her. The ransom demand that had hastened her father's death, the interminable waiting for release on Lantau: all these were obliterated by the blind assurance that at last she would be one with the man she loved. Only when Eli laid her gently down beside a brook did he return her to human consciousness with a kiss.

The first kiss of their lovemaking began hesitantly, the response gradually awakening, overcoming resistance growing in response into a dedication, so that sight, smell, sound − all were obliterated. Never before had Milly known the overwhelming joy of belonging to another. In all her girlhood's years this moment had been feared: now within the gasped endearments, Milly remembered her maidenly curiosity on the subject and smiled, for this was a pleasure she could never have anticipated.

Later while Eli slept beside her, Milly rose, and going to the brook, washed her face and hair. And Eli, finding her gone, held out his arms to her, and she returned to him and knelt beside him on the grass. Then he drew her down to him again so that his lips were close to hers, and said:

'I love you, and I know now that I've loved you from the moment we met.'

It was enough: no more, she thought, need be said, and hearing this, her heart at rest, she lay down beside him, and also slept.

29

'When is the Portuguese officer going to arrest Eli Boggs?'
asked Yung.

It was a few days later, Yung, coming from the Lantau
monastery to visit Anna, had met her aboard her Mist and
Flower sampan, which was anchored in Stanley Bay.

'When he arrests him is da Costa's business, not mine,'
came Anna's curt reply. 'I've taken him to the gunpowder
factory; the rest is up to him.'

'And when this pirate is safely behind bars, that is the end
for you?'

'My brother,' said Anna, touching his cheek, 'have I
ever lied to you? I asked your help to kill the pirates and
bandits; this you did, and I am grateful. But now our task
is finished.'

'I have committed murder and my heart is breaking,' said
Yung, and he held up his monk's saffron robe to hide his face.
'Everlasting hell shall be my punishment, says my Master in
the Bell Tower.'

'If you believe all this mumbo jumbo you are a bigger fool
than I took you for,' snapped Anna. 'Do not the villagers of
Fu Tan now flourish?'

Yung nodded, drying his tears.

'Then be thankful that our duty is done, Small Brother.
Now, do not pester me, for I have other work to do.
Tomorrow, with luck, I am returning to domestic service.'

'You are going back to the nuns of the Catholic Mission
School?' In anticipation Yung threw his arms about her.
'Gold Sister, that is wonderful!'

'Idiot! I'd rather be dead than scrub their floors again. No, I am taking a new position.'

'As a scrubbing maid?'

'Fool! As an assistant housekeeper. My scrubbing days are over. No more humility, no more going on my knees. If you have any sense you'd follow my example.'

'Gold Sister, humility is strength, not weakness.'

'Then call my god the Devil, for I am finished with such stupidity,' said Anna. And her face, in the brilliant light of the summer morning, became contorted with hatred.

'When do you start your new job?' asked Yung, sighing.

'In a day or two, I hope. I am going to meet the mistress of the house today.'

'Where?'

'On Victoria Peak, at a house called the English Mansion.'

Yung, being content that a happier future was now assured for her, did not ask more.

As Mamie entered the drawing room of the English Mansion, her expression was glum.

'The new Assistant Housekeeper has arrived, Miss Milly.'

'Show her in.'

'She ain't the right one for us, I reckon.'

'I'll be the judge of that, Mamie.'

'She scarce comes up to ma shoulder.'

'Size is not important.'

'A Chinee, an' all.'

'I know. Mr Wedderburn has already interviewed her at his club.'

'They don't work so good, these pint-sized little beggars.'

'Show her in!'

Mamie wept, her apron up to her face. 'Miss Milly, I wouldn't have believed this! Is folks sayin' I ain't been doin' ma job?'

'Mamie, it's only until you're quite well again!'

'She smells strange, too.'

Milly rose from her chair. 'Look, you stay here. I'll see her in the garden.'

Unbidden, Anna No Name was already awaiting her there,

201

standing by a fountain. Rarely, thought Milly, had she set eyes on so beautiful a woman.

Anna No Name was dressed in white, the standard dress of the young virgins of Our Lady the Immaculate, the patron saint of the Fu Tan Mission School. Her flowing hair, shining black in contrast, was tied at her neck with black ribbon, which was a sign of purity in Fu Tan; her dress, pleated at the knees, flared out to her ankles and her arms, brown to the shoulders, were steeped in sun. At her throat she wore a small golden crucifix.

'Good morning!'

Hearing Milly's greeting, Anna turned from the fountain, bowing.

'My name is Anna Fu Tan,' she said. Milly became aware, not of the cultured voice that greeted her, but of the exotic perfume that had swept the air, filling her senses.

'My husband tells me you have applied for the position of Assistant Housekeeper?'

'That is so, Lady.'

'And he has already interviewed you and confirmed your appointment. You understand that the position is temporary — until the health of our permanent housekeeper improves?'

Anna's eyes drifted over the young woman before her. Passably handsome, she thought, but with few European women available in Hong Kong, even rich masters such as Mr James Wedderburn could scarcely pick and choose. And young, thought Anna; younger even than herself, but possessed, unless she was mistaken, of a wisdom beyond her years. For the calm blue eyes that were now assessing her were unmistakably perceptive in her fair-skinned English countenance.

So this, thought Anna, was what Eli Boggs preferred! An overgrown English schoolgirl with freckles on her face. Girls like this, she had learned, had been known to hook and hold, by charms unknown to Orientals, the most wayward and feckless lovers, and Eli Boggs was presumably one of these: a fool who didn't recognise beauty or sensuality when it was under his nose.

'How old are you, Anna?' Milly smiled encouragingly.

'I shall be twenty-one in the days of White Dews.

'You speak beautiful English!'

'And a little French, should the occasion arise.'

Milly scanned the letter Anna had brought. 'The nuns of Fu Tan give you an excellent reference. Did my husband mention the salary?'

'It has already been agreed between us.'

'You understand that I have little to do with such things. He takes responsibility for the running of the house.'

They stood together in the sun, smiling. Milly found Anna oddly disconcerting; although the meeting was taking place in her own house, where she was mistress, the girl before her seemed, with her imperious eyes, to control the situation utterly. Even her strange perfume seemed somehow to project a refined, indefinable evil. It was ridiculous that this should be so, Milly told herself; the girl was well educated and possessed references from the highest source. Yet the impression persisted.

Anna, for her part, was thinking that the sooner she could dispense with the formalities of this appointment, the better. Eli had rejected her as brutally as he would a common whore, and the girl responsible for this rejection was now standing before her, clearly an innocent in a world of tigers.

The black woman – she who had opened the door to her – would have to go first; with access to the kitchen she could bring the woman's illness to a simple and early conclusion. Other people in the house – apart from the master whom she had already met – would have to be eliminated as opportunity presented. But the wife, whom Eli loved, was the important target.

Within the evil that encompassed Anna No Name, there had once existed a small gleam of hope. She, during her brief lovemaking with Eli, had known a nobler emotion than her customary instinct of the hunting animal; Eli's rough but kindly courtship engendered within her a new generosity which had temporarily blinded her elemental lust to kill. Now, following his rejection, this had vanished, leaving her pitiless.

Smiling beautifully now, she said to Milly, 'It is agreed, Lady, that I should work for you?'

'Of course!'

'I am a trained cook also, you know. You will not regret your decision.'

'Why, that's marvellous! Although my housekeeper does the important cooking.'

'So I understand.'

Bowing, escorted by a frowning Mamie, Anna No Name left the house.

'I doesn't trust that one,' announced Mamie, returning to the drawing room.

'But why not?' asked Milly. 'I think she's charming, and her perfume — heaven knows what it is — is exquisite!'

'O, aye? Well, I tells ye, when a girl's face shines, look behind her ears. When she smells that good there's some'ut wrong with her.'

30

Three days after Anna began her duties as an assistant house-keeper, with Milly and Mamie still at the Rest House on Green Island, James Wedderburn, gripping a bottle, was staring through the windows of the drawing room of the English Mansion with the befuddled rigidity of the drunk.

Swaying in the middle of the room, he suddenly straightened, fighting for sense, for faintly he could hear music – distant music – the plucked strings of an ancient instrument accompanying a woman's voice.

Going to the door, bottle in hand, James pushed it open. As the sounds increased he lurched into a corridor and listened, disbelieving his ears.

Now, following the music, James staggered towards it through the main staircase hall and into the servant's quarters. Pausing by a door where the singing was loudest, he turned the handle and entered.

The music ceased abruptly. And Anna No Name, squatting on the bed with her *p'i pa* in her arms, raised her face in undisguised terror.

With nothing but a white robe covering her, she flung away the *p'i pa* and leaped from the bed; the robe, slipping down her body, exposed her nakedness. With her fists clenched in panic, her body began uncontrollably to shake.

James, stunned by the speed of events, stared down at the vision with astonishment as Anna, recovering, snatched up the robe at her feet and rushed to the door. But James blocked her path.

'Please, Master!' Anna beseeched.

His senses swimming, James gazed down into her tearstained face. 'Good God,' he muttered.

'Oh please, I am so sorry!'

Now speaking in Cantonese, her mother tongue, a torrent of apology poured from Anna, and James, not fully understanding, grinned idiotically. But in less embarrassing situations than this, servants had been instantly discharged by outraged employers, and Anna knew it. Pulling her long hair down over her face, a Chinese sign of shame, she rushed past him to the bed, throwing herself upon it, cowering as one expecting a blow. James, now close to her, smoothed back her hair from her face.

'Sorry? What are you sorry for?' he asked, his voice thick.

'You will not have me discharged?'

'Good God, no, woman! That's the last thing I had in mind. You're manna from heaven.'

'Then,' and her eyes begged him, 'you will please be gentle with me, Master? I am convent born and know nothing of men.' Saying this she went to the door, closed it, and, leaning against it, raised her face smiling bravely through her tears.

Book Three

31

It was a month before Milly's twenty-first birthday, and a morning of incinerating heat, when all the mothers-to-be in Hong Kong were complaining about their lot. No woman, said Mamie fanning herself, should be allowed to give birth east of Arabia in summer.

'Might the heat soon affect you personally?' asked Milly mischievously.

'An' what do you mean by that?'

'Just wondered. This is the baby season in Hong Kong!'

'Don't you wonder none about this Mamie, Miss Milly. Ah've lived long enough to take care of such things.' Mamie mopped her sweating face and smiled her whitest smile. 'But, mark me, since that Black Sam came into ma life, I've sure done some outstanding poodlefaking.'

'I've heard that word before. What does it mean?'

Mamie shrugged. 'Suppose it means hoppin' around the fellas. Mind you, married to Rastus so long, I didn't expect to get a second wind. But he's dead and I'm alive, says Sam.'

'And Sam's right. When are you seeing him again?'

'Two o'clock this time next week down on Blake's Pier. He's taking me over to Stonecutters' Island, and that ain't even inhabited!'

'My, you're stepping out! Even I haven't been there. Have you got those pirate's earrings off him yet?'

'He's handin' them over a week next Sunday, on the day I gets him beside me in church for morning service.'

'No!'

'Oh, yes,' asserted Mamie. 'My Rastus went to church

like any respectable fella should do, so I said to Sam, "You behave the same as ma Rastus and you can stand straight before your Maker." "But I ain't aimin' to meet my Maker just yet," says Sam. "Have a heart, girl – Ah'm a pirate." "All the more reason why you should go straight and honest; otherwise, no more perambulations with this Mamie for the next couple a' weeks."'

Milly giggled. 'What did he say to that?'

'Well, to date we're still activatin'.'

'My! You know how to handle them!'

'That's right. When God gave Eve the gift of love He told her how to use it.' And Mamie bent to her mirror, sniffed, and put ashes of roses behind her ears.

'And how are you getting on with Fu Tan?'

Mamie shrugged. 'I say one thing for her, she's some housekeeper. I ain't done a dang stroke since she arrived.'

'Keep it that way until you're really better.'

'Mind, I never trusts anyone whose eyes go shut when they's ought to come open.'

'What do you mean by that?'

'She's a Black-eyed Susan,' said Mamie. 'She's sure one sultry piece o' woman.'

The eyes of the new housekeeper were not black, thought Milly, but brown and as innocent as a young calf's, and the house had run like clockwork since her arrival.

In the hall Milly met James going out to the gravel drive, where a sedan chair and two coolies were waiting to carry him to his city office. The white-columned portico of the English Mansion gleamed regally in morning sunlight; but James looked soiled and morose.

'Sorry I missed you at breakfast,' said Milly, amiably.

James grunted an inarticulate reply, his eyes red-rimmed and puffy. Nobody, Milly reflected, had the right to look as her husband did first thing in the morning.

With an effort he said: 'The post included birthday cards. Rather early, aren't they?'

'It's the girls from school,' Milly answered. 'They've got the wrong date, but already I'm feeling old!' While he pondered this she added, 'Incidentally, because my Trust money is due soon, I paid a visit to the bank yesterday.' James moved to go, but she delayed him. 'With at least a couple of thousand dollars due in my account, I was surprised to find there was practically nothing in it.'

'Then you'll have to start living within your means, won't you!' he retorted flippantly.

'That's ridiculous! You pay into my account five hundred dollars a month − or you're supposed to, according to the Trust − and when I want fifty the cupboard is bare!'

'Be patient!'

'What kind of answer is that? All I'm asking for is a few more dollars of allowance. Honestly, James, one would think it was your money!'

'It is, until you're twenty-one.' He sighed tolerantly. 'Look, your solicitor, Mr Goodchild, will transfer your money legally when it's due on your twenty-first birthday. Until that happens you are still a Ward of Court, bound by strict financial rules. If you want more money, see your solicitor.'

'I will! I'm supposed to receive monthly interest, and I don't get it. I'll see Goodchild today!' And Milly watched the sedan chair carry James to the end of the drive.

Going into the drawing room she was surprised to see Anna clearly within earshot. It was amazing, she thought, how the girl had the ability to appear in unexpected places with such speed. Moments ago the room had been empty.

Dusting a bookcase, Anna turned. 'Good morning, Fu Tan,' said Milly.

Anna bowed. 'The day is hot, Lady.'

'It will be hotter still when the sun comes up.'

Cool, collected, Anna smiled, saying softly, 'You have a bad head?'

'No.'

'The poor Master has, I think; I spoke and he did not reply. I have little experience of gentlemen; perhaps they do not talk greatly first thing in the morning?'

'This particular Master does not.'

'He is unwell, do you think? You will forgive me, Lady, but during the three weeks I have been here, I have grown fond of you all. Apart from my brother Yung, I have no family; therefore it is agreeable to me that I should consider

211

you as mine. When you are sad, I am sad also.'

'That is a most kindly thing to say, Fu Tan.'

'And this being so, I have begun to regard you as relatives. We Chinese have strong family ties, as you know. You are also sad, Lady?'

'Why do you ask that?' Milly was intrigued.

'Because I see sadness in the face of the Master. Perhaps he has worries; men of business always have such faces. In the world where Yung and I live there is nothing but laughter.'

'You are also a Buddhist?'

'No. I worship Christ the King, as you do,' Anna lied. 'I have seen you going to the Christian church of St John's — the one to which Miss Mamie is soon to take her man.'

Milly smiled. 'Ah, you heard us discussing it! Don't believe everything you hear of us or you will never get your work done. Have you ordered the menu for tiffin and dinner?'

'I have already done this. Miss Mamie is going to Stone-cutters' Island with him?'

'Perhaps — but that is her business, is it not?' Milly was curt.

'Of course, but snakes live on that island. When she is there she must be careful to cover her legs and ankles, also to beware of oleander, the pink or white flowers, which, if picked, make the fingers sticky and poison the mouth.'

'I will mention it to her.'

'Have you been there?'

'Excuse me, I must go,' said Milly.

'I only asked if you had been there. If ever you go to Stone-cutters' Island, do take great care,' Anna smiled brilliantly.

'It is good of you to be concerned about us all.'

The sun burned down on Hong Kong with scorching heat. At Blake's Pier the sea of the harbour glowed, jewel-like; the little breakers crested and danced to the wash of sampans and ferries.

Here, along the Praya, were the waterfront houses of the wealthy elite; before them, bordering the waterfront, were the Mist and Flower bawdy houses, behind whose ornate shutters tiptoed the Chinese and Portuguese ladies of doubtful virtue and cleanliness. An encounter with just one of these, the legend went in the old Artillery Barracks, could set a man up in his coffin for the price of a dollar a time.

Milly walked slowly, fanning herself against the sun-shot midday. Sedan chairs and half-naked coolies, bent double under loads, scampered past her down Queen's Road. The old shore line, now under reclamation, simmered and baked from Murray's Battery to Ice House Street and the Old Government House, where, in dignity, their ample wives shaded by bamboo parasols, walked the Civil Servants of the Secretarial Buildings with sweating, red-faced visitors come in for the day barging unceremoniously about them.

The offices of Messrs Goodchild and Goodchild stood next door to the old Matheson Bank. Milly walked purposefully across the cool mosaic floor of its interior and went to a counter marked Inquiries.

'Mr Goodchild, the senior partner, please,' she said to the reception clerk.

'Who shall I say, Madam?'

'Mrs Mildred Wedderburn.'

'May I know your business, please?'

'It is of a private nature.' Milly toyed with the ivory handle of her parasol; its whiteness, like her full-length, pleated dress, emphasised the drabness of the solicitor's furnishings.

The sallow-faced clerk, with pince-nez spectacles on the end of his nose, did not move from his high stool.

'Madam, it is necessary to insist. Mr Goodchild's room is at the top of the building. It may prove necessary for him to bring down the file of your related subject so please tell me the reason for your visit.'

Milly sighed. 'It concerns money held in Trust for me.'

'Ah yes. Unfortunately Mr Goodchild the elder is out visiting a client.'

'Then kindly ask Mr Goodchild junior to receive me.'

'Mr Goodchild the younger is ill, I fear. The fever, you know.'

Milly bowed briefly. 'I offer my condolences. Is there anyone at all in the firm who can discuss this subject with me?'

213

'I fear not.'

'You realise that there is a great deal of money involved?'

The little eyes of the man screwed up into crows' feet behind the spectacles. 'No doubt, ma'am. Such financial Trusts are usually of considerable proportions.'

'Then the fact is that nobody in the firm is prepared to see me. That's the truth of it!'

'Oh, no, madam! That is furthest from their intentions. I will advise one of the partners to call upon you at the earliest opportunity – perhaps when Mr Wedderburn is also at home.'

'You will do nothing of the sort,' snapped Milly. 'I've reason to know that Mr Goodchild is in the building, and I demand to see him immediately. If he doesn't come down, I am going up!'

'Madam, please!' wailed the clerk; as Milly went past he barred her way so that she had to push him aside. A uniformed bank guard came running; he and the clerk seized her arms and customers in the bank watched as Milly, now furious, struggled to break free.

'Madam, Dr Schofield's surgery is also in the building,' the clerk said suddenly. 'You can put your complaint to him.'

Milly glared at him. 'I understand that you are a patient of Dr Schofield . . .' he added meaningfully.

Dishevelled, shaking with anger, she found herself being led out into the street. Clearly James had been in touch with the Goodchilds before she had asked for the interview. Clearly, also, she thought ruefully, the confrontation with the clerk had been a mistake.

The heat was oppressive; Hong Kong was at its most extreme that morning. Walking slowly under her parasol Milly wended her way through the labouring population. Farmers shouting their wares were waving scraggy chickens upside down in batches; butchers bargained at fly-blown stalls on the pavements; and quack-quack medicine men shouted out a remedy for every known condition, from lotion for head lice to powders to be taken for birth control. Coolies hurried by under bouncing shoulder poles; funeral directors, beloved of the Chinese, were 'bawling the road' in their Make-way-for-the-Dead advancing cortege of sobbing relatives and professional mourners, the latter employed to wail at fifty cents a time. Although no rickshaws (a Japanese invention) had yet arrived in Hong Kong, sedan chairs were everywhere down Pedder Street and Queen's Road. Harlots and Mist and Flower ladies shrieked their charms from the quayside barges, inviting bachelors to partake within of heavenly delight; long-haired priests of every denomination clutched at their drab robes, lost in the mystical reveries of fanatical beliefs. All this was a microcosm of Hong Kong life, with everybody hastening to nowhere amid a hawking, squawking bustle. Milly saw them all, wondering at the marvellous complexity of Hong Kong, a Hades already infested with scores of dif-ferent Satans.

On a corner of Pottinger Street, malefactors were being flogged for multifarious misdemeanours, more dangerous criminals being despatched in chains and loaded with their *cangues* − neck-boards disallowing escape − for beheading in Kowloon City, beheading being the standard sentence for piracy and murder. Eli, please note, thought Milly. Thirteen coolies, wailing in anticipation, were squatting on the pavement: sentenced to flogging, she learned later, by the dreaded magistrate, Colonel Caine, whose infamy had spread to the British House of Commons. Here the incoming Gov-ernor had already raised questions concerning Hong Kong's crime and punishment − reports had been received of fifty-four Chinese flogged in one day. Biting her lip, Milly passed by them, not oblivious to their pleading hands, but aware that she could do nothing to save them. In Hong Kong humanity was cheap, compassion a rare commodity. With the cries of the flogged coolies ringing in her ears, Milly, sickened, hailed a sedan chair and directed the bearers to take her back to the English Mansion.

On her way, passing the old Artillery Barracks, she stopped the chair to watch British soldiers drilling on the square. Their ranks were thin; scarcely enough, she thought, to save Hong Kong from the constant threat of invasion by pirates and Taiping rebels from the Chinese mainland, for their numbers were constantly being decimated by fever −

largely because the companies, living in tents near Flagstaff House, were hosts to hordes of mosquitoes.

The sight of the drilling soldiers, listless as they appeared, filled Milly with apprehension. James was always talking about the Yellow Peril and what butchery would occur should the Colony ever be seriously attacked.

Under the Treaty of Nanking of 1842 the uneasy peace between Britain and China had so far been maintained, but now there was talk of another Opium War. China, it was said, had for a dozen years been smarting under the penalty of twenty million dollars payment to Britain in reparation for her earlier resistance to the drug; and now the Peking government was again rattling the sabre, promising to throw all Hong Kong's foreign devils into the sea should the importation of the opium be continued. Perhaps, concluded Milly, it was time for all reasonable Europeans to leave Hong Kong, if only to preserve their skins.

When Milly arrived back at the Mansion, she was a little surprised to find Mamie in bed. The summer heat, she thought, was enough to exhaust anyone. Later, wandering in the garden, she went to the highest point, overlooking the harbour, and saw a string of big junks line up astern on the cobalt sea. With their bat-winged sails billowing in a fine sou'wester, they were making in the direction of Green Island. Vaguely, Milly wondered if this activity had anything to do with Eli; there had been a great deal of junk movement lately and she had seen little of him.

Events were shaking Hong Kong from its midsummer lethargy. Soon, Milly recalled, the new Governor, Sir John Bowring, would arrive to replace Sir George Bonham. And although neither she nor James yet realised it, Sir John was a tyrant when it came to maladministration.

216

32

While Mamie was out shopping in Central Market, Milly was surprised by a call from Dr Schofield. Anna No Name ushered him into the drawing-room with quiet servility.

'She's a beauty,' he said, as Anna shut the door behind him. 'Where did you find her?'

'Ask James,' replied Milly. 'He advertised.'

'To tide Mamie over her illness?'

'That was his idea. Can I offer you any refreshment?'

'Too early! Have you seen James this morning?'

'No. For the past week he's been over on Green Island. Why?'

'I hear he's very upset about the disturbance you had at the bank last week.'

'Disturbance? What disturbance?'

'You should know − you were the cause of it!' Schofield's mocking grin widened in his cadaverous face. 'The reception clerk was very angry. You really should try to control your tantrums in public. Go on like this and you'll give the Wedderburns a bad name!'

'I haven't the faintest idea what you're talking about!' Milly said. 'I knew Mr Goodchild was in his office, so I asked to see him; the clerk refused and I tried to insist.'

'By shouting and pushing him to the floor?'

'*What*!' She was on her feet.

'That's what you're accused of! Indeed, according to the Goodchilds the clerk wanted to file a complaint for assault.'

'I don't believe I'm hearing this!

'It was only with the greatest difficulty that Goodchild talked him out of a civil action against you. The man was only trying to do his job.'

'This is a lie from beginning to end, and you know it!'

'That's not how the clerk sees it!'

Closing her eyes, Milly subsided into a chair and the doctor sat, too.

'I think I'll have that drink after all. I can see this is going to be difficult.' He slopped gin into a glass and drank it at a gulp. 'Milly, this is only for your own good. For some time now I had hoped you would manage to control yourself . . .' Schofield hesitated.

'Come on, say what you think!' She was defiant.

'That is why I've come. To begin with, the confrontation at the Governor's reception did you no good at all.'

'*Confrontation?*'

'Well, your insistence – in front of the Colonial Secretary, if you please – that you recognised someone at his party as one of the two men responsible for holding you to ransom. The whole affair did nothing to convince me that your mental state had improved. Please sit down, Milly – this is difficult enough . . .'

Milly subsided and the doctor continued, 'You succeeded in embarrassing everybody, not least the gentleman himself, who turned out to be none other than Akil Tamarins, the Dutch Ambassador to Peking. To his face you damned him as a liar despite his protests that he had never met you.'

'It was Hans Bruner,' whispered Milly, clenching her hands in her lap. 'I don't know what's going on here, but it *was* Hans Bruner!'

'My dear girl, it was not! All you succeeded in doing was make an exhibition of yourself, and now you've done it again. Not to mention these quite astonishing allegations about your discovering manacled dead men on the beach on Green Island. If I did not know you better, I would suspect you are saying these things to impress the newspapers, who have had a field day at the Government's expense. However, bearing in mind your past history, it can only be part of your further mental deterioration.'

218

'The more you try to call me insane the less you'll succeed!' Milly said evenly.

'Everybody mentally ill says that!' Schofield snapped, as he had on a previous occasion.

'I'm saner than you, and you know it.'

'Then there's this other business — something of a most private nature.'

'Oh yes. Something else, is there?'

'And more than delicate. It concerns James.'

'I can imagine. You've always been most keen to defend his interests.'

'And the — personal side of your marriage.'

'Do you mean my marital relations?'

'As a matter of fact, I do.' Schofield glanced up as Anna entered with a tray of coffee; tight-lipped, Milly waited until the girl had gone.

'We were discussing marital relations,' said Milly. 'Though what it's to do with you I can't think.'

'Milly, Milly! I'm not only the personal physician to the family, I am also your friend. James has sought my advice. Apparently, all is not well between you in this respect, and he's at his wits' end to know how to put it right.'

'Tell him to spend less on whisky and more time at home.'

'Really, I'm sure you do him a gross injustice.'

'He drinks too much, which renders him incapable of performing a natural function, then blames me!'

A silence came; Schofield's eyes drifted over her. The ugly duckling straight out of school had turned into a swan, he thought; not a beautiful swan, true, for her features were too irregular for flawless good looks, but beautiful nevertheless, because she was young. But in terms of loveliness the girl who brought in the coffee earlier was possessed of every quality and he vaguely wondered how James managed to exist within reach of such attraction without succumbing to temptation. He decided to be forthright; after all, Milly was a woman now.

'You have a lover?'

'It's no business of yours!' Milly exclaimed. Schofield has the ability to peer into a woman's soul, she thought. The

219

hypocrisy of the situation assailed her in waves of intensity; here she was indicting James for infidelity while she, at every opportunity, was engaged in clandestine meetings with Eli. She wanted to shout into this man's face that her affairs were hers alone; wanted passionately to declare that the man she truly loved would come to her at the raise of a finger, that the trickery which had trapped her into this apology for a marriage hadn't worked. Above all she longed to say that, however hard they tried, she would steer her father's legacy into her own hands, if only to release their hold upon her. This, she knew, was the reason for Schofield's continuous interference in her life. But she did none of these things. To have revealed her feelings would have been to play into his hands, allowing her love for Eli to be bandied around the gossiping set. And, even a mention of a lover would betray all Eli stood for in her heart.

'Perhaps nobody would blame you,' said Schofield.

Milly was momentarily lost within the intensity of her thought, 'I beg your pardon?'

'I was saying that your life appears to be such a damnable waste.'

Milly got up. 'Better not to pursue this conversation. I don't confide in anyone – least of all you.'

'I was only saying that you should not throw away your life,' he replied. 'You're an attractive woman. Even Mamie, it appears, is learning how to live more fully, if the rumours reaching me are true.'

'I know nothing about that.'

'At last she has learned to forget old Rastus!'

'Mamie will never forget Rastus.'

'Not in the arms of another? I find it difficult to believe this. She and her sweetheart have actually been seen in church together.'

'I'm delighted for them.' Milly could feel his eyes upon her.

'If Mamie, why not you?' he said.

Milly got up with the attitude of one bringing the conversation to an end. 'With people like you watching me like hawks, I'd be a fool to cause a scandal. If this marriage is doomed, blame James, not me.'

'Oh come! I only wish you well.' Schofield stood, betraying signs of embarrassment.

'Well, is that all?' Milly asked.

'You don't trust me, do you? That's a pity.'

'Whose fault is that? If you'd had your way I'd be in an asylum by now.'

Schofield smiled. 'Ah well, we do insist on making our own private hells in this world, don't we! If you did but realise it, I'm your friend: conversely, I can be your enemy.'

She did not reply.

'I'll see myself out,' said Schofield.

Mamie returned from Central Market with Tang, the houseboy, carrying her purchases. 'I saw that old Schofield down at Blake's Pier,' said she. 'He looked as if somebody had done him an injury.'

'Give me time,' said Milly.

'He's been here?' Mamie sat down, gasping.

'Yes.'

Mamie fanned herself. 'I'm tellin' you, this is one queer house. That Fu Tan girl gives me some strange old looks; she don't talk none, ye know. An' that young monk comin' and goin' in the kitchen do give me the shivers. Being Church of England, I doesn't go a lot on monks.'

'She's a good housekeeper. Admit it.'

'But no cook. You ain't eaten decent since I got meself retired!'

'James seems to love everything she gives him.'

'That's because his eyes ain't in his belly.'

'What do you mean by that?'

'What I say. When you're an old girl like me, you got to be good; when you're a juicy young morsel like her, you gets away with murder.'

Milly laughed. 'You eat everything she cooks, don't you?'

'Maybe so, 'cause I'm polite. But sometimes I don't feel so good, Miss Milly. I reckon her pans are too rich for ma stomach. Ma Rastus were the same, mind, a'fore he went down.'

'What a strange thing to say! Are you not well?'

221

'Not particular so. I ain't yet got over the aches I got off that Ah Lum, I guess. Ma ribs are still skinnin'.'

'You can't blame Fu Tan. I eat the same as you; so does James, and we're all right.'

'When a maiden's turned forty the stomach ain't that healthy, I suppose. It's like my Sam says, "Once you've had forty years, you ain't the same".'

'How is Sam?'

'Thrivin'! He's some man!' She glowed, her big eyes glistening.

'I hear you've got him into church! You might have mentioned it!'

'Missy,' said Mamie, getting up in grunts and wheezes, 'I ain't lettin' on to anyone the plans I got for that big Sam before I gets him to the altar. And if he plays his cards right, I'm handin' him a bunch o' babies before the change o' life. Yessir!'

33

Milly had already discovered that if she stood upon the highest point of the English Mansion garden, which was reached by the steps of a tiny pavilion, she was granted a panoramic view of Hong Kong harbour. This discovery allowed her and Eli to communicate without risking an exchange of letters. Therefore if, at an agreed time of night, a junk in the harbour made the Sign of the Cross, this was a signal for a meeting at a given place and time.

On the last day of September, with autumn colours tinting the trees of the Praya, the rendezvous was at a lonely quay near Victoria Point. The time was midnight.

The secret of living at peace in the English Mansion, Milly had discovered, was to reveal as little as possible about her activities. To this end she ensured that Anna and James were ignorant of her plans. Now, with a prospect of a clandestine meeting with Eli on Green Island, the great thing was to impress on the household (less Mamie, whom she trusted) that she was going for a day or two in the opposite direction, to Macao, involving a four-hour ferry trip through Chinese waters.

At Macao, Milly claimed, one could laze in the sea off the Praya, dabble one's feet in crystal-clear water, sleep the clock round in a Portuguese hotel, and at night eat the delicious sea-spiders washed down with free wine from Oporto: the nectar of the gods.

And, if James was suspicious of a lurking lover, so much the better. For something was going on under the roof of the

223

English Mansion — unless she was very much mistaken ...

Anna Fu Tan, the new housekeeper, was surpassingly beautiful and James was never averse to taking his chances where he found them.

'I think I'll have a short trip to Macao,' she told James at breakfast, with Anna within earshot. 'The sea air will be invigorating.'

'Excellent,' answered he, the prospect of Anna in mind. 'Please don't hurry back. When are you leaving?'

'This very moment, if you don't find it inconvenient.' She smiled brilliantly over the table.

'How long will you be away?'

'Only a couple of days.'

'You're aware, of course, that if an enemy gunboat decides to snatch you in Chinese waters, it could be for a couple of years,' James replied.

Milly laughed. 'But you will not miss me. After all, the delightful Anna is here to take care of your needs, is she not?'

James smiled. His unspoken protest told all: his was now a delightful, abandoned game of adultery. A game at which more than one can play, thought Milly.

James rose from the breakfast table. 'I'll see you next week, I take it.' He kissed Milly's face. 'Do try to enjoy yourself!'

'I am sure I will,' replied Milly.

Locking her bedroom door, for Fu Tan was likely to appear at unexpected times, Milly changed into the ragged jacket and trousers in which she had left Lantau Island. Sitting before the mirror of her dressing-table she then proceeded to turn her face into that of a Chinese.

First her lips, which she painted pink, not red. With burnt cork she darkened her eye-lids and shaded their corners. Plaiting her long black hair in pigtails that fell either side of her face she examined the effect in the mirror, and considered that where earth-coolies were concerned, she looked as good as any for a woman travelling incognito.

So intent was Milly in her preparations that she did not see the mask of a fox silhouetted against a nearby window.

On her way through the house Anna met James coming in. Earlier he had crossed the Sulphur Channel from Green Island. The sea had been rough and, soaked, he followed Anna into the kitchen.

'Where is my wife?' James asked.

'In her room, already asleep, perhaps. She has gone to bed early with a bad head, she says.'

'Then I'll get these wet things off and be with you after my meal. It is ready?'

'Of course. All is as you would wish it.'

'Including sharing a bed with you tonight?'

'In my room, Master? That is not possible.'

'Why?'

'Because my young brother, the novice monk, is visiting me from Lantau.'

'Damn all monks and your brother in particular! Good God, I haven't enjoyed you for a week! Can't you postpone his visit?'

'It is not possible. Already he will be on his way. Please — ' And Anna went to him and put her arms around his neck, kissing him on the mouth. He bent over her, but she said, her breathing hushed: 'No, Master — not here. It is very dangerous.'

'My wife is sleeping. Why not?'

'No, please!'

'Oh come, woman!' They sank together to the floor of the kitchen, his breath, laden with the fumes of whisky, was a profanity against her face.

'What if the servants come?' Anna whispered in panic.

'Lie still, damn you!'

Yung did not come to the front door, but tapped on Anna's window as he always did when visiting her at the English Mansion. The serenity of the monastery had redeemed his youthful good looks, smoothing away the lines of his face, but tonight he was a boy in panic.

'Quickly!' he whispered, as Anna opened the door of her room.

'Why is life so hurried?' she asked placidly as Yung hastened within, shut the door and leaned against it.

225

'They are coming!' he said.

'Who are coming? Talk sense, or not at all!' Tight-lipped, she flared at his weakness, for his face was wet and his saffron robe was stained with tears.

'The soldiers from Macao — they are asking questions!' he said fearfully.

'What questions?'

'About the disappearance of Captain da Costa. Already they have talked to the temple elders of Hong Kong; now they are visiting the islands and soon will be at Lantau.'

Anna held her breath. Yung said, 'You asked me to bring the captain to you so that he would arrest the pirate Boggs and now he has disappeared,' Yung went on. 'What has happened to him?'

'I do not know. I showed him the whereabouts of the gunpowder factory and have been waiting for Eli Boggs to be arrested. When he is, that will be the end of the pirates and bandits.'

'You do not know where the officer is?'

'No, I swear it, Little One.'

Yung grew calmer. 'There is also talk around the islands that a young monk called at the Macao Customs house and the captain went away with him. What if I am questioned?'

Anna took his face in her hands and kissed both cheeks. 'That is simple. Deny everything.'

'But that would be lying! A mortal sin.'

'Oh, dear!' she said facetiously, 'how very prim we are! Have you never lied before?'

'Not since I took holy orders.'

Anna smiled at him lovingly. 'You will not have to lie. Just obey my last request, Little Brother, and I promise that we can return to our village in peace.'

'You promised that before!'

'Now I swear it — on the grave of our mother.'

Yung, however, was no longer a child to be commanded as she willed. Nor did he trust her, his suspicions concerning her having been confirmed by his elders, in whom he had confided. 'Your sister is a woman possessed,' the elders had told him: 'her soul has been invaded by fur and claws: she

226

will not know peace nor find serenity of the soul, until the animal within her is exorcised. Gain her confidence and do as we command you, and you can make her clean.'

Remembering this Yung asked: 'What is this last request you make of me?'

'I will tell you all in good time,' said Anna. 'Meanwhile, Little Brother, remember this. I have made you a promise, and I will keep it.'

After he had left her to return to Lantau, Anna took from a drawer in her room the key of the Gunpowder Factory which she had earlier stolen from Eli's junk; she wrapped this in a packet and enclosed a note in English, which read: 'This is the key to the Stanley Gunpowder Factory, also a map showing its position near the village.'

Addressing the packet to the Customs Officer, she went down to Victoria and put it in the box provided by the postal authorities in Pedder Street.

It was a time for lovers' trysts that night in the English Mansion, though some were more successful than others.

'Is you in there, Mamie Malumba?' whispered Black Sam outside her bedroom door, his bangle earrings gleaming in the moonlight.

'I is — but you ain't with me,' replied Mamie.

'Open this door or I'll put me fist through it,' said Sam.

'Oh, aye? Well, if you think I'm yours any time you fancy, you've another think comin'.''

'Let me sing you *The Song o' Solomon*.'

'I've been hearin' that feller mornin', noon and night. I don't want him round here.'

'Oh honey, what have I done?'

'You done broke a promise, Black Sam. Ma Rastus never broke one in his whole married life.'

'What promise?'

'You said you'd come for the pastor's Bible readin', and you never showed up.'

'Honey, I'm a pirate. I was out robbin' people.'

'And that's another thing; this pirate palaver has gotta stop! I'm havin' those bangle earrings off your ears. Meanwhile, get goin', for you've got no prospects.'

227

There was a pause on the other side of the door, then Black Sam said, 'There's more fish in the sea, ye know. This boy jist hollers and women come runnin'.'

'Oh, aye? Tell me another. A man's on a ball and chain when once he's tasted Mamie – that's what you said, remember?'

'Have pity,' said Sam. 'D'you realise it's a week? You'll have me as skinny as a Pentecostal monk.'

'You can be a heap of shanks and shinbones for all I care; but you ain't comin' in, Black Sam.'

Meanwhile, the Pedder Street clock was striking the hour as Milly and Eli ran hand in hand along the beach of Green Island, where the two dolphins, as if expecting them, were cavorting with each other, leaping out of the breakers.

'I love you, I love you!' said Milly. Eli kissed her and the kiss left the taste of brine upon her mouth. Then they stood together in each other's arms, watching the Green Island lighthouse beams flashing across the Sulphur Channel.

'We ought to make the best of this,' said Eli. 'Now the new Governor's arrived, things are going to be different.'

'Different?'

'He's bringing changes with him, they say. This place will be out of bounds, for a start.'

'Oh no! Not Green Island!'

'Sure thing. Questions have been raised in Parliament about crime and punishment in the Colony, and there's things he don't agree with. Coolie trafficking for one, and your James is up to his ears in it.'

'You know the way I feel about that,' said Milly.

His eyes narrowed against the flashing light. 'Something's got to be done. I ain't particular where bad money comes from, but I draw the line at a slave trade, and this is all the Smith and Wedderburn shipments are. D'you know that over twenty provinces, from Anhwei to Kwangtung, tens of thousands of coolies have been shipped out from here? Governor Bowring will try to stop it.'

'What about opium smuggling?'

'That's different.'

'Oh, no, it isn't! It's as bad as coolie trafficking!

228

Just because you're profiting by it, it doesn't make it legitimate!'

'I don't think you approve of me!'

'And it's dangerous. Every day of the week they are beheading pirates in Kowloon City.'

'First they'll have to catch me.'

Milly put her arms about his neck. 'I love you, and want to keep you safe.'

'If you love me, keep out of my business. I've been breaking laws since I can remember; and I ain't changing now.'

Later, lying with Eli on the beach, Milly realised that this was the man for whom she had been born. Her experience of men before she had met him had been limited; first there had been the youthful love of Tom Ellery, whom she now saw only in dreams, then the enforced courtship of James which she had endured through wifely duty. True, Eli was not a person of gentle persuasion; his character, like his hands, was tough and calloused. Yet there was about him a certain refinement which tamed his rough masculinity. Eli was his own man, nothing more; one could take him as he was, or reject him. Of one thing she was certain: none could bend him.

Lying back, Milly watched him with half-closed eyes, seeing his jutting profile carved against the starlit sky. He was eating the food Mamie had prepared for them; this he did with an animal grace. Eating was to Eli a process whereby a man kept alive, nothing more; while with James it was a voracious drool, each heaped forkful being hauled up to his loose-lipped mouth, there to be snapped at like a dog snaps at flies, and noisily masticated while his little eyes searched for more. The way a man eats, she thought, was an indication of character, if these two men were examples. She remembered, from her schooldays, the legend of an ancient seer who had once suggested that, of the seven deadly sins, gluttony was the worst since it embraced the other six: envy of the neighbour's larger plate, covetousness of its contents, slothful of sharing, anger at a smaller portion, pride in one's ability to gorge oneself and a lust for more despite the belches and rumbles of an outraged digestion. It was a strange phenomenon, Milly considered,

229

smiling up as Eli turned his eyes upon her, that so rugged a lover could inspire a woman's respect by the simple process of eating to live, instead of like James, living to eat.

'One day they will take you from me,' she said unaccountably.

Eli seemed not to hear her; jumping up he took her hand and raced her along the beach to a quiet place beyond the Rest House. Here, in an arbour of rocks they were united in lovemaking, as the moon shone down upon them.

Down along the Praya of Hong Kong, Milly thought, sit the Chinese harlots behind their white-toothed smiles; with gesticulating hands, their fingers tipped with red as if dipped in blood, they called to their paramours at a dollar a time. How do I compare with these? she thought. The apparently respectable married wife of a wealthy merchant, lying with such an abandoned lover on such a foreign shore.

'Am I hurting you?' Eli whispered.

She did not reply. To have done so would somehow have broken the spiritual bond now forged between them; in life or death, this must never be severed, she thought. So while her body endured her man's gasping strength she knew a joy transcending all endeavour: a light of happiness that blinded her to everything but the sublime moment.

Yet what would follow, she sometimes wondered, if I were to bear a child of this illicit love? That which appeared so beautiful would, within the glare of accusation and revelation, become sordid and immoral, a topic for gossipers within a colony where indiscretion could strip away every last vestige of respectability from a woman, however lofty her social position.

'What if you conceive as a result of this?' asked Eli afterwards, reading her thoughts.

'Please do not discuss my private affairs.'

'It could happen. Then our love would be public knowledge.'

'Do not let us talk of it, or even think of it. Don't I please you a little?'

'You will please me to the end of my life.'

'But you have known many women.'

'And you please me best of all.'

'That delights me. I am now a valuable commodity?'

'Do not talk that way!'

Milly sat up and he saw her profile against the moon which, full and beautiful, was sailing over distant mountains. And Eli knew that the child he had known during her first voyage to Hong Kong had now grown into a woman, with whom he intended to share his life. Raising himself, he kissed her face, but her thoughts kept her separate and she did not turn to him.

'Soon we will leave here,' said Eli.

'Together?'

'Of course.'

'It is not possible!'

'Trust me. I shall take you away.'

'Dear me, Eli Boggs, for a pirate you are a great dreamer!'

Eli brushed the sand from her body. 'It is already planned. Below your Rest House is stored a fortune in opium casks. It belongs, strangely, not to Smith and Wedderburn, but to Hans Bruner.'

Milly's mouth fell open as he continued. 'With the money your father paid me for your ransom, he bought two tons of it for fifty thousand Mexican dollars and stored it in the Rest House until the price of opium rose. Now, with another Opium War coming, the rate is soaring, so I intend to appropriate it.'

'But Old Soong, the caretaker, guards it with his life!'

'Old man Soong has already been bought,' said Eli. 'Look upon it as a bridal dowry provided by an adoring husband.'

'Beware of dreaming, Eli. James will also have a hand in this, and while Hans Bruner may be a fool, James is clever.'

'And then we will sail away to the rim of the world,' Eli went on, ignoring Milly's caution. 'We will laze on a foreign shore all day, eat oysters, and drink French wine out of the reach of anyone.'

'It sounds wonderful, Eli; but it can never be.'

'Mrs Wedderburn! Are you aware that you lie unclothed and without a shred of respectability?'

231

'I could lie here forever with you.'

'That isn't possible, for there is work to be done.'

Rising, he seized her hands and drew her to her feet and they stood together, unashamed.

34

During the autumn events quickened in Milly's life; so much happened that it is better to repeat it in its chronological order. The events included Eli's trial for piracy and murder; the latter accusation being based upon the finding of Captain da Costa's body in the Stanley Gunpowder Factory, of which Eli of course was the legal owner.

Sulen, the daughter of Papa Tai, was the first to experience the weight of the police investigation.

With Hong Kong bathing in an aura of heat, Sulen was immersed to the chin in the waters of Stanley Bay when Papa Tai, struggling in the arms of two Portuguese policemen, bawled from the beach: 'Sister of iniquity! Spawn of a noseless beggar, come ashore at once!'

But Sulen, as naked as in the arms of the midwife, dreamed on, with waves rising and falling about her small, pink ears. With eyes tight-shut against the molten glare of the sun, she dreamed, her sun-fed body dark-hued beneath the iridescent water.

One of the policemen fired his revolver into the air; the report echoed and reverberated. Sulen, opening her eyes, saw Papa Tai and the policemen and trod water.

'*Come ashore*!' The command now reached her. So she, with nothing on her conscience and less on her anatomy, crossed her brown arms over her pink-tipped breasts and tiptoed into the tide-swim where Papa Tai flung his padded coat about her, which naturally dismayed the policemen.

'She is an idiot, you understand!' exclaimed Papa Tai. 'She has the body of a woman and the brain of a louse. Believe me, you will get nothing from her!'

'Come girl,' said one of the policemen, and all four squatted on the sand in the manner of sea-coolies. Sulen was shivering; not with cold but with the excitement of her situation.

'Tell us,' said the second policeman, 'and truly, or you will be thrashed. Have you ever known a Portuguese Customs Officer by the name of da Costa?'

'No!' said Papa Tai.

'Yes,' said Sulen, while her father cursed her. 'Often he would come to me, saying I was beautiful.'

'He was looking for a Gunpowder Factory, was he not?'

'What Gunpowder Factory?' asked Papa Tai.

'He was looking for me,' said Sulen, and rose, dropping the coat at her feet, which changed the subject.

'Clothe yourself, you strumpet!' yelled Papa Tai, and flung his blue-veined arms upwards, wailing at the sun. 'See what my woman landed me with – a baggage, a doxy! May Buddha forgive such a wife for being alive!' And then he leered at the policemen, saying: 'Look well upon her beauty, nevertheless. Have you such a woman at home? Fifty dollars in my hand and she is yours. Take her home, lads, and forget about dead officers.'

'When did you last see Captain da Costa, child?' asked the younger of the policemen, ignoring this unseemly interruption. He still had the down of boyhood upon his cheeks, which were blushing at Sulen's nearness.

'Not for three months. Perhaps more.' Sulen was holding up a sea-shell for inspection, turning its mother-of-pearl this way and that, so that it flashed in the sun.

'And what of you, old man?' asked the other policeman.

'Me? On the soul of my grandmother, I have never set eyes upon him!' Outraged, Papa Tai beat his breast.

'But you are the owner of the Gunpowder Factory. Da Costa is bound to have come to you.'

'I am not the owner,' said Papa Tai.

'He sold it,' interjected Sulen.

'To whom?'

'To Eli Boggs.'

234

'The pirate?'

'The same,' said Papa Tai, sensing danger.

'When?'

'More than three months ago.'

One held up a key. 'Is this the key of the factory? Do you recognise it?'

'Of course,' announced Sulen with finality. 'Often, Captain da Costa would take me in there and make love to me.'

'Would he indeed!'

'It is a lie,' shouted Papa Tai. 'She is a virgin!'

'Oh, why say such a terrible thing?' cried Sulen, now tearful.

'Captain da Costa was a man of honour,' a policeman stated. 'If this girl is no longer a virgin, the fault was not our captain's.'

'It is enough that he has been murdered,' added the older man. 'We will not have his name defiled. Come!' And he hauled Sulen, still naked, to her feet.

'Give her a turn of the thumb-screw, lads!' shouted Papa Tai, 'and for once you may get the truth; something she has never told in her life. But murder? No, I can assure you that neither of us have ever set eyes on the honourable captain. Sulen is mistaken.'

'Let it not be said that we Portuguese lack finesse when it comes to such beauty.' The old policeman bowed. 'You will allow me to entertain you while your father is interrogated?'

'Sir, the pleasure will be mine,' replied Sulen. 'You have me — Papa Tai can have the thumb-screw.'

'They both possess crooked tongues,' said somebody, 'but the thumb-screw will straighten them out.'

So Sulen and Papa Tai were hauled off shouting and kicking. Torture to obtain confession was disallowed in Hong Kong under British law, but this law did not apply under Macanese jurisdiction; nevertheless, Papa Tai, being a coward, did not suffer for long, and Sulen did not suffer at all. 'Stop, stop — we will tell you everything!' they cried.

'First,' said the Inspector, 'what is the name of the woman you say you guided to the Gunpowder Factory?'

'I do not know her name,' Sulen replied. 'She gave me

money and I took her to it. I know only that later she was the lover of Eli Boggs, the pirate, and that she wore upon her clothes a perfume like the scent of musk.'

'Nothing more?'

'Nothing,' said Sulen. 'Only that she lived with him aboard his pirate junk.'

'But wait!' said another interrogator. 'There is talk of a novice monk: one who called at the Customs Office. It is said that Captain da Costa went away with him.'

'I know nothing of this,' said Sulen.

'Nor I,' added Papa Tai.

'The murderer, it appears to me, is this accused pirate, Boggs,' the Inspector cried. 'Clearly he killed the captain when he discovered the whereabouts of the illegal factory. Arrest him!'

'That may be impossible, sir,' said his assistant. 'He is never in one place for more than five minutes.'

'Naturally, we will arrest him with a certain degree of reluctance,' sighed the Inspector. 'The finest jade and ivory I possess at home came from his pirate horde. So seek our friend Eli, but not too rigorously. We all have our livings to earn — including pirates!'

'And after all, sir,' said the assistant, 'nothing can now raise our beloved captain from his grave.'

35

'You are troubled in your heart, my son?' asked the Master of Novices in the Buddhist temple on Lantau Island.

'I am sorely troubled, Master,' replied Yung, sitting cross-legged before the table of three bald elders.

'Then your sadness will be lessened by sharing it with us.'

'I beg your indulgence,' answered Yung, and began as follows.

'You will recall, Master, that before I took holy orders, I confessed to assisting Anna No Name, my sister, in murdering the bandits of the Pearl River'

'For which you received our Absolution,' said the Master.

'Now I worry for the soul of my sister. I believe her to be possessed. You warned me of this possibility.'

'Explain this.'

The three elders leaned forward on their trestle seats, the better to hear, and Yung continued.

'During the early murders I did not suspect that my sister was possessed by a beast. But when Chu Apu, the pirate was attacked, such were his injuries that his body was shredded as if by the claws of an animal. Now, deranged, he hauls himself on all fours along the fishing quay of Stanley village. I questioned him: although nearly incoherent, it appears that he awoke from sleep to find himself in the arms, not of his concubine, but a giant fox.'

'Enough to addle any brain,' said one of the elders drolly.

'But why suspect your sister?'

'Because this man, Chu Apu, was the next one on her list to be murdered. And, when lying with her in our sampan, I heard strange sounds coming from her throat as she lay sleeping.'

'Ah!' whispered an elder.

'Pulling down the dividing blanket between us, I saw my sister's bare arm in the moonlight. Her skin is dark — for she is not Chinese, but a sun-fed Moslem — and upon it grew a sheen of yellow hair. And the sounds she was making were those of a vixen calling to its mate.'

'The moon was full, Novice?' asked the Master.

'The night was as bright as day.'

'And then?'

'Then,' continued Yung, 'the noises ended, and I settled to sleep. But later in the night I awoke again and looked upon the face of my sister and in the brightness of the moon I saw the face of a fox.'

At this the elders became vociferous, and Yung waited while they argued among themselves.

'Are you addicted to opium?' the Master asked eventually.

'I have never smoked in my life!'

'Nor eaten it?'

'Nor partaken of it in any way, Master.'

'Have you indulged in saki — rice wine?'

'Never! Saki is a curse.'

'How then do you account for this phenomenon? Could it not have been a dream?'

'For a long while I have noticed that foxes appear to abound when I am with her.'

'Ah,' said an elder, and drew his saffron robes closer about his naked body. 'In the fields?' he asked.

'Even by day I see them roaming.'

'One fox, or many?'

'In sunlight foxes look identical; by night I see only their eyes.'

'The same fox, probably,' said an elder. 'This sister of yours: I recall you saying that her body exudes a perfume.'

'The perfume of musk; it is hereditary.'

'Pleasing?'

'As the scent of musk is pleasing.'

'But not a human smell, nevertheless.'

'It is one which men certainly find attractive.'

'No doubt. But the body of a fox also emits a smell that is not pleasing.'

'The smell of this woman is not important,' said the Master. 'I have known people of charm and deportment who smell abominably. Only in the facial changes am I interested. Certainly she could be demoniacally possessed.'

'Then her soul is already condemned,' sighed another.

'Is this usual — this metamorphosis?'

'It is commonly found in cases of demonic possession,' replied the Master. 'A vixen will seek a comfortable home; to enter a human body through a maiden's vagina is as good an entry as any. Its soul then lodges comfortably in her womb, like the embryo of a child; a happy enough situation.' He smiled amiably. 'It also provides an inexpensive mode of travel.' One of them chuckled.

'Can we discuss this without levity?' asked the third, 'we who are bound by laws of delicacy?'

'Of course,' replied the Master, 'but it is also necessary to speak of the laws of life.

'Do not our people know that lotus leaves burned to ashes are a remedy against pregnancy, while the seeds of that same flower are esteemed as an aphrodisiac? Or that the nursing mother needs red sugar after her delivery and that dropsy can be cured by eating the refuse of burning water-melons? Likewise chicken's livers are excellent for babies' stomachs; eye trouble is alleviated by eating pig's liver steamed in chrysanthemum juice, and whooping-cough is cured by swallowing powdered sea-sparrow.

'Many and varied are the conditions of humans. How abnormal, then, is the transmigration of a fox fairy into human form? Not at all!'

'Your knowledge appals my ignorance, Master,' whispered Yung. 'But what do I do about my sister?'

The Master said carefully, 'In ancient China it was accepted that the guile and cunning of high officials was atributable to their being possessed by foxes. This is why the fox is not only respected by the Chinese, but has become a deity.

239

'The person possessed is abundant with either charity or wickedness; in a maiden, Yung, the lease of her body could be permanent until her beauty fades. Therefore the spirit should be exorcised as soon as possible. It appears that her designs to date have been evil, have they not?'

'Most evil. And she is planning more!'

'Then meet with her. Discover her future plans: if they be so evil, humour her to put her off her guard and then exorcise the demon for the good of her soul. Her body is not important in this. So, if necessary, you must kill her.'

'How do I exorcise the spirit of the fox?' Yung asked faintly.

'This will be made known to you. Go now!'

Yung rose, bowed to the elders, and tearfully left them.

36

Two days later the *China Mail* reported:

> Yesterday an attack was made upon the Rest House at
> Green Island, a property owned by Messrs Smith and
> Wedderburn, the Hong Kong merchants. Certain com-
> mercial assets were stolen by piratical forces belonging, it
> is thought, to the American pirate, Eli Boggs whose illicit
> activities in the Colony have recently been highlighted in
> this publication.
>
> The goods, believed to be opium (although this has not
> yet been confirmed), were removed in darkness and taken
> seaward to a destination on the Chinese mainland.
>
> Mr James Wedderburn, the firm's spokesman, claims
> that he knows nothing of the affair. Opium trading is
> now undertaken, not openly, but by smuggling; while
> respectable merchants abide by the terms of the law,
> pirates, naturally, possess no such scruples.
>
> Meanwhile, the sooner Elias Boggs is apprehended and
> brought to an untimely end, the better.

'You know, Black Sam, you're an uncommonly ingenious
fellow when you want to be,' Eli said jovially. 'How did
you manage it?'

Sam yawned nonchalantly. 'With Soong the caretaker
already bought, me and the others just walked in and
loaded it. Lucky Mamie weren't around!'

'Where was she?'

'Hong Kong side. I'd rather have faced the British Navy
than enter that place without her permission!'

241

'Did she know it was opium?'

'She does now. There'll be ructions.'

'Go to church twice come Sunday! She'll come round!'

'When we finishin' with the opium runnin', Boss?' Sam asked.

'When we've scared Wedderburn good and proper.'

'Ain't we done with him yet, then? I thought whoppin' up him and Bruner was the end of 'em.'

'Give me time,' answered Eli.

'Ah sure hopes you knows what you're up to, Boss,' said Sam.

Eli's lead junk, the *Ma Shan*, was one of the three rounding the most southerly point of Sulphur Channel. Spindrift was in the wind now, with the late sun putting on his bonnet and thinking it was June. There was a fine canvas breeze coming from the south. 'Good sailing when we hit the Pearl River, mind you!' Eli remarked and Sam, at the wheel of the junk, narrowed his eyes to the radiance of the morning.

'When do you expect to sight Wedderburn's ships?'

'Any moment,' answered Eli.

'More likely a British frigate on this tack, I reckon.'

'Probably now the new Governor's come. He doesn't agree with the Coolie Convoys.'

'That don't mean he'll let you get away with piracy? And when he gets news we've lifted that opium, all hell will break loose!'

'That's a chance I take. The time to fix Wedderburn is now. With his convoy running to Macao with four thousand coolies, we'll never get a better opportunity.'

'And what about Bruner?'

'Bruner's opium and Wedderburn's coolies – two birds with one stone!' Eli chuckled.

'You're a likeable feller,' said Sam, 'but I don't aim to rot in gaol with you.'

From the high poop deck above them came the look-out's wail: 'Sail on the port tack!' And Eli's deck-hands scampered into action; for the coolie ships were coming.

It was a convoy of three ships bound for Macao. They came in line astern with dead sails; each ship linked to the one in front, the whole being towed by a powerful steam-tug, its twin funnels billowing smoke.

Some four thousand coolies were in the convoy, each ship carrying their miserable share of humans battened down under hatches. The human cargo was in transit to the brokers of Portuguese Macao, there to be revived and shipped abroad: a third was destined to labour in the coal and iron industries of Philadelphia and Pittsburg; others would go to the farmlands of Australia, and the rest would find themselves in the Argentine, building railways. Less than three-quarters would survive the journey. Many would succumb to fever and exhaustion en route and some would die during the forced labour awaiting them. Few, if any, would be reunited with their families, as promised in the terms of their indentured labour. Half naked, huddled together in the airless holds, they listened to the thumping of the tug-boat's engine, the sighing of the towing lines and the battering of the sea against the hulls. Crying with fear, they clutched each other as a cannon-shot boomed and reverberated under the hatches; as the *Ma Shan*, Eli's lead-junk, put a round-shot across the tug-boat's bows.

'Run out the port cannon on grape-shot!' Eli bawled. 'Hold her at that, Sam, God bless and reward ye.'

'They'll be passin' loose on cannon shot, Boss,' Sam shouted back. 'Shall I pay her off?'

'Take her into irons!'

With the junk bending windward and the sea running down her shanks the half naked fisher-pirates of Amoy were working up to their waists in water. A fine sturdy sight the *Ma Shan* looked, as with her single bat-winged canvas billowing, she stood momentarily motionless before the tide took her to port and the wind held her starboard. Shivering her every timber as her canvas flapped, she then leaped like a tiger off the leash with her forty foot spar crashing over in a howl of the wind.

'Now run her goose-winged!' shouted Eli, and the junk put her nose down and barged straight across the bows of the coolie convoy. Hans Bruner, seeing the *Ma Shan* coming, slackened his tug-boat to two knots, and picked up a megaphone.

'Pay off, you damn-fool Boggs. Ease off! Are you mad?'

'Take us on,' commanded Eli, as the iron-clad prow of the *Ma Shan* shaved the bows of the steam-boat, then went about in a crashing of main-spar and blustering wind, to land up alongside. Eli and his crew leaped down from the rat-lines and Black Sam seized the wheel, as Eli sent Bruner flying with a backhander.

'Right!' shouted Eli as Bruner clambered to his feet, and struck him again with a vicious right-hander that sent him flying backwards against the thwarts.

'Don't kill him,' said Sam. 'We're in enough trouble as it is.'

'Get this lot stopped and boarded,' commanded Eli, and hauled Bruner to his feet. 'Then set compass for the Bogue Forts.'

'The Bogues? You're mad! They'll blow you out of the water,' shrieked Bruner, half-crazed with fear.

'If they do, you're coming with me,' said Eli. Standing on the prow of the tug-boat, naked to the waist, with a cutlass in his hand and his chest jutting, he looked like some Viking invader spewed up by the sea.

'Two points west, Sam — secure all tow-lines and take it slow!'

'Where for, Master?'

'West of Lantau and up the Canton River.'

'The Dragon's Mouth? Bruner's right — you *are* mad!'

'You do as you're told,' said Eli.

'The whole bloody convoy?' asked someone in disbelief.

'The whole convoy — all four thousand coolies.'

'*What*!' shouted Bruner, astonished.

'Do as the man says,' commanded Black Sam.

The following extract concerning the activities of Eli Boggs appeared in both the *Canton Register* and the *Eastern Globe* on September 15th:

Following the theft by piracy of stored opium from the premises of Messrs Smith and Wedderburn on Green Island, it is now reported that Eli Boggs, the pirate sought for the murder of Captain da Costa of the Portuguese Customs, yesterday attacked the same firm's convoy of three ships bound for Macao. Boggs successfully boarded and re-routed the entire convoy from its original destination and escorted it to the Chinese authorities in Canton. Here it successfully passed the Bogue Forts, which have so far deterred the British Navy, unchallenged, and docked at Whampoa, where four thousand coolies were returned to their homes.

The loss to Messrs Smith and Wedderburn (who had already paid the indentured labourers) is considerable, to say nothing of the debt incurred by the firm to the Macao brokers, who are now demanding compensation for breach of contract.

Accordingly, the price of shares in Smith and Wedderburn has dropped dramatically. So far it has not been possible to ascertain the pirates' motive for this unwholesome venture: whatever the motive, when apprehended, they will suffer the full penalty of the law.

Mr James Wedderburn, the director of the firm, declined to be interviewed on the subject.

37

At weekends, particularly after Sunday church, Milly and Mamie often took a trip by palanquin down to Ladder Street, not only to see the pirate loot being smuggled into the stalls there, but also to watch the worshippers in the great Man Ho Temple.

This temple, although not the oldest in Hong Kong, was ceratinly one of the most beautiful. It was dedicated to two gods: the King Emperor Man and the Holy King Emperor Kwan, deities who were worshipped as having the well-being of humans in their care. Therefore it was to this temple that worshippers often flocked to seek the solace of spiritual help.

It was at the Man Ho Temple that Milly had often seen Anna Fu Tan come to pray. Milly thought this rather strange, since Anna had claimed to be Catholic.

The day was bright, with just enough of a nip to put a dew-drop on a baby, said Mamie. Milly wondered if Anna Fu Tan might be in the Temple that day. But Anna was not to be seen, instead, her brother Yung, deep in a dedication of his soul, prostrated himself before the altar of Kwan, seeking spiritual help for the arduous task he was about to undertake – the exorcising of a devil from the soul of his sister.

'Grant me strength,' pleaded Yung. 'You who are the personification of righteousness, give me the courage to undertake this task.' Mamie, standing near with Milly, heard this prayer in Cantonese, which she understood well after her years in the Colony.

'He prays for courage, that young monk,' Mamie whispered.

'Are we intruding, being so near?' Milly asked.

The Master of the temple, hearing this, glided over. Leaning his bewhiskered face close to Milly's, he said in English, 'It is of small consequence, Daughter. That you should hear his prayer is part of his contrition. He is a novice from the great Po Lin monastery on Lantau Island.'

'But I know that island!'

'You know of Lantau and the Ming Dynasty temple, which is much older than this one? There the Precious Lotus monastery flourishes as happily today as it did three hundred years ago.'

'And this young monk is of that Order, you say?'

'Indeed, Daughter.' His shattered face, ancient with age, stared into Milly's in the half-light. 'He comes to pray for the soul of a beloved relative — one bewitched.'

'*Bewitched*?'

'Oh, my!' whispered Mamie. 'I don't feel so good. Let's get out of here.'

'No, I want to hear more,' said Milly.

But Mamie caught her elbow and hurried her outside into the sun. 'Bewitching sure puts the breeze up me, girl. Let's go! If I ever arrive back here it'll be too soon.'

The old Master watched them go — as did another. With tear-filled eyes Yung watched them also, not knowing that his destiny would soon be irrevocably linked with theirs.

In Milly's absence a very different ceremony was being conducted in the English Mansion up on Hong Kong Peak.

Anna No Name, dressed in white for purity, was positioned in a suitable window. In a gown that reached her feet, her eyes narrowed to the glaring light of early morning; she stood motionless, with the curtain held discreetly aside. Scarcely breathing, she watched the arrival of James's associates with her fox-like interest.

First, on horseback, came Dr Schofield. Splendid in riding breeches and frock coat, he dismounted from the fine black mare, tossed the reins to a waiting ostler, and walked to the mansion entrance as if he owned the place. 'Good morning, James,' he shouted. 'What's happened?'

'You'll soon know,' snapped James. 'Where's Goodchild?'

'Unless I'm mistaken, he's on his way,' said Schofield. 'But James you look dreadful. Are you going to ...' He broke off as Goodchild, the solicitor, arrived with Denning, the acting deputy to the new Governor, Sir John Bowring.

Goodchild approached with the air of a man who suspected the worst, even if it had not yet been officially confirmed; only Wedderburn having so far been appraised of the extent of the disaster. With the palanquins lowered, the two stepped out to be ushered into the inner sanctum of the drawing-room by Tang, the houseboy.

'I came the moment I could. For heaven's sake, what has happened?' said Goodchild apprehensively.

'This frightful business of the kidnapped coolies!' Denning replied.

'You knew of this, yet failed to give me the details?' Goodchild was outraged.

'I was trained as a diplomat,' Denning retorted, glaring resentfully at James. 'This is Wedderburn's privilege; I suggest he uses it to his best advantage.'

'I suggest he explains exactly what is happening!' exclaimed Schofield. 'Kidnapped coolies? Stop talking in riddles!'

'The game's up, gentlemen,' James said dully. 'We meet here to avoid the next step on the road to possible bankruptcy. The entire coolie convoy of four thousand men has been run off course by Eli Boggs, and deposited back on the Chinese mainland!'

Goodchild sank into his chair slowly, disbelief upon his face; vacantly, the others stared at James, dumbstruck.

'You can't mean it!' groaned the solicitor.

'Vanished! Pirated under our noses. By now the entire cargo will have returned on foot to their homes.'

'Four thousand lost? I don't believe it!' whispered Schofield.

'Read it in advance copies of the *Eastern Globe*, man – it'll be there for all to see in the morning. Or don't you read unpalatable news?'

248

'It will mean the end of my political career,' said Denning said flatly.

'To think that we actually persuaded Boggs to join the partnership!' Goodchild spat.

'Which emphasises the stupidity of mixing business with piracy,' said Denning bitterly.

'It's a nightmare!' whispered Schofield.

'It will be after the lawyers have done with us,' said Goodchild. 'How much have we lost?'

'Four thousand times fifty per head on the coolies alone,' James said, staring at the floor.

'Two hundred thousand dollars for a start,' calculated Denning.

'And that, I fear, is only the beginning,' James went on. 'Demurrage on three ships − for the Chinese will probably impound them − and loss of profit claims from the Macao brokers under breach of contract. There is also the matter of the destruction of Bruner's tug-boat.'

'Where is Bruner?'

'Bruner? Ask Boggs. There's a rumour that he landed him on Lantau.'

'Which is tantamount to holding him to ransom. Have you thought of that?'

'Of course I have. At this moment I wish I'd never set eyes on Hans Bruner.'

'What about the opium?' asked Denning. 'Bruner was going to cut us in on the sale.'

'That's in the past now,' sighed James.

'It won't be in the past when the new Governor hears of it,' said Denning.

'What do you mean by that?'

Glass in hand Denning cleared his throat. 'As you know, I'm staying on here for the next month as an official adviser − and I wish to God I hadn't agreed to do it. Bowring's a boot-faced puritan, crime and punishment are meat and drink to him.' He took a long draught of whisky. 'This couldn't have come at a worse moment. Time was we could have hushed it up and cut our losses, but now ...'

'Even if we take the losses four ways, like the profits, I

stand to lose over half a million Mexican dollars,' said Schofield. 'And I simply don't have it.'

'Then,' said James, 'you will simply have to find it. This isn't a game – I warned you at the outset of the risks.'

'Less than half that amount will ruin me,' said Denning.

'I could cover such a loss, of course, but with the utmost difficulty,' Goodchild murmured.

'So you, my wealthy friend,' Schofield said pointedly to James, 'will simply have to see us all through our present pecuniary difficulties.'

'Oh, no,' came the reply. 'That would not be possible. I could not afford it.'

'You cannot afford not to, sir,' said a voice, and Anna No Name entered the drawing-room.

She walked with the dignity of a medieval princess; when she spoke her voice had changed utterly.

'Gentlemen, only two of you know me, so let me introduce myself,' she said in Cantonese, 'I am Anna Fu Tan, Mr Wedderburn's housekeeper; some know me as Anna No Name. But remember this – it is in your interests that I have come.'

'Who is this?' asked Goodchild.

'We neither know nor care who you are, madam – this is a private meeting,' snapped Denning.

James rose in open-mouthed astonishment. 'Anna! Have you taken leave of your senses?'

In precise Cantonese she answered. 'For too long I have spoken hateful English in this house. Now I address you in my mother tongue, the dialect of the Pearl River.' She turned her attention to Denning. 'You speak Cantonese, so kindly translate what I have to say.'

'Get her out of here!' cried Schofield.

'Wait!' said James.

'She's your housekeeper, man! Where are your social graces?' Schofield was becoming choleric.

'I *was* the housekeeper,' corrected Anna, 'but not any more. So listen to what I have to say.' She paused, smiling. 'If I go, gentlemen, you're all financially ruined.'

Silence fell upon the room. James, for one, was rendered speechless. The woman before him was no longer the ingratiating servant whose convent manner evinced her absolute subservience. Even the way in which she held herself – a mixture of arrogance and disdain – demanded attention.

'I am aware of all your difficulties,' Anna went on, 'and I have certain remedies to offer.' She wandered over the big Peking carpet, smiling down at each in turn. 'It would appear that in promoting this coolie traffic, you have been using much of Mrs Wedderburn's fortune – money that is held in Trust.'

'Oh, no!' ejaculated Schofield, getting up. 'I refuse to listen to these lies.'

'Sit down, man!' James actually pushed him. 'Let her speak.'

Anna continued, 'But now events have overtaken you, have they not? Ever since Eli Boggs began to take an interest in your affairs.'

Nobody moved; even Schofield, his belligerence diminished, sat silently.

'Had it been possible to finance your coolie project from the partnership funds, all would have been well. But now your capital will have to be subsidised by Mrs Wedderburn's, which will entail fraud. Isn't it true that her fortune has soon to be paid into her account?'

There was no reply.

'Am I not correct, Mr Goodchild?' Anna repeated.

'You may be,' muttered the solicitor.

It was as if, thought James, staring up at her, she had been replaced by a mandarin from a distant past: possessed, suddenly and inexplicably, of an intelligence that was not her own, but another's. The effect upon him was almost hypnotic, as if he were in the presence of something supernatural.

Anna went on. 'The coolies are already lost to you; China has them and you will never get them back. Boggs holds Bruner on Lantau. You are heavily in debt to the ship-owners, the insurance companies, and to the Macao brokers, they who control the Triads who enforce payment of debt. Then there are the casks of opium, the holding of which is a crime under Chinese law.' A slow smile

251

spread over Anna's face. 'In fact, you are in a hopeless position.'

'And you, I suppose,' interrupted Schofield, 'have the solution to all our problems!'

'Yes,' replied Anna.

'You, a mere housekeeper, can solve what experienced merchants and men of education cannot!' He laughed falsely, slapping his thigh.

'Sir, I am no housekeeper.' Anna's eyes danced.

Schofield glared at James. 'Have you enjoyed a liaison with this woman?'

James shifted uncomfortably, eyed by the others.

'It appears that you've made a damned fool of yourself,' said Denning abruptly, 'but it's no concern of ours.' He turned to Anna. 'So what have you to offer?'

She rose, looking regal. 'Your fate is in the hands of Eli Boggs, who has outwitted you. But I, and only I, control Boggs's fate. If I raise a finger, he will be arrested.'

'We've already put out a warrant for his arrest,' snapped Goodchild.

'Yes – but only for piracy. And piracy carries no death penalty. Yet if you trust me, Eli Boggs will be executed.'

'Don't be ridiculous! People only hang for murder in this colony.'

'And that will be the charge!'

'Who has he murdered?' Schofield cried.

'Captain da Costa.'

'Who?' asked Goodchild.

James explained. 'She persists in this allegation and says she has the proof. Until now, I had not believed her.'

Goodchild rose slowly to his feet. 'If that's true it puts a different complexion on things. You refer to the Portuguese Customs Officer?'

'The one who's been missing for weeks,' said James flatly.

'Get Boggs on a capital charge and everything else becomes irrelevant,' Goodchild mused. 'But that doesn't solve our present predicament.'

'But it does,' said Anna. 'And if you want Mrs Wedderburn's money you can have it, for I can also

252

give proof of her completely irrational state.' She faced James. 'Are you aware that she is carrying on an adulterous liaison with Boggs?'

'I know she admires him — but ...' muttered James, startled.

'For the crime of adultery in old China, she would be carried down to the river in a pig basket, and all her worldly possessions distributed among her relatives.'

There was no sound in the room but the ticking of a clock on the mantelpiece.

James was first to break the silence. 'You have proof of this, you say?'

'To the satisfaction of any court of law.'

'If this really is so, your wife is certainly in a very delicate position, James,' Goodchild said. 'Should we not examine her mental state once more?'

'Immediately, I suggest,' said Dr Schofield.

'And how do you personally, Miss Fu Tan, profit from the demise of Mrs Wedderburn?' Denning asked, with deceptive charm.

Anna moved slowly to the door. 'I want the head of Eli Boggs. For personal reasons. I also intend to become mistress here as a wife, not as a concubine. The removal of Mrs Wedderburn can easily be arranged. Indeed, on the evidence I can supply, she could be transported back to England in a straitjacket; something which Dr Schofield would no doubt, be delighted to arrange.'

38

'I think,' announced Milly, 'that Mamie and I would like to spend a few days at Macao once more.'

Anna, in the process of serving breakfast from a sideboard, froze.

'Nothing much happens here at this time of year,' Milly added. 'And it's still so appallingly hot ...'

'It's possibly hotter in Macao than here − but if you insist, my darling.' James smiled with forced sweetness.

The sarcasm was lost on Mamie, but not on Milly. 'It's the sea-trip I go for,' she went on, obstinately. 'To sit in a deck-chair and go rolling along over the South China Sea is my idea of unbridled pleasure.'

Mamie, now dining with them on Milly's insistence, rolled her eyes to the ceiling. 'I recalls when your pa was alive. He spent more time in Macao than ever he did in Hong Kong.'

'That was because he preferred the Beca de Roza girls to little Cantonese whores,' sneered James brutally. 'It had nothing to do with the climate.'

'That's as may be, Mr Wedderburn,' said Mamie, 'but he were a wonderful man.'

'One who spawned a particularly difficult daughter,' came the reply; 'someone who is welcome to go to Macao or any other damned place just as soon as she likes.'

'I do appreciate your kindness, my darling,' said Milly. 'Are we not a model of conjugal love?' Turning to Mamie, she said, 'We must hurry. The Macao ferry leaves at ten.'

Anna No Name turned from the sideboard and gave

254

James a meaningful look, which he returned with a wink.

Later, in bed, Anna said to James, 'You're aware, I suppose, that they're going nowhere near Macao, but to Green Island?'

'Don't be ridiculous!' James sat up angrily.

Reaching up, she drew him down to her. 'For Eli Boggs, you see, has run the blockade of the Dragon's Mouth and is at this very moment, sailing for the Green Island Rest House.'

'Look, how can that be?' James said testily. 'The Navy's got him trapped in the estuary; his junks are pinned down under the guns of the Bogue forts and two British frigates are astride him.'

'He has slipped through their blockade.'

'But only last night the Governor's office reported that they had him cornered.'

'You don't know Eli Boggs.' And Anna, drawing him closer, covered his face with kisses.

But James was not to be deterred from his purpose. Spiritedly, he pushed her away. 'What proof have you that Boggs has escaped the net?'

'Come with me tonight to Green Island and watch him row ashore from the *Ma Shan* in darkness, to keep an assignation with your wife.'

James laughed. 'We'll have to move to catch the pair of 'em — Macao's fifty miles west!'

'My friend, how foolish you are!' admonished Anna. 'They are both on their way now in the steam pinnace to Green Island, I tell you! And if you doubt this, I suggest we go to the Rest House on Green Island and see for ourselves.'

'They wouldn't dare!'

'I am afraid it is all true. While you think Mamie and Mrs Wedderburn are in Macao, they are secretly meeting Boggs and his black friend.'

James, naked, jumped out of the bed. 'I'll get the Marine Office on to it at once!'

Anna smiled. 'Do that! No doubt your Deputy Governor will be very interested.'

255

'What do you mean by that?'

Anna shrugged. 'While the Navy is searching for Boggs he has escaped from under their noses. There will be some red faces in the Marine Office tomorrow — and the reddest will be yours, if you start inquiries.'

'Then what do you suggest I do?'

'Just as I instruct you,' said Anna. Getting out of bed she stretched her slim limbs with feline grace. 'Forget your Marine Office. Contact the Navy by semaphore and bring one of their frigates round to Green Island. Order it to send a boat ashore with ten armed marines to arrest Boggs and his crew. And bring your wife and her servant back here under escort.'

'Arrest my wife? It would be the scandal of the colony!'

Anna shrugged. 'Does it matter? She is mentally unstable! Everyone will understand how difficult it has been for you to tolerate her. Pour disgrace on her head — but do it before her money runs out!'

'It has already run out,' replied James dolefully. 'I used it to pay the Company debts.'

'That is a little unfortunate ... This new Governor is made apoplectic by the mere thought of fraud and corruption — the Island is rife with it, he says. But think how delighted he would be if you, James Wedderburn, managed to bring Eli Boggs back to Hong Kong in irons to stand trial!'

James regarded her with interest. 'You know,' he said softly, 'you are the complete enigma, Anna. One could be forgiven for believing that you have second sight — that you are somehow *possessed*. Possessed of an uncanny ability to predict the future. You are sometimes a totally different person to the one I engaged to run this house.'

'I am not enamoured of the word "possessed".'

'I'm going to look a fool if it turns out that Milly and Mamie are over on Macao, and Boggs is still bottled up on the Pearl River delta,' said James ruefully.

'That's the chance you take. Either you choose Milly — or you choose me.'

And James fell silent.

256

39

Eli the Locust, as the Chinese called him — like the locust he had the ability to travel rapidly from one place to another, devouring all in his path — turned the prow of his lead-junk south for Hong Kong, after taking his leave of the Chinese port authorities.

Earlier, through astute use of flag-semaphore, he had obtained official Chinese permission to take his coolie convoy of three ships under the noses of the cannon on the Bogue Forts, with which Imperial China protected the vulnerable estuary serving Canton, to land his coolies at Whampoa Docks.

There, joyful at their release from what they had realised was bond-slavery, each with James Wedderburn's fifty dollars in his pocket (a fortune to a rice-field farmer), they had flooded back to their village homes, there to convey to excited families their escape from a living hell. Many were leg-ironed and manacled; local blacksmiths were commanded to strike these off, leaving them free men.

Eli, presenting his credentials to the Chinese Governor General, Two Kwang, bowed to the throne and promptly moved out again before anyone changed their minds.

Sufficient for the day was the evil thereof: this was Eli's creed. Having successfully bankrupted Smith and Wedderburn and returned their slaves to their villages, he had reason to feel moderately pleased with himself, believing he had earned a peaceful sojourn in the arms of his true love on Green Island.

'You have alerted the Navy?' asked Anna.

'They are under orders to sail for Green Island under cover of darkness,' James replied. 'It is all arranged.'

'And a British frigate will lie off-shore beyond telescope range?'

'There is no moon; she will remain hidden until the landing.'

'The armed marines, what of them?'

'Ten marines will row ashore at midnight and surround the Rest House. It is all as you suggested, Anna. But what if you are mistaken, and my wife and Mamie are in Macao?'

'It will not be so,' said Anna. 'I swear it on my ancestors. These people have to be eliminated; Boggs by hanging and your wife by medical opinion.'

'Proving that she is mentally deranged and consorting with pirates will not make you Mistress here,' James ventured carefully. 'Only her death would grant you that.'

Anna recoiled like a wounded animal. 'You are suggesting *murder*?'

'What else? Already rumours are growing about our own relationship. Servants do chatter ... Never would you be accepted as mistress in my house if we did not marry. All you could be is a concubine if Milly stays alive.'

'And were she to die – say at the moment of capture ...'

James considered it. 'It could be so arranged. Perhaps an over-zealous marine during the arrest?'

'No,' said Anna. 'The coincidence would be too great. Not only have we a morality-crazed Governor in Sir John Bowring, but a fearsome advocate of British justice in Major Caine, the Prosecuting Counsel. If your wife is to die before Eli comes to trial, let it be arranged carefully, not by the blunderings of a frightened soldier.'

'I suspect that you have a plan,' James said. In the light of a dim moon, he regarded her. The scent that pervaded her presence was accompanied by an inexplicable sense of evil, which until now he had failed to comprehend.

'I would rather be your friend than your enemy,' he said.

He did not see her smile in the darkness.

'The frigate is coming,' called a nearby soldier, James seized a telescope and looked seaward where a quick blaze of the moon raised a masthead out of the layering sea mist. On high ground, James, Anna and two soldiers watched as, coming inshore, the frigate lowered a quiet anchor. A boat swung out amidships from her black hull, its muffled oars glinting from the dark.

'Ten marines, eh?' a soldier said, chuckling, 'This pirate must be God Almighty.'

'He is Eli Boggs,' said Anna. 'Ten may not be enough.'

Out of sight of the Rest House the boat grounded sand and the attacking marines waded ashore.

Within the Rest House Milly and Eli, abed, were sleeping in the peace that comes to spent lovers; in their world existed no sound save rhythmic breathing, and the distant crashing of the breakers along a dim-lit shore.

East of the Rest House Black Sam and Mamie wandered hand in hand in the shallows of the incoming tide. They did not speak, for to talk at such a time, with the moon blazing overhead, and the night cool, seemed superfluous. It was enough that they were together.

'Always, when we come this way, we finish up at the grave of Rastus,' Black Sam said, breaking the silence eventually. 'I tells you, missus, although he's in the right place by ma reckonin', Ah still get that fella rolled, boned an' punched.'

'That ain't fair, Sam,' replied Mamie. 'If you'se got a pair o' soled and heeled shoes half worn, does you cast them off and buy others?'

'Then I reckon you should have worn that feller out a'fore you started on me,' said Sam intolerantly.

Mamie raised her eyes to the moon in mock despair. 'In the village in Carolina where I comes from, us girls always worked it so we had one man on the go and another in reserve. And ain't that the same with old men like you?'

'It ain't. Since I met you I'm a one-woman feller; though I bounced around a bit in the past.'

'Hush your mouth,' whispered Mamie. 'What was that?'

259

They stood still, listening to the screeching of a night owl; then came distant whispers.

'We ain't alone.'

'Seems not,' said Sam, listening intently.

'Oh, come,' exclaimed Mamie, 'it's nothin'. Let's get goin' back to that ole Rest House.'

'You ever reckon on travellin' again?' asked Sam as they walked back.

'No, sir,' said Mamie. 'I done enough travellin' for the rest of ma life.'

'You ain't gone no place yet, girl – only as far as Hong Kong, comin' from England. No, I means travellin' to the end of the world.'

'You needs your head examined, Black Sam!'

'I sure do, for getting myself mixed up with a woman like you, when I could have had the pick o' the fillies down that new Wanchai.'

'Pick half a dozen! I don't care!'

'If I stay all ma time with you, Mamie Malumba, I can see myself in a monastery – and that's a mite strange, seein' that I'm supposed to be a pirate.'

'But you ain't a pirate no more, Sam. I made you respectable.'

'Being respectable sure goes against the grain, though. Especially churchin' around here for the rest of ma life. Like Eli says, I'm all for travellin'.'

'Where to, for heaven's sake?' asked Mamie.

'Down south to the Philippines: buy a sardine boat and swarm out the nets for sprats and lobsters, and sell 'em in the market for two dimes a throw. How does that suit you?'

'Not for me, Black Sam. I'm a land-lubber!'

'And so, we go our different ways, do we?'

'I ain't travellin' no more.'

'You're sure one opinionated lady, Malumba.'

'I ain't, Sam. I'm bleedin' inside already at the thought of losing you, for I'll love you to everlasting. But you ain't gettin' me castin' nets for the miracle o' little fishes – I's built for comfort.'

Sam's head was cocked once more, intent; they stopped, their bare feet splayed in the sand.

'You got cockroaches in the brain,' said Mamie. 'It ain't nothin' but little sea-shrimps a'callin'. Come on!' And she hauled him along.

'Somethin's wrong,' said Sam. 'I feel it in ma soul.'

'You never had a soul before I saved it,' said Mamie. 'These terrible imaginings come because you got a guilty conscience. Not like ma Rastus — he had a soul like a raiment of fire.'

'I wonder he didn't set himself alight,' said Sam.

They wandered on, their bare feet splashing through the shallows. And James, from a hill, fixed them in the circle of his telescope glass.

'That's two of them,' he said.

At two o'clock in the morning Milly awoke. Going to the bedroom window in the Rest House, she looked down on to a beach emblazoned by the full moon.

Nothing stirred within a panorama of sea, land and sky. The moonlight had its usual hypnotic effect upon her and she stood bemused, confounded by its light.

At times such as this, her imagination often conjured up images of dead Tom Ellery; and childhood visions of the mask of a fox, teeth bared and dripping blood: a dead vixen at the moment of its beheading. But tonight held nothing of nightmares; not even dreams.

Beyond her lay Eli, asleep within a tangle of bedclothes. Earlier he had been both bold and beguiling but nothing it appeared, could now stir him from his slumbers. His was the strength which had overcome the weakness of his frailer lover; yet he was defeated now.

Milly smiled. With this man I could travel the Universe, she thought, face hunger, cold, scorch in the heat of the sun. With Eli Boggs she could share her life.

There came to Milly then the words of a poem from her schooldays; its words seemed to sound within the room, like the tolling of a distant bell:

If you should leave me, I would not die, or make
grief a trumpet to shatter the sky ...

261

Returning to the bed, she sat and contemplated the man before her, his face dark against the whiteness of the pillow. Other women had been his; this she knew. And soon he would awake and reach for her; but he had done this before with many women before she had entered his life. Would he, she wondered, one day discard her as he had discarded the others?

Moonlight from the latticed window fell full upon Eli's sleeping face. He was, thought Milly, extraordinarily handsome. Surely she had no possible right, she thought, to possess such a lover, save in the fruitless dreams of a plain woman. But reality had transcended the dream, and such a man was here beside her. The knowledge of this further chastened her spirit, and Milly faltered, knowing that she had so little to offer. James, during his vain attempts at love-making, had branded her with the responsibility of his failure, and this had rankled deeply. Had he not cruelly taunted her with her failure as a woman? 'I must have been mad to cart you over from the other end of the earth, when I could have had my pick of a dozen English fillies.' And he had turned his back upon her, leaving her staring into the dark. How wonderful it would be, Milly thought, to awake one morning, look in the mirror, and see there a woman of astonishing beauty.

Yet, Milly thought, had not Tom Ellery found her beautiful? And Eli? Surely character and an inner beauty counted for something when it came to male assessment.

Suddenly, as if disturbed by her inner misery, Eli awoke. Turning to her, he smiled, and put out his hand.

'Hello, my beauty!' he said.

His rejection Milly could have borne, but his kindness overwhelmed her and she wept.

'You could not sleep?' he asked, leaving the bed and coming to hold her.

'I slept, but dreamed that you had left me!'

'But now you are awake. And I am still here.'

She stood within his embrace, lost in the rhythm of their breathing, feeling completely at one with him. Then she spoke:

262

'You realise, don't you, that the next few days could see
the end of us?'

'Why?'

'Because everything is against us now, Eli.'

Instantly he was the brash adventurer. 'So what do we
do about it?' He moved restlessly. 'Soon you'll start talking
about paying a debt to society, and all that bunkum ...'

'You've stolen their money. You can insult them, threaten
their families, but you must *not* steal their money — for that
they will burn you alive.'

'Who would dare?'

'James, Schofield, and the rest of them.'

This stilled him, and he said, quieter, 'Aye, they'll try,
and that's for sure — like Sam said, we only got out of the
Dragon's Mouth by the skin of our feet, for they called in
the British navy! So what am I supposed to do?'

'Go, while you're still in one piece.'

'You're a hard woman, Milly.'

'I am being realistic and so should you! Go tonight — now,
if necessary, or they will take you from me for good.'

'And leave you behind?'

'It is the only way I can think to keep you safe.'

'Where to?'

'Anywhere away from this accursed place!'

'You're thinking for the pair of us, that's for sure,'
he said. 'But if I'm going to cut and run for it, you're
coming too.'

'Where?' said Milly.

'Down south to Manilla and the Carolines — to Siam and
Indo-China. There's a big new world awaitin' us along the
coasts of Australasia. And we'll settle on the beach in a
mud hut and laze all day in the sun, and make love!'

'You can't mean it!' Excitement was gripping her at the
thought of escape.

'If I don't mean it now, I never will, for I've been planning
it from the moment I set eyes on you.'

Out of the corners of her eyes Milly saw something
move along the tree-fringed shore below. Then she
saw the movement again — the tiny figure of a
man moving swiftly against the yellow sand in a

darting, swerving run. Feeling Milly stiffen, Eli released her.

'What is it?'

Instantly, she drew him away from the window. 'Down there! Look! Someone is coming!'

'Probably Sam and Mamie.'

'No, not them. Look — men running!'

There were two figures now, scrambling free of the dunes, racing for the shelter of nearby trees.

'Wait here!' said Eli, in the moment before it happened.

The door of the bedroom burst open and crashed back upon its hinges. A man barged in — a red-breasted soldier who tripped and fell, sliding towards them over the carpet, followed by another, big and burly, his brass helmet flashing in the moonlight. Eli stepped in and got him with a right to the throat. Now came a third, who caught Milly up and swung her to the floor, while a fourth, his arms outflung, fell upon Eli and wrestled him over the bed.

The room was filled with clattering, cursing soldiers, Eli fighting them off. Milly was screaming, her cries piercing the shouts and bawled commands as an officer came next: big and brawny his cutlass drawn, his bulk filling the doorway as the two of them were dragged to their feet.

'Go easy on the woman, Sergeant. But punish that big one if he wags his tongue!'

Unceremoniously, with the bedroom in disorder, Milly and Eli were bundled through the door and down to the beach.

'You hearin' things again?' asked Mamie.

'They's a comin',' said Black Sam, grabbing her round the waist and pulling her into the shadows of couch-grass. There, with his great strength, he lifted her bodily and laid her down on the sand.

'What you up to, Black Sam?' Mamie cried, breathless and startled.

'Hush you, woman!'

'Loose me!' Her voice rose.

'I said hush!'

Too late.

In silence, save for the crunching of their boots in sand, the soldiers surrounded them. Black Sam stared up into a circle of their levelled muskets. Slowly, he rose, pulling Mamie to her feet; they stood, the pair of them, within a closing circle of bayonets.

Sam cupped his hands to his mouth and yelled at the top of his lungs: 'Eli! Eli! Run for it, run for it!'

But the thunder of the incoming tide drowned the warning, and it was the last sound he made before a marine stepped closer, raised a musket-butt, and struck him down from behind. Mamie, recovering, stared momentarily at Sam's prostrate body, then attacked them, shrieking, kicking, swinging with clenched fists – until another musket blow felled her and she lay silent beside him.

'Get stretchers from the boat,' commanded a sergeant.

And a little column of men, with stretcher-bearers staggering under the weight, went from the sand dunes and into the grounds of the Rest House.

40

Hitherto, from the commencement of the Colony in 1841 until recently, the only Court of Justice had been that held by the Governor himself and his Chief Superintendent of Trade. Now, however, a Court of Judicature had been established and large crowds had gathered outside the new Supreme Court Building, on the corner of Queen's Road and Pedder, for the trial of Eli Boggs, accused of murder, piracy and abduction; charges sufficient to quail the bravest heart.

Meanwhile, Hans Bruner, one of Eli's witnesses, had been last seen making his escape to the sea, and Black Sam, said an infuriated Mamie, had gone in pursuit of him, something that should have been undertaken by the police, said she. Rumour now swept the Colony: from respected members of the Hong Kong Club down to coolies in the alleys of Kowloon, bets were being laid as to the nature of Eli's sentence: with the feared Public Prosecutor, Major Caine seeking a guilty verdict, death by hanging appeared inevitable.

The Court Room of Hong Kong's Magistracy was now hushed. Expecting a scar-faced brute of terrifying demeanor to emerge from the cells below, the people in the well of the Court allowed themselves a universal gasp as Eli, handsome and impeccably attired in a white shirt and knee-length trews, was brought up between two warders: bowing to the Court, he took his position in the dock.

Milly and Mamie, sitting side by side, were expressionless, save for Milly's ghost of a greeting smile. Anna Fu Tan (lately Anna No Name), dressed in bright red, took a seat by the wall

266

and allowed herself a satisfied glance at the condemned man. If Eli noticed any of them, he showed it not at all.

Next the jury filed into the Court: specifically chosen, according to the newspapers, for their lack of interest in the opium trade or links with the Colony's criminal element. All of them had been interrogated to uncover possible dealings with the Triads, which had tentacles in most of Hong Kong's outrageous financial deals. They were mostly Europeans, with the exception of a few Macanese among them, but none were Chinese: a white man, even a pirate, being entitled to trial by his compatriots. (Around the time of the trial a notice board had been erected in a Shanghai park: 'No Dogs or Chinese allowed'.)

'Please stand!' commanded the Clerk of the Court.

Entering in legal robes the prosecutor, Major Caine, was followed by Justice Hulme. Sir John Bowring, the present Governor, came last; all took their places with appropriate dignity. The clattering of entries ceased.

Silence. The only sound was the musical buzzing of a blue-bottle against a courtroom window. Sweating copiously, the people sat in silence as, in a stentorian voice, the Clerk of the Court announced: 'Hereafter the trial of Elias Boggs on charges of opium-dealing, abduction and piracy,' — all of which, individually and collectively, could warrant the death sentence.

Not a muscle stirred in Eli's face.

Major Caine, tall, angular and hawk-like, approached the dock. He raised a sharp-nosed face to Eli.

'Prisoner in the dock, state your name.'

'Elias Boggs.'

'You are an American citizen, are you not?'

'Yes, sir.'

'By birth?'

'By birth. My family came from Baltimore.'

Caine said thinly, 'You intend, I understand, to defend yourself. Is this correct?'

'It is.'

'A Defence Counsel is available. You are aware of this?'

'I'll defend myself.'

267

Caine gazed at him quizzically. Then, 'For how long have you lived in China?'

'Ever since I can remember.'

'What is your profession?'

'Piracy.'

To Eli it appeared that he had said nothing out of the ordinary; but James, seated beside Milly, leaned back in his chair with a satisfied expression and the people in the courtroom audibly gasped.

'You confess to the charge of piracy?' asked Caine.

'I do.'

'You appreciate the significance of your statement?'

Eli nodded nonchalantly.

'Please answer my question!'

'I realise its importance.'

'How then do you plead to the charges of murder and abduction?'

'Not guilty.'

'What is your age?'

'Thirty years.'

'For how long have you been engaged in piracy?'

'Since I was eighteen.'

'And before that?'

'Before that I was employed in the Marine Superintendent's office in Canton, where I learned the profession.'

'Explain that!' And Eli answered.

'Most employed there were also engaged in piracy. The same is true of the employees in the Marine Office in this Colony.'

A ripple of laughter went round the Court.

'The levity may suit you now, Boggs; later it may prove a disservice, so do not be facetious,' Caine snapped, his face sour. 'What may have happened under Chinese administration does not occur in this Colony — of this be assured.' And he glared around the Court.

'Oh, but it does!' said Eli cheekily. 'Things are no cleaner here than in Canton.'

There was open laughter now, with people elbowing each other on the public benches. 'Turn your situation into a comedy, Boggs, and do so at your own expense, but do not make too much of it,' Caine said coldly. 'You stand accused of the murder of Captain da Costa, lately of the Ceylon Rifles, but attached, at the time of his death, to the Portuguese Customs Office. How do you plead?'

'Not guilty.'

'That, my friend, remains to be seen, for I believe you are lying.'

'Perhaps,' retorted Eli. 'But that is for the jury to assess, and you have no right to coerce them with unsubstantiated remarks!'

'That was hardly my intention!'

Governor Bowring's controlled tones suddenly dominated the whispering of the room. 'Do make the point concisely, Major Caine, or we will be here all night. In the interim,' and here he turned his face to Eli, 'while it is excellent to be entertained, this is neither the time nor the place, as you will discover. Please continue.'

'You are the owner of what is known as the Gunpowder Factory, located near the village of Stanley?'

'I am,' answered Eli.

'One you recently purchased from a man called Papa Tai, a Chinese *compradore* of Stanley Village?'

'Aye.'

'After you paid the agreed price, this villager handed to you the key of the factory, and you held it in your possession?'

'Yes.'

'For what purpose did you use this establishment?'

'To make gunpowder.'

'To whom did you sell the gunpowder?'

Eli shrugged. 'Various clients.'

'And among your clients were fellow pirates?'

'Yes.'

'You are talking of armed pirate junks, are you not?'

'That's right. Junks carrying cannon.'

'For use against unarmed merchantmen sailing these waters, intent upon their lawful business?

'You've got to use cannon shots to slow 'em down, sir.'

'A shot across their bows, you mean?'

269

Eli nodded. Caine asked. 'Did the port authorities know the whereabouts of your illegal factory?'

'They do now − since they found the captain's body inside it!'

'Until then its location was a closely guarded secret, was it not?'

'Yes.'

'Its existence was against the law?'

'Yes.'

'Then how was the unfortunate captain able to find it?'

Eli looked non-committal.

'Shall I inform you?' asked Caine.

'No doubt you will.'

The Prosecutor took a deep breath. 'It would appear that he was lured to it, and, when safely within it, was locked inside to die a slow and agonising death by hunger. You committed this vile crime, did you not?'

'It's the first I've heard of it,' replied Eli.

'But not the first time you've heard the name of da Costa!'

'The first I've heard that I lured him to his death.'

'If not you, Boggs, who else?'

'If I knew I wouldn't be here,' said Eli.

Caine held up the factory key. 'Is this the key of your Gunpowder Factory?'

Eli took it and turned it over in his hands. 'It is. How did you get hold of it?' and Caine replied, 'It is a copy of one sent to our Magistracy by an unknown person.'

Turning, Eli looked at Anna, who calmly met his eyes.

'You are unaware who sent it to us?' asked Caine.

'I've got a fair idea.'

'What do you mean by that?'

No reply.

'I suggest,' said the Prosecutor, 'that someone of your own kind sent the key to the Magistracy, complete with instructions giving the location of the factory. The man who has absconded − your confederate − Black Sam, perhaps?'

'Not in a thousand years!' Eli said indignantly.

'Where did you keep the factory key when you had it?'

'In a cabin aboard my junk.'

270

'Now you will tell me that it was stolen from you!'
'Yes.'
'You expect me to believe that?'
'It's the truth.'
'A key, stolen from the cabin of your pirate junk, was used to cause the death of da Costa – am I hearing this correctly?'
'Yes,' answered Eli.
'And presumably the thief who stole it from you then sent it to our Magistracy.'
'Of course.'
'Why?'
'So that I'd be accused of killing da Costa.'
'Could not the man known as Black Sam, your trusted lieutenant, be the one who sent the key? I ask this again.'
'Impossible!'
'Not that impossible, believe me. I put it to the Court that your friendly villain is not so trustworthy as you would have us believe. Might he not have done this as an act of revenge? Come, tell the truth. Let me remind you that you are under oath. You quarrelled perhaps – probably over a woman.'
Eli shook his head.
'Is it not true that many women of low caste were known to have visited your junk? The girls of the Beca de Roza in Macao, for instance?'
'Not recently.'
'How recently, then, did such a harlot visit you?'
'Just before da Costa's murder.'
'You could identify this woman?'
'Yes.'
'Where is she now? In Macao?'
'She is in this Court.'
'In here, at this moment?' Caine was astonished; the jurors shifted with disbelief.
'Yes,' replied Eli. 'Sitting over there.' He pointed.
'Then identify her!'
'The woman who is sitting near the wall, in the red dress.'
'You are certain of her identity?'
'Quite certain.'

271

All heads craned in Anna's direction.

James rose. 'Governor Bowring, this is outrageous!' he said testily. 'The person identified is my housekeeper, a woman of the highest propriety. I protest most vigorously!'

'The lady in the red dress. Kindly stand, madam.'

Coolly, Anna rose to her feet.

'You know the prisoner in the dock?' Caine asked.

'I do not.'

'You are Mr Wedderburn's housekeeper. Have you ever had dealings with the prisoner at any time — before your employment with Mr Wedderburn?'

'I have never set eyes on the man in my life until now.'

'You are quite certain of this? Please be certain, madam, for soon you may be under oath.'

'Quite certain!'

James cried, his face flushed. 'Really, sir, this is an appalling situation! This servant is convent trained and has the highest possible references.'

'Please sit down, Mr Wedderburn,' commanded Caine. 'The prisoner is conducting his own defence and has a right to call witnesses.' He turned to Eli. 'Do you wish to call this lady in your defence?'

'Not at the moment.'

'When, then?'

'Later. When I have more evidence.'

Caine looked troubled. 'I sincerely hope such evidence pertains to the case!'

'Let him be given the benefit of the doubt, Prosecutor!' suddenly interjected the Judge. 'Meanwhile,' and here he addressed Anna, 'kindly be seated, madam. You have heard the prisoner's accusation. True or false, he must be given the opportunity to call and cross-examine you, should he think it necessary. To this end, please give your name to the Clerk of the Court before you leave this evening, and oblige the Court by making yourself further available during the process of the trial.'

Anna flashed an unhappy glance at James, and sat.

'I'll say one thing for this feller of yours,' whispered Mamie, 'he sure gets around.'

'But he doesn't even know Anna Fu Tan!' said Milly.

'Are you sure, honey?' replied Mamie. 'I reckon he never went short of women 'afore he met you — and don't you tell me it was only their cookin'.'

'The heat in this place is appalling,' the Prosecutor said suddenly. 'I ask Justice Hulme if he will agree to a recess until the comparative coolness of late afternoon.' Caine raised his eyes to the bench, pleading.

'Approved,' said Justice Hulme. 'This Court is in recess until the hour of six o'clock this evening.'

Amid the hubbub of scraping chairs and the confusion of people rising to leave, James leaned over. 'I hear that the absent Black Sam is indicted, too, eh? When thieves fall out, just men get their dues.'

'That's just what I was thinking,' said Milly.

Later, Milly said to Mamie, 'If your Sam doesn't come home to roost soon, he's going to be in more trouble than Eli.'

'Don't you worry, girl. When he arrives he'll have that Bruner with him.'

'Have you any idea where Bruner is?'

'Somewhere on Lantau, accordin' to Sam, but I wouldn't want to be in that German's shoes when ole Sam collars him. "I'm havin' the skin off that hooligan when I catches up with him," said he.'

'Let's hope so,' replied Milly. 'Major Caine will have the skins of the pair of them if he doesn't.'

'Honey, you leave it to Black Sam,' said Mamie.

41

The following is an extract from the *Canton Register* newspaper:

The trial of the American Eli Boggs for murder, abduction and piracy came to a halt today when the opening session was postponed by Justice Hulme on account of the excessive heat. The advent of Typhoon Ruby further delayed the trial, and it is anticipated that the legal procedure will not resume until Thursday at the earliest.

The opening of the trial was enlivened by the prisoner's allegation that Miss Anna Fu Tan, at present in service to the Wedderburns, was, at a previous date, his mistress: a statement which sufficiently infuriated Mr James Wedderburn, Head of the Marine Department, to bring him to his feet in defence of his housekeeper. Nevertheless, Justice Hulme instructed Miss Fu Tan to make herself available should the accused later require to call her in his defence, which he himself is conducting.

What was initially the trial of just another pirate has resolved itself into one of important local interest, and it is probable that the trial location will, upon resumption, be removed to chambers large enough to accommodate increased public attendance.

Certainly this reporter will be present to provide a detailed day by day analysis.'

'Call Miss Ann Fu Tan!' The voice of the Clerk of the Court echoed round the larger hall.

'I think this is iniquitous!' whispered Milly. 'For once James is right! I can't think what Eli is up to!'

Mamie gave a secret smile. 'Reckon he knows his own business better'n we do. Still waters run deep. Like I said, when a gal's face shines, look behind her ears.'

A glance from an usher silenced them; Anna's footsteps echoed on the mosaic as she took her place at the witness stand.

Eli, in jocular mood, asked smilingly: 'Your name is Anna Fu Tan?'

Anna's face, pale and strained, was cast down, her eyes reddened by earlier tears. She nodded.

'But that is not your real name, is it?'

The girl raised her head at this: a pulse in her temple was beating violently. Eli said:

'Your real name is Anna No Name, is it not?' Eli said. 'You were so called by your parents because you were a foundling. Is that correct?'

Anna, almost imperceptibly, nodded again.

'What is your nationality?'

'Chinese.'

'But you are not Chinese, Anna No Name. You are a Moslem. You told me your history in detail.'

'Boggs, this line of questioning is likely to keep us here until the next typhoon,' Justice Hulme said coldly. 'Restrict yourself to relevant facts; we are not concerned with assumed names or nationality.'

'My reasons will be made clear later,' said Eli, and he turned to Anna once more. 'You say that you have never set eyes on me before yesterday; those were your exact words. Please repeat them now, under oath.'

'I have never seen you until yesterday,' said Anna.

'And you deny that you practised as a Mist and Flower girl working among the sampan dwellers of Stanley?'

Anna's eyes brimmed with tears. Lowering her head she pressed her fist against her mouth, as if to stifle the indignity.

Justice Hulme's words cut icily into her sobbing. 'Please answer the question, Miss Fu Tan. Meanwhile, try to compose yourself; sit if you care to.'

275

Hunched and weeping bitterly, Anna said: 'It is terrible that I should be accused of such immorality! I, who was born into a reverent Taoist house, and raised by the nuns of the Catholic Mission School of Fu Tan!'

'You are a Catholic, Miss Fu Tan?' asked Major Caine.

Anna raised her tear-stained face to the light. 'Daily, morning and night, I pray to Christ the King in the manner in which I was taught. Every Sunday I receive the Holy Sacrament. How can you allow this criminal to blacken my name before all these people?'

'Prisoner at the bar, plainly you have distressed this witness,' Justice Hulme said, frowning. 'Your allegations of immorality are certainly not acceptable to the court. I myself am inclined to believe this to be a case of mistaken identity.'

'One never mistakes the identity of a woman who shares your bed!' said Eli. 'And if Black Sam were here, he'd give the proof of it!'

Major Caine said angrily, 'But your confederate, this Black Sam, has absconded from justice at a time when you need him most! There exists absolutely no proof that Miss Fu Tan was anywhere near your junk, let alone aboard it.' Caine smoothed his robes with slow, ponderous hands. 'The fact is, my friend, that having shared your licentious bed with so many, you now find it difficult to differentiate between virtue and immorality.' He turned to Anna. 'Kindly regain your seat, Miss Fu Tan; let the record show that you leave the box without a stain upon your character. Now call the next witness in your defence, prisoner at the bar — and be sharp!'

'I have no further witnesses,' said Eli.

'Wait!' called a voice.

An usher entered, whispering urgently to the Clerk of the Court.

'Apparently there are others,' said the Prosecutor, flustered. 'Let them be brought into the Court.'

From the back of the court three people entered; the Portuguese policeman, Papa Tai and Sulen, the latter two were handcuffed together. Papa Tai was in his usual wheedling mood of servility; Sulen, upright and wild-eyed, looked around with a defiant stare.

'These are witnesses for the defence, did you say?' Justice Hulme asked brusquely.

'With your permission, sir,' said Caine.

'Have them brought to the front of the Court.'

Pushing Papa Tai and his daughter before him, the policeman said: 'My name, sir, is Guard Profario. I come, Your Honour, upon the instructions of the Portuguese Ambassador in Macao ...' He faltered, raising a paper in front of him. 'May I read my instructions?'

'Please do,' said Hulme, and Guard Profario began:

'"Having read in the *Canton Register* an account of the trial of Elias Boggs, the Ambassador believes it to be in the interests of justice that the testimony of these Chinese witnesses be heard, and therefore begs the convenience of the Supreme Court."'

This done, the policeman wiped his florid face and stared up at the bench with bull-frog eyes.

'Pray continue,' said Justice Hulme.

The paper rustled in the policeman's trembling hands. '"Therefore please use the testimony of these witnesses — confessions extracted neither under torture, threat or any other provocation — and do with it as you will: bearing in mind that the Colony of Macao is much concerned by the recent murder of one of its most valued nationals — Captain da Costa."'

Nothing moved within the court room — save for a faint tapping against its topmost rafters.

For here, at its highest windows, many butterflies were beating their wings against the glass. A few, descending, circled over the heads of the immobile people: Caine himself, until now sunk into a lethargy by the heat, stirred himself sufficiently to raise his face. Only one other person moved in the whole assembly; a reporter from the *Eastern Globe* scribbling hastily upon a pad. This scribbling, and the faint beating of the butterflies' wings, were the only sounds to be heard.

Major Caine's voice suddenly boomed over the public benches.

277

'Justice Hulme, I protest at the advent of further evidence at this late stage! The prisoner's guilt is surely established to the satisfaction of the jury, despite his attempts to pin the blame upon others.'

'I also await the evidence of my friend, Black Sam,' shouted Eli.

'The evidence of his avowed friend is long overdue, sir, and the Prosecution has been more than patient,' replied Caine. 'How long is the Court prepared to wait for the evidence of one who has already condemned himself by his absence? How long can this Court wait until justice is seen to be done?'

Justice Hulme interrupted stonily. 'Perhaps we must not wait until the escaped prisoner is apprehended; but certainly we will wait until the witnesses before us are properly heard under the recommendation of the Ambassador of Macao, our esteemed neighbour. Please proceed.'

Papa Tai and Sulen, their manacles now removed, stood together at the bar; the shrivelled old man in his blue cotton suit denoting his trade of *compradore*; Sulen in the pink knee-length dress, now ragged, beloved of Chu Apu, who had bought it for her in Stanley market. But no rags, thought Eli, his eyes moving over Sulen, could desecrate the native beauty of this child-woman. In some strange way the rags only served to enhance her proud and hostile loveliness. Her chin was high, her eyes slanted down; every gaze was upon her as she replied to Caine's first question.

'My name is Sulen.'

'How old are you?'

'Sixteen.'

'Sixteen. Yet I have evidence that you consort with men. Is it not true that you are yet another lover of the prisoner in the dock?'

'Not true!' cried Papa Tai, wringing his hands. 'Never would I have allowed it, Sir! This – my beloved daughter?'

'Prosecutor, is this line of questioning going to lead us anywhere?' Justice Hulme interjected.

'It will lead us to the moral corruption of those giving evidence on behalf of the prisoner, Your Honour.'

278

'I doubt its ability to influence anything until we hear the reason for the presence of these witnesses.' The judge pointed with his plume at the policeman. 'You, Guard Profario, are holding something in your hand?'

'I am holding a key, Your Honour.'

'The key to what?'

'To the Gunpowder Factory at Stanley.'

'How did it come into your possession?

Profario, his cheeks purpling, took a deep breath before replying. 'It was sent by an unknown person to the Hong Kong Magistracy, who conveyed it to our Customs Office: with it was a map showing the location of the Gunpowder Factory itself; long had we sought it, Captain da Costa in particular.'

'And when you found the factory and entered it, you discovered the body of the unfortunate officer locked within?'

'That is correct, Your Honour.'

Justice Hulme sighed and sank back into the seat: 'Very well. But why, pray, have you brought these witnesses to Court?'

'Because I discovered that they were implicated in our officer's death.' Profario's voice was hesitant.

'Not true!' wailed Papa Tai.

'That is a lie,' shouted Sulen.

'In what way implicated, Guard Profario?' asked Caine casually.

'The girl showed a third person the secret path to the factory — this on her own admission. A woman of the junks came, she said, and offered her money to show her its whereabouts.'

'See now!' cried Papa Tai. 'I had nothing at all to do with it!'

'A woman of the junks, you say?' Caine's eyes drifted over the faces of the people in the Court.

'She sits watching us!' shrieked Sulen. 'That woman!' and pointed at Anna. 'She paid me ten Mexican dollars to show her the way!'

The Court awakened from heat prostration into excited murmuring, which Caine silenced with a raised hand. 'Let

279

the woman in the red dress approach the bench,' he said, and Anna did so.

'This woman?' he asked of Sulen. 'Think well before you reply, for it is important. This is the woman to whom you showed the way to the factory?'

'It is her! The one who came from the junk of Eli Boggs.'

'On oath you are swearing this,' said the Judge.

'I swear it again!' cried Sulen.

Papa Tai, his clasped hands raised, crowed his delight. 'Hear my daughter!' he wailed. 'In all her years, never once has she lied to her beloved father. She speaks the truth. Release me!'

The people simmered into silence. Anna stood like an animal on a leash, straining foward, her eyes upon Sulen.

'But this is not all, Your Honour,' Guard Profario went on, gathering confidence. 'On the night of Captain da Costa's death a young monk came to the office of the Custom House, and called him away.'

'You saw this person?'

'The young monk? Yes. He was dressed in yellow robes as befits a novice of the Buddhist monastery on Lantau Island. Later, according to the daughter's testimony, she saw them together on Stanley Beach, all three: Captain da Costa, the novice and a woman, talking together.'

'*That* woman!' shrieked Sulen pointing again at Anna.

'The novice went off,' continued Profario, 'and the Captain and the woman left in the direction of the Gunpowder Factory.'

'Yes! Ten stinking Mexican dollars she paid me!' yelled Sulen.

Caine did not immediately react to this. Shuffling his papers with slow, careful hands, he nodded at the Court usher. 'Remove these two to the cells. Miss Fu Tan, please take the stand.'

The effect on Anna was traumatic. Turning slowly, she faced the Court; there came from her parted lips a strange, inarticulate sound, like an animal trapped within the steel jaws of a gin. Caine raised his face. Saliva and froth were now bubbling on her mouth, and momentarily she stared, her mouth gaping in the direction of Sulen, before rushing in her direction, upending chairs and a table in a lust to attack her, thrusting two ushers aside in her headlong flight. Sulen shrieked as Anna reached her; screamed as Anna's clawing hands tore her face. Ushers, Guard Profario, Sulen and Papa Tai tumbled into a mêlée of arms and legs, until warders came rushing up from the cells below.

Justice Hulme sat motionless during the attack, saying when the commotion of flailing limbs and gasping breath subsided: 'Ushers, convey Miss Fu Tan to a place of restraint, there to await the instructions of the Court. Let the jury now retire to consider their verdict upon the charge of murder against the prisoner.'

The following is an extract from the newspaper *The Eastern Globe*:

An astonishing development occurred today at the trial of Elias Boggs on charges of murder, abduction and piracy. Miss Anna Fu Tan, lately the housekeeper to the Wedderburn family of the English Mansion, being accused by Macanese evidence of complicity in the murder of Captain da Costa, flew into a violent rage and physically attacked a witness for the defence. Only by swift action on the part of ushers and warders was she restrained and taken into protective custody. At time of going to press the jury were still considering the verdict on Elias Boggs.

Mr and Mrs Wedderburn were clearly upset by an outburst which is bound to have a far reaching effect upon the household, Miss Fu Tan until now being considered a highly trustworthy servant and family friend.

The strange affair of the attendant butterflies continues within the courtroom, the atmosphere therein being heavy with the scent of buddleia, a usual attraction for butterflies; as much interest being generated in the insects as in the trial itself.

Professor Anton Backroff, the eminent entemologist lately arrived from Paris, is presently studying the phenomenon in the Magistracy. Some varieties of the insects, he claims, date back to examples illustrated in old plates from as early as the year 1615 AD.

STOP PRESS After deliberating for less than an hour, the jury returned a verdict of Not Guilty of the murder of Captain da Costa against Elias Boggs. His trial on charges of abduction and piracy will now proceed.

42

At the beginning of the third morning of Eli's trial, the Clerk of the Court opened proceedings as usual.

'The prisoner has been found Not Guilty of the crime of murder. The trial of Elias Boggs will now continue upon the second capital indictment, that of the abduction of Mrs Mildred Wedderburn, née Smith, from on board the S.S. *Mongolia*, then *en route* to Hong Kong, for approximately four weeks during the year 1850. With the permission of Justice Hulme, may the Court proceed.'

Major Caine rose to his feet and approached Eli in the dock. 'Did you, Prisoner in the Dock, join as a passenger on the eighth day of July 1850, the steamship known as the *Mongolia*, then under the command of Captain O'Toole of the Peninsular and Oriental Shipping Company?'

'I did,' replied Eli.

'And did you, with others later to be named, capture and hold to ransom a spinster named Mildred Elizabeth Smith?'

'No, sir.'

'That was not your intention at that time?'

'No. It was not my intention when I first boarded the ship. I did not then know of Miss Smith's presence aboard.'

'Where did you board the *Mongolia*?'

'At Singapore.'

'You were known to Captain O'Toole, were you not?'

'Certainly. We were old friends. I had joined his company many times before, coming from trips to Malaya.'

'Therefore he neither suspected you nor your confederates on this occasion?'

'He did not.'

'So you took advantage of this friendship to board his vessel with others in the guise of passengers, in order to overrun his vessel and rob him?'

'We were not robbing the Captain, but his cargo.'

'Name the cargo.'

'A variety of goods of sale, including opium.'

'Opium? This is denied by the P. and O. Company.'

'They can deny it all they please — but the Captain had it aboard.'

'And you did not know of the presence of Miss Smith?'

'Not until I first saw her.' Here Eli glanced at Milly, who lowered her eyes.

'And when you saw her you decided upon a further strategy, did you not?' asked the Prosecutor.

'What strategy?'

'It struck you, did it not, that Miss Smith, if taken and held to ransom, had considerably more commercial value than two tons of opium?'

Eli shook his head. 'Not immediately.'

'What do you mean by that?'

Eli's tones were measured. 'Captain O'Toole received a signal that a typhoon was coming up, so decided to put into the shelter of the Paracel Islands. Clearly — to me, at any rate — this was a trap: a ruse to facilitate the capture of the ship.'

'By whom?'

'By Chu Apu, a pirate dominating that sea-route at the time. I warned Captain O'Toole, who disregarded my advice.'

'Advice to do what?'

'To proceed upon his original route.'

'Nevertheless, he did put into the shelter of the Paracels.'

Eli nodded.

'And immediately the *Mongolia* was at anchor, two armed junks came alongside.'

'Yes.'

284

'One of these junks was yours, the other was under the command of a Mr Bruner, your confederate?'

'Yes,' said Eli.

'Would it not also be correct to say that your advice to Captain O'Toole was given for your own advantage?'

'Of course.'

'To facilitate the capture of the opium?'

'Yes, but also to avoid the capture by Chu Apu of the lady passenger, Miss Smith.'

Caine sighed like a man in pain. 'Are you seriously expecting this Court to believe that your sole regard was the safety of Miss Smith?'

'I am,' Eli answered. 'Some pirates have principles. Chu Apu – and the Court knows this – is infamous when it comes to the treatment of women. To allow a young European female to fall into his hands would have been wilful cruelty. I was after the opium; I don't deal in the yellow slave trade or the selling of concubines.'

'Which might have happened to Miss Smith?'

'Eventually she would have been sold as a concubine, if Chu Apu had got his hands upon her.'

'Did Bruner agree to this?'

'I didn't ask him.'

'You decided to bargain with him, did you not?'

'I said he could keep the opium, if I could have Miss Smith.'

'So Bruner sailed off with the opium and you abducted Miss Smith with the intention of extracting a ransom from her father, a gentleman distinguished in the Colony?'

Eli nodded.

'What happened then?'

'The *Mongolia* sailed for Hong Kong; Hans Bruner loaded the opium aboard his junk and went south to the Malayan Peninsula.'

'You realise now that the *Mongolia* never reached Hong Kong. Apparently it foundered with all hands during a subsequent typhoon.'

'So I understand.'

'And are you telling me that you had no hand at all in

285

this ship's demise, nor in the death of some eighteen crew members?'

'I regret it as much as anyone,' said Eli.

'I put it to you, Boggs, that after you and Bruner had robbed the *Mongolia* and abducted Miss Smith you then deliberately sank the ship in order to conceal your crimes.'

'We did not! Nor have you proof that we did.'

'It would not be, I venture to sugest, the first time that such a horrible outcome had occurred in these waters after an act of piracy. Let the record show that the mystery of the *Mongolia's* disappeareance has not yet been solved, but that enquiries are still continuing. All who are proved responsible will be held to account.'

'Pray continue with the examination of the accused, Major Caine,' Justice Hulme interrupted testily. 'Investigation into shipping casualties during this particular typhoon is the business of the Marine Department.'

The Prosecutor's brow was stormy; he clearly resented such interference. 'What was your first landing with Miss Smith aboard?' he asked Eli coldly.

'Lantau Island.'

'You accommodated her there in the old Fort under guard, I understand, while you set off to demand a ransom of fifty thousand Mexican dollars from her father?'

'Yes.'

'Did you get this money?'

'I did not. A servant told me that Sir Arthur was ill, and not expected to live, so I returned to Lantau empty-handed.'

'But you would have taken the money had it been forthcoming?'

'Of course.'

'And you admit going to the English Mansion precisely for that purpose – to collect a ransom?'

'Yes.'

'You are implying that out of compassion, because Sir Arthur was ill, you did not pursue your demands?'

Eli nodded. 'Not just ill – they said he was dying.' He nodded towards Mamie. 'That woman, Sir Arthur's housekeeper, came to the window and invited me in; I smelled a rat, and made off.'

286

'What did you do then?'

'I returned to Lantau.'

'How long did you remain on Lantau with Miss Smith?'

'Until the Moon Festival.'

'So you kept Miss Smith in captivity until then. Why?'

'To see if her father would recover.'

'But he did not. He died. Do you know when?'

'No. They kept it a secret.'

'Precisely. Because Mr Wedderburn, Sir Arthur's friend and partner, realised that news of his death might cause you to act precipitously.'

'In what way?'

'With the source of ransom denied, my friend, it was feared you would kill the girl you had abducted.'

'I resent that suggestion!'

'I hardly know why you are so appalled. You had already sent what was purported to be one of her ears to her father, had you not?'

'From where I'm standing, she still appears to have two,' said Eli.

'Do not be capricious! Sir Arthur believed the ear to be his daughter's; Dr Schofield, whom I see in Court, gave testimony that the shock of it hastened the death of a sick old gentleman. And you talk of compassion!'

'I had nothing to do with the sending of the ear!'

Caine stretched himself to his full height. 'Clerk of the Court, bring Exhibit One and place the jar on the bench before the accused. After which, give the jar to the judge.'

'I have no wish to handle the grisly object, Major Caine.' Justice Hulme shuddered. 'I take your word that it is a human ear.'

'According to Dr Schofield — and I trust he is correct — this is the ear of some unfortunate peasant girl of Miss Smith's age.'

'I believe that to be the case,' Schofield confirmed.

The jar containing the ear was passed around the jury, some of whom examined it with expressions of disgust.

'Therefore,' said Caine, 'although we hear claims of a pirate's compassion for Sir Arthur's illness, he did not

287

hesitate to cut off the ear of some unfortunate woman and send it to him in a bloodstained package?'

'I have told you, I had nothing to do with it!'

Caine tapped his fingers on the rail before him. 'Doubtless the jury will have their own opinions about that. Abduction of a young defenceless woman is, to my belief, as bad as murder. He who removes a loved one from the bosom of the family and then demands money for her safe return is beyond the pale of human kind and incapable of either pity or compassion for the people to whom he causes untold misery. And this case − that of stealing away the only daughter of a dying man − is certainly the worst I have known since I first appeared in silk.

'Gentlemen, can you imagine the agony of this sick old man? Already believing his daughter to have drowned in the loss of the *Mongolia*, and having put up a tablet to her memory, he is told that she is alive, only to have a ransom demanded for her safe release!

'Can you imagine his suffering? The horror of receiving a bloodstained ear hacked from what he believed to be his daughter's head? And with the prospect of other pieces of her anatomy to arrive if he did not comply with her abductor's demands?'

Caine, his thumbs in the armholes of his robe, was now pacing in front of the jury like a caged animal.

'Put yourselves in the positon of this sick old gentleman, one of refinement and sensitivity, lying on his death-bed. Can you imagine the tragic confusion of his emotions? His young daughter in the hands of bandits, alone, her youthful virtue unprotected ... about to be cut to pieces if he did not comply....'

Justice Hulme's voice cut into the heavy atmosphere of the room. 'You have made your point, Mr Prosecutor, factually and emotionally; the bloody nature of this infamy is already known.' He sighed. 'Meanwhile, the accused has long been trying to answer your accusation and I wish him to be heard.' He nodded down at the dock.

'I'm as much sickened by what I have seen as any one in this room,' said Eli. 'But I repeat, on oath, I had nothing at all to do with the sending of the ear! Nothing at all!'

The Prosecutor stared haughtily around the courtroom. 'I understand,' he began, 'that every effort has been made by the military police to establish the identity of the person from whom the ear was taken – with negative results. Let the matter be therefore understood: Elias Boggs, and he alone, stands accused of this mutilation, despite his protestations to the contrary.'

Justice Hulme intervened. 'After this gruesome session, I trust the Court may return after recess sufficiently revived to banish the painful memories of this morning.' His weary eyes lifted to the ceiling. 'Even the butterflies, so beloved of Professor Backroff, appear to have departed. Would that, Gentlemen of the Jury, we could all do the same. Meanwhile I thank you for your patience and fortitude and order a recess of this Court until eleven o'clock tomorrow morning, during which time I instruct the Military to detain for questioning the person known as Yung, brother to Miss Fu Tan, the female at present under protective restraint, it being understood that he is presently held in custody at the Monastery of Lantau.'

The Court then rose.

Justice Hulme's statement was later proved incorrect.

Yung, on hearing of Anna's detention, had already removed himself from the Lantau Monastery, and was hiding in the family sampan concealed in the river rushes of Stanley Bay, from where he could watch the comings and going of the inmates of the nearby asylum where Anna, his sister, was being detained ...

43

'Gentlemen of the Jury,' said Justice Hulme on the fourth morning of the trial, 'I have received a letter from Mrs Mildred Wedderburn, requesting that she be allowed to give testimony as to the prisoner's character, and to this I agree. Is Mrs Wedderburn in Court?'

Milly, sitting alone, raised her hand. 'This is ridiculous!' James whispered into her ear. 'It's obvious that he's for the rope, yet you insist upon making a fool of me as well as yourself!'

'Please hurry, madam,' called the Clerk of the Court. And Milly, before the small sea of faces, took her place in the witness box. In passing Eli she flashed him a smile of confidence she did not feel.

'Your name is Mildred Elizabeth Wedderburn?'

'It is.'

'Please take the oath.' And Milly did so.

'The prisoner, acting in his own defence, may proceed,' said Justice Hulme.

'Mrs Wedderburn, thank you for appearing for my defence,' Eli said. 'I'll make this as brief as possible. During the period I held you against your will on Lantau Island, how were you treated?'

'With consideration and respect.'

'Did I ever show you violence – '

'Clearly, if you had treated the witness violently, you would not have called her in your defence,' Major Caine snapped. 'Rephrase the question.'

'Did I prevent you from trying to escape?' Eli asked.

'No.'

Caine interrupted again. 'Madam, it appears to me that since you were held upon an island, you had little opportunity for escape.'

Ignoring this outburst, Eli went on. 'For at least three weeks on Lantau you were ill with malaria? Is that so?'

'Yes.'

'During which time you were nursed by a member of my crew, an old gentleman, since deceased?'

'Yes.'

Caine yawned, apologised, and said with droll charm: 'A reasonable action on the prisoner's part. After all it was very much to his financial advantage to keep you alive.'

'I must be fair,' protested Milly, 'I was shown great care while being held by these people.' Justice Hulme said:

'The prisoner is conducting his own defence, Prosecuting Counsel, as it is his right to do. Do not intervene again unless absolutely necessary.' The Judge sighed audibly. 'Meanwhile, Boggs, do try to be reasonably pertinent. The proceedings are extremely slow.'

'Immediately I learned of your father's illness, I took you home, did I not?' asked Eli.

'Yes.'

'But your father had already died before you arrived.'

'Unfortunately.'

'Who received you there?'

Milly gestured towards Mamie in the Court. 'Mrs Malumba, then the housekeeper.'

'Do you recall that I stood near the porch, where I could be recognised?'

'I do.'

'And seeing me there, what did Mrs Malumba say?'

Milly smiled. 'It doesn't stand repeating.'

'Oh, but it does! She said "You no-good scoundrel! Did you just bring my baby home? You hold on while I fetch a gun." Or something to that effect.'

'I said more'n that, an' all!' said Mamie from the Court, which caused Justice Hulme to hammer the bench and call for silence.

'But I took you home and also took the chance of being recognised. Is this the action of a merciless murderer who will do nothing if it is not for money?'

Milly shook her head.

'What happened then?'

'You went away.'

'Did you see me receive money?'

'No.'

'Since then you've surely had an opportunity to look at your father's accounts. Did he at any time pay a ransom?'

'Yes.'

'To whom?'

'To a man named Bruner.'

'You are quite certain of the name?'

'Absolutely certain.'

A gasp rippled through the Court.

'Hans Bruner?' The Prosecutor took up the questioning now.

'That's right,' said Milly.

'How much ransom was paid by your father?'

'Fifty thousand Mexican dollars.'

'In Hong Kong currency?'

'No — in the currency of Sumatra.'

'You can give the Court proof of this?'

Milly turned. 'My husband can! He was in charge of Smith and Wedderburn's accounts at the time and it was he who signed the cheque.'

'To whom was the cheque made out?'

'To a Mr Bruner of the Bank of Sumatra.'

'Repeat this person's Christian name?'

'Yes, Hans. The name Hans Bruner was on the cheque.'

'How can you possibly know this?'

'I obtained a copy of it from the Bank of Sumatra.'

'Did you, indeed! How?'

'I wrote and asked for it.'

'And they complied with your request. So you have this cheque in your possession?'

'No, but I have a copy here.'

Caine took the cheque from her. 'Is this a true copy?'

'It's so certified.'

'Why didn't you produce this evidence before?'

'You didn't ask for it!'

Justice Hulme's voice broke in: 'With respect, Prosecutor, how does this affect evidence for or against the accused?'

'If this cheque, certified as a true copy, Your Honour, is indeed a duplicate of the original, the case against the prisoner cannot be proved, since another received the ransom money.'

'Not necessarily. The accused could still be implicated.'

'Possibly, but highly unlikely. This certainly brings another dimension to his defence, and I am reluctant to proceed.' Caine turned to Milly.

'Your husband, James Wedderburn, was your accountant at the time of your father's death, was he not?'

'That's a damned lie!' shouted James from the Court, jumping up.

'Kindly regain your seat, Mr Wedderburn,' said Justice Hulme.

'It's a lie, and she knows it!'

'Please be quiet, or I will clear the Court!'

'Then clear it!' James struggled clear as a warder caught his arm. 'I'm not sitting here listening to these appalling insinuations!'

'Sit and be silent, or I will have you arrested,' said Hulme, looking over the top of his spectacles. 'You will not turn my Court into a bear garden, Mr Wedderburn, whatever your status in the community. Your time will come. Be patient.'

James sat, fuming.

'Kindly proceed with your examination of the witness, Major Caine.'

The Prosecutor turned to Milly once more.

'You say that your husband was your father's accountant. Did you know this at the time the cheque was written?'

'I discovered it later.'

'How much later?'

'Within a week or so of arriving home.'

'You were then appraised of the situation?'

'Yes.'

'By whom?'

293

'Mrs Malumba, then my housekeeper, my father's friend.'

'And she's lying, too!' shouted James.

'Previous to this, did you know this Hans Bruner?'

'Yes. He didn't come aboard the *Mongolia* with Eli Boggs and the other tea-planters – he was already there as First Mate to Captain O'Toole.'

'But they were not tea-planters, were they, Mrs Wedderburn? So do not refer to them as such. Bruner was a pirate, like Boggs?'

'Yes – I suppose he was.'

'One intent on the same course of action as the accused, but already planted as a member of the crew.'

'I suppose so.'

'What do you mean, you *suppose* so, Mrs Wedderburn? Did he not behave in precisely the same way as Boggs, who took over the *Mongolia* and rifled its contents?'

Milly nodded slowly.

'You seem reluctant to hear the accused named as a pirate.'

'That's because she is in love with him!' shouted James.

'Clerk of the Court, please have Mr Wedderburn removed,' Justice Hulme said levelly. And James was led away.

'The Court is in recess until three o'clock this afternoon.' And the public galleries emptied.

When the Court resumed, Justice Hulme addressed the Jury.

'Gentlemen, upon reflection it appears that the business of this Court has become transferred from the trial of the accused for the crime of abduction to quite another subject: the financial irregularities of the Wedderburn family. I do not wish this to continue.

'I have now received a message from the Governor of the Colony who is in attendance this afternoon.' Here he bowed briefly to the small table where Sir John Bowring sat, papers before him. 'Sir John has stated – and I agree with him – that recent evidence, particularly that given by Mrs Wedderburn, has a peculiar bearing on the trial of the accused for abduction.'

294

He took a deep breath and continued, 'Further, I am advised that the Deputy Governor, Mr Denning, has this morning resigned his office and is already on his way back to Britain.'

The people sat speechless: Eli fluttered a wink at Milly.

'This resignation comes at an inopportune moment, since it was the intention to call Mr Denning as a witness. This, I fear, will not now be possible.

'Meanwhile, during the recess it has been confirmed by the solicitors of Smith and Wedderburn that a cheque to the value of eight thousand dollars was paid into a Sumatra bank to the credit of Mr Wedderburn by Mr Hans Bruner, and was cashed by Mr Wedderburn in the following month.' The judge raised his face. 'I have lately learned of the apprehension of this Mr Bruner, who has been brought to the court by one of Boggs' accomplices, a man known as Black Sam. Is Bruner available to the court?'

'He is,' replied an usher.

'Then bring him before me.'

This was done: Bruner stood stiffly to attention in the dock. 'I am given to understand that you are turning Queen's Evidence, Mr Bruner, is this so?' asked the judge.

'Yes, sir.'

'And that you have taken the oath?'

'I have.'

'Then explain to me what this cheque for eight thousand dollars, made payable by you to Mr Wedderburn, was for?'

'The sale of opium, sir.'

'You had profit in the deal?'

'I did sir. The total money I received from each deal was ten thousand dollars; I paid Wedderburn eight thousand, and kept two thousand for myself.'

'Was this a usual transaction?'

'When dealing with Wedderburn I got twenty per cent.'

'From the profitable business of selling opium you received twenty per cent from Wedderburn and he took the rest? Was any other person, to your knowledge, a participant in opium deals? The man Elias Boggs, for instance?'

'Not as far as I know, sir. I have asked that other such deals be taken into consideration.'

'Indeed you have, and I have a note of them.' The judge looked slowly around the court, saying, 'The jury trying Elias Boggs for the abduction of Mrs Wedderburn are directed to find the accused not guilty of dealing in opium: the crime of piracy, however, will remain on the statute. I therefore dismiss the jury trying the opium charge against him with thanks for their valuable time in seeking a justifiable verdict.

'Meanwhile, this Court is in recess and will meet again at these premises on the morning of 10th October, during which further enquiries will be made into the financial dealings of Messrs Smith and Wedderburn. In this I trust I have the Governor's permission.'

Sir John Bowring rose, bowing assent.

'Bail being refused,' said the judge, 'Mr Bruner and the man known as Black Sam will remain in custody until such inquiries are complete,' and drawing his robe about him he left the Court.

44

'Milly, with that husband of yours tampin' around lookin' murderous, I reckon we'd be safer homin' in on Green Island until all this is over,' Mamie said on the morning of the fifth day of Eli's trial.

'I was thinking that, too,' replied Milly.

'The mansion ain't big enough for the three of us, now Black Sam's returned with that Bruner feller, who's a stink in ma nose, let alone Wedderburn's.'

'Queen's Evidence people are always unpopular.'

'He's certainly unpopular. Murder will be done if your James, Mr Goodchild, or that Dr Schofield get at him. Old Denning has scarpered off to England, but he'll get his comeuppance one day.'

'We've a lot to thank Eli for,' observed Milly.

'Oh, aye? We got nothin' to thank that Eli for, nor Black Sam neither. I'm a respectable widow, and ma Rastus would turn in his grave to see me at ma age roustin' around court-rooms with pirates.'

'You'll get over it.'

'Perhaps, but I'll never be the same. Do ye think they'll call me to give evidence?'

'Not unless they discover that Sam is your sweetheart.'

Mamie huffed and puffed, indignant. 'I'll be glad when all this indecency is over and done with, and I can get back to the church and ma Pastor.'

'If he'll have you,' said Milly.

The early October sun was high in the sky as they left home for the Court. Together they walked from

297

the coolie-palanquins to the corner of Pedder and Queen's, where a crowd was already assembling at the Magistracy's doors. In a miasma of perspiration and excitement the waiting people jabbered in groups in the hope of an execution: like the hags of the French Revolution, said Milly, knitting in the Place de la Concorde.

'I don't know about that,' replied Mamie, 'but I do think we should escape from this for a time. Green Island's an easier place to run to now that ole Anna isn't around.'

'Yes ... Do you know, she's the one I'm sorry for in this sad affair.'

'Don't waste no pity on her! She is a bad one, murderin' da Costa in cold blood and puttin' the blame on your Eli.'

'I wonder why she did it?' said Milly; waiting in the queue for the courtroom she narrowed her eyes to the sun. 'Because she's still in love with him?'

An old European, overhearing her, said, raising his hat: 'Hell hath no fury like a woman scorned ...'

'Oh no!' replied Milly, turning. 'Eli didn't scorn her — he merely gave her shelter aboard his junk. There's no evidence that he had anything more to do with her!' At which Mamie caught the old gentleman's eye and winked.

'Of course not,' said the old man, bowing. 'Evil is he, no doubt, who evil thinketh.'

'It's so in this case,' said Milly, and Mamie put her arm protectively around her shoulders and led her within as the Magistracy doors swung open and the people surged in.

With Eli in the dock, the Clerk of the Court cried, 'Call the second witness for the Defence, Mr Hans Bruner!'

Bruner strolled arrogantly into place.

'Your name is Hans Bruner?' asked Eli.

'At your service, sir.'

'Where are you employed?'

'Until recently at the Marine Office, Hong Kong.'

'As a ship's officer?'

'That is correct: under Mr James Wedderburn, the Chief Superintendent.'

'From whom you receive all instructions?'

'Yes.'

'Here I must remind you, Mr Bruner,' Eli said, 'that you have turned Queen's Evidence and have taken an oath to tell the truth, despite the fact that your evidence can be used against yourself and your companions. You understand?'

'Yes.'

'Why have you chosen such a defence?'

'Because,' said Bruner, 'too much has happened. Too many lies have been told, too many crimes committed.'

Major Caine glanced up at this; his eyes beady and watchful.

'Tell me – in the business of the *Mongolia*, you were to seize the opium and take Miss Smith, were you not? Those orders came directly from Wedderburn?'

'Yes. But you arrived and took Miss Smith instead.'

The courtroom buzzed with interest.

'So you gained the opium and I gained Miss Smith. Did Mr Wedderburn know about this?'

'When he discovered it he only smiled: nothing was changed, he said.'

'What happened after I took Miss Smith aboard the *Ma Shan*?'

'The *Mongolia* sailed to Hong Kong,' replied Bruner, 'and I sold his opium in Sumatra.'

'And paid off Mr Wedderburn?'

'Of course. He gave me the locations of the ships to be attacked and I paid him off.'

Eli smiled triumphantly at Milly. 'And the ransom money I was to receive – where did that come from?'

'From Sir Arthur Smith's account in the Oriental Bank of Hong Kong, part of his estate.'

'Of which Mr Wedderburn was the sole executor, under Sir Arthur's will?'

'That's right. Fifty thousand dollars, accounted through the books as ransom money paid to you, finished up in Mr Wedderburn's account.' Bruner grinned hugely. 'Everything was proceeding smoothly for us, and for Wedderburn in particular. Not only was he the sole executor, but also Miss Smith's guardian. He had a free hand.'

Major Caine intervened, 'Mr Bruner, may I remind you

299

that you are under oath? You talk of "us": it appears that you are about to make allegations involving others. I advise you to take care. Who are these people?'

Said Bruner: 'Mr Goodchild, Dr Schofield and Mr Denning, the Deputy-Governor.'

People in the Court gasped with astonishment.

'You are now accusing these eminent gentlemen of being partners in a scheme to obtain Miss Smith's money by fraud?'

'Of course. This is why she was brought out from England,' said Bruner.

'Was it, indeed!'

'According to Wedderburn she was deranged, and Sir Arthur wanted to marry her off to someone who would take care of her.'

'Wedderburn being selected for the task?' asked Eli, and sighed at the ceiling. Mr Caine, the Prosecutor interjected:

'Wait, this has already gone too far! Honourable men have been mentioned in what is proving to be scandalous matters completely removed from a trial for piracy and abduction, I object most strongly.'

'Objection sustained,' said Justice Hulme. 'But, while such a removed line of questioning cannot be allowed to continue, a situation clearly exists involving other people at present under police investigation. Therefore, I am going to order a recess until such investigations are completed, when I may think fit to allow this trial to continue. The Court is adjourned until I receive the police report.'

Judge Hulme reopened Eli's trail for piracy and abduction after a week's recess, with the following announcement:

'Gentlemen of the Jury, upon the defendant's request I am going to allow a degree of reference to the affairs of a case at present still under investigation, since I am persuaded that an overlap of evidence occurs.' He nodded at Eli. 'Please continue your examination of Mr Bruner, the witness giving Queen's Evidence, but remember that only persons at present residing in the Colony may be mentioned.'

Eli, giving a wry smile, began to question Bruner once

more. 'Please tell the Court who first gained control of Miss Smith's finances.'

'Mr Wedderburn,' replied Bruner.

'And to this end he employed yourself, Mr Goodchild, the solicitor, Dr Schofield and the Deputy-Governor?'

The judge instantly intervened. 'No reference to the Deputy-Governor, please! He is not here to defend himself.'

Eli unperturbed, continued. 'What was Mr Goodchild's role?'

'It was he who advised Sir Arthur legally to make his daughter a ward of court under Wedderburn's control. He also drew up a relevant will.'

'You have proof of this?'

'I can show you copies of the correspondence.'

'And Dr Schofield − what part did he play?'

'It was his job to prove that Miss Smith was mentally deranged and in need of special care and protection.'

'What gave the doctor reason to think this?'

'Apparently there had been something of a scandal concerning her when she was at school.'

'Dr Schofield was the medical advisor to her school in England. She was one of his patients there, was she not?'

'I don't know the details.'

'So it appears that there was a concerted attempt to prove that Miss Smith was mentally incapable from the moment she arrived in Hong Kong.'

'Not by me!'

'But you knew of Schofield's intentions!'

'Yes.'

'Now I ask you this: did you at any time impersonate another in order to give emphasis to the allegation of mental instability?'

'Yes.'

'When?'

'At a reception given at Flagstaff House.'

'Miss Smith had already met you, had she not?'

'Of course. I was First Mate aboard the *Mongolia* when she was abducted.'

'And, knowing that she would recognise you as such, you impersonated another?'

'Yes.'

'Whom did you impersonate?'

'Akil Tamarins, a Dutch Ambassador.'

'Why?'

'To confuse Miss Smith so that she would make a fool of herself.'

'And publicly prove that she was deranged?'

'Yes.'

'Whose idea was this?'

'Schofield's. He wanted to have her legally certified as insane.'

'Whose idea was it to send the amputated ear to Sir Arthur?'

The Court was hushed.

'Schofield's.'

'Can you give any details?'

Bruner took a deep breath before replying, 'Apparently he paid money to an old crook, who found a ten-year-old beggar child. Schofield cut off her ear, only to find that it was too small, so he purchased another. This isn't unusual in China — beggars have been mutilating their children for centuries.'

'And the second ear? This was from an older person?'

'A brothel prostitute sold one of hers to him — for fifty dollars.'

'So this was the ear that was sent to Sir Arthur, with a note saying it came from me?' asked Eli.

'Yes. I posted it myself from Pedder Street.'

'What was the effect upon Sir Arthur?'

Bruner shrugged. 'I wasn't there, but I know he died two days later, just before you brought his daughter home.'

'He died of a broken heart,' said Eli, and paused as Justice Hulme raised a hand, saying curtly:

'That will suffice. I suggest we've had enough horror for one day. Let the record show that the defendant's case is proved.'

302

A journalist's report in the *Canton Register* of 30 of October stated:

> The trial of Elias Boggs, on a charge of piracy, has resolved itself into a series of recesses, the latest being this morning when Justice Hulme delayed proceedings yet again after certain gentlemen were mentioned by name by the prisoner, who is conducting his own defence.
>
> It is known in financial circles that police inquiries are in hand concerning the affairs of Mr James Wedderburn when acting in the capacity of Miss Mildred Elizabeth Smith's guardian (she is now his wife), in which Mr Goodchild, the well-known solicitor, Dr Schofield, her medical adviser, and Mr Denning, former Deputy-Governor of the Colony, are also involved.
>
> The case being at present *sub-judice*, nothing more can be disclosed, but it is hoped that a fuller report can be made public immediately the legal situation has been resolved to the satisfaction of the presiding judge.

Within days of this report, Milly and Mamie, to avoid sharing the English Mansion with an intemperate James Wedderburn, packed their belongings and took up residence in the Rest House on Green Island.

It was an important event of which Yung, the brother of Anna No Name, took note.

Within the shelter of his sampan's hooped canopy, Yung watched with sad eyes the coming of his sister while on nightly exercise with the mad people of Stanley Bedlam, which was then the official name of Hong Kong's lunatic asylum.

Among the inmates was one named Chu Apu, once the husband of Sulen. On all fours came Chu, on a lead like an animal, his face ravaged by lunacy; behind him, tall and stately in a white gown that reached her feet, was Anna. With her black hair flowing free in the wind she advanced; when clear of the attendants, she stooped beside the sampan and saw Yung's yellow robe within its canopy.

'Is that you, Small One?'

'It is I,' said Yung.

303

'You come to save me, as you promised?'

'In the name of our parents, I come,' Yung answered. Seeing that the attendants were otherwise engaged, he whispered urgently: 'I have news of Elias Boggs. Do you remember?'

'How could I forget him?' asked Anna. Her face in that dusky light, shadowed under the eyes, was otherwise sheet-white: the face of a corpse, her eyes bright with an inner fire. 'He is the last to die, is he not? The very last one, as we swore would happen!'

'Be patient,' whispered Yung. 'Let them continue to believe you mad and I will come on the night of the next full moon. And then, while Elias Boggs sleeps in the house on Green Island, I will take you to him.'

'How will he die?' she asked.

'By claws, like Chu Apu: his soul will be destroyed, though his body remains alive. By claws, Gold Sister.'

Anna wrung her pale hands together, looking up at the rising moon.

All was satisfactory to her: Yung, in revenge for the world's treatment of his sister, had apparently change his tune . . .

45

On the seventh day of the trial of Eli Boggs, after listening to Justice Hulme's summing up, Milly and Mamie watched Eli and Black Sam arraigned in the dock to receive sentence. Trembling, they heard Justice Hulme deliver his grim warning.

'You, Elias Boggs and you, the man known as Black Sam, have pleaded guilty to the charge of piracy upon the high seas. Do you have anything to say in your defence before judgement is passed upon you?'

'No,' replied Black Sam defiantly.

'Yes,' said Eli.

Lord Justice Hulme sighed wearily. 'Do so, but pray make it brief. The trial has been long, the weather hot, and the jury is becoming restive.'

'What I say will be reported officially?'

'This is a court of British Justice,' replied Hulme coldly.

'Very well,' said Eli, and began to address the jury.

'I stand here accused of the crime of piracy – but does not piracy exist within every corner of this colony? In every level of its society, from the highest financier to the lowest criminal Triad?

'For days you have listened to a rigmarole of allegations, all of which are true and none of which concern me and my companion. You have heard how the Chief Superintendent of the Marine Department has swindled a ward of court out of her rightful inheritance under the law.

'You have listened to a catalogue of claims and counter claims of slanders and libels against one official or

305

another. So now I read you this from *The Times* of England.

'"Here in Hong Kong people are in prison, going to prison, or coming out of prison on prosecutions by one or more incriminated officials! Every man's hand is turned against his neighbour."'

Eli paused, breathing heavily.

'We are indicted, Black Sam and I, on a charge of piracy. But I can tell you of dreadful, heinous crimes being committed here by those in high places. Has not the Chief Justice of this Colony himself been suspended for drunkenness ...?'

Hulme bowed his head in shame.

'Has not the Registrar General been dismissed for accusing the Attorney General of consorting with pirates? Was not the last Captain Superintendent of Police proved to have more than an official interest in the proliferating brothels? And the Colonial Secretary charged by a local editor, now in prison, of having connections with the illegal opium monopoly?'

'Boggs, for heaven's sake sit, and be silent!' Lord Hulme said miserably. But Eli went on. 'The Lieutenant-Governor has been accused of taking commission from the stall-holders of the Central Market, while the Governor himself has been pilloried by the newspapers for giving preferential treatment to private contractors. The same Governor, mark you, whose son is privately employed, to his family's advantage, by one of the richest of the merchant Hongs?' Eli glared at the jury. 'If all this be innocent, how do Black Sam and I stand in the business of piracy? For ours is the gathering of a little merchandise for selling in Ladder Street – no more, no less. If we are corrupt, Gentlemen, how do these others stand? Guilty as charged – and you know it!'

'Have you quite finished?' asked Justice Hulme, raising a weary countenance.

'God help me,' shouted Eli, 'I have not started! If Black Sam and me are going to dangle our heels, we're going to do it in style. For there is no law in Hong Kong except the law of greed, where the rich get richer and the poor starve.

'I ask you to examine this man Wedderburn. He and his likely lads stood to gain a fortune before I happened along – four thousand miserable coolies raked from their

306

homes and put on the high seas for God knows where in the name of money! You talk of piracy? Tons of opium are being smuggled into China under your noses, despite the pleas of China against whom we are again about to go to war to maintain the profits of your disreputable merchants. And now we have a Deputy Governor smuggled away to England before there broke upon your heads the biggest public scandal Hong Kong has ever known! A group of men prepared to lock a woman in a lunatic asylum, in order to steal her two million dollar estate – how stands that for theft?'

Hulme's voice rose to a shout. 'Sit down, or I will have the warders eject you!'

'I wouldn't try it,' said Black Sam, looking ugly.

Hulme subsided weakly. 'Allow me to pass sentence upon you; which, if only you will stop this rhetoric and listen, could possibly be to your advantage!' He hammered on his desk with frustration.

'One day,' shouted Eli, 'historians will call this, the Pearl of the East, a den of iniquity, a filthy hive of corruption, where English gentlemen far from home can swindle and fornicate away their lives!'

'How dare you!' bellowed Justice Hulme, while Caine fumed silently. But Eli would not be stopped. 'You have created a cess-pit where the weakest die and the strongest prosper. This is a land of moral decay. While the poor starve, you live in a profusion of luxury, maintained by those who live in misery! Sentence us, then, and we'll shake the dust of this godforsaken country from our feet!'

Lord Justice Hulme, cowering in the face of Eli's outburst, raised his head in the ensuing silence. 'In the name of God,' said he, 'have you really finished?'

Eli did not deign to answer; Black Sam, standing rigidly by his side, glowered a challenge around the courtroom.

'Because if you have,' continued the judge, 'you will allow me to pass upon you the sentence of this Court. It is this:

'That you, Elias Boggs, be released in one week from today upon agreement that, from that moment, you will depart yourself from this Colony and never again return. And that you, the man known as Black Sam, whose future

307

conduct has been vouchsafed by a lady who chooses not to be named, be released under your own cognisances and placed in her care until she thinks fit to release you into society.'

A shout went up from the courtroom.

'Meanwhile,' Justice Hulme added, 'remain on the premises until you are given premission to depart, and reserve any further allegations against the dignity of this Colony until you are given permission to do so.'

There was no sound in the courtroom now save that of a single butterfly beating its wings against the glass of a distant window.

Then the judge called shrilly: 'Clerk of the Court, next case please. Bring up Messrs Wedderburn, Goodchild and Schofield to face charges of fraudulent conversion of money to their own advantage.'

'Bring up Wedderburn, Goodchild and Schofield!' cried the Clerk.

46

'We're best out o' that stinkin' Hong Kong island,' Mamie
said, looking out of the window of the Rest House on Green
Island. 'They tell me the soldiers are dying like flies in the
barracks – malaria again.'

Milly nodded. 'It's the drinking water – they forget to
boil it – you know how careless soldiers are.'

'Queer, though. Back home we used to say it was caused
by mosquito bites.'

'Really!' exclaimed Milly. 'Who ever heard of mosquitoes
causing malaria?' And she put down her hair brush and stared
at herself in the glass. Could it possibly be, she wondered,
that the plain, freckled schoolgirl who had arrived in Hong
Kong was at last a woman – and a passably good-looking
one at that?

'Girl, you're that pretty these days that you takes ma
breath away,' said Mamie, as if reading her thoughts. 'When
they release that Eli, he'll just swing you up and carry you
away to Baltimore, and he'd be foolish if he don't.'

'God willing!'

'And leave me wi' that pesky ole Black Sam?'

Milly turned to her, for the mirror was reflecting tears. 'Oh,
Mamie!' and her arms went about her friend. 'Black Sam and
the Rest House, all to yourself – what more do you want?'

'That's the trouble,' sobbed Mamie. 'He has me, but I
only have him!'

Milly laughed. 'Isn't that enough?'

'Maybe.' Mamie dried her tears. 'You see, I still bill and
coo for my big black Rastus.'

They stood together while Mamie sobbed. 'I loves you to everlastin', see? And that Eli, he's goin' to take you to the ends of the earth.'

'Don't be too sure,' said Milly.

Anna No Name, in another part of Hong Kong, was looking at the moon.

The mid-Autumn Festival had come and gone, and although a full moon was blazing, Yung, her brother, had not come for her in the sampan as arranged.

Earlier Anna had heard that a poor Mrs Lloyd, abandoned by her lover, Lieutenant Rogers, had been found dead on a refuse dump in Spring Garden Lane. Anna had thought to herself that this, perhaps, would be an appropriate end for one like Mildred Elizabeth Wedderburn: clawed and left to die, then put on a refuse dump where the ladies of the road, bawdy in their language and of saucy airs, smoked their long-stemmed pipes and accosted the sailors. Ah yes, thought Anna – such an end would only be just.

But first she must seek her vengeance and nothing less than the death of Eli Boggs, the last of the pirates, he who had cheated the hangman's rope, would suffice.

Soon, thought Anna, crouching in the rushes awaiting Yung's sampan, Eli would be free to sail away with his woman. And so Anna waited.

Yung came when the moon had waned to three-quarters.

'You are there, Gold Sister?'

'I am here,' replied Anna.

'Elias Boggs is alone on Green Island,' said Yung. In this he lied, for Eli had not yet left Victoria Gaol.

'Just take me to him, and I will do the rest,' said Anna, and they set off together in the sampan, Yung paddling in front, Anna paddling behind.

Eli was indeed about to leave Hong Kong, in accordance with the instruction of Lord Chief Justice Hulme. That night he went aboard his junk, the *Ma Shan*, and prepared the new crew to sail.

Milly, in her bedroom in the Rest House, watched and waited. In expectation of Eli coming for her, she had assumed

310

her old disguise of a Chinese girl, in order to travel with Eli wherever he wished without fear of recognition. Her eyelids she painted, using burnt cork at the corners to turn them up high; her face she changed from English paleness to the sun-blackened visage of the Hakka woman; upon her head she put a tribal hat, heavily fringed with beads. About her throat she wore the chunky jewellery which Hakka women love; her hair was arranged in two simple plaits. This done, she stood before the mirror, thinking that for a Chinese girl going to the ends of the earth, she looked better than some.

The disguise complete, Milly went down to the servants' quarters to make her farewells to Mamie. But the house-keeper was absent: on her bed lay a note: 'I'm on the beach with my sweetheart, Black Sam.'

Milly returned to her own bedroom to wait for midnight, which was the time the *Ma Shan* would tie up at Green Island Wharf.

Supposing, she thought now, sitting on her bed, Eli did not come? Supposing he had had his clearance from Victoria Gaol and had sailed off alone? What would happen to her then? Would she be alone for the rest of her life in the great rooms of the English Mansion, waiting until James, her legal husband, came out of prison? Mamie would make a new life with Sam: all that would remain to Milly then would be a solitary return to England. It was a terrifying thought. And in her loneliness, she remembered Tom Ellery. Supposing Tom had not died, and she had married him? Her life then would have been that of a rustic: waiting in a tied cottage for her man to return from the fields. A life of harrowing, hoeing, ploughing and sowing; but nevertheless real, substantial. Would that Eli were equally substantial! All he had so far offered was a future uncertain at best: the mistress of a pirate aboard an armed junk roaming the seas!

Now, lying upon the bed in a doze of dreaming, a vision of Tom Ellery returned to Milly with astonishing clarity. He suddenly and perversely assumed the proportions of absolute reality, impinging himself upon the disorder of her mind. And his features, at first indistinct, slowly transformed into recognisable reality: first the eyes became brighter; then the chin and forehead took form, then his smiling mouth.

311

She blinked to banish the vision. But Tom's face did not disappear, but stood suspended before her. The shock of this awoke Milly from her dream-like state, she sat up, focusing her eyes anew, and slowly the apparition vanished.

This was the onset of the old delusion that had haunted her since girlhood. Next, out of her infancy, would come the blood-mask of the beheaded fox and the warm smear of its blood. When this did not happen Milly breathed more freely, yet within her was growing a new and foreign dream.

Perfume.

She could smell a perfume; at first indefinable. Then a breeze blew from the open door of the bedroom where the lawns stood stark and clear in the moonlight beyond, and the perfume strengthened, to grow in power and intensity; waves of showering musk were suddenly fragrant on the wind.

Milly went to the door, looking out on to the night. Afar, at the edge of a line of poplars, two eyes were glowing from the dark. A fox? Milly nodded to herself: many were to be seen in the gardens at night.

The tide was slack through Sulphur Channel; dark velvet waters lay placid in silver light under the moon. Yung turned and faced Anna in the sampan; she, seeing the reflecting waters dancing upon his face, drew closer.

'You love your brother?' he asked.

'As the kittens love the cat,' she said, as she had done when they were both children.

'You realise that you are ill, Gold Sister?' asked Yung.

'Ill?'

Anna's face which, until now, had been radiant, took on a menacing cast.

'An illness that has come down through the generations,' said Yung, drawing his saffron robe about him. 'For many days I have talked to the elders, seeking their advice. It is an illness of which we both know, and never speak. So if you love me, as you say, why not let me cleanse you?'

Anna's eyes became extraordinarily bright in the light of the moon, and the perfume of her body reached Yung's nostrils.

'Your illness is not unusual, Gold Sister,' he reassured

312

her quickly. 'Since the beginning of time the great mandarins, those of superior intelligence, have been entered by the spirits of clever foxes; for good, and, at times, for evil. You were once a Taoist. Do you recall the Taoist Pope who bottled evil souls and kept them corked in his cellar for the good of the human race? I beg you to remember the teachings of our parents!'

'This,' said Anna, 'is the gabbling of a simpleton, not my brother.'

'Because you are my sister, I would die for you,' Yung said. 'As me to save your soul by giving my own life. I beg you, let me say the prayer that will exorcise the vixen that has invaded your womb!'

'You are an idiot!' whispered Anna, hatred in her face. 'Always I have suspected it, now I know! Have I not lived long enough with idiocy in the madhouse where people wail at the full moon and grip tombstones?' And she rose, swaying, to her feet, staring down at him, froth foaming upon her mouth so that the spittle dripped upon her gown.

And even as she stood there, while the sampan moved in circles on the tide, Yung began his priestly incantations. Wild-eyed, Anna watched him light tapers that spluttered at her feet; and he raised his hands in supplication to his gods, crying hoarsely:

'Evil one! Spirit of the Fox! Depart and burn within the fires of holy Buddha. All-Powerful god of earth and heaven, hear my prayer? Depart, depart!'

The effect was instant. Anna struck out; as Yung fell she was upon him, shrieking and beating at his face with her fists. And when he cried aloud and fought her away, her fists became claws that ripped and tore his flesh, so that he fell back, seeking escape. But there was no escape from the fury of her onslaught. And when, in desperation, he tried to throw himself over the side of the sampan, she snatched at him and pulled him to his feet with astonishing strength, so that momentarily they stood clutched together, swaying as in a last embrace, before toppling headlong into the sea. As they fell, the sampan floated away, leaving them stranded in the middle of the ocean.

Anna was screaming; Yung was silent. Beneath the water

313

he saw her girl's body, lithe and strong; surging up into the air he held her, gasping, but the one he held was not his sister.

At the first plunge, his hands beneath her billowing gown had known the satin-smoothness of a woman, but now he knew the kicking thrusts of sinewy legs, coarse fur and floundering paws that tore his skin. Instead of Anna's face he saw a slavering mouth of snarling jaws and serrated teeth. All this Yung knew in a moment, before the attack upon him suddenly ceased, and the long slim body of an animal slid away into darkness, calming the tumult of the sea.

With this sudden respite came silence. Yung saw beside him a woman spent, her body floating lifelessly.

Gathering Anna to him Yung struck out for distant Green Island, but the tide had now turned and the channel was running in spate. Brother and sister tumbled within the angered waves, for little stayed alive in the full bore of Sulphur Channel.

Later, under a misted moon, locked together in a drowned embrace, they drifted at the wish of the tide, slowly but inexorably carrying them away, into the relentless waters of the South China Sea.

And the Great Fox, the spirit which had possessed the body of Anna No Name, clambered out of the sea and glared up at the Rest House, where a solitary light glowed in a bedroom window.

47

Milly, awaiting midnight, turned down her bedside oil lamp. She was about to draw the curtains when she noticed Mr Soong, the old caretaker, wandering about in front of his chalet at the bottom of the garden. Longing for company of any sort, Milly went down to join him.

'You leave here now that trial business all over, Missy?' he asked.

'I hope so,' Milly replied.

'Perhaps Miss Mamie stay on here, now she got another sweetheart like her Rastus?'

'Perhaps. I don't really know her plans, Mr Soong.'

'But you go and never come back?'

'Oh yes — one day we will return.'

'All English people say that, but never come back.' His old face, lined with the years of China's hunger, creased up. Suddenly, to Milly's astonishment, he bowed, took her hand and kissed it. 'Like Chinese people say — you savvy me, I savvy you, you belong my very good friend, I am very happy for you.'

Sweetcorn's words came out of the past: it was one of China's ancient goodbyes, full of dignity and sincerity. 'Goodbye, Mr Soong.' She returned his bow.

Milly knew it was the last time she would see him, for she had no intention of returning to Hong Kong; but she did not know the old man would be dead within the hour, dying in the manner Sweetcorn had died.

From the undergrowth that fringed the old man's dwelling two eyes watched.

Back in her room, with a packed trunk lying beside the bed, Milly looked at the clock; the hands showed ten minutes to midnight. She wondered vaguely where Mamie was: strange, she thought, that at this late hour she wasn't in her room as the time drew near to saying goodbye. Stranger still that Sam hadn't offered to carry her luggage. And then she smiled, for when romance was in the head, sense was out. Full of apologies they would no doubt be waiting on the *Ma Shan*.

It was then that she heard the scream.

The scream was more terrible than anything she had heard before: it was the long, high-pitched wail of a man. And even as she stiffened, the scream came again and again, before dying into gasps and sobbing.

Momentarily disorientated, Milly swung around, focusing upon its direction, then ran to the french doors, pulled them back and listened. In the window of Soong's distant chalet a yellow light bloomed suddenly; instantly appeared the figure of a man wandering in the garden, his hands out in front of him, blindly searching the air. On he came against a background of redness; then suddenly, in a blaze of the moon, Milly saw him more clearly, knowing it for Soong. Fire struck her mind. The old man must have stumbled and set his clothes alight; the chalet behind him was now blazing.

Milly ran, snatched up a blanket and raced across the lawn. But at the moment she reached him, the old Chinese fell at her feet.

'Mr Soong!' Kneeling, Milly spread the blanket to douse the fire, but the old man's clothes were soaked with blood. And no longer did he possess a face, for it had been ripped and clawed; his eyes were no longer eyes, but sockets within an horrific mutilation.

Horrified, Milly began to tremble: the trembling slowly transfixed her being before releasing itself in a single shriek. Standing, she stared down at the body of Soong; then, as if on an inner command, one of his bloodstained hands rose slowly and pointed skywards before he sighed and slipped easily into death. Milly staggered away, running for the safety of the bedroom.

It began to rain; gently at first, then louder, drumming on the flat roof of the bedroom, an obliterating roar of sound.

It was as if the moonlit heavens, in anger, had opened in a deluge that threatened to drown the island.

Now within the safety of the bedroom, Milly froze. At her feet, leading across the carpet from the open french doors to the corridor entrance, were wet footprints.

Not human footprints, she decided, but the indefinable wet smudges of a large animal: a ghostly animal, too, for she had neither seen nor heard its arrival. Regaining her senses, she slammed the french doors shut, locked them and rushed into the corridor entrance, holding high the bedside oil lamp for guidance.

New imprints of muddy paws stained the corridor's lush white carpet.

Gasping with fear, she was enveloped by the roar of the rain, the glass skylight in the bedroom roof accentuating the downpour. Distantly, within the servants' quarters, she heard the crash of splintering glass: the shocking sound jolted her from the apathy of her fear, and she put her ear to the door, listening for the return of Mamie and Sam from the beach. Unwarned of the thing within the rooms, they could blunder into the same horrifying death that had overtaken Soong.

Loyalty and terror vied within her for dominance, loyalty winning, she carefully opened the door and, with the lamp held high, tiptoed out of the bedroom. Lightning momentarily lit her path towards the servant's corridor, flashed and flashed again, before dying, leaving only the yellow circle of wavering light from her lamp.

Milly paused, listening in the corridor. Nothing stirred.

And then she heard it: a faint padding along the white mosaic of the corridor, the unmistakable sound of an approaching animal whose claws were clicking as it approached. Nearer, nearer it came, then stopped. Was it listening? Listening to her?

Turning down the lamp to a faint glow, the will to survive forced her to be clear-headed. Whatever it was — animal or human — it would kill as it had killed before; the embedding teeth holding the victim still, the rending claws mercilessly raking out a life, as a cat kills a rat. In such a manner Soong had died; with horror, Milly remembered Sweetcorn's warnings and the supernatural visitation of Lantau.

317

A giant fox?

Milly turned out the lamp and listened to the panting of the animal confronting her. It was ten yards away — perhaps less, she did not know — until a low growling galvanised her into self-preservation. Beside her was a laundry cupboard, Mamie's pride and joy; feeling for its handle, Milly slipped within it, and stood in its darkness, hearing nothing, save the creaking of the old timber-framed house.

Then arrived a new sensation, the claustrophobic knowledge of the totally enclosed space. She realised the error of using such a hiding-place, for the evil awaiting her in the corridor would have the advantage the moment she emerged. Then, to Milly's astonishment, she heard Anna's soft voice.

'Miss Milly, are you in there? No good hiding in there, Miss Milly ...'

Milly's eyes widened in the cupboard's darkness. Disbelieving her ears, she listened. The animal panting had begun again; this time it was even nearer, directly outside her door. In the eye of her mind Milly saw Mr Soong's torn features, overlaid with the gaping jaws she had known in her dreams; the lolling tongue, the bared fangs. Images followed images across the tortured spectrum of her imagination in a terrifying phantasmagoria that brought the sweat pouring down her face. And again, this time unmistakably, she heard a voice:

'Miss Milly ... Miss Mamie's come back ... she's in her room ...'

It was true, thought Milly. Unaccountably, impossibly it was the voice of Anna Fu Tan.

There came a low scratching, and the door shook. Then followed a louder, more energetic scratching that grew into a frenzy of effort as the door held: now a growling, the wild ferocity of an animal being cheated of its prey. The door of the cupboard rattled and shook to the onslaught of an even more violent attack as the animal howled, as a wolf howls, an unearthly sound that instantly ceased, as if the thing were listening for signs of life within. Gripping the handle, Milly slowly sank to her knees; near fainting, she fell against the protecting door. In this position, all her

318

senses gripped within the rigidity of total fear, she slipped slowly into unconsciousness.

Regaining her senses, Milly stirred within the stifling atmosphere of the cupboard, gasping for breath. Her awareness renewed, she listened.

The animal, or whatever it was, had presumably given up the chase, for Milly could now hear its claws padding upon the attic floor above her. Her lungs demanding air, she pushed open the cupboard door, falling headlong into light.

Thunder was now rolling and clattering on the rim of the world; within its pauses the sounds of the animal above her intensified. Inspired by new hope of escape, Milly lurched back into her bedroom and, trembling, locked the corridor door behind her with shaking hands. Restoring the lamp to its bedside table, she struck a match and with fumbling hands re-lit the oil lamp. Light glowed yellow, gratefully restoring to her a world of light: light in all its glorious rays that exposed the beautiful space of the big room after the pitch-blackness of the cupboard. It was a glorious return to safety. At last she felt the phantom of her animal pursuer had been banished.

Then, glancing upwards she saw it, glaring down at her through the glass of the bedroom skylight.

No phantom this time: with its forelegs astride the skylight, it stood, enormous, its form outlined by lightning flashes. And Milly knew that she had seen it before – on Lantau, before the death of Sweetcorn: a gigantic fox of sleek and terrible beauty. Bigger than a fully-grown dog, its eyes, between the lightning flashes, were yellow orbs glowing from the dark.

Licking its lips, the thing began to stamp its fore-paws on the roof skylight, and the glass bellied and cracked. Milly stood frozen, her legs unresponsive to command; thus rooted she stood while the animal stamped upon the skylight, pausing only to throw back its head and howl at the leaden sky. Only when the skylight glass began to shatter did Milly regain control of her senses; with a brief scream, she stumbled towards the french doors that led to the garden. Tripping upon the carpet, she fell full length and on all fours snatched at the bed to haul herself upright. In doing so she barged against the bedside table, sending the table-lamp flying.

As the glass above her shattered beneath the stamping paws, she staggered across the room, gripped the door handles and turned them. *Locked!* Crying aloud she fumbled with the key, and managed to open the door in the instant before the animal fell through the skylight to lie on the floor, momentarily stunned. Now, howling with pain, it twisted upright and leaped across the room at her, striking the french doors with the full impact of its weight – just as Milly, by now on the other side of the door, reversed the precious key in the lock, snatched it out and fell headlong into the teeming rain.

Lying in the grass, stunned by the impact of her fall, Milly opened her eyes.

The animal, trapped behind the glass of the french doors, was becoming increasingly frantic to escape; for the lamp was flaring and fire was taking a hold on the curtains. Unearthly howls came as the animal cast about for air in the flames and smoke: time and again it hurled itself against the french doors, but the glass held. Incapable of further effort, drained of her last reserves of strength, Milly watched with dull eyes as the room caught fire, sending upwards a vortex of smoke and fire, using the shattered skylight as a chimney. The flames roared. The animal's fur caught fire; howling piteously it suddenly appeared framed in the glass doors in Milly's full view, before sinking down into the fire.

Milly climbed to her feet. The fire was really taking hold, the flames pluming up in the teeming rain, the steam and smoke unearthly in the night air.

She was wandering aimlessly near the road to Green Island Wharf, when Eli came running through the rain.

'Where have you been?' Reaching Milly, he threw his arms around her. 'A *fire*? For God's sake what happened?'

Black Sam and Mamie came now, the latter in wobbling pursuit, and they gathered about her, all three, Eli still demanding to know why she hadn't been at the Wharf at the appointed time. Words beat about Milly in stupid repetition, jabbering senselessly, until they resolved into a single unintelligible blur.

'She's fainted,' Eli said.

'You madman, shouting at her! Give her to me,' demanded Mamie.

'Is she burned?' asked Eli.

'She'd be hollerin' if she was,' said Sam.

'Put that woman down!' Mamie was strident in her command. 'I ain't never known such a pesky lot o' nincompoops — you sure don't know how to handle a faintin' woman.'

'Get her aboard and out of the rain,' said Eli, and pushed Mamie away, lifting Milly effortlessly.

The crew of the *Ma Shan* — 'and you ain't never seen such a ragged, bob-tailed set o' cutthroats,' said Mamie — watched unspeaking as Milly was carried down to a cabin. With hawsers in their hands, waiting for the order to sail, they stared from one to the other. Then Black Sam put his head out of the narrow companionway, and bawled: 'Ain't you never seen a faintin' woman before? Cast off, cast off, ye stupid oafs!'

Lumbering before a southerly wind, the big junk left Green Island Wharf while the fire of the Rest House was still blazing, and turned its foam-crested snout west for the wastes of the South China Sea.

48

The *Ma Shan*, with her bat-winged sails billowing in a strong sou'westerly, rattled along at a merry pace through the Straits of Cupsingmoon.

'Did you think you'd be having Mamie and Sam aboard?' asked Eli.

'I did not,' replied Milly. 'I thought they were all for hiding themselves up in the respectability of the Rest House, and to the devil with anything to do with piracy.'

'With the pickin's as good as they are today?' shouted Sam. 'Could you ever imagine me with ma feet up on cushions, livin' out a life in a palanquin, and twice to church on Sunday?'

'And teaching in the Sunday school, too, if I'd had my way,' said Mamie. 'I was born in a pastor's bed back home in Carolina, and here I am on the high seas consorting with pirate riff-raff. It's enough ...'

' ... to make your Rastus turn in his grave,' finished Sam. 'But your Rastus ain't here no more, so you're takin' orders from this feller in future!'

The waves billowed as the old *Ma Shan* heeled to the wind, taking the great hissing sea of the China Run down her shanks. Up in the rigging the wind was singing a Cantonese opera.

'One thing's certain sure,' complained Mamie, 'since there ain't no money in virtue, and if Eli and Sam are goin' to mend their ways, I'm straight into sack-cloth and ashes, and to hell with the damned old cookin'.'

'Woman,' cried Eli, up on the fore-deck, 'it ain't that

bad, for we'll head straight for the First Oriental Bank the moment we reach Sumatra.'

'Don't tell me you've got loot stashed away in Sumatra!' said Milly.

'Loot in plenty, and then some!' came the reply, and he tipped her under the chin. 'Just follow your Uncle Eli, the pair of you, and hold your hats on.'

Down in the cabin again Black Sam hauled a sea-chest from under a bunk. With a shaft of glowing sun streaming in through the starboard port-hole, Eli unlocked it and lifted its lid. The chest was full to the top with silver dollars; kneeling, all four peered down.

Mexican silver lit up their faces with reflected light.

'Good gracious!' whispered Milly.

'Count it, if you like, but it'll take you all day,' said Eli. 'Two million dollars plus, and add ten Chinese dollars a cattie for two tons of opium belonging to poor old Bruner − I burned it in front of the Canton warehouses with half the population dancing round the flames!'

'Is all this pirate loot?' asked Mamie, her eyes like saucers.

'Legitimate salary, girl, for services to China,' replied Sam. 'Paid to Black Sam − '

'Paid to *Elias Boggs*,' corrected Eli, 'under the terms of Tei Po − the recent Chinese peace offer to Britain, which Britain has ignored − for the delivery of three ships, hitherto the property of Smith and Wedderburn, plus four thousand indentured coolies returned to their homes in Kwangtung Province.'

'Nigh three million Mexicans in all!' added Sam. 'More, Miss Milly, than old Wedderburn stole from you in the first place.'

'Well, I hope it's real legitimate,' said Mamie, getting up in wheezes. 'It's bad enough livin' in a state of sin without spendin' its wages.' She prodded Sam in the ribs. 'I agreed to come on this harum-scarum trip to please Miss Milly, but I'm gettin' you before a pastor the moment we reach Sumatra, to make me into a respectable woman.'

'What about you?' Eli asked Milly. 'You're silent all of a sudden.'

'Just thinking,' she replied.

Later, with the moon lying on its back among ghostly clouds, the *Ma Shan* heeled to a gusty tack, clattering along in a shower of spindrift, with the crew up for'ard and Mamie and Sam arm in arm astern, watching the ocean sea-lights.

In the port cabin, Milly and Eli were very much awake.

'Well now, ye darling thing,' said he, 'could you ever have imagined yourself finishing up with a pirate on the South China Sea, and living the life of Riley in Sumatra?'

'Take care,' said Milly. 'You're going Irish again.'

'Aye! If you've lived your life on the edge of the law like me, it pays to use a worldwide tongue! A Portuguese accent for the Beca de Roza women, and an English one when you're chasing Sussex canaries.'

'Am I a Sussex canary, pray?'

'No more talking,' whispered Eli. 'Just lie quiet, and don't move. I will remember us like this until the end of Time.'

'I couldn't move if I wanted to,' said Milly. 'Is it always going to be like this?'

'Indeed. For when it comes to women, give me a Sussex canary every time.'

Later, with Eli sleeping beside her, Milly suddenly opened her eyes, awakened by a sound within the cabin. She saw, beating its wings against the porthole glass, a giant butterfly of pure white. And there came to her nostrils a perfume of musk from the open cabin door, which was creaking in a wind from the sea.

Then to her astonishment, the form of a little fox cub took shape. Sitting upon the threshold of the open door, it watched her intently. Motionless, it sat, dripping with water like some hostile spirit clambered out of the sea. And Milly saw through its furry mask the grain of the door, and knew it for an apparition.

Aware of her watching eyes, the cub waddled uncertainly towards her, its little teeth bared as in a smile of greeting.

Speechless, Milly continued to stare.

324

Ice was in her womb.

The butterfly beat its wings vainly against the moonlit glass.

'Eli,' she called, '*Eli*!' ...

The little fox crawled closer.

Epilogue

The following is an extract from the *Canton Register*:

Earlier this week the body of Anna No Name, together
with that of Yung, her brother, were found on the most
southerly point of Green Island. These were the young
people who had cleared the delta of bandits to whom the
villagers had been forced to pay tribute.

According to reports brother and sister, both drowned,
were found wrapped in each other's arms.

This publication has learned that the sister, although she
once stood accused of Foxism, was known as the Butterfly
Girl, since her body exuded a perfume akin to musk and the
buddleia bush, which butterflies are known to frequent.

It is also said that her brother, Yung, was a novice monk
at the monastery on Lantau Island before his death, but
this has not been confirmed.

DESOLATION ISLAND

The Works of Patrick O'Brian

Biography

PICASSO
JOSEPH BANKS

*Aubrey/Maturin Novels
in order of publication*

MASTER AND COMMANDER
POST CAPTAIN
HMS SURPRISE
THE MAURITIUS COMMAND
DESOLATION ISLAND
THE FORTUNE OF WAR
THE SURGEON'S MATE
THE IONIAN MISSION
TREASON'S HARBOUR
THE FAR SIDE OF THE WORLD
THE REVERSE OF THE MEDAL
THE LETTER OF MARQUE
THE THIRTEEN-GUN SALUTE
THE NUTMEG OF CONSOLATION
CLARISSA OAKES
THE WINE-DARK SEA
THE COMMODORE
THE YELLOW ADMIRAL

Novels

TESTIMONIES
THE CATALANS
THE GOLDEN OCEAN
THE UNKNOWN SHORE
RICHARD TEMPLE

Tales

THE LAST POOL
THE WALKER
LYING IN THE SUN
THE CHIAN WINE
COLLECTED SHORT STORIES

Anthology

A BOOK OF VOYAGES